BOOK FOUR IN THE RAIDING FORCES SERIES

ROMAN CANDLE

PHIL WARD

A RAIDING FORCES SERIES NOVEL

This book is a work of fiction. Names, characters, businesses, organizations, places, events, and incidents are either a product of the author's imagination or are used fictitiously. Any resemblance to actual persons, living or dead, events, or locales is entirely

ISBN: 978-0-9895922-4-6
Published by Military Publishers, LLC
Distributed by Military Publishers LLC
Austin, Texas
www.raidingforces.com

Cover design by Stewart A. Williams

For ordering information or special discounts for bulk purchases,

please contact Military Publishers LLC at 3616 Far West Blvd., Suite117, Box 215, Austin, TX 78731.

First Edition

DEDICATION

~ ~ ~

THIS BOOK IS DEDICATED TO WILLIAM "BILL" CLARK.

On 3 June 68 his son, Brian, was killed in the Battle of the Plain of Reeds under my command. I wrote the letter. Bill read it and forwarded the letter to President Lyndon Johnson. From the White House, the letter worked its way through the military system. Six months later or so, while on an operation, orders arrived for me to report to the division headquarters. They had the letter. I was taken out of combat. Some say life is a circle – Bill Clark most likely saved my life.

The letter had a life of its own. The staff officer who interviewed me about it (a future Lieutenant General commanding the Virginia Military Institute) wrote a book. In it he told the story of the letter and quoted from it. Forty plus years later I met Bill Clark for the first time. He introduced me as "the one who wrote the letter." I asked if he still had a copy – mine had been sent to him. No, he had mailed his to the President. So, I bought him the book.

.

RANKS, DECORATIONS AND NICKNAMES

RANK PROTOCOL:
The first time a person is named in a chapter or after a chapter break their full rank and name is given. Addressing military personnel by their rank is a mark of respect. At all levels rank is earned and those who have it from a corporal to a four star general are proud of it.

DECORATIONS:
In the British military officers are authorized to put the initials of their decorations after their name. In the Raiding Forces Series the protocol is the first time an officer is introduced in a book the initials of his decorations are listed following his name. After that for the rest of the book they are not.

In the U.S. military officers do not have the same privilege.

NICKNAMES:
In the British military nicknames are endemic. Radio operators are called Sparks, red heads are called Ginger, tall people are called Lofty but sometimes short people are called that too etc.

In the U.S. military there are a lot of nicknames but nothing like the British.

RANDAL'S RULES FOR RAIDING

Rule 1: The first rule is there ain't no rules.

Rule 2: Keep it short and simple.

Rule 3: It never hurts to cheat.

Rule 4: Right man, right job.

Rule 5: Plan missions backward (know how to get home).

Rule 6: It's good to have a Plan B.

Rule 7: Expect the unexpected.

INTELLIGENCE REPORT

NUMBER 1

Situation: The Force N Advance Party consisting of Major John Randal, Royal Marine Butch Hoolihan (promoted to the temporary rank of Bimbashi which is higher than a Major in the Sudanese Army and lower than a British Second Lieutenant) and Kaldi the interpreter have jumped in and are on the ground in Abyssinia. The parachute containing the team's radio roman candled and it was a complete loss. Headquarters in Khartoum does not know if the men are alive, much less when and where to send in the guns, money and additional personnel required to carry out their mission and Force N has no way to contact them.

Mission: Force N is to raise a guerrilla army in advance of an invasion of Italian East Africa. The planned attack out of Khartoum and Kenya designed to drive the Italian Forces from the Red Sea coastline in order to qualify the Middle East Command for Lend Lease supplies shipped direct from the United States.

Execution: There is no execution. (Force N is Missing in Action.)

Administration & Logistics: On hold.

Command & Signal: None.

1
DON'T GET BIT

"THE MOST IMPORTANT THING TO REMEMBER ABOUT tracking a wounded lion is don't walk right up to it and get yourself bit," Mr. Waldo Treywick said as he and Major John Randal, DSO, MC, stood looking at the four blood trails leading off into the bush.

The spoor had been left by four man-eating lions wounded the night before when the two of them had sat up in a small boma using themselves as bait. Fourteen man-eaters had been put down from one pride, which must have been some kind of record.

Now Maj. Randal had to follow up the injured big cats and kill them. The reason for hunting the lion had been to curry favor with the local villagers in order to win recruits for the guerrilla army that he had parachuted into Abyssinia to raise. Force N was not going to win any hearts and minds – or gain any recruits – if he left four wounded man-eaters on the loose in the neighborhood looking for payback.

" 'Cause if you do get munched on you're pretty much as good as dead," Waldo rattled on..

Waldo Treywick had been held captive by a bandit Ras for five years until Maj. Randal shot the shifta chief and freed the old man along and two slave girls nicknamed Rita Hayworth and Lana Turner. Waldo had only the two girls to speak English with for his entire captivity. The girls understood the language perfectly but stubbornly refused to speak it, so for five years all his conversations in English had been one way. Now that he had been "emancipated," Waldo had not stopped yapping, accustomed as he was to all of his conversations being one-way.

"We'll just skip on past the details, Major, about how a lion likes to bite their prey on the back of the neck and the throat simultaneously... killin' it more or less instantly by breakin' its neck or smotherin' it, though there ain't no absolute guarantees on that. As you may recall, I have already done pointed out that sometimes you get drug off and ate alive."

"Roger," Maj. Randal said. "How could I forget?"

"The most important thing about huntin' big cat is don't get scratched neither – like you already done did. Now I ain't brought it up before, not wantin' to be insensitive to your injured condition, Major, but out here in the bush if a man gets clawed he nearly always dies because the wounds generally always turn septic. In your case, you're either a fast healer or that Zār Cult mumbo-jumbo Rita and Lana performed done did the trick on you, 'cause your wounds ain't infected. Except'n for that nasty-looking scar runnin' down your face, you're almost as good as new.

"I'll go ahead and explain how she works if you do get clawed by a man-eater so you'll know what it is you're dealin' with. Then you can make real sure not to let it happen – again."

"Go ahead," Maj. Randal said. "Run it down."

"The thing is, lion's claws – and leopard's too, is all hollow inside. Man-eatin' cats kill and eat people with 'em and when they do, little pieces of human meat gets trapped inside the hollow part. So what happens is the next time they swat somebody, the putrid meat particles trapped inside the claw gets into the scratch, it turns septic, gangrene sets in, the swat-ee gets real sick and dies a horrible death – ain't real pretty."

"I see," Maj. Randal said, wondering what the chances were Waldo might run out of steam or die of old age so he could get on with tracking down the four wounded lions.

"Make sure you don't get yourself bit or clawed anymore 'n you have to a' followin' up those bad boys. You ever tracked anythin', Major – somethin' that might bite you at the end of the trail?"

"Huks."

"Well, there you go," Waldo said in a failed attempt to sound cheerful. "Here's how I think we ought to handle this. You tackle the first one a' followin' up one of these here blood trails and we'll see how you do.

"After that I think maybe it might be a good idea to send out parties of native trackers to scout up the other three. We can save a lot of time that a' way. The trackers can signal us when they have a big cat run to ground. We'll ride up easy on our mules, then you can dismount, wade in and bust it. Or maybe we'll try to run the lion out into the open with beaters where we can shoot it at long range."

"Sounds like a plan."

"OK, but the locals kind of need to see you kill one on your own first, Major."

"Let's do it."

"I ain't goin' to be able to go in with you all the way on this safari. I'm too crippled up and would probably only get in the way. You need to be nimble fightin' cat up close. Lana and Rita will serve as your gun bearers. They're real good at it. I trained 'em myself. When we ride up, one of the girls and I'll stay back to hold the animals while you and the other girl move in and make the kill."

"Sir, I want to go with you," Bimbashi Butch Hoolihan said eagerly.

"Negative," Maj. Randal said. "You're my troop commander. Your mission is to get on with recruiting. Go through the same drill, sort out the rifles and ammunition, keeping only the weapons that fire Italian Army-issue rounds – pick your men."

"Sir, I would really like to come."

"Butch, number one priority is to raise an army. So far you only have two men. We've got a long way to go. Wrap up your recruiting in a hurry. I plan to pull out right after we deal with these lions. No reason to hang around and give the Italians a sitting target."

"Yes, sir," Bimbashi Hoolihan said. "Not bloody fair you get to have all the fun."

"You'll get a crack at a lion, Butch. Just not today."

THERE ARE FEW ENDEAVORS MORE DANGEROUS THAN tracking a wounded man-eating lion. Following-up a wounded big cat with a voracious appetite is not a sport recommended for the faint of heart or weak of spirit, a vivid imagination being a handicap.

The ability to shoot fast and straight is a plus.

"Once a hunter goes in after a wounded man-eatin' cat," Waldo said, sounding like he was having second thoughts about the wisdom of the morning's endeavor, "the most important thing to remember is only one of you is goin' to come out alive.

"Now Major, the minute you set out on the trail a' huntin' this here lion, the cat is already huntin' you. Don't never forget that."

"I understand, Mr. Treywick."

"Don't forget your Big Cat Down Shoot Again Procedure. In fact, you keep workin' the bolt and trigger on that slicked-up Springfield till it runs dry. Then just stick out your hand and the other one will be in it quick because Rita or Lana will be right there to hand it to ya'. I trained both girls and, like I said, they're reliable."

"Good luck, sir," Bimbashi Butch Hoolihan called, sounding about as worried as a Royal Marine is ever going to sound in public.

Major John Randal moved out on foot.

A whole crowd of locals were on hand to see him off. The villagers hoped to tag along, hang back and watch the show from a nice, safe distance. Having been preyed upon by these man-eaters, they wanted to see them dead. The Force N interpreter, Kaldi, was under orders to keep the spectators well back.

The blood trail was easy to follow and led straight for a patch of thorn bush half a mile distant. The grass in the open savanna was almost waist high, making it necessary for Maj. Randal to move slowly and carefully with the M-1903 A-1 Springfield at the ready. The cat could be laying in ambush, hidden anywhere in the long grass. Or it could have button-hooked back to attack from a rear quarter, one of an African lion's favorite tactics. Waldo had covered this trick in his series of endless ruminations on the subject of hunting the big cats.

Sitting on his mule a few yards back, Waldo called a reminder, "By the time you spot the cat, the kitty will have been watchin' you, Major. From the second the lion senses you in the bush he's goin' to have a plan and he's already workin' at executin' it while you're still on the scout."

Maj. Randal ignored him, concentrating on the spoor. Right at his heels was his gun bearer, Lana Turner, recognizable by the Royal Marine insignia on her multi-colored turban. He had given her the badge as an identifier because it was so difficult to tell the two girls apart. She was like his shadow, floating along silently everywhere he moved, never getting in the way.

In the Philippine Islands during his tour with the U.S. 26th Cavalry Regiment, Maj. Randal had spent two years operating against the elusive Huk guerrillas. He noted that the experience of following up the lion felt not much different from tracking a wounded Huk who would kill you at the end of the trail if he could. With the lion there was the added primal element of knowing that what he was trailing wanted to eat him.

A Huk would not do that.

The spoor was not hard to follow. Cats are known for being soft-footed, but this lion weighed between four hundred and five hundred pounds. It left unmistakable pug marks that were plain to see for anyone who knew the rudiments of tracking.

The lion had been shot, but how severely hit was impossible to tell. The bullet wound was leaving a trail of blood, though there was not a great deal of it. The widely dispersed reddish brown splotches were there to be followed, provided of course the tracker knew how to read spoor.

From time to time, Maj. Randal lost the blood trail. At that point he would simply stop and move in a half circle in the direction of march, casting until he cut the sign again. The wounded cat had bounded away from the boma the night before, leaving a lot of signs with its giant strides. A skilled African hand could have told a detailed story from reading the clues.

No doubt if Mr. Treywick had been doing the tracking he would have been able to tell the cat's height, weight, age, sex and IQ from the spoor, but Maj. Randal only knew that the sign pointed him in the general direction the wounded lion had taken. There was, however, no guarantee. The man-eater might have curled back in the grass to ambush his back trail. In that case, knowing the animal's original line of flight could provide a false sense of security.

Maj. Randal reminded himself not to forget the cat was likely aware of his presence by sight, sound, smell, or all three. The man-eater already had a plan to kill him and was working out the details of how best to put it into action. He moved slowly, edging his way carefully forward using the method known as still hunting, taking his time, letting his eyes scan the brush looking for anything, for everything, but especially something out of place – a color, a shape, the flicker of an ear or the ripple of a tail.

Progress was steady but painstakingly slow – sweeping the brush with his eyes trying to see through and behind it, peering inside the brush line letting his eyes adjust, but working them hard. Maj. Randal had better-than-perfect eyesight and his peripheral range was extraordinary. Today he could have used X-ray vision.

Following up the lion was as spooky as anything he had ever done. He was hunting the man-eater, but he knew the man-eater was hunting him too. There was the unmistakable feeling the animal was studying him right this very second, licking its lips. Maj. Randal was clicked on.

There was no sign of the lion, only the occasional brown blood splotches and the pugmarks. Up ahead the grass thinned, and the visibility improved marginally. He could not see anything but thorn bushes and intermittent turfs of savanna grass. Inside the bush line the grass thinned out, and the dirt was packed.

Lana Turner had closed up tight, brushing against him with the spare M-1903 A-1 Springfield rifle ready to trade off. She also had his 12-gauge Browning A-5 slung over one shoulder for close work. Walking up on this lion felt like a really stupid thing to be doing. Maj. Randal wondered what Lady Jane was doing right this minute. He thought about being the Blue Plate Special.

The lion exploded from a clump of grass that would not have concealed a quail, streaking for him like a flaming arrow. The speed with which the big cat covered the ground was incredible. All Maj. Randal saw was a tawny yellow flash; then the M-1903 A-1 Springfield was to his shoulder, his finger was curled around the two-stage military trigger taking up the slack in its first stage, the post front sight centered rock solid under the raging man-eater's gigantic incisors through the Marine No. 6 aperture sight, and the weapon boomed – only he had no memory of causing any of those things.

The man-eater and Maj. Randal locked eyeball to eyeball as he cycled the bolt. Too late he remembered you are not supposed make eye contact with a lion, it infuriates them. The rifle quickly banged three more times.

Dead from the first shot, the lion kept charging. Maj. Randal continued to fire even after the animal plowed into the ground chin-first, piling up three feet from where he was standing. The M-1903 A-1 Springfield rifle boomed once more as if it had a mind of its own, then his spare rifle was in his hands. Lana was inserting a stripper clip into the empty weapon and he could hear her racking the glass-smooth bolt to chamber a .30 caliber round.

She was very good.

All in all, the event was similar to a dream sequence. It felt as if he were having an out-of-body experience, looking down on the drama unfolding from a height of about fifteen feet. Maj. Randal was familiar with the sensation, having experienced it in combat before.

From the beginning to the end of the attack – which had taken less than three seconds – he had not made one conscious decision. Like most life and death encounters, the fight was over quick. Every action had been automatic.

Then Waldo and Rita Hayworth arrived with a host of jubilant natives swarming around. The death of a man-eating lion was always a happy occasion.

While studying the dead cat, Maj. Randal lit one of his few remaining Player's cigarettes with his battered U.S. 26th Cavalry Regiment Zippo,

"Nice goin', Major," Waldo praised as he rode up on his mule. "Standin' your ground with a man-eater comin' for you ain't for everyone. You sure followed your BCDSAP right quick, like I taught you. That Springfield was really talkin'. Lions come at you fast, don't they?"

"What's the chances one or two of those other cats we winged last night might already be dead by now, Mr. Treywick?" Maj. Randal said.

"We can always hope, Major. Optimism is a good thing to have in the man-eater huntin' business. Lion in the wild, especially those that has been makin' a livin' eatin' people on a daily basis, ain't the loveable furry creatures they make 'em out to be in the movies, is they?

"Noticed the macabre detail that differentiates your man-eater from your regular run-of-the-mill lions yet, have you?"

"Negative," Maj. Randal said, confident Waldo was going to point it out for him.

"Human meat is marbled meat with a high fat content. Man-eaters is plump and sleek. Look a lot like contented show kitties – only there ain't no such thing as a contented man-eatin' African lion."

"Warm and cuddly as a Nazi SS-storm trooper," Maj. Randal said.

"Well you're the man wanted to be a lion killer. You ready to start lookin' for a less adventurous line of work, Major?"

"Not until Hoolihan has all his soldiers recruited."

"In that case, I was you," Waldo said, "I'd advise Butch not to be so choosy a' pickin' his men."

THE VILLAGERS CLOSED UP ON THE KILL. THEY WERE FIRED with enthusiasm to go after the three remaining lions now that they had seen one put down. Militarily, Major John Randal noted this might be a good sign, an indication that – if well led – the men might fight. The natives were eager to set out.

First off, Waldo relieved every one of them of his rifle. The men were not supposed to shoot at the cats. Besides, the natives had more confidence in their ability with their spears. But they were not expected to spear the man-eaters either. Their job was to follow up the blood trails and signal when they had a lion at bay.

"The last place you'd ever want to be is anywhere in the area when these boys is armed with loaded firearms and facing a mad cat," Waldo said. "They're likely to bust a cap on anythin' that moves, but the only thing they're goin' to hit is what they *ain't* aimin' at. You got enough problems, Major, without havin' to dodge friendly fire."

The plan was for Maj. Randal and his entourage to rest easy in the shade of an acacia tree and wait for developments. Three parties of spearmen were dispatched to track down the blood trails of each of the remaining wounded lions. When any of the three groups of trackers felt like they had the lion cornered, they were to dispatch a runner to guide Maj. Randal to the scene; he would then ride up, dismount, go in and finish off the wounded animal.

The idea was to get the villagers involved with saving themselves and at the same time help Waldo identify any native who demonstrated ability as a tracker so he could be recruited for later field work. And, Maj. Randal got a respite from the high stress inherent in following up killer cats.

Maj. Randal reclined under the acacia, smoking a cigarette. Rita and Lana were nearby twittering like canaries. Waldo sat easy in the saddle of his mule. A group of villagers were squatting under other trees observing the events.

A native dashed up, shouting excitedly. The old elephant poacher called, "Mount up, they done got one run to ground!"

Parachute, the big white mule, shied away when Maj. Randal attempted to step aboard. He must have sensed the excitement. The mule picked the wrong time to get temperamental. Maj. Randal took two running steps, vaulted into the saddle and once aboard, kicked the animal hard in the ribs to get his attention.

The native messenger took off at a dead run. Parachute gave a couple of little crow hops before coming around on a tight rein and loped after him.

Waldo and the two girls were hard after the white mule. Rita was toting Maj. Randal's spare rifle and shotgun and would be serving as his gun bearer on the second stalk. Lana would dismount and hold the mules while Waldo stayed in the saddle with his 8mm Steyr-Mannlicher ready, providing backup and rear security in the event the cat circled back.

The riders trotted through the bush following the native guide until Maj. Randal spotted a small clutch of natives gesturing wildly with their spears for them to hurry. He had the United States Marine model M-1903 A-1 Springfield with the No. 6 aperture sight in one hand with the steel butt resting on his right thigh.

As he rode up to the small group of natives, the lion exploded out of the thick cover, leapt at Maj. Randal, missed, sailed over the back of Parachute and locked onto the rear haunch of Waldo's mule with all four claws. The natives screamed and scattered.

Parachute was not of the temperament to appreciate this development. In the blink of an eye, the mule leapt high into the air, fish-hooked and let fly with both heels a vicious kick at the man-eating lion, catching it flush on the ribcage. The vicious cat was knocked loose from Waldo's braying mule.

But Parachute's unexpected move pitched Maj. Randal over his head and sent his rifle flying.

The snarling lion and Maj. Randal slammed into the ground at about the same time, separated by only ten yards. The Raiding Forces (RF) officer hit so hard he bounced. The fall really hurt, and for the second time in his short career as a lion hunter he was facing an enraged man-eater at close range with no rifle. By the time he rolled over, struggling desperately to get back in the fight, Rita was right there kneeling beside him. She handed him his .12-gauge Browning A-5 in time for him to pump three rounds rapid fire into the angry cat from the prone position. Waldo managed to get his mule under control enough to get off one shot before the natives swarmed in with their spears to finish the monster off.

"I musta' forgot to warn you – the most important thing to remember about mounted lion huntin' is to make real sure you don't ride your mule up too close to where they got the lion bayed," Waldo said after the situation was under control.

"Things get real excitin' real fast if you do."

Maj. Randal was kneeling head down on the ground spitting out dirt, battered from the fall, hurting all over. The scratches on his chest from his first encounter with a lion had fired up, the pain glowing like neon lights and the stitches in the long wound on his face were throbbing.

The Force N commander had heard enough of Mr. Waldo Treywick's lion hunting commentary for one day. And he still had two more wounded cats to deal with. Lion hunting may be the sport of kings, but it is not without its vicissitudes.

On the plus side, he was beginning to grow attached to Rita Hayworth and Lana Turner, which was a good thing, since, technically, by Abyssinian rules, he owned them.

2

MAN WHO WOULD BE KING

"WHAT?" MAJOR JOHN RANDAL DEMANDED.

"The head knocker ain't goin' to keep his word," Waldo repeated. "He ain't lettin' his personal bodyguard join up like he promised if we killed all those man-eatin' lions like we done. And he ain't even goin' to let Butch recruit men from his village for Force N."

"Well, he's a lying skunk."

"Yeah, and he says it's time for us to ride on out. We done out-stayed our welcome."

"You're kidding."

"No I ain't, Major. The fact is, I'm playin' it down some. We can bivouac here tonight, but we've been ordered to leave in the mornin'. Thanks for killin' all 18 of them bad cats, but goodbye – and don't let the door hit you in the ass."

"Get Butch and Kaldi in here."

When the two arrived, Maj. Randal had Waldo repeat what the village headman had said.

"Bastard!" Bimbashi Butch Hoolihan snarled in anger.

"It's what one could expect, sire," Kaldi said, "from a village devious enough to devise a plan to drive a pride of man-eating lions over to their two neighboring villages to devour their blood-feud rivals."

"Look where that got 'em," Bimbashi Hoolihan said in disgust. "What are we going to do, Major?"

"Attack at dawn."

"Whoa," Waldo cried in alarm. "Let's not overreact here. There's about fifty hoochs in that village, which would normally translate into maybe fifty to seventy-five fightin' men except that them man-eaters reduced the pool a' manpower quite a bit. All we got is you, me, Butch and Kaldi plus Butch's two recruits. Don't be hasty, Major. We ought to think it through. You're supposed to be good at that."

"You said Rita and Lana were good shots," Maj. Randal said. "How far can they hit a standing man?"

"Any upright individual standin' still at two hunert' fifty yards is a dead man if those two girls crack down with their Carcano 6.5s."

"Well then, we've got them too."

"That's great, Major. I didn't make it very far in school back in Tupelo, Mississippi, but even I can do the math and, best case, they got us outnumbered ten or twelve to one not countin' their women. If it came down to it, they'll fight too. War out here is for all the marbles."

"You told me," Maj. Randal said, "when Abyssinians do battle they form up in a line facing each other and then one side gets its courage up and attacks the other in a rush."

"That's right. It's a medieval deal and it's the side with the most men that makes the charge every time. These low-lifes can get real brave when they got the numbers workin' for 'em," Waldo said. "I run 'em down a lot, but the fact is, it's pretty hard to stop an Abyssinian once he commences to makin' a charge. They ain't got a brain in their head so at that point 'ya got to kill 'em or they'll overrun 'ya. Generally speakin', it's the side that makes the charge wins every time."

"When they line up to do battle, how far apart are the two opposing forces?"

"I'd say about seventy-five yards or so. These fools can't hit anythin' with their rifles so it's pretty much a spear deal and then finish off the wounded with swords, knives and rocks to the head 'cause bullets is money. There's never much shootin' goin' on."

"You and Butch drift over and recon the village, then come back and give me a detailed report on the layout."

"Major, like I done told you, I'm a reconnaissance man. Me and P.J. Pretorius was scoutin' out German positions when you was wearin' diaper pins. I done reconned the village. Doin' stuff like that is second nature to me. I majored in it. Tell me what you want to know and I'll save us the trouble."

"Scratch me a diagram of the village on the ground, Mr. Treywick – like a military sand table, paying special attention to where the mules are kept, the location of the headman's hut and anything else of tactical importance," Maj. Randal ordered.

"Kaldi, you draw up a note to the chief stating we intend to attack him tomorrow at sunrise. We'll send it over just before nightfall. And draft invitations to the other two villages to come see the show."

"Sire, what message do you want me to convey to the village we plan to attack?" Kaldi inquired.

"Tell 'em any man that doesn't want to stand with Force N can feel free to stand in front of it."

"I was safer when I was a slave," Waldo said. "You ain't nuthin' but a lightnin' rod hopin' for a black cloud."

"Get moving, Mr. Treywick," Maj. Randal commanded. "Put some effort into that mock-up."

"Sir," Bimbashi Hoolihan asked when the two were alone, "why not simply ride out? The Swamp Fox Force men told me at Calais you used to say 'run away to fight again another day.' "

"Can't, not this time Butch," Maj. Randal said. "If we let this bunch double-cross us, we're dead men. The word will go out that we can be had. After that, no matter how many man-eaters we eliminate you won't be able to recruit the troops we need. Eventually either the lions will get us or bandits will kill us for our weapons and animals."

"Major, you always taught Raiding Forces to never launch an operation unless the element of surprise was in our favor."

"That's right, Butch."

"How do we accomplish that, sir," the young Royal Marine officer queried, "if you send a note into the enemy camp telling them when and where we are going to attack, and then invite the neighbors over to observe the battle?"

MAJOR JOHN RANDAL DISAPPEARED WITH THE ZEISS binoculars he had taken off a Panzer leader at Calais. When he returned, he assembled every English-speaking member of Force N. They huddled around the terrain map of the village that Waldo had constructed on a smooth patch of dirt. As advertised, the former army scout was a professional. The Commando instructors at Achnacarry would have been impressed with the detailed diagram he had constructed of the enemy camp.

Maj. Randal briefed the operation. He did it by the book – Situation, Mission, Execution, Administration & Logistics and Command & Signal. A lot of time was spent on the "Concept of the Operation" paragraph that came under Execution.

When he was finished, every person – including Lana Turner and Rita Hayworth – knew their assignments. Maj. Randal would have liked to conduct rehearsals, but that was not possible. Villagers were wandering around the Force N camp. There was no problem signaling the enemy what Maj. Randal's intentions were but no need to show them how they were planning to actually carry them out.

Surprise on the battlefield is much misunderstood. Everyone knows you are supposed to achieve it, but few people understand how. The unexpected happens all the time in combat, so simply doing the unexpected does not really count as the element of surprise. To have any military value, surprise has to throw the enemy into a panicked state of confusion and give an overwhelming tactical advantage to the side achieving it. And, that advantage needs to be anticipated so it can be rapidly exploited.

After the briefing, as Waldo was obliterating the map of the village with his boot, he confided to Bimbashi Butch Hoolihan, "The Major may be a military genius."

"Think we can pull this off, Mr. Treywick?"

"We'll find out," Waldo answered. "If we don't, we're all dead."

"Maybe the headman will change his mind when he gets Maj. Randal's message."

"Yeah, and maybe we'll stumble across the pot a' gold at the end of the rainbow," Waldo said. "This whole shebang rests entirely on your shoulders, Bimbashi. I'm gonna' be a' countin' on you to get 'er done."

"I thought it depended on you, Mr. Treywick."

"We all got our part, Butch," Waldo said, "Don't you never forget this is a fight to the death. There ain't no second place out here in Africa. One side or the other is gonna' get rubbed out."

As the sun began to wane, the villagers visiting the Force N encampment started to drift away home. Abyssinia is not a safe place to be after dark. The locals wanted to be back in their mushroom-shaped huts before last light. Three messengers were recruited and dispatched to carry Kaldi's carefully drafted messages in the traditional forked stick, which granted the bearer safe passage.

When the camp was clear of the visitor's prying eyes, Bambishi Hoolihan and Kaldi briefed the two native prospects for Force N, their pages, wives, female slaves, mule tenders and assorted camp followers on what was going to transpire when the sun came up. Each of them had a specific assignment. There was work to be done, and much of it had to be carried out in the dark, something none of the Abyssinians had ever attempted before – with the exception of Kaldi, who had participated in night field-training exercises during his two years at the French military academy, St. Cyr.

Maj. Randal's plan was simple, but the execution had to be flawless if Force N was to have any hopes of winning. Military schools teach that the attacking force needs to outnumber the defenders by a ratio of four to one. Five or six to one is better. Since that was clearly not going to happen, Force

N had to come up with some way to level the playing field and swing the odds in its favor.

For tactics, Maj. Randal decided to combine an old Apache trick with a variation from Kipling's short story *The Man Who Would Be King,* which he had been assigned to read by his English Literature student teacher – the reigning Miss UCLA at the time. Except for Miss UCLA, the story was the only thing he remembered from high school English Lit.

The plan was for Waldo to take up a position on a ridge overlooking the battlefield with his Steyr-Mannlicher 8mm rifle on the right flank of the Force N battle line approximately three hundred fifty yards from the enemy village. Rita and Lana would take up a position on the military crest of a small kopje on the left flank with their Carcano 6.5 carbines approximately two hundred yards from the enemy village. Bimbashi Hoolihan would take two teenage pages and swing around far to the rear of the enemy village. All of them were to be in position before first light.

As dawn approached, Maj. Randal, mounted on Parachute, would lead the remainder of Force N – consisting of Kaldi, the two prospects, their wives, female slaves, camp followers etc., all armed and dressed as men in a battle line facing the enemy camp. In addition, the prospects and each of the camp followers would be carrying a scarecrow Abyssinian warrior built on a spear, complete with Tom Mix straw hat, shield and sword. When they came on line, the dummy fighting men would be staked upright in the ground. The entire line would be spaced out with approximately ten yards between each notional Force N trooper and each real war fighter.

The Force N position was planned to be approximately three hundred yards from the enemy camp, which was over three times the distance Abyssinians normally set up their battle lines. Maj. Randal did not want the opposing force to be able to recognize the deception for what it was. More importantly, he did not want the villagers to get their courage up too soon and make a rush.

When the sun came up, it would be rising from behind the Force N battle line, which had been carefully positioned with this in mind. Maj. Randal would ride out in front of his troops and appear to be leading them forward to close the gap between the two lines, anticipating that the villagers would take up their line right outside their village, which they would want to protect. He would initiate the Force N attack by firing a single shot from his M-1903 A-1 Springfield rifle.

When the single distinctive .30 caliber round was heard, three things would happen more or less simultaneously. Waldo would start knocking down enemy personnel with his 8mm Steyr-Mannlicher on the right flank; Rita and Lana would do the same with their 6.5 Carcano carbines on the left flank. Bimbashi Hoolihan, accompanied by two page boys who would have looped around the enemy village unseen in the dark, would stampede the villager's mule herd through the village to the rear of the enemy battle formation, all the while setting fire to as many straw-roofed huts as they could.

As this was taking place, Maj. Randal would dismount, take up a prone firing position and open on the center of the enemy line with his rifle. The Force N troops to his rear would stand fast. They had been admonished not to fire a single round since their marksmanship skills were so bad as to be hazardous to themselves and other Force N personnel – particularly Maj. Randal who was to their immediate front. Since the only ammunition the troops had in their possession was their own, there was little to no chance they would shoot any of it since, to them, bullets were money.

All that was required from the handful of Force N native troops was to make a demonstration. While the two prospects and the camp followers were clearly apprehensive, the chance of earning one Fat Lady per day if they could sign up permanently was expected to help the men and their vassals overcome their fear. Money is a big motivator in a country where there is not much of it and life is cheap.

The concept of the operation was to throw the enemy force into a panic when they started taking causalities from long range, saw their animals stampede, and realized their village was burning. Abyssinians gain courage from their group, and they can lose it the same way. More importantly, the villagers were not disciplined troops who would likely stand in the face of a withering fire.

As nightfall set in Maj. Randal asked, "What do you think they're doing over there, Mr. Treywick?"

"Oh, that's easy, Major," Waldo replied as he wiped down his rifle with an oily rag. "They're a' chewin' bhat... gettin' stoned to build their courage up. And the headman's a' braggin' about killin' us all except for the wimmen which'll make good slaves, and all the loot they're goin' to capture. They ain't doin' no detailed plannin' like you done. Their only idea is to line up, charge, go to work with spears and swords and that's it."

"What do you anticipate the reaction of the other two villages is going to be?"

"Now that's the wild card, ain't it?"

NO MILITARY ENDEAVOR EVER GOES ACCORDING TO PLAN. AT least none of Major John Randal's had. However, with the exception of Bimbashi Butch Hoolihan and his two pages playing at Apache Indians by sneaking around to strike from an exposed flank, setting fire to the village and stampeding the animals while the main force demonstrated to the front, the battle plan was a fairly straightforward proposition.

"Go get 'em, Butch," Maj. Randal said to the young Royal Marine officer shortly before sunrise. "Wait until you hear my shot."

"Yes, sir," Bimbashi Hoolihan said, Royal Marine cool. Then he disappeared into the dark with his two page boys. They were all armed with unlit torches that had been soaked in kerosene. In addition, the Royal Marine carried his cherished .45 caliber Thompson submachine gun. It was hoped he might be able to work into a position behind the enemy battle line where he could bring the submachine gun into play. However, that was a secondary mission – subject to opportunity.

Rita and Lana moved out next. The two girls had their Carcano carbines slung over their shoulders and an extra bandoleer of 6.5 mm ammo belted around their waists. Before they vanished into the night, Maj. Randal looked each one square in the eyes (both girls had amber eyes which contributed to making them virtually impossible to tell apart) and said, "Wait until you hear my signal, then open fire."

Since the girls steadfastly refused to speak English even though they understood it perfectly, the two did not say anything – but they flashed beautiful, white-toothed smiles and were gone.

Waldo was last out. For once, the talkative ex-slave, ivory poacher, and army reconnaissance man did not have much to say. There was no mention of P.J. Pretorius. He simply gave Maj. Randal a nod and stepped into the darkness.

Not long after Waldo departed, sounds of banging drums and cymbal hats were heard in the distance up in the hills. From two different directions, torch light processions could be seen snaking their way through the mountains toward the scene of the upcoming battle. The spectators were intending to arrive before the show started and were making a big production of it to drive off any surviving man-eaters that might be lurking. Both villages intensely hated each other, but they hated the village Force N planned to attack even more because it had originated the idea to drive man-eating lions down on their villages to eat them. Even by Abyssinian rules that was a foul.

The sky streaked burnt orange at the tips of the mountains, and then faded to pale gold. Maj. Randal led Force N out to do battle. Across the valley in the distance the enemy force was arrayed on line, right where expected. There looked to be hundreds of them, but in fact, there were less than fifty armed men standing to.

For once, Parachute seemed to sense the gravity of the situation and was as docile as a lamb. Calling cadence, Kaldi marched at the head of the Force N troops right behind the tall, white mule. Not one of the Force N prospects or any of the camp followers disguised as fighting men had any idea what counting cadence was, but they stumbled along with their spears, swords and rifles, carrying their diversionary dummies close to their side so that from a distance, in that light, the enemy would not recognize the fake fighters for what they were.

When Maj. Randal had Force N in position he ordered, "Do it now, Kaldi! Set 'em up."

Militarily speaking, it was not a thing of beauty but the Force N assault line finally got itself sorted out. Across the three hundred yards between the opposing lines, the increase in their numbers must have come as a surprise. After all, the locals had been in Force N's camp and thought they knew how many fighting men to expect. Mock-ups in the ground and the remainder of the personnel dressed right (sort of) and ready to fight – it was almost time to get this battle underway.

There was one last thing. In a stroke of improvised genius, inspired by Miss UCLA and her homework assignment, Maj. Randal pulled his Fairbairn Fighting Knife from where it was strapped on his chest and, holding it high over his head, walked Parachute toward the center of the enemy line. The villagers had been chanting, jeering and shaking their spears to get their fighting spirit up – egged on by their headman who was riding back and forth in front of his spear line on a black mule urging them into a fever pitch. But they went silent suddenly when they saw Maj. Randal's nickel-plated knife, made by the famous sword maker, Wilkinson's, flashing in the morning sun. Everyone knew it was a magic saber. That story about him killing a man-eating lion with a hand-held knife had traveled far and wide over the bush telegraph.

Holding up the silver knife, Maj. Randal rode the length of the enemy line from a distance of less than fifty yards out, then back again. The villagers, arrayed for battle, were mesmerized. No one fired a shot.

Up in the mountains, the spectators gasped and rose to their feet for a better view. No one on either side had expected anything like this. Then Maj. Randal walked Parachute back to the center of the opposing force's line of battle. He sheathed the Fairbairn knife, pulled his M-1903 A-1 Springfield rifle from its saddle bucket, brought it to his shoulder and shot the headman off his black mule. *BOOOOMMOOOOMM.*

Waldo began knocking down villagers as fast as he could work the bolt of his Steyr-Mannlicher 8mm. Lana and Rita opened, dropping men with every shot. Random firing broke out in the village behind the enemy battle line accompanied by whooping and yelling as Bimbashi Hoolihan and his crew stampeded the mules. Huts began exploding into flames as their dry thatch roofs were torched. The Thompson submachine gun started... *RRRRRIMMMPHH, RRRRRRIMMMMMPHH, RRRRRRIMMMMMPHH.*

The enemy villager's line of battle wavered and broke.

Spectators from both neighboring villages acted as one. They came streaming down off the mountain, full bore into the valley, screaming war cries at the top of their lungs, intent on seeking blood feud retribution, and the slaughter was on. To cap it off, acting on their own volition, the Force N troops charged, carrying a startled Parachute along with them. In the blink of an eye, Maj. Randal found himself caught up in the middle of a swirling, spear-stabbing and sword-swinging mêlée.

A lot of old grudges, real and imagined, were being settled.

Maj. Randal managed to get his rifle back into the boot, pulled a Colt .38 Super and attempted to shoot his way out of the fighting mob, not entirely sure he was shooting the right people. Four or five men went down, then Parachute fought clear. He loped off a short distance, then turned and back to watch the battle. Waldo rode up. Soon Rita and Lana trotted up on their mules.

"How do we get this stopped?" Maj. Randal asked.

"We don't," Waldo said. "It won't last long."

"We've got to get Butch out of the village," Maj. Randal ordered, setting out at a gallop in a wide circle around the fighting. The party of four rode in to the little town, past crackling hot, mushroom-shaped huts that were burning ferociously. In minutes they spotted Bimbashi Hoolihan and his two pages perched on top of the headman's hut.

Waldo trotted forward with his rifle out, pulling security, while Maj. Randal and the two girls rode up to the hut. The Royal Marine and his two boys jumped down on the back of the mules and, riding double, the party galloped out. Bimbashi Hoolihan was hanging on to Maj. Randal while holding his Thompson submachine gun. As they rode into the abandoned Force N camp, Kaldi was the only person in sight.

"Sire, I never gave the order to attack."

"Don't worry about it, Kaldi," Maj. Randal said. "Nobody could have held 'em back."

"Butch," Maj. Randal said, "good job, stud."

"It sure was," Waldo seconded. "Bold, very bold indeed, Bimbashi. You sure stampeded those long ears at the exact right time."

Bimbashi Hoolihan and Kaldi mounted their mules, and the Force N Command Party sat easy in the saddle and watched the battle winding down across the way. It was hard to determine who was fighting whom. From the looks of things, it appeared the two neighboring villages had turned on each other in the killing frenzy. When it seemed like all parties were on the point of exhausting themselves, Maj. Randal led the Force N group slowly forward at a walk.

On the ride over, Waldo said, "What was that crazy stunt ridin' right up in their face wavin' your shiny knife? You got a death wish, Major? You ain't no good to me if you get killed, which I recall havin' mentioned to you once or twic't before."

"You're the man who told me the natives wanted to see the Fairbairn," Maj. Randal said. " 'Make a big production of it,' you said."

"I didn't say ride up and show your blade to fifty of 'em crazed with blood lust and stoned on bhat," Waldo said, "gettin' ready to stab your ass with spears."

THE FIGHTING CAME TO AN END WHEN BIMBASHI BUTCH Hoolihan fired his .45 caliber Thompson submachine gun in bursts over the combatant natives' heads. The Royal Marine hated to waste his precious ammunition, but there was no other way to get their attention. Dead and dying men were strewn about like rag dolls. Women were howling in anguish. No one was quite sure exactly who the victor was.

One thing was clear. The men from the original village – the one that had started the man-eater driving and that had refused to honor their promise to Force N to supply troops to fight the Italians – had paid a heavy price for their bad behavior. The village chief shot dead. Most of the rest already down or being held captive and undergoing rough treatment.

All the participants in the battle were exhausted from their exertion. Spear and sword fighting takes a lot out of a man. To the victor go the spoils, but who exactly was the victor? Major John Randal immediately made it clear – Force N owned the day.

The two neighboring villages were ordered to separate into their individual groups under the control of their headmen. Casualties were left intermingled where they lay dying or wounded. There were no medical facilities to be had. Wounds had to heal on their own, or the injured parties die – on the other hand, there was a business opportunity for the two enterprising Zār Cult priestesses, Rita and Lana. The least-damaged men from the enemy lion-driving village and their women were herded into a group under guard of the Force N prospects and their pages.

Using Waldo to translate, Maj. Randal ordered the two neighboring village chiefs to have their men immediately ground their rifles. They were allowed to retain their spears and swords. The rifles from the dead, wounded, and the prisoners were stacked in a separate pile. Rita and Lana were dispatched to organize a party of the Force N camp followers to round up the mules Bimbashi Hoolihan had stampeded.

The headmen from the adjoining villages looked on sullenly until Maj. Randal explained that any of the women and all the plunder in the huts not deemed of military value would be divided equally between the two villages after the men needed for Force N had been selected. On hearing that announcement, the village chiefs perked up. Politicians down to the ground, with the promise of booty settled, the headmen immediately pitched in to exert their civic authority over their individual village groups. All hands were eagerly awaiting the distribution of the spoils.

Wasting no time, Bimbashi Hoolihan began his selection of recruits. Waldo was assigned to inspect the weapons and to commandeer any that fired Italian military rounds regardless of which village they came from. He was instructed to seize any weapon, caliber notwithstanding, if he thought it might be of use to Force N. This caused signs of unrest among all interested parties until it was explained that whoever owned the weapons appropriated would be compensated.

First off, Bimbashi Hoolihan inspected the survivors from the village Force N had attacked. Then he moved on to the other two village groups. Virtually every man wanted an opportunity to earn the magnificent sum of one Fat Lady per day.

When he completed his selection from all three villages, those chosen were allowed to gather their wives, servants, slaves and page boys. Then the prospects and new camp followers were marched off in the direction of the Force N camp. The men not selected from the defeated village were informed that they would be considered for a slot on the Force N roster if they showed up with an Italian rifle, ammunition and a mule. Then they were ordered to leave the area immediately with their life spared, which by Abyssinian rules was an out-and-out miracle.

At that point, Waldo brought the two neighboring headmen together and allowed them to begin the process of sorting the remaining women they wanted as slaves.

"Are you sure about this, sir," Bimbashi Hoolihan asked uneasily when he saw what was happening, "allowing them to be forced into servitude?"

"Those women were dead or doomed to be slaves the minute the headman of their village decided to double-cross Force N, Butch," Maj. Randal said. "Look at this way, we can't take them with us, and if we hadn't put a stop to it, all their men would have been executed on the spot. Abyssinians play hardball."

Bimbashi Hoolihan had no idea what "hardball" was, but he got the picture. It pays to be a winner in Abyssinia.

"Maybe the men can obtain Italian rifles, win a place in Force N and earn enough money to buy their women back later," the Royal Marine said hopefully.

"Don't count on it," Waldo told him. "Wives is small change in Africa. Somethin' happens to yours, you get yourself another or a couple more. No problem. Ain't a bad system when you study on it."

"How many rifles, Mr. Treywick?" Maj. Randal asked.

"Twenty-two from this village that Butch can use, another forty-three commandeered from them other two villages. We made a good haul, captured another thirty-six guns that don't shoot Wop ammo, mostly junk. What do ya' want me to do with 'em, Major?"

"Keep every captured weapon," Maj. Randal said. "You said the Italians have a buyback program, so let's sell 'em to them. I don't see any reason not to let the Blackshirts help finance our war for us."

"Now that's a plan, Major," Waldo said. "Kinda' gettin' into the spirit of all the dirty double dealin', ain't ya'?"

"Yeah, you might be right, Mr. Treywick."

After a day-long orgy of looting, when the sun began to sink in the sky, Maj. Randal ordered, "Boots and saddles... we're moving out."

Waldo and Kaldi were exhausted from refereeing disputes over which village got what loot and seizing items deemed of military value to Force N. The day was long, and it was hard work. Tempers had flared at times, though the battle had taken most of the fight out of the Abyssinians. The people from the two spectator villages were happy to have had such an unexpectedly profitable day.

"Burn it," Maj. Randal ordered, "every last hut."

As they rode back into the mountains, the only thing remaining of the village that had tried to double-cross Force N was a black smudge on the valley floor and a giant letter "N" painted on a boulder. The drums beat in the night. The message that went out over the jungle telegraph was simple, "Cross the Emperor's man at your peril. Support him and you will be rewarded."

No one seemed to think it the least unusual that Force N was now made up primarily of men who had been fighting each other that very morning.

26…..PHIL WARD

3
SPOTLIGHT

"ABYSSINIANS IS A WEIRD PEOPLE," MR. WALDO TREYWICK elucidated as Force N marched through the mountains. "They take great pride in the ancient days, some of which is misplaced bein' based on pure raw fiction. And they live in a sorta' rigid heraldic nobility, the lords of a handful of grass huts shaped like mushrooms.

"Just because they ain't got nothin' don't mean they ain't proud. Your native has a delicate sensitivity that probably derives from livin' in pellucid sunlight all the time. Then again, maybe it's the thin air of a country so high up it's called 'The Roof of Africa' – that may have somethin' to do with it. Or the influence of their illiterate Coptic priests, possibly their spicy diet... could be it's the strain of havin' thirteen months in their calendar – who's to say?"

"I can see where that might cause a strain," Major John Randal said.

"Your average Abyssinian is a vain son-of-a-bitch, Major. You got to understand their character if you're a' plannin' on commandin' an army of the delicate little fellows. Your local native is susceptible to taking quick offense, can be as fickle as a virgin bride, ferocious in his anger, gentle on rare occasions and even loyal, though you can never turn your back on one of 'em. You got to ride 'em with a loose rein – at the same time they expect to be ruled with an iron fist. Fail to be firm they'll think you're a sissy. Weakness is somethin' a commander of Abyssinian troops can never show. It's the kiss of death."

"So I've heard," said Maj. Randal.

"Now the feudal system goes back to time immemorial, and it's way too subtle for your average outsider to ever get a handle on 'cause it don't make a whole lot o' sense even to Abyssinians. The system is based on serfdom to the King of Kings without hardly any money in it. And since the big King – meaning the Emperor – ain't here, having deserted his post when the Italians invaded back in '35, the idea for the citizenry to be subservient to the royal peckin' order has fallen on hard times.

"Blood feud is the drivin' force. Don't never forget it, Major, because everythin' that happens in this entire psychotic country is based on it. Payback is a' happenin' round the clock with somebody always schemin' and a' plottin' to get some and that's the motor that drives this here loony bin of a nation."

"I'll keep that in mind," Maj. Randal said.

"Murder is taken casually. Ya' can generally smooth over any killin' with blood money if ya' change your mind after you done did the deed. Or maybe if the dead man's kin makes things too hot for ya' after you whacked their favorite siblin' you can buy 'em off with hard coin."

"In Abyssinia every tinhorn Ras is only in it for hisself – there ain't no such thing as national unity. Patriotism don't exist in any form I ever seen, and teamwork is limited pretty much to the bandit level but only as long as the shifta *tillik sau* keeps dishin' out the loot.

"Now I've been a' givin' some thought to spotlightin' lion," Waldo said, switching gears. "Those flashlights you taped to the end of our rifles don't throw out enough candle power to dazzle the man-eaters sufficient enough to suit my fancy. We need somethin' to really zap 'em."

"What do you have in mind, Mr. Treywick?"

"If I was to get my hands on an Italian truck or maybe a motorcycle it would probably be fairly easy to take out a headlamp or two and rig us up some really powerful spotlights."

"What do you propose?"

"That's your department, Major. You're the tactical mastermind at designin' and executin' cuttin' out operations – don't forget I done read your book. And you did right nice plannin' that fight the other day. You figure out somethin' about the lights. I only wanted to let ya' know I've done come around to the opinion maybe ya' stumbled on to somethin' spotlightin' lion, only we need to hone our technique some."

Maj. Randal said, "OK, I'll give it some thought."

"The big thing is, killin' the man-eaters like you've been a' doin' is workin' to make you into a real genuine *tillik sau*. You may not realize it, Major, but you're on your way to becomin' a livin' legend, turnin' into a regular Fredrick Selous – which is like sayin' the Davy Crockett of Abyssinia. I'm beginnin' to think maybe there's a whisker of an outside chance ya' might actually pull off this crazy idea of raisin' a guerrilla army."

"Glad to hear you're so positive, Mr. Treywick."

"Well, I am, provided ya' don't get ate up first, on which there ain't no guarantee because unless ya' can get your hands on a bunch of money or a pile more of guns somewhere you're gonna' to have to kill a passel more of man-eatin' lions to bring in the amount of Patriot manpower you're gonna' need.

"By the way, whoever thunk up the name 'Patriot' for these back-stabbin' slime is some special kind a' dumbass. 'Minute Men' is more like it – these idiots have the attention span of a' sand flea. One minute is about as long as you can count on any of 'em."

Maj. Randal started to say something, then thought better of it.

"And whoever the man is that came up with the idea of Force N parachutin' in here like that to ferment a rebellion in the first place is a rank idiot, and I do mean the genuine article. Whoever he is, the man ain't playin' with a full deck. You might want to keep that in the back o' your mind if and when we ever do find some way to reestablish communications with your headquarters."

"I'll do that."

"But it sure was audacious of you and Butch to give 'er a try and Abyssinians *do* admire pluck. They just ain't apt to display much of it themselves unless it's out of pure bravado, ya' know, gettin' swept away in the exuberance of the moment caught up in a mob or when they's stoned on baht and just can't help themselves."

"We're not wasting our time then, killing lion?" Maj. Randal asked.

"Major, to these people you're the first person that has shown any interest at all in their personal health or welfare since the Italians invaded five years ago and ran the Emperor off with his tail between his legs like the sorry dog he is.

"Like I've done told ya' – Abyssinians bask in the glory of ancient days that never really happened. With these folks, if it comes down to a choice of history or legend, if the legend is better they go for it every time no matter how unbelievable it is.

"Now in the olden days, the king was supposed to protect the people from the wild beasts, says so right in the Bible – which every joker in the entire country lies and says he's read – Abyssinia havin' the most religious criminals in the whole entire world.

"St. George, who the Coptic Christians claim built a castle single-handed up in Gondar province a' wearin' full body armor the whole time no less, well, he is internationally famous for slayin' dragons. Now, how St. George the dragon killer and castle-builder is supposed to have hauled hisself all the way out here to this remote corner of Africa from somewhere in Europe way back then is anybody's guess, but the thing is, Major, you're the primary dragon slayer around here now a'days, and the word's gettin' out about it."

"That was the plan, Mr. Treywick," Maj. Randal said.

"Well, it's kickin' in. I'd have to say you're doin' real good so far in the winnin' hearts and minds department, not that these ingrates would ever let ya' know it seein' as how the words 'thank ya' don't even exist anywhere in any of the local languages.

"Which brings us back to the subject of spotlights.

"If we can manage to get us a couple of real good ones with a lot a' candle power, maybe we can turn our man-eater eradication program into somethin' a little less resemblin' hand-to-hand combat. So far it's been a little too authentic for my personal appetite."

"I'm for that, Mr. Treywick," Maj. Randal said. "Besides, it's about time my troop commander gets a chance to lead his first combat patrol."

A map was produced, Bimbashi Butch Hoolihan summoned, and the three of them immediately conducted a map reconnaissance. The Italian Army was basically a road-bound force. They had a few native cavalry squadrons called *Banda* that ventured cross-country from time to time, but other than that, the Italians stayed close to the road network. The good thing from Force N's point of view was that there were virtually no roads in Abyssinia, so if they made camp far away from the few that did exist, they were relatively safe – from Italians anyway.

The nearest hardtop road was thirty miles due north from where the three were huddled around the map. The road ran through hilly and rugged terrain interspersed with thick forest, particularly where it crossed a stream.

Dotted along the hardball thirty to fifty miles apart were army outposts called Forward Operating Bases (FOBs). They were located on the top of hills wherever possible and consisted of company-sized elements tasked with the mission of guarding the road. In fact, all the bases accomplished was to tie up most of the available military transport in the entire country, running re-supply convoys to sustain the troops in the FOBs, and the only thing the soldiers in the base camps were guarding was each other.

Tactically, it is impossible to guard any stretch of road not under direct observation. From the beginning of organized warfare, occupying armies have been failing to learn that one simple truth. The Blackshirt forces in Italian East Africa (IEA) never did.

Being stationed at one of the remote bases was tantamount to being sent to a prison work camp. The way the Italian troops saw the situation, they were confined in a small, isolated fort surrounded by a teeming jungle filled with dangerous animals and homicidal natives who had a long-standing tradition of collecting their enemies' precious body parts as trophies. And, there was a decided lack of quality female companionship to be had.

The garrison had to be supplied regularly with food, ammunition, mail and in many cases, water. The only way the Italians could do that was by road. Remote roads are the easiest of all targets to ambush.

The plan was for Waldo and Rita to drift away later that morning to conduct a clandestine reconnaissance of the nearest point on the road with the idea of selecting a likely spot for an ambush. The two would travel alone. Force N did not trust any of the Abyssinians to accompany them, it being well understood that the Italians had spies, or more accurately, collaborator-type agents who would sell information in every village. There was a possibility that they had recruited some of them. If no one knew the plan then they could not tip off the enemy.

In two days' time, Maj. Randal would lead Bimbashi Hoolihan and his band of irregulars – variously now called "Butch's Gang" or "Hoolihan's Heros" – to a pre-selected rendezvous with the recon party. So far the Patriot volunteers were all still rated as prospects – Bimbashi Hoolihan had yet to issue a single M-1903 A-1 Springfield rifle. He was taking his time evaluating the candidates. There were a lot more volunteers for the promised one Fat Lady per day positions than he had weapons to assign, so he could afford to be selective.

Before he departed on his recon mission, Waldo had one last piece of advice, "Don't do nothin' fancy, Major, while I'm gone. If you feel like ya' just have to hunt lion tonight, find yourself a tall tree and sit up in it and I do mean tall this time. Like thirty or forty feet high."

"Roger that."

"And if ya' should shoot one, don't get down out of the tree to check his pulse until well after sunrise and don't forget your Big Cat Down Shoot Again Procedure."

"Try not to get caught by the Italians, Mr. Treywick."

"I been a' slippin' in and a' poachin' German and Portuguese ivory with P.J. Pretorius and sneakin' it out across the border about twict as long as ya' been born, Major. If I don't want to be seen, I'm a ghost. Worry about gettin' yourself gobbled, soldier boy."

Maj. Randal intended to take Waldo's advice and be very careful in his choice of lion hunting technique while the old ivory poacher was gone. In fact, he was seriously considering taking a break. A full night's sleep sounded good for a change.

Unfortunately, a delegation of elders from a nearby village showed up shortly after Waldo and Rita had departed the area. They reported that within the hour a lion had attacked a woman in broad daylight in her hut not more than a mile away and carried her off into the bush. "Would the Major please come and dispatch the evil spirit?"

This had not been part of the plan, but having no other option he could think of, Maj. Randal and Lana followed the group to the scene of the grisly attack. When they arrived at the victim's hut, the sign was clear. According to the delegation, the man-eater had gone into the woman's mushroom-shaped hooch, pounced on her while she was preparing a meal and dragged her off screaming "I am being eaten by a devil."

While Maj. Randal had his doubts about the authenticity of that as an exact quote, the sign left by the man-eater was plain enough. He and Lana carefully followed the trail out of the village and through the bush for over a mile until he came to where the lion had been joined by his mate. From the sign it looked like the two big cats had fought over the victim.

The only remains were the woman's head and a severed left hand with a thin silver band on it, bitten off at the wrist. The head did not have a single mark on it and both green eyes were wide open – staring. She had pierced ears and was still wearing a pair of copper loop earrings. Nothing Maj. Randal had ever seen hit him as hard as looking at the expression of terror registered on the dead girl's face.

Maj. Randal made the decision to sit up for the two cats. He told the villagers to leave the girl's remains where they were in hopes the man-eaters would return. Then he gave orders for a perch to be built in a tall tree about fifteen yards from the bloody patch where the girl had been devoured.

Using the green-eyed girl's remains as bait was cold blooded, but he wanted to kill the lions, and it seemed like his best chance to get them. Maj. Randal could not ignore how attractive the victim had been. The green eyes were almost, but not quite, the same color as Lady Jane's. That haunted him.

Maj. Randal decided he hated lions.

Later that night sitting in the stand built in the top of the tall tree with Bimbashi Hoolihan, who was experiencing his very first big cat hunt, Maj. Randal and his young Royal Marine protégé listened as the two African lions walked boldly through the jungle in the dark, roaring back and forth to each other.

The lions sounded like they were headed directly toward the tree the two officers were sitting in. Bimbashi Hoolihan was quivering with what Maj. Randal hoped was anticipation. He was shaking a little himself, probably just a chill – it was cool out.

"I thought lions were supposed to be silent hunters, sir," Bimbashi Hoolihan whispered.

"They are," Maj. Randal said. "Those two ain't hunting, Butch."

"You are bloody right, sir. Those cats are coming straight here to eat us – no hunting to it!"

"They have to get us first, Butch."

"When Lady Seaborn sent me out to Africa with your gear, she made me give her my word that I would take care of you," the Royal Marine said in a shaky whisper. "Right this minute, sir, it does not feel like I am doing a very good job of living up to my promise."

"Don't worry, lions won't climb a tree," Maj. Randal said, imparting some of his recently acquired lion knowledge and hoping he sounded a lot more confident than he actually felt. "Not with us in it, armed and ready."

It was nice to know that Lady Jane had been concerned about his safety. Involuntarily Maj. Randal glanced down at the green luminous digits on the black-faced Rolex diver's watch she had given him. He thought about her every time he did, which on any given day was a lot.

Suddenly the two man-eaters quit roaring – a sure signal that the animals *had* started hunting. The silence did not make either of the two British Commandos feel all that much better. They realized they were being stalked.

There was no chance either of them would get bored and fall asleep, particularly as they had each brought a canteen full of high-quality Arabica coffee to help keep them awake. The same coffee that, according to legend, had been discovered by the sheep herder who had noticed his flock becoming "animated" after eating "cherries" and that had kept the monks up for days at a time praying. The coffee tale was one local fable Maj. Randal did not have any difficulty believing. One sip and your eyes zoomed open wide, stayed open wide, and you became very aware. Waldo claimed the stuff would actually improve your night vision.

For three hours, the two officers could sense the lions circling them out there somewhere in the dark. Lions are careful hunters – they take their time. The trepidation mounted, and while there was no way the killer cats could get up to them, there are no sure things. When you know you are the cheese in a mousetrap, the fact that the mouse is eventually going to get its neck broken is not all that much reassurance. What if either of them slipped, lost their balance and fell out of the tree... what about that?

"Mr. Treywick told me that people are nothing but groceries to a man-eater."

"He talks too much, Butch."

From below there was a deep sigh. The sound indicated that at least one of the killer lions was very, very hungry. A giant cat sighing in anticipation of gobbling them up did nothing for morale. Now was no time to get careless. Simply knowing a hungry, five hundred-pound cat was right down below made both of them wobbly. Maj. Randal secretly regretted not having taken the precaution of tying themselves off with toggle rope safety lines.

"Mr. Treywick also told me an African lion has to consume on average fifteen pounds of meat per day," Bimbashi Hoolihan said nervously. "He claims the big advantage a man-eater has over other lions is that they do not have to hunt very hard – they can simply head for the nearest native village – it's the man-eater kingdom's equivalent of a takeout restaurant..."

"Now, Butch," Maj. Randal whispered, cutting him short – they both switched on the flashlights taped to the barrels of their .30 caliber M-1903 A-1 Springfield rifles. Standing below them directly under the tree was a large, savage lion with a thick, black mane staring up right where they were perched. The lion's golden yellow orbs lit up in the twin circles cast by the flashlights. Neither man could actually see the animal licking his lips in anticipation, but both officers felt it was a sure bet that's what he was doing.

Bimbashi Hoolihan's rifle boomed and the lion was knocked down, falling sideways; but quickly sprang back to its feet. Before it could take a step, the young Royal Marine racked the bolt on his M-1903 A-1 Springfield and squeezed off a follow-up shot, dropping the big cat in his tracks.

"Hammer him once more," Maj. Randal ordered, "don't forget your BCDSAP."

BOOOOOOM!

The RF officers shone their lights through the bushes in a 360-degree circle hoping to pick up another set of golden eyes, but did not see any sign of the other cat. After a while they gave it up and waited for daylight.

Taking a sip of the delicious coffee, Maj. Randal said, "Now, Butch, the most important thing to remember about hunting lion…"

4
CHEAP BRIBE

THE MORNING AFTER MAJOR JOHN RANDAL AND BIMBASHI
Butch Hoolihan killed the man-eating lion, a motley band of armed men
numbering approximately thirty arrived at their encampment. Led by a one-
eyed rogue, they were distinguished by their tall, cone-shaped, pearl gray,
Tom Mix-style cowboy hats. When they rode in, Lana Turner hissed "shifta"
as if she had seen a poisonous snake.

They appeared friendly, but in a country like Abyssinia, "friendly" is
a relative term. What it meant in this case was that no one had killed anybody
yet. Kaldi went out to meet with the one-eyed villain while Maj. Randal sat
in his canvas camp chair conspicuously swishing his ivory-handled whisk,
the one with the Emperor's Seal engraved on the sterling silver cap, the black
lion's tail for a chaser and a long, thin, razor-sharp stiletto blade concealed
inside the handle. He pulled the silver Fairbairn Fighting Knife out of its
sheath and laid it in plain sight on the small camp table next to his chair.

"Bimbashi Hoolihan, unlimber that Thompson gun of yours."

Standing just inside the entrance to the tent, the Royal Marine said "Standing by, sir," as he discretely held the weapon down by his side by its finger-grooved pistol grip.

Lana had her Carcano carbine in her lap and was fingering the curved rhinoceros-horned dagger at her belt. She never took her eyes off the troop of bandits as she stood up and edged around behind Maj. Randal's chair. Clearly the girl did not like what she saw.

Several members of Butch's Gang drifted over with their rifles. Maj. Randal had wondered how they might react. The men were all still only prospects and might choose a moment like this to decide the life of a soldier was not all it was cracked up to be. You never know with untried indigenous troops.

Bimbashi Hoolihan was also observing and making book on how the volunteers were responding to the unexpected development. This could turn into a gun battle at any second, and he wanted to know which of his lads could be counted on to stand with him and who was not so sure. Anyone hoping for a shot at a permanent slot in Hoolihan's Heros had best not hang back now.

The young Royal Marine officer privately regretted there had not been more time to drill the men – the forlorn hope of combat leaders of all grades from the beginning of standing armies.

Kaldi came back looking concerned. "These are shifta sire, dangerous men. They say they have heard the British are passing out rifles to those who want to fight the Italian occupiers. Do you wish to speak with their leader?"

"What do you recommend, Kaldi?"

The slim young Abyssinian advised, "You cannot trust these people, sire. They are bad men, murders, stealers of women, land pirates and the like, who prey off the weak – professional brigands. Men like these outlaws are a stain on my country."

"Will they kill Italians for us?"

"Only when it is to their advantage, sire, for plunder. You can never depend on shifta. They are blood parasites." Kaldi added, "Shifta are not true Patriots; they are common criminals who fight only for treasure."

"Bring the man over," Maj. Randal said.

The shifta chieftain was an evil looking scoundrel with a long white scar running diagonally across one empty eye socket. He removed his big sombrero and bowed five times as he made his way up to Maj. Randal's canvas camp chair, which was the exact protocol required on being admitted to the presence of the Emperor. No one present actually believed the land pirate was quite that sincere.

"Sire, this is Gubbo Rekash, the leader of this banda of... ah... Patriots."

Lana was now standing close beside the canvas camp chair, brushing up against Maj. Randal. Over his left shoulder, she was staring hard at the one-eyed bandit like he owed her money. She stifled a giggle at the introduction. He wondered what that was about.

A chair was procured for the shifta chieftain and Maj. Randal indicated for him to sit. Kaldi ordered one of Butch's Gang to bring coffee. The wicked old rascal sat grinning, displaying a set of rotten teeth as the dark, golden liquid was poured into tiny porcelain cups. The bad teeth looked like termites had gotten at them. Personal hygiene was obviously not a shifta priority.

The old bandit rattled off something.

"Gubbo Rekash is curious to know how you received the wound to your face, sire," Kaldi interpreted.

"Lion."

On hearing the response, the outlaw chief shook his head gravely, flicking his one rheumy eye at the huge ten-foot lion skin stretched for curing on the rack beside the tent. Then Gubbo checked out the silver Commando dagger lying on the camp table. Clearly he knew the tale about the knife.

"He says that he has heard you are a great killer of demon lions."

"Well, tell him this one tried to French kiss me."

"Sire, I do not believe he will comprehend," Kaldi said, sounding like he was choking. "French kiss will be most difficult in translating."

"Ask him what he wants."

After a lengthy discourse, Kaldi explained, "He says it is his intention to rally to his Emperor, wage war against the Italians and drive the filthy dogs from this country. He says Blackshirts are neither Christians nor Muslims, but fascists, and they are bad for business."

"What business might that be?"

"Murder for hire, robbery, kidnapping for ransom, sire. Possibly the occasional forbidden trade in slaves and stolen ivory. Also, my guess is the brigand is a mule thief," Kaldi said without bothering to consult Gubbo Rekash. "He is lying of course, about rallying to the Emperor out of patriotism, sire, but the man does appear to have a genuine hatred for fascists."

"Tell him to go kill Italians then."

Another lengthy conversation transpired. "As soon as you supply him with the necessary rifles and ammunition he promises to eradicate many Blackshirts," Kaldi interpreted. "The man claims he has heard that the guns being supplied in Gondar are of an inferior quality. What he requires are modern repeaters, not the old-style single-shot Martini-Henrys that are being passed out on the Sudan border by British agents."

"I'm not giving him any rifles," Maj. Randal said.

Surprisingly, the old land pirate did not seem offended by the rejection. He babbled to Kaldi and grew animated, waving his hands about.

"Gubbo Rekash inquires if you are the one who killed the six shifta and displayed their heads on stakes. He says that the Italians are very disturbed by that. The gang leader you shot was a famous Ras, a *tillik sau.* Word has spread throughout the countryside of his death. He wants to know what the letter 'N' that was painted on the mens' forehead stood for."

"Tell him."

"Sire, I do not know what the 'N' stands for."

"Say it means death to fascists."

"The bandit is also curious to know why you put their heads on the poles after you killed them," Kaldi said.

"You tell him Butch did that," Maj. Randal said. "He's a blood-thirsty British Royal Marine. In fact, you say we call him 'Headhunter Hoolihan' and that he can't wait to chop off more heads. Tell him Butch doesn't care if they are Italian or not – he's a trophy hunter."

Out of the corner of his eye Maj. Randal could see Bimbashi Hoolihan blanch.

Kaldi babbled to Gubbo Rekash who listened solemnly to every word as if it were a national address being made by the Emperor, King of Kings, Elect of God, The Lion of Judah, etc. The old bandit discretely flicked his eye over to the young Royal Marine officer as Kaldi finished, being careful not to make the slightest eye-to-eye contact. A man did not live as long as he had in the banditry business in a wild, disorganized country like Abyssinia by making foolish social *faux pas,* especially with anyone named "Headhunter."

"He asks if you know the Italians have put out a large reward for you, Major."

"Tell him I said for them to come and collect it."

The shifta chief smiled when he heard the reply. He finished his coffee and stood up, bowing his way out of the camp. As he was leaving, Maj. Randal ordered Kaldi, "Tell the man I pay cash for dead Italian soldiers."

When the crazy old villain was gone, Maj. Randal turned to Lana and demanded, "What were you laughing at?"

"Gubbo Rekash," she replied in her soft, whispery voice. Her reply was the first time either of the slave girls had spoken a word in response to anything he had ever said, though Lana was, in fact, not actually speaking English, she was merely repeating an Abyssinian name.

"It means *cheap bribe*, sire," Kaldi said with a big grin.

Later that morning Force N broke camp and moved out for the rendezvous with Waldo and Rita. Maj. Randal let Bimbashi "Headhunter" Hoolihan take charge. This was going to be his inaugural debut as a combat troop commander leading a movement to contact. Maj. Randal knew that no matter how many times you have done it before, the approach march to an enemy contact will always give a troop commander butterflies. Should it ever fail not to, something is seriously wrong.

When the little command moved out, the commander of Force N got the requisite butterflies even though he was technically only a spectator. For once, they were a strangely comforting feeling. At last, for the first time since he had parachuted into Abyssinia, he was setting out to perform a task he was confident he knew how to do.

Maj. Randal felt like a soldier again… a hard, edgy, in-charge feeling he liked.

When they struck camp, Gubbo Rekash and his ragged band followed suit and mirrored their move. The "Patriots" stayed behind Force N, plainly in sight, doggedly shadowing their line of march. Maj. Randal was not sure if the shifta were waiting for an opportunity to attack or simply wanted to tag along to see the show, though the bandits had no idea what Hoolihan's Heros were setting out to do.

No one did.

The little guerrilla army was growing rapidly even though Force N had yet to swear in their first official recruit. Three-fourths of the native personnel consisted of women camp followers of one kind or another, boy pages, and now a troop of confirmed bandits. Force N was definitely nothing to write home about. As military forces went, it was a throwback to another age – every single man armed with a rifle, a spear, a short sword and carrying a shield.

Most of the men sported oversized straw sombreros typical of the 1920s-era Hollywood Western movies except for the Muslims who wore tassel-topped fezzes. The cowboy hats were not Abyssinian in origin – they were an affectation imported from Europe. Waldo claimed that when you saw a pearl gray Tom Mix hat, you knew the man wearing it was a bandit – they could afford it... or better yet steal one.

When they stopped for the night, Maj. Randal dispatched Kaldi to invite Cheap Bribe over for a joint strategy session. The shifta chief arrived promptly and was instructed to have his men pitch in and help build a boma large enough for both groups to post their mules inside. The bandit chief seemed more than a little surprised to be included in the Force N night defensive laager and agreed to comply without hesitation.

Maj. Randal ordered Bimbashi Hoolihan to organize a 25% alert, meaning that one out of every four men in Butch's Gang had to be awake and on guard at all times. The shifta were *not* included in the night-guard duty rotation.

One member of the command party was to be awake on duty at all times. Kaldi had first shift, Bimbashi Hoolihan the second shift and Maj. Randal took the last watch so he would be awake at sunrise, the traditional "stand-to" dating back to the French and Indian War when the Indians liked to attack at dawn. All Force N troops would be up, alert, armed and ready to fight well before the sun came up – the first Force N Standard Operating Procedure (SOP) had been established. Force N would stand-to every morning from now on.

Maj. Randal made a big show out of his evening inspection tour of the camp, swishing his ivory-handled whisk against the side of his leg, Lana Turner trailing one step behind at his heels. Making his rounds, he encountered Gubbo Rekash supervising his shifta as they labored to construct a section of the thorn bush boma. When the old robber spotted the Force N commander, he began screaming at his men, haranguing them to work harder, faster. The bandit leader gave his shifta a real tongue lashing, putting on an impressive performance of his own – theatrics being the order of the day with both commanders badly overacting.

Maj. Randal nodded with a thin smile, touched the brim of his cut-down Australian slouch hat with his whisk and continued on his rounds, fully intending to shoot out Gubbo's other eye first thing should there be even the slightest hint of a double-cross. He tried hard to convey that impression without actually having to come out and say it.

Fortunately, the night proved uneventful. Next morning, Force N, with attachments, pulled out early and after four hours of steady marching encountered Waldo and Rita. The two were sitting on their mules waiting for them on the military crest of a ridgeline, alongside a twisting goat trail a mile from the road that Waldo had selected for ambush.

When Waldo spotted the band of shifta, he recoiled, "Where'd you pick up that trash?"

"They rode in right after you left."

"You ain't plannin' on lettin' 'em hang around, are you?"

"We need every man we can get."

"Ya' can't never trust scum like these robbers –ain't nothin' but criminals, blood-thirsty murderers and defilers of anythin' or anyone they can get the upper hand on. They'll turn on you, Major. I thought ya' had more common sense."

"I have to fight with what I have, Mr. Treywick, not what I want – you find a suitable site?"

"As long as we don't bite off more than we can chew, this whole stretch of road is one good ambush location after another. You can take your pick. A couple of Eyetie trucks has already done gone by since we've been here. They'd a' been real easy to knock over. Dependin' on how ya' work it, this ought to be a lead pipe cinch."

Bimbashi Hoolihan joined them, accompanied by Kaldi. Waldo cackled when he heard the story about "Headhunter Hoolihan's" new nickname.

"I bet that gave the old hyena somethin' to think about, the idea of Butch loppin' off heads. Sounds like I'm goin' to have to sleep with one eye open myself from here on out; I sure wouldn't want to get my head chopped."

Somewhere along the way, the Royal Marine had acquired a young page who now accompanied him everywhere. Riding on a little black mule, the boy carried a small red, yellow and green Abyssinian flag mounted on a short, stubby bamboo pole. Bimbashi Hoolihan was beginning to take on the trappings of a guerilla troop commander in the field.

"Bimbashi Hoolihan, take charge of your troops and set up an ambush at a location of your choosing somewhere along the road to our immediate front," Maj. Randal ordered, going by the book.

"Sir," Bimbashi Hoolihan responded with a parade-ground salute. "Mr. Treywick, would you be so kind as to escort Kaldi and I on a leader's reconnaissance of your recommended site?"

"Hell Butch, what do ya' think I'm sitting here a' waitin' to do?"

Turning over command of the operation to his young subordinate took every bit of self-discipline Maj. Randal possessed, but it had to be done. In time of war, each officer has to have his baptism of fire as a combat commander. It's a rite of passage that has to be earned – it cannot be bought for any amount of money, learned in the classroom or acquired on field exercises – no matter how realistic.

The only way to become a veteran combat officer is to actually be in a war zone in command of troops and lead a mission in which shots are fired in anger. For the good of Force N, the sooner Bimbashi Hoolihan got his initiation over with, the better. Maj. Randal could improvise most everything with the one exception – junior officers. He intended to groom the only one he had available with great care.

Being allowed to command a combat operation free to make his own decisions while Maj. Randal remained in the background, available to consult when and if he ran into problems, would exponentially enhance the young Bimbashi's professional growth as a troop commander. All the training in the world does not equal the experience gained leading one mission against a real live adversary.

The fact that he understood the importance of handing over the operation and was willing to stand by and allow it to happen was a mark of Maj. Randal's maturity as a commander. Even so, he really wanted to conduct the operation himself.

While attached to the Philippine Constabulary he had the privilege of being schooled in the art of the military ambush by a couple of the best NCOs who had ever worn a U.S. Army uniform. Now he was just as meticulously grooming Bimbashi Hoolihan the way they had him.

That's how it works in the army... when it's done right. Still, Maj. Randal was surprised at how hard it was to stand back and observe. He wondered if Hammerhead and Tiger Stripe, his team sergeants, had felt the same way back in the days when they were operating against Huk guerrillas.

Sitting in the shade of a tall eucalyptus tree smoking a thin cigar, Maj. Randal felt time was dragging as he waited for the leader's recon party to return. He would have liked to tag along, but then it would not have been Bimbashi Hoolihan's recon. The green hands on his Rolex were frozen in place, locked down tight, time seeming to stand still. Sitting nearby holding the reins of the three mules, Lana Turner and Rita Hayworth were being unnaturally silent for a change, seeming to sense his mood. Normally the two girls twittered like canaries.

Suddenly the reconnaissance team rode in on their mules. They were moving quickly as Bimbashi Hoolihan rattled off a string of orders to Kaldi, who moved out immediately to issue them to the waiting native troops. Butch's Gang mounted their mules with a rattle of weaponry as they took their rifles from their pages.

"What do you want me to do with Cheap Bribe and his lads?" Bimbashi Hoolihan asked, never taking his eyes off his soldiers as they went about their preparations for battle.

"I thought we might let him sit up on the ridge and watch the show," Maj. Randal said, "subject to your approval, Bimbashi."

"Very good, sir," Bimbashi Hoolihan said, absorbed by the machinations of his men. The anticipation of an upcoming fight was thick in the air.

"Have those people dismount," he ordered abruptly. "We are moving out from here on foot."

Maj. Randal had been wondering when the Royal Marine was going get around to figuring that one out. He checked a smile. Bimbashi Hoolihan was not doing all that bad for his first mission.

"Any further instructions for me, sir?"

"You know your job," Maj. Randal said in a clipped tone. "Go get 'em, stud."

There is something in the United States Army called the KISS principle. Some people say KISS stands for "Keep It Simple, Stupid" while others claim it means "Keep It Short and Simple." No matter, the idea is the same. Maj. Randal had passed along the KISS principle to his men in RF. It was one of their rules, and Bimbashi Hoolihan intended to apply it to the mission today. He had decided to set up a linear ambush, the most basic and easy to control. A prudent choice considering he was commanding raw native troops who had never fought together as a unit before.

The site selected was a straight stretch of road that led into a sharp, S-shaped curve. Any vehicle coming from either direction would be forced to slow down to enter or negotiate the curve. The far side of the road disappeared into thin air – an eighty-foot drop off a steep cliff.

On the near side, thick scrub brush right up to the edge of the roadway offered excellent concealment for the ambushing force. As sites went, it was textbook perfect. Waldo had proven again to understand the concept of military reconnaissance inside and out, exactly as he had claimed.

Maj. Randal violated every known principle of setting up an ambush by stepping out in the middle of the roadway and walking the length of the killing zone to inspect it. He simply could not help himself, he had to check it out. Besides, stepping off the kill zone of an ambush site is a real adrenalin rush. Bimbashi Hoolihan gave him a disapproving look, which he pointedly ignored. However, Maj. Randal got the message and moved off to a position from which he could observe the action and be out of his subordinate's hair.

Rita was back over the ridge holding the mules while Maj. Randal and Lana awaited developments at the ambush site. Waldo was with Bimbashi Hoolihan, standing by. His assigned task was to take the toolbox out of one of the targeted vehicles and use the tools to dismantle the headlamps in order to remove them from the truck.

The pages and camp followers were with the mules on the reverse slope of the ridge with instructions to close in on the road once the firing stopped. Bimbashi Hoolihan intended to depart the area as fast as possible when the time came to break contact. Hit and run, Swamp Fox Force style – the way the Calais veterans had described their tactics against the 10th Panzer Division to him in a million bull sessions.

Up on the ridge Gubbo Rekash and his crew were sitting like eager spectators waiting for the start of a football match. Along the edge of the road, the Force N prospects were waiting in concealment in their firing positions, eagerly anticipating the arrival of an unsuspecting Italian convoy and Bimbashi Hoolihan's signal to initiate the ambush.

Few things are as dull as waiting in an ambush site for the target to arrive. It is hard to understand why that is so. You are standing by to kill your enemy who will certainly kill you if he can, and yet you are bored nearly to tears with the waiting. It is the same every time.

Maj. Randal decided to pass the time by practicing his language skill on Lana. Not being an accomplished linguist, he knew he would probably make hash of it, but he gave it a shot anyway. "You and Rita," he stumbled, mixing English in with the Amharic he was studying out of a small paperback phase book, "have *konjo geug ma leut*."

He was trying to say the girls had "beautiful smiles" but was uncertain if his finger had slid down far enough, causing him to read the wrong line, accidentally substituting the word "smell" for the word "smile"... uh-oh!

Lana rewarded his clumsy effort with a beautiful smile anyway. And since she and Rita were in a dead heat for second place behind Lady Jane for the most beautiful smiles in the whole world, he felt like he had gotten a lot of bang for his buck.

Deciding he had enough foreign language work for one day, Maj. Randal put the phrase book back into one of the breast pockets of his jungle-green battle dress uniform (BDU), leaned back against the trunk of the tree and watched the empty road. He wondered what Lady Jane was doing right this minute. How long would it be before the Italians came... if they came?

He sat chewing on his thin, unlit cigar. Ambushes were always like this – BORING!

5
CAMP CROC

THE HUDSON, CARRYING CAPTAIN THE LADY JANE SEABORN, OBE and Lieutenant Pamala Plum-Martin, OBE, RM landed at Nairobi Airport where it was met by her father's old Kenyan business manager who had continued to run the farms after the Lady's family was killed. Lady Jane's father, Colonel Lionel Fairweather, had been an avid sportsman who loved Kenya and spent as much time there as possible. He had accumulated a number of properties in the country, all of which were described as "farms" even though they did not grow any crops.

The plane required servicing, and the aircrew needed rest before the last leg of their odyssey. The manager whisked the women to the Mayfair Court Hotel where Lady Jane and Lt. Plum-Martin immediately disappeared into their suites and proceeded to soak luxuriously in king-sized sunken tile baths. The flight had been long, hard and not without hazard. Portions of it had been through airspace well within the combat patrol fan of Italian C.R. 42 fighters.

Early the next morning the Hudson took off, en route to Marsabit on the shore of Lake Paradise, the location of Lady Jane's most spectacular Kenyan property. Some authorities rate Lake Paradise as one of the ten best-kept secrets in the world, while others have declared it to be one of the most exotic travel destinations anywhere – only almost no one ever went there. Why? Marsabit was ten hours north of Nairobi by road, surrounded by the Chalbi Desert beginning three hundred kilometers south of the even more remote Lake Rudolph. Locally, the lake area was known as "bad bush" – meaning the conditions were primitive, the natives were hostile, and the road was "bad" (for an African road to be described as "bad" it has to be basically impassable).

In the high jungle forest covering the hills above Lake Paradise lived the largest concentration of big elephants carrying the heaviest ivory anywhere in Africa. The elephants came down to water at the lake in the evenings and made wonderful viewing from the veranda of the Seaborn Paradise Farm. The beasts were oversized even for jumbos – there was something odd about their genetics.

A noted zoologist who had studied the Lake Paradise elephant herd speculated that they were a lost link, or possibly a remnant herd, surviving from prehistoric days. The size of the Lake Paradise elephant skulls measured significantly larger than any other known species of African pachyderm.

Lady Jane's father owned the entire jungle forest, and he had made it into a private game preserve. Hunting was strictly forbidden except to cull the herd. Not only had her father been a keen sportsman, he had been a passionate conservationist. A small private army made up of local tribesman under the command of a former Kenyan game warden was constantly on patrol, waging a never-ending battle against poachers. Lady Jane had not visited the place in the sixteen years since her family's plane crash.

The Hudson set down on the dirt strip located at the edge of the lush oasis, stopping only long enough to pick up the farm manager and the ex-game warden, and then taking off immediately for the remote northwestern shore of Lake Rudolph. The final destination was her father's fly camp for Nile perch fishing.

The lake sported perch averaging two hundred pounds apiece, and they had been known to reach up to four hundred pounds in size.

In addition to monster perch, Lake Rudolph also claimed the largest assemblage of Nile crocodiles in Africa. It was said that twenty-two thousand of them lived in the lake, though no one was exactly sure who had counted them. The crocodile, like the perch, were gigantic. No claim was made that they were a genetic throwback – all crocodile are prehistoric. The vicious Nile crocs in the lake were simply giant, hungry reptiles. You had to be extremely cautious fishing from the bank. No one in their right mind ever went wading or swimming, and even small boats were not immune from attack.

If there had ever been a perfect location to locate a clandestine military base of operations for incursions into a neighboring country, Lake Rudolph was the site. It was the world's largest desert lake. Situated in the Great Rift valley, it is completely surrounded by a barren alkaline volcanic desert, the Chalbi, and inhabited by some of the fiercest and most hostile natives in the world. By any measure a remote, desolate and mysterious place, the lake was virtually inaccessible except for the extremely determined. The only way to reach it was by air or camel caravan, and the ground route was subject to attack from the natives.

The lake lay not far from the junction of the Abyssinian, Sudan and Kenyan borders and actually encroached into Abyssinia. Because the border had been closed since before the turn of the century, the area was called the "Forbidden Zone." Anyone not connected to the Fairweather or Seaborn family wishing to go there had to receive a government permit. Few permits were issued. Not a single one had been approved since 1935.

The fishing camp, jocularly known as "Camp Croc" by Lady Jane's father, was a monument to the determination of a rich Englishman to enjoy both his sport and his creature comforts. The house was as handsomely outfitted as any Gun & Rod club anywhere. Every stick of furniture, glassware and hardware, to include a generator for electricity, had been painstakingly trekked overland to the lake by camel caravan contracted from the hardy desert natives of the Rendille tribe.

On the Northwestern shore of the lake, where Camp Croc was situated, there were seasonal herds of migrating plains animals: lion, cheetah and a huge flamingo population. Natives living around the lake – the Turkana, Rendille, Galla and the El Molo – were noted for their ferociousness. A constant state of semi-war existed among the tribes, and none of them welcomed outsiders.

You have to be tough to survive in a barren, volcanic land as unforgiving as the Chalbi Desert, and the tribesmen certainly were. All four tribes tended to shoot first and ask questions later... and they hated most white men.

When viewed on a map, Lake Rudolph was shaped like a giant green jalapeño, and it was frequently called "The Jade Sea." As the Hudson approached, the colossal green lake was glimmering in the distance like an exquisite jewel in the bone-dry desert. Lady Jane remembered as a little girl her father had teased that it was the color of her eyes.

Well, not quite.

The Hudson landed on the desert next to the house. After a quick inspection tour, Lady Jane issued detailed instructions to the farm manager she had brought from Lake Paradise to arrange to have the house put in order. Camp Croc was going to be organized initially as a base to support Sqn. Ldr. Paddy Wilcox, DSO, OBE, MC, DFC, and his aircrew. The idea was for the Jade Sea to be the jumping-off point for the supply mission planned to leapfrog up the chain of lakes into the heart of Abyssinia. And eventually it was going to serve as a secret way station for the officers and men who would pass through en route to operate with Force N.

"Camp Croc is going to become a major supply dump in the immediate future. There will be a sizeable permanent staff stationed here. In addition to quarters for them, you will need to organize separate permanent living arrangements for at least five of my female Royal Marines," Lady Jane ordered.

Lieutenant Karen Montgomery would arrive shortly to set up a parachute rigging station. Most of the men assigned to Force N and a large portion of the supplies would be going in by parachute.

The ex-game warden was ordered to recruit a security detachment from the Turkana, the tribe in the immediate area. Once operations commenced, no one was going to be allowed inside Camp Croc and if anyone should wander by – on purpose or by accident – they would not be permitted to leave – detained for the duration. Lady Jane informed the former game warden that he could turn over responsibility for the security detail to Lieutenant Harry Shelby, MC, Sherwood Foresters, and return to protecting his elephants once the RF officer arrived overland with his "Shelby's Scouts."

Then, with time being precious, Lady Jane and Lt. Plum-Martin boarded the Hudson, and the pilot immediately took off for the return trip to Nairobi. From there Lady Jane would begin coordinating the shuttling forward of men and equipment while Lt. Plum-Martin flew back to Khartoum to report to Major Sir Terry "Zorro" Stone, KBE, MC, and take up her position as the Force N intelligence officer (IO).

"Camp Croc was my father's favorite place," Lady Jane commented as the plane skimmed over the brackish, desolate desert lake. "He would have rather been up here fishing for giant perch than anywhere else in the entire world."

Looking up from filing her blood red nails, Lt. Plum-Martin said, "Men are sick!"

Upon arriving again in Nairobi, Lady Jane enjoyed a long, hot soak in her hotel suite at the Mayfair. After changing into a fresh uniform, she asked the hotel to supply a driver to chauffeur her to the Headquarters (HQ) of Major General Alan Cunningham, the commander of East Africa Force (EAF) – the troops who would be making the attack from Kenya into Abyssinia. She did not have an appointment.

Maj. Gen. Cunningham was not the kind of commander who suffered drop-in visitors, outright refusing to meet them in most cases. However, Lady Jane was a formidable woman, and he agreed to see her right away for two excellent but entirely different reasons.

The first reason being that he vaguely knew "The Razor," a close friend of his seagoing brother, and was aware Lady Jane was related to him by marriage. No one in their right mind in any branch of the service who valued their career would antagonize the old Admiral by snubbing a member of his family – the nickname "Razor" had nothing whatsoever to do with shaving.

The second reason was that Lady Jane was reputed to be one of the most beautiful women in England. No military man would turn away a woman of that ilk – no right-thinking soldier, regardless of grade, is ever that busy.

After the courtesies were out of the way, Lady Jane explained without fanfare the purpose of her unscheduled call. She needed one hundred trucks to transport military stores from Nairobi to Lake Rudolf. From there the supplies were to be airdropped to the secret guerrilla army operating inside Abyssinia in support of his upcoming invasion of the country.

When Maj. Gen. Cunningham heard her request, he found it difficult to keep a straight face. In fact, it was only with a great deal of iron-willed restraint that he did not break out in loud guffaws. Clearly the woman was perfectly serious, but it was equally clear she had no idea of the impossibility of the request. The truth was, Lady Jane might as well have asked for a thousand trucks... or even ten thousand. There were no trucks.

Currently he was in the middle of the marshalling phase for the southern prong of the upcoming invasion of IEA. When it kicked off, he was to command the main thrust intended to drive all the way up the coast of the Red Sea – and secure it so that the Middle East Command would qualify for American Lend Lease. There were two distinct phases of the operational plan, which were state secrets, but from Lady Jane's demeanor he was pretty sure she was fully aware of them.

The first phase was to assemble his forces for the invasion. To accomplish that, he was going to have to move his troops to the start point on the border of Abyssinia across the waterless, trackless Chalbi Desert. To do that, he was going to have to build a road every step of the way while carrying his water, fuel, military stores and equipment with him. Militarily, that is a tall task.

The second phase was to drive the Italians – who badly outnumbered him – out of the Red Sea corridor.

All things considered, the combat was probably going to be easier than the nightmarish logistics involved in transporting his army up to the line of departure. One hundred trucks – ha! She might as well have asked for a magic carpet! EAF was not able to count on one stick of material support from Great Britain. To solve the shortage, South African Field Marshal Sir Jan Smuts had taken the draconian step of nationalizing every single civilian automaker in his country to build army trucks. Then the trucks needed to be

driven straight off the assembly line one thousand miles overland to Kenya
– before they could start the trek across the desert to the Abyssinian border.
Getting the trucks to the start line in time for the invasion was going to
require a military miracle.

"Lady Seaborn," Maj. Gen. Cunningham explained gently, "for
reasons I am not at liberty to discuss, I shall have to disappoint you in your
request. I do not have a single truck to spare at the moment. And it would
not be fair to you to leave you with the impression that the situation in
regards to wheeled transport will remedy itself any time in the foreseeable
future. I sincerely wish I could be of more help, but it is simply impossible."

Lady Jane was not pleased with the General's response. However, she
was not surprised, knowing a considerable more about the details of the
planned invasion of IEA than she was willing to reveal. But she was not to
be deterred. Once Lady Jane set out to accomplish a task, she never let
anything stand in the way. Her father had taught her to never give up.

The Royal Marine officer left Maj. Gen. Cunningham's HQ and
proceeded directly to the Nairobi office of Special Operations Executive
(SOE).

"Lady Seaborn, my instructions are to render you all the support it is
in my power to provide, on penalty of being interned in the Tower of London
for the duration should I fail to do so," the Chief-of-Station informed her. "I
have been working night and day to try to find a way to move Force N's
supplies from the Port of Mombasa to Nairobi.

"The fact is, while I may be able to accomplish that, I have no idea
how to transport the stuff to Lake Rudolf once it arrives here. Every civilian
truck in Kenya has already been requisitioned by the army."

"We have been promised a Catalina. Will that help?" Lady Jane asked.

"Yes, but it has not been forthcoming. Besides, it would tie up one
aircraft flying around the clock seven days a week for two months merely to
ferry all the men and supplies needed for Force N up to Lake Rudolf. Then,
take another four to six months to leapfrog the stuff forward up the chain of
lakes to where we believe Force N is currently located. We do not have the
luxury of that kind of time. The campaign will be over by then."

"In that case," Lady Jane said, "I suppose a handful of Walruses will
not be much in the way of assistance?"

"They will help in shuttling the personnel forward," the Station Chief replied, fully aware that Lady Jane had a certain "leap over tall buildings in a single bound" reputation. He appreciated "leap over tall buildings" type operators – they were hard to find, and he did not want to insult her or make it sound like he was talking down to her or was a know-it-all. Nor was it his intention to discourage her. He simply was at a loss to solve the logistical problem. The amount of material to be moved, the lack of available transport, and the long distances to cover compounded by the primitive conditions in the northern desert region of Kenya –created a situation that was all but insurmountable.

"All right then," Lady Jane announced, sounding determined, "you concentrate your efforts on having the supplies delivered to Nairobi, and I shall arrange some way to transport them up to Lake Rudolf."

"Very well, Lady Seaborn. I must say, you have certainly volunteered to take on the Herculean share of the task. You can count on me, and if there is any service I can perform to help you accomplish your end of the bargain, rest assured – I shall. All you have to do is ask."

"I need you to send a cable for me."

"Certainly. What do you wish to convey?"

"To Commodore Richard Seaborn, routed through the Khartoum office – 'Urgent you meet me Nairobi ASAP.' "

"The signal will have gone out before you return to your hotel."

"There is one other thing," Lady Jane said. "I should like for you to contact the Phantom Group in the UK and request Captain David Niven by name to come out to Kenya to organize a long-range communications station at Camp Croc, capable of covering all of Italian East Africa. It shall not be necessary for him to remain on station for the duration of the mission, but I would like David to personally supervise the installation."

"My pleasure," the Chief-of-Station said. "Phantom and SOE have established a working relationship. In the interim I shall arrange for a temporary SOE signals team to be established at Camp Croc."

The next stop for Lady Jane was the Nairobi branch of Barclays Bank. In the heavily-paneled chambers of the bank president's luxurious private office, she informed him, "I wish to purchase a fleet of amphibious transport airplanes of the Catalina-Shortland class. Perform a worldwide search on availability through your international offices and report back to me at my hotel at your earliest convenience this afternoon."

"Might I inquire for what purpose, Lady Seaborn?"

"No," Lady Jane said. "I am at the Mayfair."

SOMEWHERE DEEP IN THE ABYSSINIAN CENTRAL HIGHLANDS, Major John Randal was alerted by the sound of three loud wood-on-wood *thunks*. It was the pre-arranged signal for "Enemy in Sight" generated by Bimbashi Butch "Headhunter" Hoolihan hammering the side of a tree trunk with a small green log. In this case, the enemy was not actually in sight but the sound of an approaching vehicle could be heard. The wooden *thunk, thunk, thunk w*as the preparatory equivalent to the command "Stand Ready," making it no longer boring to be lying in wait in an ambush position.

Maj. Randal rose up on one knee, taking pains to stay well-concealed behind the tree under which he had been reclining. He studied the designated killing zone of the ambush to his immediate front one more time. He had a clear, unobstructed view. The sound of a truck was coming from the left which meant it would have to decelerate to negotiate the sharp S-curve.

Bimbashi Hoolihan had made a mistake when he set up his ambush and Maj. Randal wondered if the young Royal Marine had realized it yet. His young protégé had failed to put out an obstruction to force the truck to come to a complete halt before Butch's Gang initiated the ambush. This was not necessarily a fatal flaw – however, if the truck driver survived the initial burst of firing and kept his wits about him he could accelerate and drive right through the kill zone.

Since today was, in effect, a live-fire learning experience for his Bimbashi – a right of passage into the ranks of blooded combat troop leaders who have actually commanded men in action – Maj. Randal had elected not to point out the oversight. Trial and error is the best teacher, particularly when it comes to battle. Tactical blunders made in the field during an action are never forgotten – not ever.

Bimbashi Hoolihan would gain a lot more out of the exercise if he were allowed to make his own mistakes and see the results first hand. Besides, tactics are not written in stone. The best tactic that fails goes in the loss column, while the worst tactic ever devised is a victory if it works.

The thing to keep in mind: it is paramount to not get killed during the learning process.

Suddenly, a Fiat 38 truck rolled into view. Inside the open-topped cab were two Italian soldiers sporting dark-tinted goggles. Standing in the bed, leaning against the back of the cab were two armed askaris wearing khaki shirts, shorts and sola topees. The fascists seemed blithely unaware of the danger they were in. That was good.

The signal to initiate the ambush was to be Bimbashi Hoolihan firing a burst from his Thompson submachine gun. The choice of signals was sound because it was simple, easy to recognize by all the troops in the ambush party and inflicted causalities on the enemy immediately. As initiating devices went, the Thompson was a lot better than blowing a whistle which might be heard by the opposition, therefore giving him a slight window of opportunity to take evasive action or perform counter-ambush measures.

BAAAAAARRRAAP. BAAAAAARRRAAP. Bimbashi Hoolihan fired two carefully aimed bursts, chopping down the two native askari riflemen. The driver of the truck, a stocky, black-haired Italian soldier without any headgear, immediately hunched down over the steering wheel and floored the accelerator. The khaki-clad soldier in the passenger seat fell out of sight onto the floor of the cab.

The initial two bursts from the .45 caliber Thompson submachine gun were quickly followed by a ragged volley of rifle shots from the brave stalwarts of Hoolihan's Heros. Maj. Randal noted it was about the most uncoordinated fusillade a group of armed men could perform. As far as ambushes went, this was one for the record books – all-time worst shooting by a concealed party of riflemen at point blank range.

After the first few hesitant rounds popped off, the firing picked up in intensity and enthusiasm as Butch's Gang warmed to the task – particularly since the troops realized nobody was firing back at them. Then Hoolihan's

Heros really poured it on – only they were not hitting anything. The Fiat 38 truck rolled on through the kill zone.

Maj. Randal winked at Lana Turner who was crouched next to him observing the action with a concerned look on her golden face. The fascists were clearly escaping. He wrapped his arm in the M-1903 A-1 Springfield rifle's sling, stood up, shouldered the weapon and shot the bare-headed driver center of mass, causing him to slump over the wheel. The truck immediately lost speed, swerved to the right, then crashed into a large boulder at the side of the road. Steam spewed up from the radiator.

As soon as the truck wrecked, Bimbashi Hoolihan led his troops out into the killing zone, putting in the final assault. The move was perfectly timed. The prospects were bolting and firing their rifles as they advanced, laying down marching fire exactly the way he had drilled them. Only they were still not hitting anything. Rounds were ricocheting off the gravel road, knocking leaves out of trees and zinging off into the great unknown. There was not the nice, neat cone of fire hammering the target Fiat 38 truck into junk metal as intended.

Up above on the ridgeline, Gubbo Rekash was watching with his band of shifta. When they noted the Italians and the askaris were down, there was no return fire and the assault wave was going in to get the loot, the land pirates could no longer restrain themselves. The shifta streamed off the hill making warlike screams and rushed down into the killing zone of the ambush with the wild abandon of a platoon of U.S. Marines who had just heard the words "FREE BEER."

Maj. Randal, Hoolihan's Heros and Cheap Bribe's bandits all arrived in the killing zone of the ambush at more or less the same time. Waldo went straight to work dismantling the headlamps from the Fiat 38.

The screaming shifta caused Butch's Gang, who had been attacking on line like a well-oiled fighting machine, to become concerned that the bandits would get first dibs on the plunder. In the blink of an eye, Bimbashi Hoolihan's highly disciplined fighting force disintegrated into a disorganized mob of want-to-be looters.

Bimbashi Hoolihan was shouting out orders, Kaldi was interpreting them as fast and loudly as he could; meanwhile, a riot had broken out in the back of the Fiat as shifta and Hoolihan's prospects battled each other for treasure. The kill zone of the ambush had deteriorated into a swirling mass of a heavily armed men crazed with the idea that someone else might be able to steal more than they could.

Maj. Randal opened the passenger door of the Fiat, reached in and pulled out the Italian soldier who was curled up on the floorboard with his hands over his head. When the terrified Italian soldier saw the chaotic scene swirling around the truck he burst into tears. He had a pretty good idea what these demented Abyssinians had in mind for him.

Lana shoved the unresisting man face down to the ground in the middle of the gravel road with her boot and putting the point of her curved dagger against his neck to keep him from moving, pulled out a rawhide string and lashed his hands together behind his back.

"Kill him if he tries to escape."

"Please do not hurt me," the Italian soldier pleaded in flawless English.

"If he makes a run for it, shoot him, Lana."

Walking around to the front of the Fiat 38 truck, Maj. Randal inquired, "How's it going with the headlight, Mr. Treywick?"

"Just about done, Major. These idiots shot out one of 'em. The only target Butch's boys hit all day was the one thing they wasn't supposed to shoot at."

Going back around the Fiat 38 in the middle of the mêlée taking place, Maj. Randal found that Bimbashi Hoolihan had Gubbo Rekash down on his knees with the Cutts compensator of his Thompson submachine gun pressing against his forehead square between the eyes – only one of which, like the headlamps on the enemy truck, was still operative. Cheap Bribe was begging for his life.

"Go ahead, shoot him, Butch," Maj. Randal said conversationally. "It'll save me from having to do it later."

Bimbashi Hoolihan gave him a look, then in a threatening tone ordered Kaldi, "Tell Gubbo to call off his men, now!"

Kaldi screamed at the bandit chief only to receive loud squawks of protest in response. Maj. Randal walked back around to the front of the truck to check on Waldo again. The job was completed, and an empty light socket was all that was left of where the left front headlamp had been.

"Let's get the hell out of Dodge, Mr. Treywick." They had already spent longer at the site of the ambush than he cared to – Maj. Randal liked to hit hard, get in and get out fast.

"P.J. Pretorius hisself couldn't have said it any better, Major," the old hunter agreed as he carefully put the headlamp into a burlap bag and started tying off the end in preparation of pulling out.

Suddenly a Bersaglieri wearing the signature plumed light infantry sola topee roared up on his powerful Moto Guzzi Alce (Elk) motorcycle. The troops and shifta were still doing battle with each other over what was in the back of the truck; consequently, no one was in a position to do much about it.

The dispatch rider took one look at the wild mêlée taking place in the middle of the road in front of him and without a moment's hesitation gunned his motorcycle, shot through the killing zone of the ambush, navigated around the wrecked Fiat 38, swished through the S-shaped curve and was gone, poof. He disappeared in a flash without as much as a single shot being fired at him.

Later, galloping out of the area on their mules, Maj. Randal shouted over to Bimbashi Hoolihan riding alongside, "Butch, start thinking about expanding your command to a company-sized element."

"You want me to be a company commander after today, sir?" the Royal Marine called back in disbelief. "I was thinking more along the lines of a Board of Inquiry."

"You did fine, Butch," Maj. Randal said as they pounded along. "If we don't get some help in here I'm going to turn you into a battalion commander as soon as you recruit the troops."

"Sir, have you been smoking more of that bhat?"

Later, when the Italian rescue force arrived at the ambush site, they were greeted by the unspeakable sight of the decapitated heads of three men displayed prominently on the hood of the Fiat truck, like ornaments – one was still wearing sun goggles. The fourth man was missing. The initial reaction of the troops in the relieving unit was revulsion followed by violent anger. However, that wore off soon enough, to be replaced by the onset of pure, raw fear.

A capital "N" had been finger-painted prominently in blood on each of the three dead mens' foreheads. The Italians all knew that had to mean something… but what, exactly? Every single man in the relief party had a story to tell when they returned to base.

The legend of Force N was beginning to grow.

6
HEADHUNTER'S DEBRIEFING

THE DAY FOLLOWING THE AMBUSH, MAJOR JOHN RANDAL
called a war counsel consisting of himself, Bimbashi Butch "Headhunter"
Hoolihan and Kaldi. Waldo Treywick sat in along with Rita Hayworth and
Lana Turner close at hand, the girls not wanting to be left out of anything.
First, Maj. Randal had Waldo lead off with his version of events – starting
with his reconnaissance of the ambush site and proceeding through the order
to withdraw from the ambush killing zone after he had collected the
headlamp from the Fiat 38. Next Maj. Randal had his Royal Marine officer
talk through the entire mission. Finally, he stood up and debriefed the entire
mission from start to finish.

The purpose of the exercise was two-fold: for Bimbashi Hoolihan to
have an opportunity to talk through every minute detail of the operation from
the time Force N departed for the target area until they reached safe haven
following the successful execution of the ambush, and also for him to have
an opportunity to hear other people describe what had taken place. That part

is always instructive to the mission commander since no two participants ever see a combat action the same way.

It also gave Maj. Randal an opportunity to recite his version of events, so that he could point out tactical errors, omissions, and mistakes without seeming to be overly critical because, by definition, a debriefing is supposed to be a critique.

Debriefings are learning vehicles. Everyone involved has a chance to explain the operation from their personal perspective, and any controversial decisions or actions that may have taken place in the heat of the engagement can be pointed out and examined in detail in a calm setting.

There is no such thing as the perfect military operation. Things go wrong, equipment malfunctions, events unfolding on the ground are misinterpreted, resulting in incorrect decisions. People forget things under stress, communications fail, etc. The list of challenges to getting an ambush right are endless – before ever even taking into consideration any countermeasures the enemy initiates to defeat your plan. That's what makes being a combat commander so incredibility interesting.

Using the debriefing method, Maj. Randal was able to conduct a full-scale public review of his Bimbashi in the spirit of a colleague analyzing the mission with an eye to learning from the experience, rather than as an omnipotent commander dishing out criticism. And it did not seem quite as much like he had been looking over his young subordinate's shoulder judgmentally from start to finish – even though that was exactly what he had been doing.

Maj. Randal realized it was extremely important at the end of the day, after all the finger-pointing was done, for Bimbashi Hoolihan to feel validated in his actions as a troop leader and for there to be no petty disagreement between the two of them about who did what, as so often happens after combat actions when it comes time to pass out the blame or receive credit.

Giving Bimbashi Hoolihan the chance to speak provided the Royal Marine a golden opportunity to point out first that he had failed to take into consideration a method of blocking the road, so that way Maj. Randal did not have to, sparing the young officer unnecessary embarrassment. There was no need to disparage Bimbashi Hoolihan. He would never make that particular error again – not ever – no matter how many ambushes he set up during his career. He would make other mistakes, as would Maj. Randal, but he would never again fail to block a high-speed avenue of approach.

In fact, the ambush had been a resounding success, all the melodrama notwithstanding. Even if the Fiat 38 had rolled on through the ambush and escaped, they would have accomplished two out of three of its primary goals – to bloody Hoolihan's Heros and to get Bimbashi Hoolihan's first combat mission as an officer under his belt. Ambushes are not nice and neat. Things go wrong.

For a first mission, Maj. Randal was well satisfied, and he made a point to let his protégé know it. Recognition, he believed, was vital for a commander to pass out if he was interested in obtaining maximum performance from a junior officer. Commanders who understand the value of praising their subordinates motivate them rather than stooping to the more common practice of ridiculing their junior's mistakes, are rare individuals.

"Butch, the purpose of the exercise was to obtain a headlamp so Waldo can rig up a spotlight. We got one, your men were able to see how Force N expects them to conduct ambushes and we sent a message to the Italians – the price of poker has gone up. You looked good out there when things got a little crazy. Nice job, stud!"

"Thanks, sir," Bimbashi Hoolihan said, meaning it. Few things in life are ever more rewarding to a combat officer than being complimented on the handling of his first battle assignment. This is true across the board, from the lowest-ranking junior officer to the highest-ranking general.

"What are your questions, Bimbashi?"

"Sir, why are we still chopping off enemy heads?"

Maj. Randal responded carefully, not wanting to lose the respect of an officer who looked up to him and who was clearly troubled by the extreme violence inherent in guerrilla war. "What's the first Rule of Raiding?"

"The first rule is there ain't no rules, sir."

"Exactly," Maj. Randal said. "We're in an unconventional situation, Butch, that requires us to be creative. One of the few things we have to work with is the knowledge the Blackshirts are terrified of the Abyssinians they conquered."

"Yes, sir. But what does Force N mutilating dead soldiers have to do with that?"

"Psychological warfare," Maj. Randal explained, "makes the Italians' fear work for *us*. The object is to cause the bad guys to dread leaving the safety of their fortified bases by convincing them a blood-thirsty Force N guerrilla with a sharp knife is hiding behind every bush."

"Your dago is a real macho individual," Waldo waxed philosophically. "Deep down inside he is seriously concerned about the idea of some native doing a little trophy hunting on his private parts – particularly if he ain't quite dead at the time."

"The fascists have never followed the Geneva Conventions, Butch," Kaldi pointed out helpfully. "Clouds of poison gas, sprayed from the heavens to fall on innocent women and children, is much worse than the cutting-off of the head of your dead enemy in order to advance your military objective. Besides, in this country the vanquished must expect harsh treatment. The Blackshirt invaders have inflicted many massacres on the Abyssinian people."

"Force N policy is to never allow a live prisoner to be abused, Butch," Maj. Randal said firmly. "One day we're going to want the bad guys to surrender. The only way they will is if they trust us to not maltreat them."

"How do we convince the Wops to trust us to protect them if we keep leaving the decapitated heads of their soldiers everywhere, scaring the bloody hell out of them, sir?"

"Easy, Butch," Maj. Randal said as he stuck a thin Italian cigarillo that he had captured from the truck between his teeth, "We blame the shifta – we'll say Cheap Bribe did it. When the time is right, we'll march right up to an Italian base camp, inform the commander they're surrounded and if he doesn't surrender right this minute, we'll pull out and leave 'em to the tender mercy of Gubbo's gang of cutthroats – take your choice."

"Sir, that may be the best plan I have ever heard!"

"I'll second that," Waldo said. "You may turn out to be as good as they say in your book. I sure wish P.J. Pretorius was here right now to hear how slick you got this deal all lined out."

"Butch," Maj. Randal said, changing the subject, "are you prepared to copy?"

"Sir!"

"First, mobilize all the pages into a platoon we'll call the 'Bad Boys.' I intend to use 'em for minor sabotage projects – juvenile delinquent-type missions."

"The men are not going to like the idea of having their gun-boys taken away, sir."

"Put your troops on the payroll as of now, but it's a prerequisite for membership that they have to send their retainers to serve in the Bad Boys," Maj. Randal said. "Tell the men it'll make Hoolihan's Heros a leaner, meaner, harder hitting fighting machine – sell it to 'em, Butch."

"Yes, sir. What kind of sabotage do you have in mind?"

"Everywhere we go, we'll send the Bad Boys out in small teams to operate against the roads for miles in all directions. I want them scattering spikes to go after the Italians' shortage of tires. Have 'em knock down the telephone lines. And order 'em to paint, scrape or nail the letter 'N' on everything not breathing."

"How do I decide who to issue the Springfields to?" Bimbashi Hoolihan asked with a ring of excitement in his voice. Force N's private war was clearly stepping up the pace. "We only have a dozen rifles."

"Don't issue a single one," Maj. Randal said. "Troops always want equipment they can't have."

"I think I understand, sir," Bimbashi Hoolihan said. "You want me to continue using our handful of Springfield rifles to drill new recruits so when we eventually *do* make contact with Force N Rear and they start air-dropping big lots of M-1903 A-1 Springfields to us, we have a large force of men dying to get their hands on them, trained and ready to put them to good use."

"That's the idea, Butch."

"What else, sir?"

"Take half of your platoon and move out this afternoon to conduct another road ambush at a location of your own choosing anywhere in this general area," Maj. Randal ordered casually, pointing out the new area of operations (AO) on his map. "You're on your own, Bimbashi. Link up with me in four days' time at these grid coordinates. What are your questions?"

"When do you want me to have the Bad Boys ready to commence operations, Major?"

"Today before you move out will do just fine."

"Yes, sir," Bimbashi Hoolihan said. Conducting an ambush under the direct supervision of your commanding officer is one thing. It is quite something else to be sent out to do it all by yourself.

"Move out, Bimbashi," Maj. Randal said. "I intend to try out Mr. Treywick's new spotlight tonight. Then at first light tomorrow I'll take the other half of your men and conduct my own ambush somewhere along this stretch of road... right about here," Maj. Randal tapped the map in the general vicinity he intended to operate. "Don't worry, Butch, I'll take Cheap Bribe with me so you won't be saddled with him this time out."

"I should have shot that bloody brigand when I had the chance, sir."

"Yes, you should, but now you know why we need him."

"So we can blame him for everything?"

"You're a fast learner, Butch."

Gubbo Rekash was summoned to Maj. Randal's Command Post (CP). Maj. Randal proceeded to read him the riot act for his shifta's actions. Waldo translated. The shifta chieftain was ordered to parade his men. Once assembled, the bandit troops were instructed to produce every item of equipment that had been plundered at the ambush site.

Maj. Randal stood out in front of them swishing his ivory-handled whisk and made it clear that in future operations it was a penalty punishable by being boiled in marinated peacock oil, or possibly tarred and dipped in baby blue ostrich feathers, to confiscate war material from the Italians and fail to turn it over to Force N. He made a big show of his displeasure.

The Emperor would extract serious retribution from any man found in possession of unauthorized booty and as the agent of the King of Kings, the Lion of Judah, Elect of God, etc., Maj. Randal would take it upon himself to dish out the punishment personally posthaste and not bother to burden his Imperial Highness with the petty details.

This harangue was met with an indifferent silence from the motley crew of Abyssinian bad men. The shifta were, after all, professional criminals – stealing was what they did. Cheap Bribe's crew was used to people not liking it. Not one of the offenders was concerned about threats emanating from distant Khartoum, even if this officer was promising to carry them out here and now on his own recognizance.

Basically, it is impossible to intimidate thugs like the shifta with mere words. Maj. Randal knew that. He marched over to one of the outlaws who was brazenly wearing a pistol belt with a Fascist eagle on the buckle. The buckle had been taken from one of the askari who had been killed in the back of the ambushed Fiat 38 truck. Maj. Randal tapped the buckle with his ivory-handled whisk.

"Mr. Treywick, order Cheap Bribe to recover this piece of captured enemy equipment."

Waldo relayed the command to a startled Gubbo Rekash. The robber chief suddenly found himself in a dicey situation, one he had not seen coming or had time to develop a strategy to deal with in advance. Caught between a rock and a hard spot, he could side with his men, which is what they all expected of him, or he could cave in to the Force N commander – something he was loath to be seen to do.

Shifta potentates rule by strength, guile, fear and fidelity to the band. Plus, they are generally a little smarter than the troops they command. Paramount chiefs of Abyssinian robber gangs are cagy local politicians with guns who like to see which way the wind blows before they commit to action. Political missteps generally being fatal in Abyssinia, Maj. Randal did not actually blame the man for his reticence.

"Do it now."

Gubbo Rekash had a wild, panicked look in his single eye, not caring at all for the way things had developed. Forced to make a choice and to make it quick, right there on the spot, all of his finely-tuned survival instincts were screaming that this was a really good way to get himself in a lot of trouble one way or the other – double fast.

A drawback to being a shifta CEO is that you don't have a whole lot of people to go to for advice in a pinch, and never anyone to bail you out if you make the wrong call. The crafty one-eyed felon did the math. There was a good chance the Emperor might have him shot on sight for various crimes and misdemeanors if he ever got the chance – if and when he ever returned.

Then again, there was the equal possibility that the King of Kings might reward him for services rendered to his representative, Maj. Randal.

But if he failed to back up his men in this showdown they might mutiny, a genuine possibility never far from his mind on any given day.

Gubbo Rekash did not really like the odds – a long shot on the Emperor against a sure thing that his men expected him to back them up. On the other hand, there was the complicating factor that Maj. Randal would most likely react badly if he failed to follow his orders.

Not bothering to announce his decision, Cheap Bribe suddenly commenced a savage, businesslike beating of the man wearing the pistol belt with his sturdy riding cane. As he continued to slash his man methodically with the thick stick – the type favored by Abyssinian gentlemen who rode mules on a regular basis – the shifta fell to the ground cowering.

Finally putting a stop to the assault, Maj. Randal ordered, "Have every item of equipment your men stole stacked up front and center – right now."

A long tirade from Gubbo Rekash followed Waldo's translation. Exercising his prerogative, Cheap Bribe had clearly elected to improve on the original message. The Patriots broke ranks, and the men raced back to their encampment while their fallen gang member lay crumpled on the ground, moaning. Within minutes, the robbers were back with their plunder.

Acting on their boss's instructions, the stolen booty was piled up. One of the shifta thought to unbuckle the offending pistol belt from the bleeding bandit who was lying semi-comatose on the ground. Clearly the outlaws feared their one-eyed leader who they regarded as a big-time *tillik sau*.

The pile of captured Italian equipment did not amount to much. Bimbashi Hoolihan had already secured the weapons carried by the enemy askari. According to information gained from the prisoner, the truck had been returning empty after having made a mail run. There had not been much on board to steal.

"Pick out a piece of gear, Waldo."

"We don't need any of that junk, Major."

"Take something anyway."

"I guess we could use that tarp there."

"Get it," Maj. Randal ordered, "then kindly inform Cheap Bribe to distribute the rest of the stuff to his bravest, most deserving patriotic freedom fighters for the heroic performance of their duty today."

Waldo did a double take, "You went to all this trouble to give it all back?"

"That's right."

Gubbo Rekash listened to the translation with open incredulity. No official backed by the Abyssinian ruling class in any position of authority had ever publicly validated his command position before, even remotely. The old bandit puffed out his chest and attempted to assume what he imagined was a rendition of the proper military position of attention and actually managed a reasonable salute, which Maj. Randal gravely returned with his ivory-handled whisk. The two men were looking hard at each other, eyeball to eyeball, though of course, Cheap Bribe only had the one.

"From now on," Maj. Randal commanded, "all enemy equipment captured will immediately be turned in to Gubbo Rekash for safekeeping. The chief will personally make the decision how it is to be distributed after first consulting with me or my designated representative. Any man caught trying to keep any captured material will immediately have his rifle and mule confiscated, then he will be stricken from the rolls of Force N and banished."

A hushed silence came over the shifta when they heard that last dreadful pronouncement translated. Being driven out was a punitive sentence more ominous than the threat of a firing squad or the favorite Italian spectator sport, hanging. Strangers in the Abyssinian countryside are viewed with dark suspicion, seldom welcomed. A man alone in Abyssinia was always in grave peril. Unarmed, they would be easy prey for any aspiring youngster looking to score his first kill.

Not one of Gubbo Rekash's men had a home village they could return to for sanctuary, it being accepted that when you become a shifta you burn your bridges. Maj. Randal had threatened them with the single worst punishment in the book – being cast out.

It was a masterstroke.

The Force N commander had one more ace up his sleeve, and now seemed as good a time as any to whip it out. "Ask Cheap Bribe if he can read and write."

"The man says he can," Waldo translated. "My guess is he ain't no Rhodes Scholar."

"Stand that empty foot locker up on one end about ten yards down range."

Waldo gave him an inquiring glance, then dragged the empty metal footlocker, which had been used by the Italians to secure their mailbags, ten yards away and stood it up on one end. The shifta watched curiously with more than a few misgivings. Maj. Randal was clearly preparing to give them a demonstration of some kind, and in their world, most object lessons included some form of pain.

"Stand clear, Mr. Treywick," Maj. Randal ordered, producing an ivory-stocked Colt .38 Super from the chest holster on his harness.

The pistol banged ten times evenly spaced. Waldo sauntered over to evaluate the footlocker for damage while Maj. Randal changed magazines.

"Well, Major, you managed to hit the box all ten times but you ain't a whole lot better pistol shot than you are at huntin' lion. Them bullet holes is scattered all over kingdom come. I thought you could handle a handgun a lot better'n that considerin' all the men I seen you shoot with one."

Maj. Randal ignored the critique, raised the Colt .38 Super and cranked off the next ten rounds fast. As he was recharging the pistol he ordered, "Tell Gubbo to check it out."

Waldo Treywick and the bandit chieftain strolled over to inspect the footlocker. When they reached it, the two men both started shouting in different languages. The shifta fell out of formation, ran down and gathered around to see what all the excitement was about. A buzz of amazed delight broke out when the gang saw the cluster of bullet holes.

Magically the metal container had the letters "G R" neatly stitched in the side. Even these functionally illiterate itinerant outlaws recognized their boss's initials when they saw them. Among professional fighting men, proficiency with weapons is universal cause for respect.

What they had witnessed was, by Abyssinian standards, a skill level so highly advanced it appeared to be supernatural. Most of the bandits present could not have hit the footlocker with their rifles at that range. Maj. Randal had to be some kind of magic wizard.

Captain "Geronimo" Joe McKoy would have been proud. Even Waldo was impressed – and it took some doing to get that old ivory poacher's attention. He had seen his share of fancy shooting during his days on the African frontier.

"You ought to be in the circus, Major. You're a' wastin' your talent in the army."

Gubbo Rekash supervised the hauling of the trunk back to his camp. There, he carefully cut out the side of the metal container with his initials stitched on it. Then he had his most skilled artisan remove the paint, burnish the metal to a brilliant shine and craft the bullet-punctured sheet to the front of the little round fighting shield the bandit chief carried on his left arm at virtually all times.

Without a doubt, Cheap Bribe was the only man in the whole of Abyssinia to display his initials shot in a string of bullet holes as a coat of arms. He thought it made a nice statement – the shield was definitely eye-catching. The pirate decided it might look natty if he mounted matching rubies in each of the bullet holes.

The problem being, he did not have any rubies.

74.....PHIL WARD

7

TWO MISSIONS

SPECIAL OPERATION'S EXECUTIVE FORMALIZED ITS MISSION in Khartoum by setting up what it called a "GR" office under the command of Major General James "Baldie" Taylor, OBE. In theory, SOE ran the show and everyone in the West African theatre of operations worked for it, including the Kaid, Major General William Platt and Major General Alan Cunningham – or at least they thought they did.

Only it was not true. GR was only a cover. Behind the scenes in London, from the billiard room of his club White's, Colonel Stewart Menzies, DSO, aka "C" – the chief of the British Secret Intelligence Service (SIS) MI6 – was the actual puppet master and everyone danced to his tune.

The number of people in Khartoum who knew this was precisely one, Maj. Gen. Taylor. The number of people who suspected it was also one, Major Sir Terry "Zorro" Stone. In Kenya, Captain the Lady Jane Seaborn, Lieutenant Pamala Plum-Martin and Squadron Leader Paddy Wilcox could be added to the number of people who suspected. In Cairo, Lieutenant

General Sir Archibald Wavel and Lieutenant Colonel Dudley Clarke were the only people who knew.

Attached to GR was Captain George Steer of Political Warfare Executive (PWE), the super-secret organization so hush-hush that Steer claimed to be working for SOE, a group itself so covert that even its initials were classified and no one would acknowledge it was present in the theatre. For public consumption, Capt. Steer was in charge of the Propaganda Department, a job no one, whether military or civilian, ever takes seriously. His arrival came about as a direct result of Major John Randal's request to have a PWE operator sent out from England. PWE was also planning to send out a second officer who would serve in the field with Force N once contact had been established with the advance party or another element sent in to replace it.

PWE had a history of working with RF.

When you do not have the requisite guns, material and manpower, it is a good idea to find some way to make your enemy think you do. Maj. Randal described psychological warfare as "smoke and mirrors." He liked to make it a part of RF' operational plans whenever possible, and he wanted some big brains supporting OPERATION ROMAN CANDLE, particularly because RF did not have very much else in the way of material assets.

A recent addition to GR was Captain Douglas Dodds-Parker. His assignment was to coordinate Abyssinian Activities with the Kaid, Maj. Gen. Platt. Previously Capt. Dodds-Parker had served in the Sudan Political Service both as a District Commissioner and in MI-5, the Secret Security Service, aka counterintelligence. When the war broke out, he had departed Africa to seek a more active role in the military, only to find himself in SOE being ordered straight back to his old stomping grounds.

Capt. Dodds-Parker had his work cut out for him. The Kaid was suspicious of Abyssinian Activities, the Emperor, the burgeoning number of want-to-be Lawrence-of-Arabias who were flicking their eyes lustfully at Abyssinia, and anyone out from England who might interfere with his plans.

Major Edwin Chapman-Andrews was another new member of GR, being assigned to hold the Emperor's hand during the run-up to the invasion. He had been seconded from the Embassy in Cairo and – in the quirky fashion the British have for dealing with unexpected military exigencies – gazetted into the Royal Sussex Regiment for the sole reason that the appropriate regimental badges could be obtained locally in Khartoum.

The Major's military identification card was carefully marked, "No pay or allowances from Army funds," which spelled out loud and clear he was not military. Whoever had managed Maj. Chapman-Andrews' records at SOE might as well have stamped the words "DIPLOMAT, BUREAUCRAT, SPY" on the cover of his file in bold red ink. That is not supposed to happen in the secret agent business. It was becoming increasingly clear that SOE Cairo was not cut from the same cloth as SOE London, which, while it made its own share of blunders, was learning fast.

Lt. Plum-Martin flew in from Kenya and gave Maj. Gen Taylor and Maj. Stone a detailed briefing on the status of the Lake Rudolf/Camp Croc project. She described Camp Croc as "the most dreadful place on planet Earth, tailor-made as a staging base for a clandestine war in Abyssinia."

The Royal Marine then took up her duties as the Force N IO. The first item on her agenda was to develop an Enemy Order of Battle appreciation. This proved to be a reasonably straightforward proposition. The Blackshirts did not rotate units. Italian outfits that had taken part in conquering Abyssinia five years before were, by and large, the same units still occupying the country now.

The exception was the local colonial units that had been formed out of ex-soldiers from the Imperial Guard and other Royalist Army outfits disbanded after the Emperor fled the country. The process of developing a completely accurate picture of how many locally-raised formations existed, the type of unit, troop strength, and where they were stationed was going to take some sorting out.

Lt. Plum-Martin also began creating a biographical sketch of each of the major Italian commanders in IEA. Her task was made easy by a fatal flaw in the fascist communications system. The British Y Service was able to intercept, decode and read the Italian secret wireless communications almost as fast as the Italians could. The enemy dispatches proved to be a treasure trove of information. The only problem was that the Blackshirts had very few radios. Most communications in Abyssinia was by landline, so while she was able to read the enemy wireless transmissions, and there were not a lot of them.

Two intriguing items came to light in the massive pile of intelligence reports Lt. Plum-Martin was working through. The first was that the Italian High Command was deeply concerned about the possibility of British officers infiltrating Abyssinia to raise guerrilla forces. *Seven Pillars of Wisdom* by T.E. Lawrence had been a best-seller in Italy too. Clearly, the senior officers in Addis Ababa had all read it and were worried that Abyssinia was ideal ground for a modern-day repeat. Messages to subordinate commanders throughout IEA inquired about reports of British officers in the country. The responses were always the same, "No sign of British officers at this time."

Second, several intercepts made reference to the heads of Italian soldiers or their Abyssinian auxiliaries having been cut off and displayed on stakes. The decoded fascist's messages were backed up by agent reports trickling in from border station interrogations on the Sudan side. Several line-crossers had also made mention of heads being mysteriously stuck up on poles like trophies.

Something seemed not quite right. Lt. Plum-Martin did some checking but could find no previous history of headhunting in the country. Abyssinians had a well-documented history of cutting off precious body parts of their enemies as trophies – but not heads. Decapitation was out of the ordinary even for a place as weird and unpredictable as Abyssinia. What was wrong with this picture? Maybe nothing, but her curiosity was aroused.

One specific detail in particular caught her attention. Several of the intercepts made mention of a "lightning bolt" painted between the eyes of the heads on the poles. Lt. Plum-Martin sketched out the outline of a head and then played with drawing a bolt of lightning. Could the people making the reports be mistaking a crooked or poorly drawn "N" for a bolt of lightning? Being a highly-trained intelligence operative, she decided to keep that possibility to herself until she could get confirmation. Still it was possible and gave her reason to hope.

Lt. Plum-Martin would have felt a lot better if she had found some indication of a British officer actively raising a guerrilla army, but so far no joy.

MAJOR GENERAL JAMES "BALDIE" TAYLOR BROKE GR DOWN into two separate self-contained elements – Mission 101 and Force N.

Mission 101, named after the fuse on an artillery shell that caused it to explode, was presently under the operational control of Major Orde Wingate because its commander, Colonel Dan Sanford, was across the border inside Abyssinia with its advance party. Col. Sanford's team had been discovered and was on the run from the Italians.

This was the first attempt to liberate an Axis-occupied country, and everyone, including Maj. Gen. Taylor, was learning how to do it on the fly. It was becoming painfully clear that it had been a bad idea to send the commanders of Mission 101 and Force N into Abyssinia with the advance parties. Both Col. Sanford and Major John Randal were out of radio contact with GR at the exact point in time they were most needed to make crucial decisions about their commands.

On paper, the stated purpose of Mission 101 was to enter Abyssinia in company with the Emperor, his entourage, a caravan of twenty-five thousand camels, five thousand camel handlers, thirty trucks, a fortune in Maria Theresa thalers, arms and ammunition, escorted by the Frontier Battalion and the 2nd Abyssinian Battalion with the intention to raise a rebellion and restore the Emperor to his throne... or maybe not. Strictly off the record, there was no rush to get the King of Kings to the capital city of Addis Ababa.

Abyssinia had no strategic value once the Red Sea corridor was cleared of Italian Forces – none.

Not a single one of the officers and men of Mission 101 knew that restoring the Emperor to his throne was not their true objective. Mission 101 was a brilliant diversion carefully crafted by Lieutenant Colonel Dudley Clarke to help address the lopsided imbalance of Axis troops to British troops. Its real purpose was to draw the eyes of the Italian High Command in Addis Ababa away from where the two spearheads of the actual invasion would strike.

No one had explained it that way to Mission 101.

Neither Maj. Wingate nor the Emperor had the slightest idea their column was a decoy. Both were operating under the grand illusion that Mission 101 was the big show. The Emperor thought restoring him to his throne was the primary objective. Maj. Wingate believed he was on a mission from God.

A retinue of reporters had been assigned to travel with Mission 101, none of whom had anything to report on except the press conferences Maj. Wingate held in his hotel room. These were conducted with the major lying nude on his bed brushing his body with a toothbrush. His particular favorite topic was the failings of the officer corps of the regular army of which – he seemed to forget – he was one. He gloried in calling them "military apes."

Because there was nothing else for the press corps to write about, the reporters wrote about Wingate, creating a Wingate legend. The journalists realized early on that they had a much better chance of their articles being accepted by their editors if they were writing about a superhero. So they made Wingate into one.

What never occurred to any of the newsmen or to Maj. Wingate was that since the Official Secrets Act and military censorship were omnipotent, the mere fact that the stories were allowed to be published had to mean that someone, somewhere, for some reason, wanted the information out there.

For a self-proclaimed genius on the art of guerrilla warfare, Maj. Wingate did not have the first idea about the meaning of operational security. He told everyone he was "going into Abyssinia to foment a rebellion." Encountering Captain the Lady Jane Seaborn in the restaurant of the Continental Hotel, he loudly invited her to go along as his "personal secretary." She was not amused.

The Italians had an intelligence network that was very good at gathering information, particularly when the information was published in the newspaper. The High Command soon became convinced that Maj. Wingate was the next Lawrence. From Addis Ababa, the Blackshirts carefully watched developments in Khartoum, making plans to shift troop dispositions to counter Mission 101 the minute it crossed the border.

When Maj. Wingate and the Emperor did eventually affect entry into Abyssinia, the eyes of the Italian High Command – and for that matter the entire world – were going to be locked on Mission 101.

Why Maj. Wingate did not realize what was happening is not easy to understand. He claimed to be a military visionary. And, he convinced a lot of others who should have known better that he actually was.

Mission 101 was a freak show.

From Cairo, Lt. Col. Clarke watched and exulted. The mad major was the star in his Abyssinian misinformation campaign. For the purpose of military deception, the man was priceless. Had Maj. Wingate not actually existed, Lt. Col. Clarke would have had to invent him.

The second element of GR was Force N under Maj. Randal. Its mission was to enter the interior of the country and raise a guerrilla army. The plan was to initially support Major General William Platt attacking out of the Sudan through the Kern Pass, and later to assist Major General Alan Cunningham who would be knifing up from Kenya.

Dissipating the vastly superior fascist troop strength was crucial for the Imperial Forces to have any hope of success. The plan was to compel the Italian High Command to draw off ever larger numbers of Italian forces from where they were most needed – defending the Kern Pass and the Kenyan border – to counterattack Mission 101's column or to go chasing after a highly mobile Maj. Randal's Force N who would be hitting and running, raising merry hell in the interior.

Force N was the catalyst that would make all the pieces of the three-pronged invasion come together because the Italians would have no choice but to react to it.

Maj. Randal's guerrilla army was tasked to cut Italian lines of communication by aggressively ambushing the Blackshirt mobile columns on the roads and cutting the rail lines. Force N's mission was to restrict the Italian High Command's ability to rapidly shift reinforcements from one front to another, thus neutralizing the Blackshirt advantage of having short interior lines.

It does not matter how superior the enemy's troop strength is if they can't get their units to the fight.

Force N's battle plan was classified "Most Secret – Need to Know Only." So while Mission 101 had no idea at all of Force N's intentions, the Force N Rear people and interested newsprint readers worldwide knew everything there was to know about Mission 101's plan of attack, except for the parts Maj. Wingate was dreaming up nights and not telling anyone.

The dilemma facing Major General James "Baldie" Taylor was that the Force N Advance Party and its commanding officer were missing in action. GR was either going to have to re-establish contact with Maj. Randal soon or reconstitute the mission like it had done with Mission 101 – putting Maj. Wingate in command to replace it's missing in action commanding officer. No one wanted to write off Maj. Randal yet – but then again, no one was wagering any money on finding the advance party alive either.

Currently the staff of Force N Rear consisted of Major Sir Terry "Zorro" Stone in temporary command, Captain Mickey Duggan, DCM, MM, RM, the recently field-commissioned Royal Marine serving as Chief of Signals and Lieutenant Pamala Plum-Martin, IO. Six more men from RF had arrived from England on the morning plane from Cairo. They were waiting transshipment to Nairobi, then on to Camp Croc.

Lady Jane flew in aboard the Hudson to pick up the six RF personnel and to consult with Maj. Gen. Taylor and Maj. Stone. She advised them that Barclays Bank had located three amphibious transport airplanes in Brazil, owned by a copper mining conglomerate that was using them to ferry miners and supplies to its more remote mines in the Andes.

Arrangements had been made to purchase the three planes. Commodore Richard "Dickey the Pirate" Seaborn, VC, OBE, RN was en route to Rio, accompanied by Squadron Leader Paddy Wilcox and two of the bush pilots he had recruited for Special Operations (SO) duties to fly the planes to Africa. From Rio to Sierra Leone the distance was seventeen hundred air miles, and then it was on to Nairobi, Camp Croc and points north into Abyssinia.

That evening, Lt. Plum-Martin arranged to have Evelyn Waugh, the best-selling novelist, give a background briefing on the military conditions in Abyssinia when Mussolini had conquered the country five years previously. Waugh, who was passing through Khartoum on his way to London to enlist in the Royal Marines, had covered the 1935 Italian invasion as a freelance reporter and had written several books about his adventures.

Khartoum was an "Empire country club" living in a state of complete denial. The Italians were capable of capturing the city within seventy-two hours anytime they wanted. All they had to do was launch the attack. However, for the expatriates, the normal peacetime round of cocktail parties, black tie dressing for dinner, tennis parties, river sailing and picnics continued to be the order of the day. A real disconnect existed between the war fighters who were planning desperate operations and civilian officialdom in the river city who acted as if they had no idea there was a war going on. A parallel to Nero fiddling while Rome burned was difficult to ignore.

The atmosphere made the Force N personnel feel angry and isolated.

Lt. Plum-Martin arranged reservations in a private dining room off the terrace overlooking the Nile in one o the better restaurants. Maj. Gen. Taylor made it a point to attend. After dinner, over brandy and cigars, the famous author held forth on his views of all things Italian and in Abyssinia.

"I must admit I have never been in love with Italians," he said. "I have traveled extensively in their country and found them to be pompous, overbearing, petty bureaucrats living off the glory of the past Roman Empire.

"I was educated at Oxford University where it was fashionable to raspberry when the comic opera Duce with his pompous iron chin and effeminate plumed cap – officially called, I believe, the 'Fascist Fez' – appeared on the silver screen in newsreels at the campus theatre. A government that tells universities what they can teach, newspapers what they can print and writers what they can write is evil in its core.

"There is bad blood between the Italians and the Abyssinians dating back to the Battle of Adwa in the last century when the Italian prisoners got the chop, being… ah… castrated by the victors. The army held a grudge that Mussolini set out to avenge.

"What the fascists were going up against in 1935 when they invaded was a million-man army commanded by Emperor Haile Selassie. However, the army was not what it appeared on paper. One tenth of the troops served out of loyalty to Christianity, one tenth from loyalty to the Coptic Church, one tenth from local loyalties, one tenth were only willing to serve as guides but would not fight, one tenth were women, and one tenth priests. At the end of the day, the Emperor had only about one hundred thousand actual fighting men. And they were not prepared to fight a major European power.

"The army was made up of armed groups centered around the local Ras – roughly equivalent to our medieval dukes. The Christian groups were suspicious of the Muslim provinces and vice versa. There was also the little problem of more or less constant internal warfare, political intrigue, blood feuds, etc. The concept of national unity was – and is – basically a non-starter.

"When Haile Selassie became Emperor he fired the Swiss military advisors and hired Belgian advisors, which proved unfortunate. To their credit, the Belgians did replace the army's antiquated small arms with modern Mannlicher rifles purchased in Czechoslovakia. The Belgians also organized the Imperial Guard.

"In early 1935, many of the sons of noblemen and traditional military leaders were sent for officer training in Europe while an Officers Training School was established locally. The cadets were, by all reports, highly intelligent, averse to physical exercise, full of confidence and embedded with a natural tendency to overestimate their own capabilities.

"Foreign advisors and mercenaries played a major role in the development of the Abyssinian Army. There were two Belgian Missions – one actually being styled the 'Unofficial Belgian Mission.' Alas, the two groups did not get along, refusing to salute each other.

"For some reason, relations between the Belgians and the Emperor's Turkish advisors were frosty. The Belgians described the Turks as a' bunch of lawyers, shopkeepers and comedians.' The senior Turkish military advisor was General Mehmed Wehib Pasha, a rather elderly, short, stout man who always wore gym shoes.

"As the showdown approached, the train delivered a colorful cast of characters straight out of a Hollywood back lot to the capital daily. I used to greet each and every arrival at the station simply for the pleasure of seeing who would get off next. There were doctors, missionaries, journalists, adventurers, arms dealers, moviemakers, Nazis, pacifists wanting to serve in the Red Cross, anti-fascists, Anti-Slavery Coalition volunteers and even some animal rights activists from California.

"There were a handful of Irish 'Wild Geese' mercenaries, a retired English Master of Foxhounds, a former French NCO of Armenian origin hired to help bridge the cultural gap between Belgians and Abyssinians, a Russian electrical engineer, a Cuban aviator or air gunner – which, exactly, was never quite clear – who became the personal machine gunner for a ras on the Northern Front, a Bavarian Count who flew an air-ambulance; and a negro pilot from the United States – Colonel Hubert Fauntleroy Julian, 'The

Black Eagle of Harlem.' The Black Eagle crashed the Abyssinian Air Force's last remaining aircraft.

"How much actual military value these people provided is open to debate," Evelyn laughed, taking a large sip of brandy to fortify himself. "Would have been a bloody dull war without them.

"The Imperial Guard was the only unit in the Abyssinian Army that wore a uniform and even *they* did not wear boots. In fact, the Emperor personally banned footgear. He felt boots inhibited his soldier's ability to cross rough terrain. Branch of service was indicated by a color-coded collar patch – red for riflemen, dark green for machine gunners, black for artillery, blue for cavalry and pale blue for radio telephone operators.

"If the Abyssinian Military Command had any central war strategy, I never understood what it was. In battle, the ranking commander's troops were placed in the middle of the line with the formation having a center, left wing, right wing, rear guard and vanguard. These are tactics as practiced by Genghis Khan.

"The Fascist Italian Army, I was reliably informed, had undergone major modernization since the World War I," Evelyn continued after another sip. "Since I was never allowed anywhere near the scene of the actual fighting I have no way to verify that.

"Most of my time was spent in various bars drinking hard liquor with the foreign mercenaries while listening to marvelously creative excuses about why they were miles in the rear and not at the front earning their pay.

"What are your questions?"

"Did you have experience of decapitations during your time in Abyssinia, Evelyn?" Lt. Plum-Martin asked.

"Well, yes, actually I did, Pamala," Evelyn replied. "After the fighting was over and the Italians had taken Addis Ababa, a general bloodbath ensued. The fascists were executing any educated Abyssinian, any member of the noble family they could lay hands on, and murdering quite a lot of the clergy. A photo of the severed head of an Abyssinian soldier carried on a silver tray with his chopped-off arm beside it like he was giving a salute made the rounds. The Italians thought it was hilarious."

"Any cases you know of Abyssinians ceremoniously cutting off heads and displaying them on poles as trophies?"

"None I can think of. Why do you ask?"

"I have been reading reports that mention severed heads," Lt. Plum-Martin said.

"The only chopped head I know about – the Wops did the chopping."

ACROSS TOWN AT THE *PINK PALACE*, EMPEROR HAILE SELASSIE was growing more restless by the day. For political reasons he had been kept out of the public eye ever since he had arrived in Khartoum. The Emperor began to grow despondent when he realized how little was being done to support his return to the throne. Major General James "Baldie" Taylor decided something had to be done to perk the droopy-eyed little fellow up, so he consulted with his PWE advisor, Captain George Steer, and they came up with the idea of a "photo op."

The Emperor thought it a grand idea. With full pomp and ceremony due a head of state, he was publicly flown down to Gedaref in the Sudan's biggest, most impressive airplane – an obsolete Vickers-Valentia – to meet with a few Patriots. The King of Kings traveled with complete court regalia, including the world's only Imperial State Umbrella, his entire retinue, plus his favorite niece.

Capt. Steer, taking personal charge of the advance work, did the Emperor proud. There was a colorfully embroidered tent waiting for him on the polo grounds when he arrived. The West York Regiment's officers were introduced to him in grand style while the droopy-eyed little potentate sat comfortably in the shade of the State Umbrella, which was held aloft by a slave.

The King of Kings, Lion of Judah, Elect of God, etc. was protected by his personal bodyguard, a giant armed with a leather rhinoceros-hide whip. His primary responsibility was to beat back the overzealous crowd of Abyssinian Patriots who dashed forward screaming shrilly from time to time to prostrate themselves at the Emperor's feet. Many were beaten, no one killed, few permanently injured and a good time was had by one and all.

Capt. Steer was possessed with the active imagination and cynical sense of humor essential to a successful PWE operator. After the event, he obtained a photograph of the Emperor meeting the West York officers and had it copied with the caption, "Emperor Haile Selassie meets with high-ranking officers of the General Staff." PWE saw to it the photo received mass distribution and was published in newspapers worldwide.

The highest-ranking military luminary depicted in the picture was Major Edwin Chapman-Andrews, and he was not even a real army officer. It said so right in his records. He was a spy.

8
LIVE BAIT

MAJOR JAMES HAMILTON AND MAJOR COURTNEY Brocklehurst flew into Khartoum with A brand new concept of the operation for the liberation of Abyssinia. The proposition they put forward was a real blockbuster. Both men were considered "local experts" and they wanted to rewrite the script for the invasion of Abyssinia – casting themselves in the starring roles.

Maj. Brocklehurst was a former game warden from the Galla country. He had known Colonel Dan Sanford, the Commander of Mission 101, prior to the Italian invasion. And he knew the Emperor. The King of Kings knew the major too and had vetoed him for the job of commanding officer of Mission 106 – now in-country operating under a new name, Force N – because he was a dyed-in-the-wool supporter of the Galla tribe.

Maj. Hamilton was a six-foot, four-inch former heavyweight boxer, the winner in his class of the Sword of Honor at Sandhurst, and had served for seven years as the Political Officer in British Somaliland. He was en route to take command of the Mobile Force in Aden, known locally as the "Mobile Farce."

The two officers proposed to do away with Mission 101 – the column that was to escort Emperor Haile Selassie to Addis Ababa. Maj. Brocklehurst disagreed with the basic premise of Mission 101, which was – at least for public consumption – to reinstall the Emperor to his throne.

Like all Galla men, he detested the Amhara – the Emperor's tribe. There were Galla experts, and there were Amhara experts. The prevailing Galla expert's point of view was that the Amhara experts were involving a naïve, ill-informed British government in a dastardly attempt to impose Amhara rule on the Gallas. What was needed – they said – was an independent Galla nation.

The duo arrived in Khartoum to put forward the idea, offering the Galla the promise of double liberation – from the Blackshirts and the just-as-hated Amhara. Their unsolicited political bombshell of a plan screamed in and detonated just when the entire Abyssinian Operation was at its shakiest.

Lieutenant General Sir Archibald Wavell was not interested – the Kaid, Major General William Platt, wrote the two off as classic examples of wanna-be Lawrences. The Emperor and Major Orde Wingate were apoplectic – the Maj. Wingate even issuing the order to shoot Maj. Brocklehurst on sight should he be encountered anywhere in Abyssinia.

But the Foreign Office saw it from a different perspective.

The Foreign Office had always harbored doubts about restoring Haile Selassie to the throne. At the same time, they suspected Col. Sanford, the Commander of Mission 101, had overstated the Emperor's value as a rallying point for Abyssinian Patriots. And quite likely, he had.

Major General James "Baldie" Taylor was livid at the distraction brought about by the last-minute political intrigue. He had grown skeptical about "local experts" as time went by. By nature of the job description, they automatically had built-in bias. He had come to the conclusion that "local experts" had value as regional political advisors but not much else except to comment on the flora and fauna.

What the Galla or the Amhara did once the Italians were ejected from the coastline of Abyssinia was of no interest to Maj. Gen. Taylor. His assignment was to clear the Red Sea corridor of Italian naval units and land-based attack aircraft so it could be declared safe passage for American Lend Lease shipping. After that was accomplished, the two tribes could fight it out to the death, for all he cared.

In London, Cairo, and Khartoum the political debate raged. The fate of millions rested on the final decision. Great men jockeyed to be able to take credit for what was decided.

What finally settled the issue was Lieutenant Colonel Dudley Clarke sending an "Eyes Only Most Secret" cable to "C", Colonel Stewart Menzies, stating he needed Mission 101. Upon receipt of the message, the chief of MI-6 arranged to have a quiet word with Prime Minister Winston Churchill at *Chequers* later that evening. The result was a directive settling the matter that was sent out the following morning over the Prime Minister's signature.

The Emperor was going in.

Maj. Wingate believed he had won a major political victory. But it was not true. The Emperor had the green light to return to Abyssinia, but Mission 101 was still nothing more than a diversion.

The Prime Minister, Maj. Gen. Taylor and Lt. Col. Clarke were all reading from the same page. No one gave a fig about Abyssinian politics. Hamilton & Brocklehurst were sent packing, which came as a surprise to some, considering Maj. Brocklehurst was married to Prime Minister Churchill's cousin.

SOMEWHERE IN ABYSSINIA IN THE MOUNTAINOUS CENTRAL highlands, Major John Randal was blithely unaware of all the international political machinations, the double dealing, backstabbing, empire building, career enhancement and personal agenda advancing, not knowing one tribe from the other. From the beginning, he had adopted a hands-off policy of noninvolvement in local politics. His only interest was to raise a guerrilla army.

The last thing he wanted was to allow himself to be drawn into any blood feuds, intertribal rivalries, personal squabbles, or be forced to take sides in a regional dispute. How could he know what faction to align with? His local expert, Waldo, professed to be an equal-opportunity despiser of all tribes.

He advised Maj. Randal to never trust any Abyssinian – which set the tone of Force N's political agenda – "Kill bad guys, don't take sides."

Maj. Randal was sitting outside his tent at a small camp table cleaning his personal weapons with a shaving brush and enjoying himself immensely. The plan was for him to take the chief of the local village they were currently visiting with him that evening to sit up in a tree, waiting for a pair of man-eating lions that had been terrorizing the local villagers off and on for the last six months or so. Tonight would be his first opportunity to try out the field-expedient spotlight Waldo had rigged up.

Bimbashi Butch "Headhunter" Hoolihan had already departed the area on his first independent ambush mission. Waldo was making preparations to ride out to conduct a lone reconnaissance of a new AO one hundred miles from their current location. Maj. Randal knew the Italians would come out *en masse* searching for Force N after he and Bimbashi Hoolihan each conducted separate ambushes in the next few days. He planned to relocate, operate for a time in a new area far away, then move a long way off, set up and start all over again.

Shoot, move and communicate – exactly the way they had taught at the U.S. Army Cavalry School at Fort Riley, Kansas – only he was not going to be able to do much communicating without a radio. If the Blackshirts were going to run Force N to the ground, he intended to make them work at it or get lucky. By necessity, Force N was living the life of nomads.

Waldo walked over, leading his mule. The old army scout was traveling alone on this trip. He slid his rifle into the boot on the left side of his saddle.

"I'll meet you in ten days at the base of that mountain we picked out on the map, Major."

"Sure you don't want to take Rita or Lana with you?"

"I'm travelin' light. I only take the girls along for company anyway, and you're the man that's gonna' need company. Lana told me you'd been practicin' your language skills. Said you told her she and Rita had a real nice smell. Finger hit the wrong line in that phase book of yours, did it?"

"What makes you think I need company?"

"Major, the chief of this here village is goin' to send the commander of his personal bodyguard on down ahead of ya' to the tree where you're gettin' ready to sit up tonight. When ya' go down there to get in your stand at dusk, they're gonna' kill ya'. The Chief plans to let the lions cover up the evidence by eatin' your remains."

"The man thinks he's planned the perfect crime."

"Really?"

"Yeah, the slime ball is on the Wop payroll, but that ain't the reason for killin' ya'," Waldo said. "He wants your ivory-handled side arms to sport around so everybody can see he's a big shot."

"How did you find out?"

"One of Butch's boys heard about it while he was in the village before they rode out. He reported it to me. Everyone probably knows by now exceptin' you," Waldo said. "Murder's the kind of thing that passes for an inside joke around here."

"Cheap Bribe aware of this?"

"Could be – it ain't no real big secret," Waldo said. "Now, the most important thing to remember about huntin' lion is don't let yourself get shot by your huntin' buddy."

"Thanks, Mr. Treywick."

"I'll see you when I see you – have yourself a nice hunt, Major."

Maj. Randal waited until Waldo rode out of camp, and then had a quiet conversation with Rita Hayworth and Lana Turner. The two slave girls listened intently to everything he had to say. Since they resolutely would not speak English, he did all the talking.

"Any questions, ladies? Feel free to jump in anytime."

The two girls looked at him with narrowed amber eyes and shook their pretty turbaned heads. There was a lot to be said for one-way dialogue with women, Maj. Randal decided. Conversation was a snap, you never had to worry about petty melodrama, there was no getting tongue-tied and you never felt stupid.

The Italian prisoner captured in Bimbashi Hoolihan's first ambush was named Guido Grazinni. He was living in terror that something horrible was going to happen to him, it being well understood what the natives did to

Italian prisoners. The reason he spoke English, he explained, was because he had lived in the United States and attended the University of Michigan's School of Hotel Management. In the summer of his junior year he returned home to visit his family and was promptly drafted into the Italian Army. He hated Il Duce Benito Mussolini, all things fascist and the Italian Army in particular. He loved America, had no quarrel with the British and wanted to be anywhere on Planet Earth but Abyssinia.

Maj. Randal gave him two options. Pull duty as the Force N cook or be turned over to Gubbo Rekash for safekeeping until the end of the campaign. What would happen if he tried to escape was also explained. Guido, who liked to be called GG, opted wisely to take up employment as the Force N chef.

GG's lifetime dream was to open a restaurant in Hollywood and cater to movie stars. He was desperately afraid of Lana and Rita, who mischievously toyed with their curved rhinoceros-horned knives every time he walked past. Whenever the girls were around, he kept his eyes cast down on the ground. No sense taking any chances.

The first meal GG prepared was a hamburger. This scored him big points with Maj. Randal. Lana and Rita were less impressed. The slave girls had never seen a hamburger before and eyed theirs with a great deal of suspicion. It almost tasted like the real thing. The new Force N chef actually whipped up some French fries to go with it.

Later that day Maj. Randal ordered GG to make plans for two guests for dinner, then dispatched Lana Turner to invite Gubbo Rekash to attend the evening meal. The village headman would be arriving soon. The schedule called for the three to dine in camp; then he and the chief would head down to the tree stand before dark.

There were only the three for dinner. Since Maj. Randal could not speak any Abyssinian language – it being hard to eat and manipulate his phrase book at the same time – and neither Gubbo Rekash nor the chief spoke more than a few words of English, there was not much in the way of conversation during the meal.

That did absolutely nothing to ruin the jolly ambiance. Maj. Randal had just handed out captured Italian cigarillos and was lighting them with his old Zippo lighter – the one displaying the crossed sabers of the U.S. 26th

Cavalry Regiment– when the tranquility of the onset of twilight was broken by the sound of two simultaneous rifle shots.

"Gee... wonder what that was?" Maj. Randal said, as he held the flame to the chief's cigar.

The chief had a curious look on his ugly face while Cheap Bribe was wearing what could be described as a quizzical expression on his. In a little while, Lana and Rita trailed into the camp. The appearance on their countenances was that of a sleek pair of pussycats who had just *eaten* the canary.

"Ask Cheap Bribe if he wants to go hunting with us tonight."

Rita translated the invitation. Gubbo Rekash's single evil eye flashed pure panic. He was either deathly afraid of man-eating lions, or aware of the chief's plan for the evening's entertainment... or both. Maj. Randal observed the shifta leader carefully through the blue cigar smoke.

The one-eyed bandit began to squirm. A world-class survivor who spent every waking moment concentrating on his continued existence, all of his senses were protesting that somehow he had managed to land himself in some serious hot water; only how could that be? Gubbo was the one man at the table who should not have been in any peril this evening.

Cheap Bribe's response was short, not really needing any translation. Gubbo Rekash had no intention of voluntarily setting foot outside of camp, not tonight. Rita shook her head, "No."

Maj. Randal strapped on his pack containing a battery taken from the ambushed Fiat truck. The field-expedient spotlight, which had been rigged out of one of the truck's headlamps, was wired to it. He picked up his M-1903 A-1 Springfield rifle, the one with the ivory post front sight for night work.

"Let's do it, chief."

The village elder was carrying an ancient Lebel rifle stoked with 8mm rounds, though he had absolutely no intention of shooting any of them at lions. Everyone knew man-eaters were spirit devils and could not be killed with bullets. The Lebel was for show. If things worked out as planned, he might fire it up into the air couple of times at the appropriate time for effect. Walking ahead, he led the way down the trail with the confident swagger of a Judas goat leading sheep to slaughter.

Before the two of them made it out of camp, Gubbo Rekash, acting on impulse, called out a warning. Maj. Randal turned to the girls; he was not expecting much help in the way of translation but was hoping for some gesture that might possibly help him understand what Cheap Bribe had to say.

"Take care," Lana whispered, speaking the first real words of English he had heard from either of the girls, other than the time when he was under the influence of multiple mind-altering substances.

"Nice move, Gubbo," Maj. Randal said, leaving the old bandit to ponder the meaning of Lana's interpretation as he turned to follow the chief down the trail.

The two men moved along at a rapid clip. Neither of them wanted to be caught on the ground after dark, but it was not far to the machan where they would take up position for the night. The chief suddenly pulled up short as they came near the clearing where the tree stand was located – the site where the commander of his personal bodyguard was supposed to be lying in wait. The fool had not taken the trouble to camouflage himself very well. The bodyguard could clearly be seen lying under a tall tree directly ahead. Involuntarily, the chief looked back to check if the Force N Commander had noticed.

He should not have done that.

The instant the chief turned his head, Maj. Randal brought up the M-1903 A-1 Springfield. With his left hand firmly gripped on the forearm and his right hand tightly grasping the small of the stock, Maj. Randal chop-popped him on the left side of the face with the tip of the rifle barrel. Then, lighting quick, rapidly reversing directions, hammered the chief on the other side of his jaw with the leading edge of the rifle's steel butt plate, executing a textbook-perfect horizontal butt stroke. The major employed a sharp, wicked, fast-snapping motion – the way he had been taught in ROTC and the U.S. Cavalry School – nearly taking the chief's head off.

Maj. Randal dragged the semi-comatose chief up to the tree where the commander of his personal bodyguard was lying face down, two fist-sized exit wounds visible in his back. He was as dead as two 6.5 Carcano steel jacketed bullets can make a man. A rope was dangling over a limb high up in the tree and tied off at the base of the trunk.

Pulling the noose that was tied in the loose end of the rope down with the front site on the barrel of the Springfield, Maj. Randal wondered how Rita and Lana had managed to place it over a limb so far up in the tree. He fitted the loop over the prostrate chief's feet and then hoisted him as high as he could pull before tying off the rope.

Climbing up into the stand twenty yards away with his pack, spotlight and rifle, Maj. Randal wished Waldo could be here tonight. This was one lion hunt the old ex-ivory poacher would have enjoyed. Maj. Randal was certainly planning to.

Later, when the chief came to, he was going to find himself dangling face down looking at his dead bodyguard commander eyeball to eyeball. Maj. Randal had gone to the trouble to roll the bodyguard over on his back with that idea in mind. At some point the chief was going to realize he was live bait.

The thought did occur to Maj. Randal that he had not been able to hoist the chief's head much more than six or seven feet off the ground. Based on his newly acquired treasure trove of knowledge about hungry man-eating lion behavior, he realized the average-sized cat could stand up on its hind feet and reach seven feet high without even jumping.

Oh well.

The chief came to, immediately realized his predicament and became hysterical. His screams could be heard as far away as the village. At the Force N HQ, the girls and GG could hear them. Gubbo Rekash and his band of shifta cutthroats over in their camp could hear them too. The terrorized histrionics went on and on and on and on and on and on. The spine-tingling yelps were ghastly, even for as cold-hearted a bunch of listeners as was tuned in tonight. GG covered up his head with a blanket to muffle the horrible sounds.

In fact, the panic-stricken shrieks were so awful people eventually began giggling, then chuckling, finally openly laughing at the chief's exertions. The headman was not in any pain, except for a world class headache – he was scared.

First, Cheap Bribe's men started laughing, then the chief's own constituents in their mushroom-shaped huts joined in. Apparently, the man was not a wildly popular civic leader.

The screams brought the hungry lion running.

The next noise the listening audience heard was a sound that could only be described as the purring of two very happy man-eaters. The sound was the closest thing to contentment anyone in hearing distance had ever heard a big, hungry cat make. Jovial man-eating lions were too horrible for even this hard-case crew of listeners. No one was laughing now.

The purring and the blood curdling screaming went on for a long time. Then the night exploded. *BAAAAAROOOOM! BAAAAAAROOOOM!* Several seconds later, this was followed by another *BAAAAAROOOOM! BAAAAAAROOOOM!*

Then there was dead silence. Normally, after the shooting stopped, the villagers would wait a suitable time to make sure everything was safe. Then, banging pans, blowing horns, beating drums and using any other noise-making device they could lay hands on, they would conduct a torchlight procession to the scene of the night's hunt. Not tonight. No one came to investigate.

In his camp, Cheap Bribe was feeling better about his spur-of-the-moment decision to give the Force N Commander a last-minute warning. Gubbo Rekash was pretty sure he had dodged a bullet. Any man merciless enough to use a village headman for lion bait would most likely hold a grudge against someone who knew there was a death plot against him and failed to give warning.

Unknown to Maj. Randal, he had won over the last holdouts of Cheap Bribe's shifta who were still unsure if he had the right stuff to be a *tallik sau*. Gubbo's outlaws were men who had respect for the word "heartless." In their book, using a captured enemy to lure man-eating lions was highly advanced creative thinking. A man that terrible deserved to be followed.

The deep thinkers in Cheap Bribe's band wondered what had made him so cruel. The consensus was it had to be a woman. To move a band of professional, career slit-throat shifta to ponder an emotional concept like that was a rare achievement.

Next morning when the locals finally cut down the traumatized chief, he jogged straight to the village, went into his hut and cowered there. Not one member of the community even acknowledged the dead bodyguard. The corpse was still lying under the tree when Maj. Randal and his troops rode out, taking with them the largest contingent of new volunteers that Force N had ever recruited from a single village.

The sound of African tom-toms thundered, and runners set forth with their messages held high in the cleft fork of sticks. News of the night's episode spread across the country like wildfire. Individual Patriots in their villages and independent banda of shifta in their hidden jungle camps learned of the event and marveled.

Many made up their minds to seek out Force N and join the fight.

9
THE LETTER N

MAJOR SIR TERRY "ZORRO" STONE WAS READING A LIST OF names of available Royal Air Force (RAF) officers in the Middle East Command to serve as his Military Air Liaison. He knew he had his man when he came to Pilot Officer Gasper "Bunny" Featherstone, DFC. The two had known each other since boyhood.

Plt. Off. Featherstone was an ace Spitfire pilot with seven hard-won victories flying with the Expeditionary Force in France and during the Battle of Britain as a member of the glamorous auxiliary Squadron 601 – better known as the "Millionaires" because of the fabulous wealth of its flyers.

When gas rationing had gone into effect in England, the pilots of 601 were having problems finding petrol to fill up the tanks of their Bentleys, Triumphs and Jaguars. Plt. Off. Featherstone, being a man of action, had whipped out his checkbook and purchased the local filling station. Problem solved.

Before the fall, operating in support of the British Expeditionary Force flying out of an airfield in France, the "Millionaires" had the honor of being inspected in the field by Prime Minister Winston Churchill out from England on a whirlwind visit to the front. The squadron lined up half a dozen Spitfires, and the pilots staggered out for a morning formation. The squadron was back from a night carousing the town – the pilots so hungover they felt like the Gestapo had worked them over with rubber truncheons.

Apparently the "Millionaires" did not look as bad as they felt.

A reporter accompanying the Prime Minister recorded the scene in a syndicated news release. "Prime Minister Churchill grinned, waved his stick defiantly and took a moment to chat with each aviator. This reporter watched the boy's faces light up as he went from plane to plane. The Air Force officers looked to this observer like angels from the heavens."

In fact, at that exact moment, Plt. Off. Featherstone was out behind his aircraft, throwing up in the grass.

Major General James "Baldie" Taylor came into the room carrying a scope-mounted M-1903 A-1 Springfield rifle. "I received a note from Wesley-Richards advising me my weapons were ready for pick-up. Since I had not ordered any, I went over straight away to see what the commotion was all about and this is part of what was waiting."

"A telescopic sight on a Springfield – that might be useful. Our Lovat Scouts have scopes mounted on their privately-owned red stag sniping rifles," Maj. Stone said.

"Not only did they mount a scope on the Springfield but they re-barreled it to 6.5mm, turning it into something called a 6.5-06. According to Wesley-Richards, this is the flattest shooting shoulder-fired rifle in the world – capable of hitting a standing man at one thousand yards with no holdover. They built Force N a dozen of them."

"Never heard of that round," Maj. Stone said, interested. Like most members of his class he was an avid sportsman.

"Hybrid caliber – what is known as a 'wildcat' – neck the .30 caliber case down to 6.5mm and shoot a pea-sized bullet at high velocity. The steel-jacketed military round will penetrate about anything. The idea was that the shooter could save the Springfield's brass and reload it in the field using captured Italian 6.5 rounds – so ammunition resupply is never a problem.

My immediate reaction was this is the ultimate sniper's weapon until the Wesley-Richards people brought out one of the Boys Anti-Tank Rifles they had mounted the No. 32 Mk1 scopes on."

"Wesley-Richards mounted telescopic sights on Boys Anti-Tank Rifles?" Maj. Stone asked in disbelief.

"Twelve of them to be exact," Maj. Gen. Taylor said. "The No. 32 Mk1 scope was originally developed for the .303 caliber Bren gun. Constructed out of solid steel, the scope is virtually indestructible. After production began, a government bean counter did the math and realized it was cost prohibitive to put one on every Bren gun in the British Army arsenal. So they simply wrote the entire project off as a bad idea and warehoused the entire lot of the first production run."

"Why would anyone possibly desire a telescope on a Boys Anti-Tank Rifle?" Maj. Stone asked. "The weapon famously will not penetrate any known armor, even at point-blank range."

"Because the .55 caliber round is capable of great accuracy at extreme range out to a mile... or even beyond," Maj. Gen. Taylor said. "Mount a scope on it and put the weapon on a tripod pedestal heavy machinegun mount – the Boys becomes the ultimate extreme long distance sniper's rifle. One mile, one shot kills. I simply cannot believe no one ever realized you could do that with a Boys Anti-Tank Rifle before now. It's the ultimate thin-skinned vehicle killer."

"What genius dreamed that idea up?"

"Captain 'Geronimo' Joe McKoy. The old cowboy placed the order before he departed to Abyssinia, to be delivered to me," Maj. Gen. Taylor said with a shake of his sun-bronzed bald head. "Geronimo Joe must have decided long-range sniping would help make up for our complete lack of mountain guns and mortars.

"Somehow he knew where to find the No. 32 Mk1 scopes – or he brought them with him when he came out to Africa. Wesley-Richards had to design the scope mount from scratch because nothing like this had ever been contemplated. The staff over there is real proud of themselves. They say they finished one 6.5-06 and a scoped Boys weapon in time for the Captain to take with him when he went in-country."

"Best have the rest of our allocation of Lovat Scouts sent out from Seaborn House," Maj. Stone said. "We have employment for them."

"I wonder what would happen if you necked a Boys .55 caliber round down to 6.5mm?" Maj. Gen. Taylor said.

AT THAT VERY MOMENT THE INNOVATOR OF THE SCOPED Boys .55 Sniper Rifle, Captain "Geronimo" Joe McKoy was nearly six hundred miles deep inside the Abyssinian border approaching the Great Rift Valley with his mule train. He was not planning on crossing the valley, which was good because it has been compared to the Grand Canyon in scale. He would not want to get caught by the Italians when he was in the bottom of the gorge. It was believed that Major John Randal and his Force N team had been dropped on the north side of the valley where his mule train was and he was hoping that proved true.

By his best estimate, they were getting close to the Force N drop zone (DZ). There was no way to pin it down precisely since the airplane and crew that had dropped them had gone MIA on a mission shortly after. All he had to go on was a set of grid coordinates provided by the RAF that may or may not have been accurate.

So far, navigation on the journey had been a snap. The mule train was following the mercenary company commanded by Sergeant Mike "March or Die" Mikkalis, DCM, and his crew of former French Legionnaire NCOs, which was now only about three days' march ahead. Since Mikkalis' Mercs simply shot anyone who strayed in their way – no questions asked – all Capt. McKoy had to do to plot his course was follow the circling vultures.

He had learned that a pack mule could travel at the rate of two and a quarter miles per hour through normal Abyssinian terrain, though scaling a steep escarpment or fording a swollen stream might take up an entire day. The caravan was able to maintain the two and a quarter mile per hour pace for a maximum of five hours, and then the mules needed to spend the rest of the day grazing. Going faster was possible for short spurts, but Capt. McKoy knew the muleteer who hurries at the beginning of a long march is only storing up trouble for himself toward the end.

The former Arizona Ranger was in his element. This trip was like a flashback to when he went into Mexico with the Punitive Expedition chasing Poncho Villa – only a lot more dangerous. Back in those days he had served as the Chief of Scouts for Brigadier General John "Blackjack" Pershing.

The exotic Abyssinian landscape consisted of some of the most incredible scenery he had ever laid eyes on. No one had told him the country was this fantastic. Parts of it looked like they were on another planet, sort of like the geography of Estes Park in Colorado – only more of it and wackier. Some of the terrain was so rugged and surreal at times he wondered if they might actually encounter moon men.

Anything seemed possible.

The caravan's escort, Merritt's Marauders, had fought three sharp engagements with shifta bandits attired in picturesque 1920s Tom Mix Hollywood movie-style cowboy hats. In two of the fights, things had gotten "down right Western" for a while. They likely would have encountered more trouble along the way except Mikkalis' Mercs were stacking up dead shifta like cordwood, blazing a trail and whittling down the number of land pirates for Capt. McKoy's mule train to run into.

Lieutenant Jack Merritt, MC, MM, was shaping up to be a first-class commander of irregular troops. Since the former Life Guards corporal had excelled at virtually everything he ever put his hand to, this came as no real surprise. Nevertheless, Capt. McKoy was well pleased with the way Merritt's Marauders handled themselves on the march.

Abyssinia was wild country, not recommended for family-oriented tourists interested in a nature tour. Everything either wanted to eat you, rob you, or in the case of the Italian Blackshirts, stand you against a wall and shoot you.

The biggest problem by far was the wild animals. The crocodiles, hyenas and lions – to mention the top three – were real trouble. They never let up. The onslaught was relentless. Giant crocodiles were lurking in every waterhole, at the edge of every lake and under the bank of every river. The hyenas were out in force every single night cackling, laughing and circling the camp. Lion followed the caravan, waiting to attack whenever they saw an opening.

Every day, every night, every foot of the way was a constant battle for survival. Caravans passing through Abyssinia could not let their guard down. Relax for a second and a hyena would dart in to disembowel a mule, a lion sneak up to snatch a native driver or a shifta jump out from behind a bush with a spear and evil intent. Capt. McKoy was having so much fun he was considering relocating here permanently after he retired.

When the mule train stopped for the afternoon's graze, he ordered Lt. Merritt to set up the radio and contact Mikkalis' Mercs.

"Mike, this is Joe, over."

"This is Mike, go ahead, over"

"Time to stop shooting all those shifta boys Mike, over."

"Why should I? Over."

"Cause we should be getting purty close to the drop zone area. You're probably right on top of it. Take some prisoners. Interrogate 'em to find out what they know 'bout the Major, over."

"Roger, over."

"You can still shoot a few of 'em, if they give you any trouble, over."

"Wilco – out."

HAVING GOTTEN OFF THE REGULAR MORNING FLIGHT FROM Cairo at the Khartoum Airport, the pale pilot officer limping across the tarmac with a cane was unrecognizable as the fun-loving playboy Major Sir Terry "Zorro" Stone had grown up with. Pilot Officer Gasper "Bunny" Featherstone looked at least twenty years older than his actual age. The Battle of France, which had been lost, and the Battle of Britain, which by some accounts had been won, had extracted their toll. He was very nearly the last of the "Millionaires"; 601 Squadron no longer existed except on paper. It had been shot to pieces. A problem inherent in being one of the legendary "Valiant Few," to which so much was owed by so many, was that the numbers kept dwindling.

Swaggering along behind him, wearing jaunty green berets cocked over one eye, overstuffed duffle bags thrown over their shoulders and bristling weapons, were six members of RF out from England. They were the second contingent of Raiders from Seaborn House being shuffled to Force N as rapidly as air transport came available.

The public arrival of the RF troopers was intentional – cooked up by that master of deceptive intrigue, Lieutenant Colonel Dudley Clarke. The fact that RF men were in town and planning to do something nasty to the Italians in East Africa was not a secret – *what* they were planning to do was. It was hoped that a fascist spy was watching the airport. The odds were strongly in favor one was.

Maj. Stone had ground transportation standing by for the RF troopers to deliver them to the safe house. Half the RF types were to be assigned the task of staffing a training/selection program under the command of temporary Captain Roy "Mad Dog" Reupart for the officers and NCOs volunteering for duty with Force N.

The RF men who were detailed to the training/selection mission had their work cut out. The new candidates for Force N were not the typical volunteers for special service. The regular cavalry officers who had volunteered had been publicly disparaged by Major Orde Wingate of Mission 101, as "scum from the Cavalry Division." The recently commissioned Bimbashis ranged in age from nineteen to sixty-three, and they had little or no military experience.

One evening in the bar at the Continental Hotel, a rear echelon staff officer temporarily up from a safe billet deep in the flesh pots of Cairo on a fool's errand of some sort sidled up and commented dryly to Maj. Stone, "I met one of your octogenarian volunteers for Special Forces the other day. I say, Sir Terry old chap, who is going to take responsibility for passing out all their pills? Ha ha."

"How would you like the job, old stick?" Maj. Stone drawled, nearly giving the staff wallah a heart attack. "I can arrange to have orders cut."

The other three RF troopers would be traveling on today with Maj. Stone and Plt. Off. Featherstone to Port Mombasa in Kenya and then on to Camp Croc on Lake Rudolf. Two rather dilapidated Khartoum taxis were standing by to whisk the Force N personnel to the seaplane dock on the Nile where they were due shortly to board a Southland Short Flying Boat.

When the group arrived at the seaplane dock, they found Lieutenant Pamala Plum-Martin waiting for them with her bags, having decided at the last minute to join their party.

She said, "Hello, Bunny."

Lt. Plum-Martin knew quite a few of "The Few."

On the flight to Port Mombasa, Maj. Stone briefed Plt. Off. Featherstone on the Force N mission. The young RAF fighter pilot listened carefully but seemed distracted. There was a far-away look in his royal blue eyes. accented by the heavy bags underneath them that no man his age should be sporting. Any sound that vaguely resembled a Bakelite-telephone ringing made him jump about a foot. He used the word "bloody" a lot.

"The bloody flying and bloody aerial combat was not so bloody bad," he said. "I can stay in the air with any bloody Hun, it is the bloody constant sitting around the bloody airstrip waiting for the bloody phone to ring with the bloody orders to scramble for the next bloody mission that bloody grinds you down day after bloody day."

"You multi-engine amphibious sea plane qualified by any chance, old stick?" Maj. Stone asked.

"Are you bloody blinkers? I barely bloody even knew how to fly a bloody single seat Spitfire when the bloody war started. The bloody 'Millionaires' were hardly more than a bloody social club when the bloody balloon went up. I did crash land in the bloody Channel and was rescued by a flying boat the second bloody time I was shot down, come to think of it. Does that count?"

"How would you like to be my liaison to the South African Air Force, old stick?"

"Now *that* I can bloody do," Plt. Off. Featherstone said. "I am very social. From what I hear, the bloody SAAF has a reputation as being a bloody hard-drinking body of men."

At this point in the flight, Maj. Stone initiated a policy he intended to continue as long as he was acting as the Deputy Commander, Force N. He had his newest officer read the medical report on conditions in Abyssinia and initial it in his presence. He did not want any man ever claiming at some later date he had not been fully warned in advance.

"How in the bloody hell did Mallory manage to arrange for Jane's bloody paramour to be marooned in a cesspool like bloody Abyssinia?" Plt. Off. Featherstone said, looking up from the medical report. "Seaborn has the bloody luck of a cat – always lands on his bloody feet."

"Personally, I never cared for the man," Maj. Stone said.

"Likewise," Plt. Off. Featherstone agreed. "Do not expect me to set one bloody toe across the bloody Abyssinian border, Sir Terry. Did you bloody read this – eighty percent syphilis rate? Is this supposed to be some kind of a bloody joke?"

"Put your initials on it," Maj. Stone ordered. "Never let it be said you were not warned, Bunny."

"Bloody well remind me not to get involved with any of Mallory's bloody women," Plt. Off. Featherstone said. "Speaking of which, I am reliably advised there are a bloody enormous number. A woman in every bloody port. Oh, for the life of a sailor!"

One of Commander Mallory Seaborn's women, his wife, Captain the Lady Jane Seaborn, was waiting when they landed at Port Mombasa. "You arrived in the nick of time. Sqn. Ldr. Wilcox has radioed he is inbound on his final approach."

They stood on the dock, all eyes strained out to sea. Over the horizon three tiny specks appeared in the azure blue brilliance of the African sky where it met the darker blue-green of the ocean. The dots came steadily on.

Flying the lead aircraft, Squadron Leader Paddy Wilcox was seated in the Command Pilot chair of a Consolidated Model 16 open cockpit Commodore, the largest, longest-range flying boat in civil aviation use. Originally designed for the U.S. Navy as the XPY-1 Admiral, these planes were the first three prototypes to roll off the assembly line and had been sold not to the Navy, but to the short-lived New York, Rio and Buenos Aires Airline (NYRBA).

When Pan American Airlines gobbled the NYRBA up eighteen months after it has purchased the three Commodores, the planes – being prototypes and therefore non-standard models – had been sold off to the Rio Tinto Mining Conglomerate. Pan American wanted to avoid the maintenance headache of trying to service nonstandard types. An underlying reason for the sale was the fact that the three were open cockpit models, which contributed to pilot fatigue from the wind, weather and engine noise.

The open cockpit was not a drawback to Sqn. Ldr. Leader Wilcox. He loved flying with his face in the breeze. The former bush pilot thought of it like driving a convertible. The Commodores were just the ticket for what he had in mind – shuttling men and equipment forward into Abyssinia, up the chain of lakes the length of the Great Rift Valley. Only they were going to have to clean out all the chicken feathers, chili peppers and goat droppings first. These long service aircraft had seen hard use.

Originally the Commodores had been the luxury airliners. Each passenger compartment had been paneled in its own shade of pastel fabric selected by a famous interior decorator hired by Consolidated. The seats were leather upholstery, and the flight deck was carpeted.

The planes sported coral-colored wings with cream-colored hulls. Below the waterline they were painted ink black. But that had been nearly eleven years ago and they had not been painted since. Nowadays the paint was peeling off in large chunks.

Configured to carry twenty-two passengers, a gross carrying weight of seventeen thousand six hundred pounds dictated the actual number of paying customers. Two 575-horsepower Pratt and Whitney engines powered the Commodores with three paddle airscrews providing a range of one thousand miles at an air speed of one hundred eight miles per hour. The crew originally consisted of a pilot, co-pilot and radio operator. Not much of the original pastel designer fabric or leather seating remained in the passenger compartment of these hard-service planes. Goats had eaten most of it.

The three amphibious airplanes lined up in trail formation and flew into the Port of Mombasa line astern. They touched down smoothly and taxied to the unloading portals. In the lead aircraft Commodore Richard "Dickey the Pirate" Seaborn, wearing a pair of oversized flying goggles, was riding in the co-pilot's seat next to Sqn. Ldr. Wilcox. The trans-Atlantic flight in the open cockpit had been one of the most harrowing experiences of his military career. Secretly, he felt he had finally earned the Victoria Cross he had received on OPERATION LOUNGE LIZARD. He would not make that flight again for one million pounds sterling. It was probably just as well that he had not been aware that the amphibians were literally flying on fumes by the time they landed.

"Bloody things have to be the most wretched excuse for bloody airplanes I have ever seen in my entire bloody flying career," Plt. Off. Featherstone pronounced in wonder and amazement, "Bloody deathtraps!"

"Welcome to Force N, Bunny," Maj. Stone said. "Get used to it, everything we have is worst of breed."

"Actually, I began to bloody suspect that might be the bloody case the moment I learned that Force N wanted me," Plt. Off. Featherstone said. "Confirmed when I saw you waiting at the bloody airport, Sir Terry."

Lt. Plum-Martin was desperate to have a private moment alone with Lady Jane. The instant the two were dropped at the hotel where they were staying, the Force N IO pulled her aside and produced a thin envelope from her handbag.

"I am not quite sure what this Y-service intercept means, Jane. We have to be careful not to read anything into the query, but I wanted you to be the first to see it."

The envelope contained a translated signal intercept of the daily traffic from an Italian battalion commander to his brigade HQ. The message was a recent low-level communication of the kind not likely to contain anything of significance and if Lt. Plum-Martin had not been a diligent professional it would have languished, unread, in the stack of intercepts delivered to her daily. The inquiry was intermingled with routine requests for foodstuffs, military stores and the other countless mundane administrative signals common to military units in all armies. "Please advise the significance of the letter 'N' as it relates to the Abyssinian resistance movement."

Lady Jane looked at Lt. Plum-Martin. They both began to cry.

10
KING'S AFRICAN RIFLES

MAJOR JOHN RANDAL WAS LYING IN AMBUSH BESIDE THE road with a black and white Abyssinian Stonechat flitting around the bush he was hiding behind. Cheap Bribe, his new best friend, had volunteered to cut the road with his shifta in a burst of uncharacteristic patriotic zeal. This was going to be the first time Gubbo Rekash's men had taken the lead in an operation. In all past engagements they had hung around on the fringes, hoping for an opportunity to swoop in and claim some of the booty.

Rita Hayworth and Lana Turner were with him, so communications were possible, one way. Not that it really mattered. Maj. Randal was only along as an observer – as full-time outlaw bandits, the Patriots were masters of the art of unexpected attack. They did not need his advice on how to set up an ambush.

The shifta shot a zebra and dragged it out into the middle of a straight stretch of road. Traffic coming from either direction would have to stop, dismount and move the dead animal in order to pass. There was a sheer drop off on one side and a steep sloping, heavily wooded ridge on the other. The ambush party was near the road, concealed in the cedar forest part way up the slope, and would be firing downhill into the killing zone. As usual, the mules were being held just over the top of the ridgeline out of sight, ready for a quick getaway.

The set-up was almost perfect. No Italian truck driver would ever be alarmed by the sight of a dead zebra blocking the road. In Abyssinia, dead animals on or beside the road were a common sight. The Blackshirts shot from the back of their trucks as their convoys rolled through the countryside as a matter of course. They fired on anything that moved, including the local denizens.

Maj. Randal was interested to note that Cheap Bribe had followed one of his tried and true techniques – planning the operation in reverse (a RF Rule). The bandit chief understood full well from a life of crime that it did not matter how much treasure was captured if he did not get away alive to divvy it up.

The only deficiency worthy of note was that the shifta's off-white shamma togas were difficult to camouflage. Maj. Randal whispered to Lana Turner, "Take a note, Lana. Tomorrow I want you and Rita to dye everyone's cloaks. Boil 'em in coffee or tea."

The golden-skinned slave girl responded with a white-toothed smile. He interpreted her response to be the equivalent of "Roger that."

They would probably have a hard time getting the shifta to let them dye their pearl gray Tom Mix hats. But the cone-shaped cowboy hats were not a problem; the Patriots had left their signature sombreros back with their mules. The tall hats with the single crease in the crown would have been virtually impossible to keep concealed.

From up the valley came the screech of a wild mountain rock baboon. Only it was not a baboon, it was Cheap Bribe's right flank security party who was keeping the road under close observation. The call was passed on, alerting the Patriots waiting in ambush that the Italians were approaching. Soon the sound of trucks shifting gears could be heard in the crisp mountain air.

The Fiat 38 truck was the standard-issue Italian troop transport. It was a workhorse. However, the fascists had never been able to produce enough of them. The military vehicles that entered the straight stretch of the road and drove unerringly to the dead zebra before coming to a halt were of five different makes. Curiously, one was a British Bedford. Now how did that get there?

The instant the vehicles stopped for the zebra and before the Italians could dismount, Cheap Bribe initiated the ambush by having his trumpeter blow a call to open fire. This is not the most effective way to signal the beginning of a fight – Maj. Randal preferred the first sound the enemy heard in the killing zone of one of his ambushes to be one that inflicted casualties – however, it did work.

The Patriots let loose a fierce volley of fire that poured into the trucks from point-blank range. The shifta were not any better shots than the average villager who volunteered for Force N, but the bandits knew their limitations and compensated for their deficiency in marksmanship by setting up as close as possible to their target. This is what the instructors at the U.S. Cavalry School called a "near ambush." Unlike with man-eating lions, the outlaws were not operating under the delusion that the Italians were spirits and could not be killed by a bullet – the trick was to hit the bad guys with one.

The Patriots positioned on the side of the dead zebra away from the truck's direction of travel immediately ran forward down to the road, crossed it and formed the base of what was taught in all military schools worldwide as an "L" shaped ambush. Maj. Randal was impressed. Tactically it was a good move.

The shifta's volume of fire gained intensity until it reached a crescendo with only a few desultory return rounds popping back from the Italians. Up to this point, the ambush had been conducted with textbook precision. Cheap Bribe appeared to have the situation well in hand.

However, when the brigands in the long part of the "L" along the length of the ambush position saw their companions make the rapid flanking advance to close up the distance to the killing zone, they became concerned that their associates might get to the trucks ahead of them and have first dibs on the plunder. Acting on their own initiative, they rose up out of their ambush positions *en masse* and rushed the convoy emitting wild, high-pitched, terror-inducing war screams.

It is accepted military practice to assault through the killing zone of an ambush. The recommended technique is to gain fire superiority, then move out slow and steady on line, shoulder to shoulder, with every man squeezing off a round every time his left foot hits the ground – executing what is called "walking fire." According to the book, this is the climactic moment in the ambush operation.

However, most commanders prefer to wait until the enemy are all down – dead or wounded – before having their troops leave the safety of concealed positions and press home their attack. Not so Cheap Bribe's boys, they were in an out-and-out footrace with each other to be the first to grab the booty. Shifta fall into two categories: the swift and the broke.

Acting against his better judgment, before moving down the slope to join the Patriots, Maj. Randal handed his M-1903 A-1 Springfield to Lana Turner and took in return the A-5 Browning shotgun she held out for him. The Italians were still popping off the odd round – in fact, they seemed to be recovering from their initial shock and beginning to fight back. Oblivious to the risk of being shot dead, shifta were swarming into the backs of the trucks in search of treasure even while fire was coming from the cab. Several of Gubbo's men were chopped down in mid-grab. No one paid the friendly casualties the slightest attention.

Maj. Randal stepped up on the red dirt hard top with Lana Turner at his heels. He worked his way down the side of one of the Fiat 38 trucks with his back flat against the vehicle. When he made it to a position behind the truck's cab, he stretched the A-5 out at arm's length and, with both hands holding the barrel, pointed at a right angle and pumped three 12-gauge rounds into the passenger compartment through the open window.

A quick head check showed the two passengers were down. Lying on the seat next to the dead driver, Maj. Randal spotted a strange looking, short barreled submachine gun with a stubby, perforated barrel that looked like a cheese shredder. He opened the door of the cab and was reaching in to scoop it up when the sound of a Lancia armored car racing around the corner was heard. The tall, antique-looking, round-turreted fighting vehicle carried three 8mm St. Etienne machine guns, and they were spitting out bullets to beat the band.

The Lancia was a high, ungainly fighting machine. The day the first one rolled off the assembly line in 1915, it was already obsolete as far as armored cars went. However, Cheap Bribe's men had no defense against it. Maj. Randal found himself running for his life with the rest of the Patriots. A hail of 8mm rounds cracked through the trees, making a terrific racket as they rushed back up the slope to the top of the ridge and into the forest. The panic was infectious. Lana was dancing along behind him with her Carcano and his Springfield slung over her shoulder.

Cheap Bribe was about ten feet in front of them going for all he was worth. Holding his Mauser 98K over his shoulder with the barrel pointed back in the general direction of the ambush site (consequently waving the muzzle almost in Maj. Randal's face), he was pulling the trigger with his left thumb while reaching across working the bolt with his right hand, all the while running up the slope. The bandit never turned his head to look back, not even once. Every time Gubbo Rekash discharged his weapon, the muzzle blast nearly blew Maj. Randal off his feet. The Force N commander shouted in fury for Cheap Bribe to "cease-fire," but the big Mauser kept booming.

The chaos did not abate when the Patriots reached the safety of the crest of the ridge. Without waiting to take a head count, Gubbo Rekash's troops piled on their mules and pounded helter-skelter down the far side of the ridgeline, trying to put as much distance between them and the Lancia as rapidly as possible. The panicked outlaws rode as fast as their mules could lope – every man for himself.

Rita was waiting with Parachute and the other two mules. Without breaking stride, Maj. Randal and Lana leapt aboard their animals and were away like the devil was after them. Rita was left some distance behind, quirting her mount furiously in hot pursuit. Even so, the three found it difficult to keep up with Gubbo Rekash's fleeing raiders. The shifta were executing the military maneuver known affectionately in RF as "getting the hell out of Dodge" with élan.

The fright was totally illogical. The armored car was road-bound – there was no way it could come up the steep incline through the jungle after them. Besides, the Lancia carried a crew of only five men, and they had no intention of leaving the safety of their armored vehicle. Most of the Italian troops in the convoy were dead or wounded and those remaining were in no condition to mount any kind of pursuit.

But no one present, Maj. Randal included, was going to wait around and analyze the situation. When breaking contact, when it's time to go – go.

Once out of harm's way, the Patriot's sense of humor kicked in. Nearly getting killed can sometimes be wildly hilarious – that is, after the danger has passed. Next, the men started calling out to each other, bragging about who had been the most afraid – great fear being something to be proud of, as every combat veteran knows. The first liar never had a chance.

Maj. Randal would have cheerfully wrapped a wire garrote around Gubbo Rekash's neck one minute and hugged him the next. When they finally pulled up to let the mules blow, the shifta were laughing uproariously. The general consensus among the semi-hysterical desperados was, "Let's do that again!"

When the victorious Patriots arrived at the Force N rendezvous point, down a narrow, winding cutback canyon, it was like riding into one of Baden-Powell's Boy Scout Jamborees with guns. Men were rallying to the flag in droves; only not all of the volunteers knew exactly what the national flag actually looked like. The Italians had banned the Abyssinian flag for the past five years, which meant most of the younger Patriots had never seen one.

Tribal warriors were streaming in from all points of the compass. The jungle telegraph had done its work. Naturally, each man brought his pageboy to carry his rifle, his wife, a slave or two to cook his meals and care for his mule, and possibly a hair stylist for his beehive hairdo. Force N was increasing exponentially with the tooth to tail ratio getting way out of whack.

Maj. Randal did not waste any time putting that right. Men signing up on the promise of one Maria Theresa thaler per day were quickly organized into fighting units. Those who did not have a rifle chambered for a round of Italian Army manufacture were sent off to "obtain one." The pages were drafted into the Bad Boys to subsequently be dispatched on missions of petty sabotage. The Bad Boys were responsible for painting, carving or scratching the letter "N" on as many things as possible in places where the Italian armed forces personnel were likely to see it in the course of their daily duties. Also, planting nails on the roads to exploit the Italian forces acute shortage of tires.

The women and slaves were left to cook, maintain the camp and perform the animal husbandry. While this dramatically streamlined the fighting units, it still left Force N bloated with a large number of noncombatant personnel.

Bimbashi Butch "Headhunter" Hoolihan sorted out the rifles and ammunition. The idea was to end up with a force of fighting men armed and equipped entirely with captured Italian weapons – or at the least, weapons that fired the same caliber of ammunition as the Blackshirt army. The Patriots could then depend on re-supply by raiding the enemy. The result would be a self-sufficient guerrilla command able to sustain itself indefinitely in the field. All they had to do was fight the Italians to re-supply.

While not a perfect plan, it was the best one Maj. Randal could come up with. What a guerrilla army really needs is a secure source of supply from across a safe border outside of the actual country it operates in. When an insurgent force has an active base of national-level military support coming in from an adjoining country, it is difficult to defeat, particularly if the local indigenous people provide a safe haven and substance to the guerrillas.

Unfortunately, in order to achieve that military state of affairs, Maj. Randal had to re-establish contact with Force N Rear in Khartoum. At the moment, he did not have a clue how he was going to be able to accomplish that task. Drums and runners have their limits, and six hundred miles is stretching it a bit for the jungle telegraph. He needed a radio.

There did not appear to be any way to capture one. The Italians were absurdly short of radio communications. None of the convoys carried radios. Not even the Lancia armored car had been equipped with one. In fact, the company and battalion-sized Italian outposts scattered along the roads did not have radios either. Fascist battle doctrine called for the military to rely almost entirely on landline communications.

The lack of radios made it virtually impossible for Maj. Randal to capture one, and it had an even worse effect on the Italians. Because there were no mobile radios in the convoys, it was impossible for the Italians to set up reaction forces to respond to Patriot ambushes with anything resembling the lighting quickness needed to catch the nimble shifta. Reliance on landline communications made the Blackshirts susceptible to having someone, like the Bad Boys, attack the cable.

Cut the wire, and the Blackshirts would be forced to send out a party of line repairmen to locate the break. Maj. Randal knew that. So whenever possible, the cut was arranged to be in some spot ideal for an ambush, where a heavily-armed band of Patriots might or might not be lying in wait. The Eyeties never knew. It took a brave Italian to walk along holding a wire looking for the break with Force N in the neighborhood.

Over time, the ease with which their communications could be knocked out would work to heighten the Italian's fear and sense of isolation. However, at this point in the operation Maj. Randal had placed a temporary hold on cutting the Italian phone lines. He was saving that trick for later; he did not want the Italians to have time to develop some countermeasure against it – though exactly what that would be was hard to figure.

Landline communications are very vulnerable.

The order forbidding the cutting of Italian landlines marked a turning point in Force N's private war, though no one recognized it at the time. Maj. Randal was beginning to get a feel for his enemy. Subconsciously he had gone over to the offense.

Each day a little progress was being made toward organizing Force N into an effective fighting force. The good news was that Patriots were coming in to volunteer to fight the Italian occupiers. The bad news was that the more people assembled in one place, the easier it was for the Italians to locate their camp and attack it.

As the commander of Swamp Fox Force at Calais, Maj. Randal had experienced first-hand the danger of air attack. He knew enemy air was the biggest threat his budding guerrilla army faced. Exactly the same as the Luftwaffe had in France, the Regia Aeronautica enjoyed absolute air supremacy over Abyssinia. Any plane in the sky was Italian.

"Butch, have all these people disperse," Maj. Randal ordered. "Pitch their tents under the cover of the jungle. From now on, whenever possible, Force N marches at night."

"Yes, sir!"

"Post air guards – they're only to give us early warning. Give the order no one fires at an airplane – under no circumstances."

"Right away, sir."

One morning, Bimbashi Hoolihan and Waldo were studying a map while Maj. Randal briefed them on his idea that Force N Rear would most likely attempt to work its way up the chain of lakes in the Great Rift Valley by using amphibious airplanes. The trio was debating the merits of sending Waldo down the chain to attempt to make contact with them.

"Just don't expect me to go all the way to Lake Rudolf," Waldo said. "I got myself in a little trouble down there back in the day when I first came out to Africa as a kid, and I ain't goin' back to see if it's blown over."

"What kind of trouble, Mr. Treywick?" Bimbashi Hoolihan asked.

"I signed on with an ivory trader, Dr. Eustace Atkinson, who had heard the Rendille tribesmen up at the lake had a lot of ivory for sale. This was my first trading safari, and it nearly turned out to be my last. Mark it down, Butch, they's bad natives living around Lake Rudolf, mean as snakes – kill you as quick as look at you.

"Now, Doc Atkinson had a hard streak himself, meaner even than the Rendille. So what he done, he called 'em all into a big tent – and I do mean all of 'em. Then Doc rolled in a big, wooden keg that he claimed was chuck full of Maria Theresa thalers he was goin' to use to buy up all the local ivory. He took a seat on the keg, lit up a big stogie, then the negotiatin' commenced.

"The Rendille drove a hard bargain, demanded more than the Doc wanted to pay. But those bad boys wasn't a' fix'n to let us say no to the deal and walk away with our keg full o' silver thalers, no sir. We was dead men then and there.

"Only there wasn't no Fat Ladys in that keg – it was a' loaded to the brim with gunpowder and rusty two-penny nails. Doc surreptitiously lit the fuse with his cigar, told the Rendille he needed to step outside a moment and discuss their offer with his associate, meanin' me. He'd be right back – smoke 'em if you've got 'em, boys.

"When that tent blew, it went sky high. The Doc pretty near wiped out the whole tribe, got the entire leadership. We loaded up the tusks and beat feet for Nairobi, only the Colonial Office down there failed to see the humor in it, confiscated our ivory. "

"What happened, Mr. Treywick?" Maj. Randal asked.

"They tried to hang us for killin' them Rendille, that's what. Had a jury trial and everthin'," Waldo said with a disgusted shake of his grey head.

"You ain't ever truly enjoyed yourself 'til you been on public trial for multiple homicide."

"There still a warrant out for you in Kenya, Mr. Treywick?"

"No Major, the jury ruled it justifiable. I ain't worried about the authorities, it's the Rendille. Some of the survivors is probably still pretty mad. There ain't no statute of limitations on payback."

"Could be a problem," Maj. Randal said.

As they were talking, a group of six men dressed in old, faded, British khaki BDUs sporting sergeant's stripes on the sleeves paraded into the camp, marching in perfect formation with a leader counting cadence. The crisp commands rang out in precise English and were smartly being executed, by the number. Maj. Randal watched from his canvas chair, bewildered, as the detail marched up to his tent and came to a halt with an elaborate stamping of bare feet. The senior man had the troops present arms with a crash.

Maj. Randal put his cigarillo down and stood up. He adjusted his jungle jacket, put on his cut-down Australian slouch hat and then walked over to take the salute. He could have hardly been more astounded if a space ship had landed and tiny green men climbed out and reported for duty.

The six men in khaki were Abyssinian tribesmen who had left their villages years ago to travel to Kenya to serve in the King's African Rifles (KAR), that legendary band of native troops commanded by British officers, who regarded themselves as the most elite fighting unit on the African continent. After completing the required twenty years Imperial service, the men had returned home to their villages to take wives and live like kings on their army pensions. Now the former KAR veterans had come to offer their service to the Crown again.

Their unexpected arrival was a stunning development for Force N.

Kaldi made a little speech about how the Emperor would reward each of them handsomely when he was returned to the throne and the Italians were driven from the country. The KAR sergeants listened politely.

Maj. Randal kept it short and simple. He promoted the six KAR veterans to Shambel, the equivalent of captain in the Abyssinian Army, on the spot. This announcement made the former sergeants euphoric with pleasure. Pride of arms is an important aspect of Abyssinian culture. Military advancement is virtually the only way a man has to improve his social position. Promotion to the officer class, while not unheard of, was a rare achievement. The man doing the promoting can generally count on the undying loyalty of the men promoted. Force N now had six indigenous English-speaking officers who would follow their commander off a cliff.

After the impromptu ceremony, Maj. Randal formally turned the new Shambel over to Bimbashi Hoolihan (who outranked them, Bimbashi being the equivalent to the rank of major) to assign them cadres so that they could start organizing the inflow of volunteers into mule companies straight away. The plan, cooked up on the spot, was for the six new Shambels to each form a unit of one hundred men. Each Shambel would be responsible for organizing the company, selecting platoon non-commissioned officers (NCOs), the men who would serve the company, and providing for their men's mules. They would also lead the mule companies in battle until RF officers could be brought in to take command.

Maj. Randal was counting on the former NCOs from the KAR living up to their regiment's reputation.

"Why are all these people suddenly coming in, Mr. Treywick?"

"Major, you probably don't realize it, but you done become an Abyssinian celebrity," Waldo responded. "Every man in the whole country knows that sooner or later the time is a' comin' when they have to take sides. The word is gettin' out that you look like a winner."

"Good thing they didn't see us legging it up the hill when that Lancia roared up with all guns blazing," Maj. Randal said.

"Those Eyetie armored cars are a problem," Waldo said. "We ain't got nothin' that'll put a dent in 'em."

"There's always Molotov cocktails," Maj. Randal said.

"Yeah, I heard some Russian big-wig politician was trying to grab credit for inventing firebombs – naming 'em after hisself and all.

"The truth is," Waldo said, "the Klu Klux Klan was a' usin' fruit jars filled with fifty percent kerosene and fifty percent moonshine liquor – hunert' and eighty proof – a long time before the Russians ever got into the cocktail business. My Pappy was a' practicin' member in good standin' of the KKK back in Tupelo when I was a kid, so I know what I'm talking about.

"The Klansmen, all bein' dirt poor, soon figured out that there was a' whole lot a' moonshine liquor available and kerosene cost money, so after a while they just made 'em out of pure white lightnin' in a jar with a rag stuck in it as a fuse. Then at night when they'd go out to do their duty, pretty soon they got to drinkin' their fire bombs.

"One night my Pappy and a group of resolute Mississippi men set out on Klan business, and after they'd drunk up about half the incendiary devices they had with 'em, they went ahead and done what they set out to do. Only my Pappy, in all the excitement, somehow managed to ignite hisself.

"My poor grievin' mother took up with a travlin' insurance salesman about two full days of mournin' after the funeral. He was a mean bastard, so I run off and stowed away on the first boat out of Mobile. When it hit Mombasa, I jumped ship."

"That's some story, Mr. Treywick," Maj. Randal said.

"What I'm trying to get at, Major – firebombs is dangerous weapons. If you believe I'm goin' to purposely arm and equip any of these Patriot whack jobs with glass jars full of flammable liquid, then pass out matches to light 'em off in the middle of a firefight, you better think again."

"Roger," Maj. Randal said, "point made."

THAT VERY SAME MORNING, WHILE THE FORCE N SENIOR staff was debating the pros and cons of Molotov cocktails, Prime Minister Winston Churchill was taking a stroll at his private country estate, *Chequers*. Walking at his side was "C", Colonel Stewart Menzies, the Chief of the British SIS, MI-6. The former Life Guards officer had not been the PM's first choice for the job of the nation's chief IO, but that was water under the bridge now. What was important was that "C" was doing a magnificent job as the country's senior spymaster. Col. Menzies had proven to be reliable and perfectly willing to do his Prime Minister's bidding without throwing up unnecessary roadblocks, which was more than the PM could say about any number of the key men holding high positions in his government.

"Stewart, there is something not right in Nairobi."

"In what way, Prime Minister?"

"The colonial government out there seems to be actively impeding the war effort," Prime Minister Churchill huffed in disgust. "First they refused to allow Abyssinian deserters – askaris from the Italian Army – men with gads of military experience, to be used for the re-conquest of Abyssinia on a flimsy technicality – some made-up argument to do with the Geneva Convention. Claim they can put them to better use as road builders. What rot!

"The Kenyan white settlers are not volunteering to serve outside the colony. The lads are joining militias in droves, we have thousands of them in uniform, but they will not fight! The whole affair is a national disgrace.

"A substantial amount of our precious military stores seem to have gone missing out there. One million rounds of .22 caliber ammunition earmarked to train new recruits in marksmanship has recently been stolen. Trucks and parts are vanishing.

"I demand action against the Italians from Kenya into Abyssinia, and all I get is half-hearted excuses or obstructionism. There is something rotten in that sinful Sodom & Gomorrah of a colony."

"What is it you would have me do, sir?"

"Identify the source of the problem, and then put it right," the Prime Minister commanded, pausing to light up one of his huge green Cuban cigars. "Action this day. There is no requirement for you to be gentle in the manner you go about it, Stewart. I need not remind you, there is a war to be won."

"I shall make inquires immediately, Prime Minister," the Chief of British SIS said. "We have long suspected the Italians might have a man in Kenya."

"Bring me results!"

11
READING FOR DETAIL

THE SUNRISE WAS SPECTACULAR AGAINST A MISTY NAVY sky. As the sun came up the mist melted and the sky faded. Major John Randal was sitting around a table in his CP tent, having breakfast with his six brand-new Abyssinian officers, formerly of the KAR. Bimbashi Butch "Headhunter" Hoolihan and Waldo were at the table, as were Lana and Rita. GG was buzzing around serving a gourmet, field-expedient meal that would have made the staff at the luxurious London Bradford Hotel green with envy. The Italian POW had recruited a couple of the younger pageboys to act as his headquarters staff waiters.

Maj. Randal was receiving an initial report from each of the Shambels on the state of the companies that they were in the process of forming. Recruits were pouring in, and the progress they were making at creating two battalions of mule-mounted infantry was better than he could have reasonably hoped for.

"You men are going to be responsible for raising, organizing and training your individual companies," Maj. Randal said. "When we establish contact with Force N Rear in Khartoum, highly-qualified British officers from Raiding Forces will be parachuted in to serve as your company commanders. You will then become the executive officer, second in command."

There was visible relief on the faces of the six grizzled ex-KAR sergeants. British officers in command was the model they were accustomed to and comfortable with. The stratospheric rise to the officer class had taken the Shambels by surprise and they desperately wanted to succeed.

But not one of them had ever commanded before and the idea was more than a little daunting for the long-service NCOs.

"If we can't make contact," Maj. Randal continued as he lit his cigarillo with his old, battered Zippo 26th Cavalry Regiment lighter, "you men are going to have to stay in command until we do."

From the serious looks on the chiseled, bronze faces around the table, it was obvious that the six acting company commanders clearly hoped communication with Khartoum could be effected with alacrity. Rank has its privileges, but it carries a highly disproportionate share of responsibility. In time of war, that can be heavy.

"Been thinkin'," Waldo said, drawing on his own cigar while Maj. Randal held out his lighter, "I'm readin' your book again, Major. This time I'm goin' for detail."

"I read it too, Major," GG interrupted, laying a platter of biscuits on the table. "I laughed out loud at the part where you gave the order to 'Kill 'em all and let Allah sort 'em out.' Did your platoon of cutthroat Commandos think it was funny?"

"The deal is," Waldo said, ignoring him, "if you're such a red hot snatcher of enemy Generals and Admirals from the arms of their mistresses in the dead of night and a genius at cuttin' out operations like they claim in the book, don't you think you could at least come up with a plan to kidnap one dinky little Italian long-range radio?"

Maj. Randal looked at him levelly.

"You probably wouldn't even have to steal the radio," the old army scout speculated through a blue cloud of cigar smoke as he rolled the stogie between his fingers.

"Hell, all you'd have to do is sneak inside some Wop brigade or higher HQ, dial up home and tell your folks where to come and find you. It's practically a no-brainer."

"Had much experience operating Italian military radios, Mr. Treywick?"

"I have sir," GG offered. "In my Headquarters Company, everyone had to rotate radio duty. I know where we can find one with sufficient range to contact Khartoum, no problem."

"Well, there you go, "Waldo said, clenching his cigar between his front teeth. "What're you waitin' on, Major? An engraved invitation from the Duke of Aosta? P.J. Pretorius would a' already gone and done it by now."

MAJOR GENERAL JAMES "BALDIE" TAYLOR FLEW INTO Nairobi to meet with Major General Alan Cunningham, the General Officer Commanding (GOC) EAF who was in the process of staging for the attack out of Kenya into IEA. Captain the Lady Jane Seaborn met him in the hotel Bentley when his plane landed, and they drove to the East Africa Force Headquarters (EAFHQ) located three miles north of the city.

EAF consisted of the 1st South African Division, 11th African Division and the 12th African Division. The last two were colonial units made up of native troops led by British officers. With all attachments, EAF was projected to be approximately forty three thousand men when it reached full strength.

From the Sudan, Major General William Platt, the Kaid, would be attacking into IEA with two divisions made up of primarily Indian troops and a handful of Free French and Free Belgians. When the balloon went up, there was going to be a smashing little colonial war right out of the pages of the storybooks.

Empire Forces would total fewer than ninety-five thousand men. The Italians had three hundred fifty thousand men, of which one hundred thousand were Italian National troops. The odds did not look good on paper; however, the British could choose the time and point of attack.

Maj. Gen. Cunningham knew the only chance he had was to concentrate his three divisions, attack on a narrow front, punch through and go like blue blazes. The general did have one thing going for him – his command was fully mechanized. In fact, EAF was the first army in history that was 100% mechanized.

The EAF had not been able to count on one stick of material transport in the way of trucks and/or armored fighting vehicles from England. Left to fend for itself, South Africa had simply mobilized every auto manufacturer in the colony, even those owned by neutral America – like Ford, GM and Chrysler. The plants stopped manufacturing automobiles and started producing nothing but trucks and armored cars. As one rolled off the assembly line, a South Africans driver was waiting to take it one thousand miles overland to Kenya on dirt roads – an epic feat all in itself.

EAF may have been small in numbers, but it was nimble and possessed of a can-do spirit and willingness to improvise. All it needed to be a formidable military machine was experience in actual battle – something for which all the training in the world is no substitute. There was a scheme in the works to correct that deficiency in the near future. A couple of small tune-up battles on the border were in the planning stages to give the troops combat experience prior to the invasion.

The meeting with Maj. Gen. Cunningham was short and to the point. The GOC said, "My staff and I are convinced the Italians have a master spy operating in Kenya, possibly in the military or high up in the Colonial Government. If the Italian High Command ever discover we are building up our troop strength to invade Italian East Africa and the date we intend to do it, the Blackshirts will be able shift massive numbers of reinforcements south to counter the threat. It is a given – if that happens, they win.

"Our only advantage is the element of surprise. If we lose it, our operation is doomed to fail."

"We are doing everything possible to create a cloud of confusion to cover your buildup, General, using a variety of means to make the Italians believe your intentions are only to guard the border," Maj. Gen. Taylor reassured him. "We have our best people on it – misinformation, psychological warfare and propaganda."

Maj. Gen. Cunningham, while bluff, was likeable and approachable, unlike Maj. Gen. Platt in Khartoum. He had an outstanding combat record from the last war, and since the beginning of this one, he had commanded three different Territorial Divisions before being appointed to command EAF. And, unlike the Kaid, Maj. Gen. Cunningham did not see himself as a modern day Pharaoh, which made him easier to confer with, it being unnecessary to genuflect.

"I voiced my concern about a master spy," Maj. Gen. Cunningham said, "now let me say what is keeping me awake nights – an Italian spoiling attack.

"Should the Duke of Aosta discover the date we are planning to invade, he will immediately mass his troops and launch a preemptive strike. The Italians will knife through the light forces we have positioned on the Northern Frontier and be in Nairobi in a matter of days."

"General, we are doing everything in our power to mislead the enemy and keep them in the dark," Maj. Gen. Taylor reiterated.

"Let me be perfectly clear," Maj. Gen. Cunningham repeated, clearly not reassured. "If the enemy manages to obtain the date we plan to invade, it will automatically trigger a spoiling attack. The Duke will have nothing to lose and everything to gain by hitting first!"

"General, what gives you reason to suspect the Italians have the means to acquire the date of your attack?" Lady Jane asked, tapping her scarlet nails on her crocodile handbag.

"Kenya Colony is shot through with fascist sympathizers," Maj. Gen. Cunningham said, dripping contempt. "More than a few people here actually believe the quality of life would be improved under fascist rule.

"To the average white Kenyan's way of thinking, the fascist's idea of a benevolent white European nation bringing law, order, education and medicine to a black African country represents the correct point of view – even if done at the point of a gun."

"Exact same problem we have in the Sudan," Maj. Gen. Taylor said.

"The playboy Duke of Aosta and his polo-playing wife were regular guests at the Muthaiga Country Club before the war started," Maj. Gen. Cunningham added. "The Duke made it clear if – meaning when – the Italians take over Kenya, everything will remain status quo, only better. My sources reliably inform me that the Duke has privately made glittering promises to more than a few of the members."

"He floated the same kind of offers in the Sudan," Maj. Gen. Taylor said. "What specifically can we do to help?"

"Effective counterintelligence is what I need... and right now! That's why I asked you here today. I do not trust anyone in Kenya to take on the task."

"Our team will commence an investigation immediately, General," Maj. Gen. Taylor promised. "We will make catching the Italian mole our top priority."

"Find the spy," Maj. Gen. Cunningham ordered, "and eliminate him."

THE NEXT STOP WAS THE SECRET BASE THAT CAPTAIN THE Lady Jane Seaborn had established twenty miles to the west of Nairobi on an isolated farm that was another family property. The term "farm" was generously applied to this tract of rugged jungle. The charm of the place, for their purposes, was its vastness. There was only one road in, and a private lake located near the center of the tract large enough to land amphibious aircraft.

No one ever came here. If anyone tried nowadays, they would run into a tough security force organized by the recently-promoted Captain Harry Shelby. The hard cases in this small company of native troops had been stiffened by white professional hunters, ex-mercenaries and former military types. They had orders to shoot to kill with their American-made M-1903 A-1 Springfield rifles. To a man, they were itching for a chance to pull a trigger.

One of the three Commodore amphibious airplanes Squadron Leader Paddy Wilcox had flown in from South America, now painted flat black, was bobbing at anchor on the lake. Another, also painted black, was making a slow pass overhead at one thousand feet. Spilling out from its rear door was a string of parachutists.

Major General James "Baldie" Taylor ordered the Bentley's driver to pull over so they could step out of the car and watch the show. The stick of jumpers was an inspiring sight. Paratroopers in the air under open canopies are something that always causes people to take notice. No matter how many times you have done it yourself, the idea that someone would actually jump out of a perfectly good airplane while in flight always seems amazing.

Lieutenant Karen Montgomery had come out from Seaborn House with a detachment of female Royal Marine parachute riggers. She had organized a parachute packing shed in one of the large, high-ceilinged barns on the farm. The girls were kept busy packing parachutes for the trainees. Chutes were in short demand. There were only enough to go around if the riggers kept packing round the clock.

The jumpers were Abyssinian volunteers from the large number of askaris who had deserted from the Italian Army. All the parachutists had volunteered to join British Forces in order to return to their native country. The askaris had been obtained from the Kenyan Assistant Military Secretary of Manpower, Captain the Lord Joss Victor Hay, only after much delay, many excuses and a great deal of effort had been expended. Commodore Richard "Dickey the Pirate" Seaborn had finally intervened and demanded they be assigned. The miles and miles of senseless red tape and bureaucratic stonewalling that had to be fought through to effect what should have been an automatic transfer of experienced soldiers from a non-combatant outfit to a fighting one had been mind-boggling.

The Abyssinian askaris were excellent material. They were currently under the supervision of Captain Roy "Mad Dog" Reupart, who had been brought in from the Sudan especially for the job. Prior to joining RF he had been an instructor at No.1 British Parachute School.

The plan was for the Abyssinian askaris to be parachuted in to Force N. There they would be supplied with mules and become one of three mounted battalions that would operate behind the enemy lines in the central part of the country. A scattering of officers and men from RF and handpicked individuals from the Cavalry Division who had volunteered for hazardous duty were commanding the companies and platoons.

At present, no commanding officer for the parachute battalion had been designated, though it was widely understood that Major Sir Terry "Zorro" Stone intended to assume command sometime in the near future. The movie star-handsome cavalryman did not intend to sit out the invasion of Abyssinia behind a desk in Khartoum.

The sight of the paratroopers descending forced Maj. Gen. Taylor to return to the problem that had been nagging at him for weeks now. There was no reason to believe Major John Randal was alive and able to continue his mission even though Lieutenant Pamala Plum-Martin had shown him the Italian radio intercept querying the significance of the letter "N."

Maj. Gen. Taylor was a veteran intelligence operative. His take on the query was not as positive as hers – it could mean anything or nothing. Besides, he was in possession of a message out of Abyssinia provided to him by the Emperor which Lt. Plum-Martin had not seen. That message indicated Maj. Randal was dead – killed by a lion.

The platinum blond Royal Marine officer had also shown him another intercepted message advising "one Australian has been sighted…" The Italians were apparently quite alarmed by this development and a flurry of inquiries had flown back and forth on the subject with no conclusive answer. The last thing the Blackshirts wanted was a modern-day Lawrence of Arabia running around loose in the interior of Abyssinia raising the natives in open rebellion – and Australians had a reputation as tough fighters.

Lt. Plum-Martin's take on the intercept was that the report emanated from the Australian slouch hats the Force N Advance Party had been wearing. Maj. Gen. Taylor was not so sure. The problem with her theory was that the team could have been killed on landing or sometime afterwards and someone *else* was wearing their headgear. Sorting out sketchy intelligence a long way from the scene of the action can be tricky.

The original report read: "One Australian sighted north of the Addis Ababa rail spur." When this was passed on, it either became garbled in the transmission or misinterpreted by Servizio Informazioni Militare (SIM) – the Italian Military Intelligence Service - to read "One Australian *Division* sighted…" This was somewhat understandable because of the odd habit the British Army had of saying the number of a division first without any tense, for example "One Australian" instead of "First Australian," like most other armies of the world. Anyone could be confused by the quirky British system of naming units.

On the other hand, a single man in a slouch hat, whoever he was, had suddenly become more than fifteen thousand to Italian Intelligence, which had to be cause for alarm to them. And that was good. In the misinformation business, perception was as good as reality. But it did not mean Maj. Randal and his men were alive.

The problem hounding Maj. Gen. Taylor was how much longer he could continue to wait without contact from Maj. Randal before appointing Maj. Stone as his replacement. He could not put the decision off much longer.

Having your ground commander go missing in action on the first day of a major operation is not a good way to start. The guilt he was carrying around for deploying the Force N Advance Party in the hurry-up fashion he had done was weighing heavy.

Lesson Learned: Never send the mission commander in with the Advance Party. Hindsight is 20/20.

12

OPEN SEASON ON MARRIED WOMEN

LIEUTENANT TAYLOR CORRIGAN, MC, HORSE GUARDS, A RF officer out from Seaborn House, reported in to Force N Rear in Khartoum. Major Sir Terry "Zorro" Stone met him at the airport and escorted him to the Force N safe house where he went through an intensive, two-day briefing on the state of their operations. Then without further ado, Maj. Stone cut orders promoting Lt. Corrigan to captain, placing him in charge of Force N Rear. Then Major General James "Baldie" Taylor and Maj. Stone boarded the next flight to Nairobi, where he was going to take command of the Abyssinian parachute battalion in training there.

On the ride over to the airport, the general finally showed him a copy of the message the Emperor had secretly provided him weeks ago describing the Force N Advance Party and what appeared to be Major John Randal's fatal encounter with a lion. The flimsy was not something Maj. Stone wanted to read and the follow-up intelligence about the word "bit" perhaps actually being the word "ate" did nothing to make him feel any better.

Lieutenant Pamala Plum-Martin was also on the flight. She had turned over her duties as Force N IO to an officer from the 9th Queen's Royal Lancers, Captain Oliver Goodwood. Capt. Goodwood had answered the call for volunteers for special hazardous duty in order to escape the boredom of being a horse cavalryman stuck patrolling the vast nothingness of Palestine with the Cavalry Division.

Lt. Plum-Martin was en route to link up with Captain the Lady Jane Seaborn to become part of the counterintelligence mission assigned to locate the Italian master spy believed to be embedded in the Kenyan colonial government or military command. Theirs might well be the most important assignment of all, but it was not one for which the women were trained.

Neither she nor Lady Jane had the least idea who the Italian spy might be. The two did have orders on where to initiate their search – the notoriously wicked Muthaiga Country Club. Whoever the enemy agent was, he would definitely spend time there. High-ranking military officers and politicians frequented the club. Every single officer or ranking official passing through the Kenya Colony made it a point to visit.

It was the perfect place to pick up information on what was going on in the colony since the well-heeled members and their guests were there every single night drinking themselves senseless. Discretion was not on at Muthaiga. Loose lips were stock-in-trade – gossip being one of the main entertainments of the establishment, second only to infidelity.

Neither woman knew the first thing about the art of counterintelligence, which was the province of MI-5. Counterintelligence is a highly specialized field. The fact that they were given the assignment showed how desperate the situation was. There were no MI-5 professionals available.

However, there were probably no two women anywhere better suited to penetrate the social scene of the Happy Valley set of white farmers who hunted big game, played polo, golf, or went to the race track by day, and then retired to Muthaiga Country Club to revel in the hedonistic pursuit of pleasure, riotous parties, wife swapping, heavy drinking and hard drugs by night. The British expatriates in Kenya were refugees from the Lost

Generation, unwilling to accept the fact that the days of the "Roaring Twenties" were long gone.

Being married was not a limiting factor for Lady Jane in the quest. In fact, it was a plus. In an effort to keep out prostitutes, Kenya had a quaint immigration law forbidding unmarried women from entering the colony unless during wartime when serving in uniform. This policy had the reverse unintended blowback of legislating in adultery. The law made married women fair game by statute since they were all there was, at least until the war started and women in uniform began trickling in.

At Muthaiga Country Club it was open season on wives.

The spectacular honey-blond adventuress Brandy Seaborn was flying in from Cairo to help. Brandy was not known to be trained in counterintelligence either. In fact, unlike the other two, she was not an intelligence operative in the true sense, though she did work for A-Force. Brandy was simply wildly good-looking and liked to have fun.

Brandy arrived via Royal Navy (RN) military transport, which landed at the Port of Mombasa. Having had her fill of flying, she elected to take the train to Nairobi. On board the train, Brandy ran into an acquaintance she knew vaguely, Sir Jock Delves Broughton, 11th Baronet and his young bride, Diana. Sir Jock was a degenerate gambler who had squandered his family fortune, though the fact of his being broke was not well known. Diana was a former cocktail waitress and "art model" with a penchant for precious metals and fine jewels, specifically matched sets of pearls. At fifty-seven, Sir Jock was old enough to be her father.

Brandy vaguely recalled there was some scandal attached to Sir Jock's record in the Great War. What she did know for certain was that no one cared for the man even though he had been an Etonian, served in the fashionable Irish Guards Regiment, and was clubbable, a member of White's, was always impeccably tailored and a self-styled "good loser" at the race track. Sir Jock bragged "he knew when to cut his losses."

What Brandy did not know, but soon found out because he told her and anyone else who would listen, was that Sir Jock was coming out to Kenya on a hush-hush mission for the SIS.

One day when Sir Jock was in White's for his usual Thursday lunch, the hall porter, Groom, had approached him with a request to follow him to the Billiard Room at the invitation of Colonel Stewart Menzies. It was well known, but never spoken of at the club, that "The Colonel" was the head of MI-6. Sir Jock consented to the request straightaway.

The conversation was brief. In Col. Menzies' eyes, Broughton was a loathsome toad, a reminder to others of what society dishes out to any man who lets the side down. In the last war, Sir Jock had served with the Irish Guards. On the day his regiment deployed to France he came down with sunstroke on a cloudy afternoon and was in the hospital, unable to sail. Sir Jock never managed to recover sufficiently to ever rejoin the troops in the trenches, which for him was fortuitous.

Rudyard Kipling, whose son was an officer in the regiment and was killed leading his men, was infuriated by the sunstroke incident. Kipling wrote about it, branding Sir Jock a coward for life. In the British upper class, men are expected to serve in time of war at the front – on the sharp end of the stick. That is the price England extracts from her aristocracy.

Sir Jock never lived down the stigma. The strange thing was he thought he had. No one ever brought up the subject of his sitting out the entire war while his brother officers were being slaughtered almost to a man in France – in his presence.

However, someone made a snide remark about it behind his back every time he left a room, or when his name came up in conversation – every single time, forever. Even the members of his own family treated him the same way. Sir Jock was a pariah, a man without the respect of his peers.

Col. Menzies also knew that Sir Jock was virtually bankrupt and that the scoundrel had committed two cases of insurance fraud – one with his first wife's jewelry, reporting it stolen from the glove compartment of his car, and another with stolen paintings cut out of the frames at one of his houses.

"Sir Jock," Col. Menzies said, "I understand that you will be traveling out to Kenya shortly."

"That I am, Stewart. I have some land awarded in the 1919 Soldier Settlement Scheme. I intend to become a gentleman farmer."

"Excellent," Col. Menzies said, knowing that was, in fact, a lie. The coward was running away from his second war, terrorized by the constant German bombing and the imminent threat of invasion. No one was getting shot at or bombed in Kenya. The fact that the Italians could invade out of Abyssinia and overrun the entire colony in a matter of days had probably not occurred to him.

"We have a particular interest in keeping informed on a matter of some delicacy in the colony. A business requiring absolute discretion, one of personal importance to me – very confidential – you understand, Official Secrets Act and all that. Do you think you might be available to perform this service while you are out in Africa?"

"Why of course, Stewart. I am always happy to do my duty."

"Come around tomorrow to this address," Col. Menzies said, extending a card. "Show this when you arrive. My will man brief you. Naturally, we are not having this conversation."

The following day Sir Jock learned that his task was nothing more than to keep a quiet eye on Col. Menzies' former brother-in-law, Captain the Lord Joss Victor Hay. For the past few years, the Earl had been masquerading as a gentleman farmer while pursuing his true life's calling, which was being a full-time seducer of other men's wives.

Col. Menzies loathed his ex-brother-in-law almost as much as he did Sir Jock.

Capt. Lord Hay had recently shown an unexpected burst of patriotism and taken on the job as Military Secretary of Manpower for Kenya, which was a surprise since he knew absolutely nothing about the military and hard work was not his style. By all reports he was doing commendable service to the Crown. The idea of his playboy ex-brother-in-law sitting behind a desk every day in an office seemed wrong. The rogue had never done an honest day's work in his entire life. What he did was live off the family fortunes of the older women he married while preying on their girlfriends, which made him a full-time practicing gigolo.

Col. Menzies wanted a pair of eyes on Capt. Lord Hay out in Kenya Colony, and he was not choosy about whom they belonged to.

On the train to Nairobi, Sir Jock took every opportunity to imply that he had "come out to Kenya to undertake hush-hush things connected with the war." Brandy had no idea what he meant by that; he did not elaborate. "Official Secrets Act and all that...," but she thought it quite extraordinary that a man would talk so openly about the covert work he claimed he could not discuss.

Something else happened on the train trip that Brandy could not help notice. When the newlywed Broughtons disembarked from the train, Lieutenant Hugh Thompson Dickinson, another Etonian, met the couple at the station. Instinctively, Brandy knew "Hughsie Daisy," as Diana greeted him, was her lover. But how could that be since the girl had come out to Africa on her honeymoon? Had Lt. Dickinson come out to Kenya ahead to be with her? Did Sir Jock know?

Brandy thought it strange. The love triangle gave her something to gossip about to Lady Jane, who was waiting to collect her at the station. The hotel's Bentley whisked the two of them to their suites. Being in counterintelligence in Kenya, the golden girl decided, might turn out to be fun.

What Lady Jane knew but could not tell Brandy because she did not have a need to know, was that Lt. Dickinson was MI-6. Sir Jock was spying on Capt. Lord Hay, had Lt. Dickinson come out to Kenya to keep an eye on Sir Jock? Did Diana know "Hughsie Daisy" was a spy? Was Diana an agent too? And if so, who was she working for?

Lady Jane agreed with Brandy – counterintelligence was turning out to be fascinating.

SQUADRON LEADER PADDY WILCOX AND COMMODORE Richard "Dickey the Pirate" Seaborn were on board a Walrus inbound to Camp Croc. Lake Rudolf really was shaped like a giant jalapeño. Late mornings to afternoon and evenings it was as green as one, though most people chose to describe it as "emerald." Early mornings the lake took on an unusual turquoise blue with splotches of white mixed in.

The former Canadian bush pilot knew the white was the tops of waves caused by the hot desert wind that blew in strong gusts from the east, down the slopes of Mount Kulal. The wind created whitecaps that made surface navigation of the lake problematic most mornings. Anyone planning to land in a light amphibious aircraft needed to know this important detail and act accordingly.

The big green lake was situated in the eastern arm of the Great Rift Valley, primarily fed by the Omo River in an inhospitable moonscape of dormant volcanoes, sun fried semi-desert, and ancient jagged lava flows.

Surrounded by volcanic slag in the south and east, and red-hot mud flats to the north and west, Lake Rudolf was approximately 160 miles long and ten to twenty miles wide in places. The absence of any outlet made the waters brackish. The salt water made the hides of the monster crocodiles useless for commercial purposes, therefore no one ever hunted them. Since they have no natural enemies, the crocodiles thrived and multiplied in its depths. Sqn. Ldr. Wilcox had heard there was an estimated 22,000 of them in the lake.

Up ahead through the windscreen appeared the three islands in the lake, cleverly named North Island, Center Island and South Island. These islands were home to large populations of pelicans, flamingos, kingfishers and cormorants. Elephants occupied the eastern shore of the lake and were known for the weight of their ivory and their aggressiveness. Hippopotamuses were found in and around the lake in great abundance.

Like all the other animals in the Lake Rudolf region, the hippos were distinguished by their ferocity. Hippos were known, as were the crocs, to attack small boats, which the Squadron Leader reckoned had to include amphibious airplanes like the Walrus. There were also lions, and while most were not man-eaters in the classic sense, they were hungry and would go for a man if the opportunity presented itself.

The wildlife at Camp Croc was decidedly unfriendly.

The north end of Lake Rudolf straddled the Abyssinian border, and there had always been a dispute between Great Britain and the Abyssinians about the exact location of the boundary line. For that reason, and the fact that armed raiders out of Abyssinia and Somalia roved the region unchecked, the entire area had been placed off limits, labeled the "Forbidden Zone" from before the turn of the century. There were no roads in or out, and a government permit, which was not easy to obtain, was required to travel there. Not to worry. No one in their right mind wanted to go there anyway.

Captain the Lady Jane Seaborn's father had established a fishing camp on the western shore of the lake, which meant that he must have had a relationship with the British SIS.

The only explanation that made any sense for the camp being allowed in the Forbidden Zone was that it provided an excellent listening post on the Abyssinian border. The place certainly made the perfect FOB to stage a secret effort to rescue and/or supply the Force N Advance Party. Failing that, it was ideal to launch a reconstituted Force N into the interior of Abyssinia by the use of amphibious aircraft.

Since the days of its discovery, it had been said travelers to Lake Rudolf needed to be bold, resourceful, unorthodox adventurers imbued with ingenuity and a dash of eccentricity. That was certainly an accurate description of the Strategic Raiding Forces team of men and women in the process of setting up the Force N FOB at Camp Croc. They were preparing to execute a logistical military exercise that had never been attempted in the history of warfare – supplying a fighting force operating behind enemy lines entirely by air.

The concept of the operation, as developed by Sqn. Ldr. Wilcox, was to set up a main supply base at Camp Croc. Men, weapons, equipment, supplies and aviation fuel would be transported by rail and by convoy from the Port of Mombasa to a secret base west of Nairobi. From there, they would be airlifted to Camp Croc by the fleet of Commodores. Then, deep inside Abyssinia, leapfrogging up the Great Rift Valley, Force N would select at least two additional lakes to establish clandestine supply dumps.

At each site, a cache of fuel and supplies would be carefully built up in a relay of night flights shuttling forward. Each cache would be permanently guarded by a reinforced company of heavily-armed men liberally equipped with machine guns for their defense.

Only lakes large enough to have islands over two miles distant from the shore were considered by the Squadron Leader. There were three reasons for his choosing islands for his supply caches. First, most islands in Abyssinia are uninhabited, which reduced contact with locals of unknown loyalties. When you ringed an island with barbed wire entanglements, land mines and machine guns, the prospects of casual looting were cut down to zero.

Second, he knew Abyssinians were not a nautical people. In fact, only one or two small tribes in the entire country possessed the skill of boat building. Abyssinian boats were, in fact, large rafts built out of reeds roped together and propelled by poling. The natives never mastered the art of using wind powered sails. They did not use oars or paddles.

The reed boats had a fairly short life span, becoming gradually more and more waterlogged. Waterlogging would eventually cause the reed boats to sink unless the rafts were periodically beached and rebuilt. The wise Abyssinian boat operator stayed close to shore at all times.

The third reason Sqn. Ldr. Wilcox hit upon the idea of islands for the supply bases was because the Italians had no patrol boats operating on any of the lakes. The only thing the cache defense platoons were going to have to worry about was pirates. Abyssinian pirates were not afraid of water.

Since there was no way to guarantee there would not be some contact with Abyssinians, it was decided that the cache defense companies should be attired in Italian Army uniforms. With all the aircraft arriving and departing at night and being painted flat black with no other markings, there would be no reason for the locals – if they ever became aware of the operation – to suspect it was anything but a Blackshirt mission. And if by chance any Abyssinian did get close enough to observe them, all they would see were Italian soldiers.

Any unauthorized person coming ashore on one of the islands would be shot or detained indefinitely.

Sqn. Ldr. Wilcox had selected Lake Margherita as the initial stepping stone. The first jump would be the longest – according to the map, approximately two hundred twenty-five miles as the crow flies. Little was known about the lake except that it was located in the Great Rift Valley, east of Mount Gurage, and fed on its northern shore by the Bilate River. By his rough measurements, the lake was approximately thirty-five miles long by twelve miles wide. What he wanted was a small, uninhabited island in the middle of the lake that Captain Harry Shelby, the officer responsible for security, could ring with automatic weapons and land mines in the unlikely event of a pirate incursion.

What was not desired was a large island that might be populated, meaning they would have to deal with the local people on a daily basis. More importantly, they did not want an island so large that shifta pirates could land unobserved, marshal their forces out of sight and mount an overland attack. Capt. Shelby insisted on a defensive scheme that would force any attacking unit to come in by reed raft and attack straight into the teeth of interlocking fields of automatic weapons fire.

Modern machine guns (though it was hardly fair to describe the Hotchkiss light machine guns (LMGs) they had been issued as modern) loaded extra heavy with tracers and incendiary rounds should be able to flame any pirate reed rafts far out in the lake. At least that was the plan – it looked good on paper.

The problem was they could not obtain any other intelligence information on Lake Margherita other than it was red. Lakes in that bizarre part of the world came in assorted strange and unusual colors. Little was known about them.

Lady Jane had scoured Nairobi, and then all of Kenya, searching for anyone with firsthand knowledge about Lake Margherita or any of the other lakes in the chain. She drew a complete blank. Not a single person could be found who had ever visited one.

The RF planners were left working off notes that had been written in 1903 by a British officer who had surveyed the Great Rift Valley – only he had been sick with malaria and scurvy at the time and may have been hallucinating.

Basically, the region was a complete unknown.

The Walrus taxied out on Lake Rudolf, roared into the sky and then swung around to the north and headed straight into IEA with Sqn. Ldr. Wilcox at the stick. Seated in the right seat was Cdre. Seaborn. In the back seats were Capt. Shelby and a RF Commando.

Today they were flying out to make an aerial reconnaissance of Lake Margherita. If possible, they would land and conduct a physical inspection of a likely island base. Strapped to the amphibious skids was a rubber raft that Capt. Shelby and the Commando would use to paddle to the island. The flight was timed to arrive at sunset, so they would not have much time to locate their target from the air.

Cdre. Seaborn was doing everything in his power to see that the operation to liberate Abyssinia was a success. He was a man carrying a heavy load of guilt because he had recommended Major John Randal to command Force N. At the time he truly believed him to be the best man for the job. He had no idea that Major General James "Baldie" Taylor would parachute the American as part of a three-man team into the middle of the country on an advance reconnaissance, which everyone now agreed was a virtual suicide mission.

It was true his cousin had written a letter to him asking to have Maj. Randal detained in Africa while he straightened out his marital problem with his wife, Lady Jane. But it was *not* true that Cdre. Seaborn had recommended the commander of RF for the Force N assignment as a result of his cousin's request.

Cdre. Seaborn was a committed RN officer whose assignment was to clear the Red Sea corridor of Italian Forces so that passage would be safe for American ships to bring Lend Lease supplies through it to the Suez Canal. He intended to do whatever it took to accomplish his mission.

Armchair strategists would argue that the Suez Canal is the most vital body of water in the world. The commodore knew it was not. If ships can be attacked and sunk before they reach the Canal, then it becomes virtually worthless. As long as the Italians had air and naval bases bordering the Red Sea they effectively neutralized the Canal – making the Red Sea the most vital body of water in the world at this particular point in time.

The mission to take down Abyssinia was given to SOE. SOE had never liberated a country before, even though they were the first national government-level sponsored guerrilla warfare organization in history. This was their first attempt.

The challenge was that SOE had hardly any men or material assets available to carry out the mission. So when asked, Cdre. Seaborn had recommended Maj. Randal for the job of organizing an internal Abyssinian revolt, knowing he was a can-do type who had demonstrated his ability to improvise and carry out independent operations. Later, when it came out that his cousin, Mallory, had written and asked him to delay Maj. Randal's return to England, Lieutenant General Sir Archibald Wavell had misinterpreted his motive and threatened to have him cashiered and sent home in disgrace if the American was killed.

Cdre. Seaborn was doing everything in his power to ensure a successful rescue mission to reach the Force N Advance Party and bring Maj. Randal out alive. Failing that, he was going to fight with every fiber in his body to make the liberation of Abyssinia succeed. He would have preferred to be at sea standing on the deck of a capital warship, but here he was flying over desert in an obsolete amphibian aircraft to land on an unexplored lake.

The mission they were flying today was about as dangerous as a mission can get. The Italian Air Force had total air superiority. Their CR-42 fighters ruled the Abyssinian skies. The Italian fighter jockeys were crackerjack pilots. To top off the danger factor, if the Walrus was shot down, there was not going to be any walking out. No one would be coming to rescue them.

To counter the fighter threat, Sqn. Ldr. Wilcox flew at anteater level. Today the Canadian pilot had his black eyepatch pulled up. He needed both eyes. They were crawling by air travel standards, the Walrus being a slow, bi-wing airplane about as aerodynamically designed as a phone booth. But to the men on board it felt like they were screaming along inches above the ground.

The Walrus zoomed over the southern end of Lake Margherita just as the giant flaming sun was plunging into the wasteland to the west. Mt. Gurage gleamed golden to the north, and the lake itself really was red. No one on board had believed that part would turn out to be true, but then why not – Lake Rudolf was jalapeño green.

Sqn. Ldr. Wilcox steered a course straight down the center of the red lake. Then in the distance they saw what they were looking for – a small speck. When the Walrus flew over, it was a tiny island with a scattering of tree cover that appeared perfect for what was needed. There was a gentle sloping beach all around for landing their stores, there was no sign of habitation, and a platoon of troops could easily secure the entire place.

Banking left, Sqn. Ldr. Wilcox racetracked far to the west of the lake waiting for the sun to set. When it did, it was like the lights in a closed room were suddenly switched off. When it gets dark in Africa, it gets dark fast.

In the pitch black before the moon came up, Sqn. Ldr. Wilcox flew back to the island and set the little bi-winged amphibian down. Everyone on board was aware that a slight mishap at this point in the mission meant they were marooned.

Capt. Shelby and the RF Commando deployed the rubber raft and paddled off into the night. Then it was just Cdre. Seaborn and Sqn. Ldr. Wilcox bobbing around in the Walrus waiting, and waiting, and waiting. Time stopped dead still.

Cdre. Seaborn remembered that hippos had been known to attack small boats, which he also realized most likely would include the Walrus. If the airplane was capsized by a hippopotamus, the two of them would be easy prey for the crocodiles. Then he remembered that the crocodiles had been known to attack small surface craft too. At least that was true for Lake Rudolf – was it true for Lake Margherita?

A night like this made him long for the days back in the dank, dark, smoke-filled basement in the underbelly of the Admiralty, routing convoys.

He reflected that Sqn. Ldr. Wilcox had spent many nights bobbing around on small lakes behind German lines in France waiting for Lovat Scout sniper teams to paddle out for extraction when he was flying OPERATION BUZZARD PLUCKER missions. The Canadian, he decided, must have pure ice water in his veins.

Several lifetimes later Capt. Shelby, followed by the RF Commando, climbed back on board and reported, "Spot-on for what we need, sir."

If Maj. Randal had been there he would have said, "Let's get the hell out of Dodge."

Every man on board had heard him say it at one time or another on some hostile shore. No one said "Let's get the hell out of Dodge" tonight, but they were all thinking it as the Walrus roared to life and they began their take off run. For once, Camp Croc was going to look really good.

13

GO, JOHNNY, GO

MAJOR LAWRENCE GRAND, THE DEBONAIR HEAD OF SECTION
"D" (Destruction) of SOE – a man known for his impeccable Savile Row
suits with a carnation pinned to the lapel, smoked glasses and custom-
blended brown cigarettes in an ivory holder – arrived by cab at, White's, the
most exclusive club in London. According to knowledgeable people in the
trade, he was one of the most dangerous men in Europe, as was the man he
was to meet. Groom, the hall porter, was waiting and immediately ushered
him to the billiard room.

Colonel Stewart Menzies, "C", the chief of the British SIS was in his
customary chair by the fire reading his papers under the bust of Edward VII
and the Champion of England boxing belt. The two were old associates.
Section D had originally been a part of SIS, but was abruptly transferred out
during wartime reorganization and hastily cobbled together with two other
government departments to form SOE.

There were some hard feelings in the ranks about the move.

Before the reorganization, Col. Menzies had been Maj. Grand's boss. He still was. It was difficult to believe that anyone could be so foolish as to actually suppose that you could simply rip out the clandestine direct action section from the most prestigious intelligence organization in the world and plop it down in a brand new startup agency without split loyalties.

Apparently, SOE did, but then they were rank amateurs.

"Hello, Lawrence."

"How are you, sir?"

"I have a matter of some delicacy I need you to front for me," Col. Menzies cut straight to the main point, as was his style. "Are you briefed on the Abyssinian affair?"

"I am," Maj. Grand replied. "In fact, sir, I personally recommended James Taylor for the assignment."

"Excellent choice of men," Col. Menzies agreed. "One can always count on Baldie not to let the side down.

"Time is short, Lawrence. The invasion of Abyssinia is set to begin sometime in late January or early February. Recent intelligence has confirmed our suspicions that the Italians have a mole embedded in the Kenya Colonial government. If this spy learns the date of Cunningham's invasion, the Blackshirts will either launch a spoiling attack or deploy enough troops to the south to stall his advance. Either move is fatal to our plans.

"I want you to travel out to Kenya and quietly take charge of the counterintelligence operation. There are detailed instructions in your brief. Familiarize yourself with them on the flight out and act accordingly. One of the items you will discover in your reading will be the name of the enemy agent.

"Only you are authorized to know how you came into possession of the Italian master spy's name. Be very careful not to leave any SIS fingerprints. Our involvement is never to be revealed. In the unlikely event your participation should ever come to light, you will maintain your cover as being SOE. Is that perfectly clear?"

"I quite understand, sir!"

"There is one item not covered in your brief," Col. Menzies concluded with a ring of cold steel in his voice. "Under no circumstances is the enemy agent to be taken into custody. Kill him. Is that clear?"

"Perfectly."

"Excellent, Lawrence. I know that you will handle this with the utmost discretion. Bear in mind you can never reveal SIS as the origin of the mole's identity. Unless Baldie's counterintelligence team manages to uncover the Italian's man, you will have to develop a cover story for how you obtained the spy's name and that is best done in the field. Lieutenant Commander Ian Fleming will be coming out from the Naval Intelligence Division as an observer. They have a vested interest in the successful outcome of your mission. Feel free to use him as you see fit. "

What Col. Menzies did not tell Maj. Grand, because the Section D chief did not have a need to know, was *how* SIS had obtained the exact name of the Italian master spy in Kenya. The answer to that was the single most precious, closely guarded secret in wartime Great Britain.

Located at Bletchley Park, codename "Station X," was a highly-classified organization of cryptanalysts. The code breakers at Bletchley had broken the German Enigma code. This was a feat so extraordinary that it was regarded to be impossible by every national intelligence agency worldwide. Station X had a little help in the form of a captured Enigma device supplied by Major John Randal's Strategic Raiding Forces as a result of OPERATION RUTHLESS.

Right at this time it would be possible to count the people outside of Station X who were authorized to know about the penetration of the German Enigma encoding system on one hand and have some fingers left over. The King of England was not on the list. It was that secret!

When he had been alerted by the Prime Minister that there was a potential problem in Kenya, the Chief of the British SIS had taken it upon himself to travel out to Station X and have all the traffic from the Enigma decrypts that referenced IEA made available for his perusal. As he suspected, from time to time the Italian High Command in Addis Ababa used a German Enigma encoding machine to transmit their intentions to their Nazi allies in Berlin.

The name of the Blackshirt's master spy in Kenya was referenced in several of the decrypted intercepts. The Italian Viceroy, the Duke of Aosta, had big plans for his confederate after the war. The highly placed mole was to be appointed the fascist's Governor of Kenya as a reward for his good efforts on their behalf. Col. Menzies was not amused when he read the spy's name, having been related to the bounder by marriage at one time.

"Your mission is extraordinarily sensitive, Lawrence," Col. Menzies said. "The risk of political blowback is high. The reputation of certain members of the Royal Family might be sullied if this is not handled with absolute discretion – silk gloves please."

MAJOR SIR TERRY "ZORRO" STONE WAS ROLLING ALONG IN an ammunition carrier with his Somali driver at the wheel and two tough Somali bodyguards in the back armed with M-1903 A-1 Springfield rifles. He had his bags packed. Today he was headed to Nairobi to meet Pilot Officer Gasper "Bunny" Featherstone for a weekend of debauchery at the notorious watering hole, the Muthaiga Country Club.

Training his Abyssinian paratrooper battalion was proceeding according to plan. Maj. Stone was enjoying being back in command of troops. He was trying to come up with a catchy moniker for his battalion. The South African units flooding into Kenya sported romantic names like Imperial Light Horse, Royal Natal Carbineers, Transvaal Scottish and the like. This was his first battalion command and he wanted a glamorous, action-filled title to distinguish it.

The only real organizational problem he had was a desperate shortage of officers. To date, the Kenyan Manpower Department had not seen fit to assign him a single Kenyan white farmer, police officer, professional hunter, or in fact any of the "Hostilities Only" colonial officers he needed to fill his platoon leader positions. Kenya should have been a gold mine of the type of unconventional soldiers who would make superb small unit leaders of irregular troops, but so far the men he needed had not been forthcoming.

The Manpower Office was proving intractable.

The battalion he commanded consisted of three rifle companies of two hundred fifty men each. While this was the standard table of organization for a rifle battalion, Maj. Stone did not care for it. He wanted a more flexible unit along the lines of a commando battalion. What he had in mind were six companies of one hundred men plus a headquarters company and a scout company. To do that he was going to need a lot more officers, and he was only accepting high-quality men.

Maj. Stone was hoping to encounter Captain the Lord Joss Victor Hay the Assistant to the Governor for the Department of Manpower at the club and evoke the old school tie network. It was said the Military Secretary had a photographic memory and knew the name of practically every white man in the colony, and the Earl was handpicking men personally for their assignments. It should be no problem to arrange for him to assign the officers he needed. The Secretary of Manpower was, after all, a former Eton man.

Capt. Lord Hay was widely known to be a frequenter of the Muthaiga Country Club. In fact, his house was situated across the street adjacent to the club property for quick access. The Earl was a local legend in Kenya – known as the "World's Greatest Pouncer," addicted to whisking amorous wives from the club to his home for brief romantic encounters, then returning alone later to meet the women's unsuspecting husbands at the bar for a drink.

With any luck, Maj. Stone would cultivate Capt. Lord Hay socially and put paid to his battalion's officer problem once and for all. There had to be some way to cut through all the red tape. However, this weekend was not strictly organized for business. Pleasure was high on his card.

Officers of Maj. Stone's class are expected to take their recreation. For example, before the war, there was never even a question of Life Guards officers doing any soldiering during the winter. Officers departed the regiment annually for two months' leave to hunt, taking with them a pair of chargers plus one or two troop horses and as many soldier grooms as was needed to look after them, along with their regular batman. British officers have a highly refined ability put aside military responsibilities temporarily and have their recreation totally free of any guilt complexes.

The Muthaiga Country Club was the perfect place to do it, a cross between Paris in the Roaring Twenties and Sodom & Gomorrah. It was founded so that the white farmers in Kenya could have their drinks properly served while they enjoyed polo, cricket, golf, tennis and exchanging adulterous glances across the bar. It was a snooty social organization that even vetted the Colonial Governor for membership. On its rolls could be found the occasional murderer, thief, con-artist, drug dealer and closet fascist, but to a man they all had impeccable social references.

The club was noted for laid-back morals, cheap gin, cocaine and the prevalence of the drug of choice among the pleasure-loving Happy Valley set – morphine. Muthaiga was like a lost world inhabited by expatriate, philandering survivors of the Roaring Twenties, all running from or toward something at full speed.

While the German Luftwaffe was pounding London into a ruin, the fast set in Nairobi was living the high life of endless parties, alcohol, drugs and wife swapping. Running just below the surface of the false gaiety was the undercurrent of a looming train wreck. This all had to end badly.

Not widely advertised, because the principals did their dead-level best not to let the secret out, was the fact that virtually every single person in the Happy Valley set was broke, socially compromised, or had some stain on their professional reputation. Even the cream of British aristocracy, the club system, and the most famous army regiments have their disappointments, and they all seemed to be drawn to Kenya like steel dust to a magnet.

Maj. Stone was unaware of much of this as the ammunition carrier climbed up the escarpment and drove into Nairobi. He had heard of the Muthaiga Country Club. It had a reciprocal agreement with his club, White's, and it was reported to be the place to stay when in the city even though it was three miles north of town. The place had a reputation. He was looking forward to an opportunity to unwind from the stress of command, enjoy himself and find out if the rumors were true.

Nairobi was a small, elegant frontier town with a population of twenty-one thousand settlers in the white community (no one had bothered to count the Africans.) The city was located on a high plateau with wide, scenic avenues and handsome colonial buildings. The Union Jack flew from the government buildings. Crisp-looking askaris in heavily starched uniforms stood guard duty at selected points here and there. All of the structures, including civilian houses, were sandbagged in anticipation of eminent Italian air attack. With all of the windows taped against the shattering effect of bomb blasts, the place had a combat-ready ambiance. Somehow the town did not seem quite real – it was more like a movie set.

The Kenyans were playing at war.

Maj. Stone and the Somalis cleared Nairobi and drove the remaining few miles to Muthaiga. Arrangements were made with the club secretary for his expenses and lodging for his three men to be put on account. Money never changed hands on premises. Members of White's were always welcome.

While his bags were carried to his room and unpacked by one of the legion of club servants, Maj. Stone wandered into the bar to find Plt. Off. Featherstone there waiting for him, hard at work trying to drink himself into unconsciousness. Even in the decadent confines of Muthaiga, where conventional values were tossed overboard and they played by Kenyan rules, certified members of the valiant "Few" were held in a state of high esteem that bordered on virtual awe. Fighter pilots were gods and Plt. Off. Featherstone, a veteran of the "Millionaires Squadron," was a god among gods.

Not only was he a surviving veteran of the Battle of Britain, he was a certified ace with seven confirmed victories to his credit and a millionaire. There were three pink gins lined up that people around the bar had sent over to him. Everyone wanted to rub up against his glory.

Maj. Stone, a military star from the glamorous Life Guards regiment and a famous Commando leader who had participated in who-knew-how-many raids on the German-occupied French Coast, was accorded equal Olympian status by the members, particularly female. The ladies had all seen the newsreel of him returning from the first British parachute operation of the war.

Had he been a big drinker, Maj. Stone could have drowned himself in free liquor right then and there. Alas, he was nearly a teetotaler by Muthaiga standards, not wanting to let alcohol impair his faculties in the event the opportunity for suitable female companionship presented itself. Maj. Stone had his priorities.

Glancing across the bar, he immediately locked eyes with a smoldering brunette who was staring at him like a hungry hyena. A few moments later he stepped out of the bar to purchase a package of Player's.

Walking through the lobby on the return trip, he found himself literally dragged into the cloak closet. The hungry-eyed brunette proceeded to give a reasonably good demonstration of the Rear Take Down and Strangle Hold, which is a fairly tricky move to perform in close quarters. She must have had private lessons – the maneuver being a restricted "gutter fighting" technique not generally taught civilians.

It can be lethal.

Because the lady had been sitting at the bar with a man he presumed was her husband (she was wearing a wedding ring, and married women were one vice Maj. Stone virtually never *intentionally* indulged in), there was a moment's hesitation. However, this was war and also a colony where the chic Happy Valley slogan was "Are you married or do you live in Kenya?" There was also the reputation of the Life Guards and RF to be considered, so he went ahead and did his duty right there standing up among the furs.

Stumbling out of the closet later, Maj. Stone realized he did not even know the woman's name. He nearly crashed into a tall captain who startled him because he looked exactly like an older version of himself. The resemblance was uncanny – an older Errol Flynn. The man was a dead ringer, though beginning to go a trifle puffy.

"Easy sport," the captain said suavely, with a wicked smile. "Hello, June. Need any more assistance in there looking for your mink?"

The tousled brunette walked out of the closet, gave the tall man a pout, patted her hair and disappeared back to the bar without a word. June's husband and Plt. Off. Featherstone could be heard in the background re-fighting the Battle of Britain, which only one of them had participated in.

"Joss Hay," the man introduced himself with a handsome rakish grin. "Welcome to Muthaiga."

"Terry Stone. I do believe you are just the man I have been hoping to run into, old stick."

"Well, you certainly did so with style, sport. Now, the way we go about things here at the club, Sir Terry – at least the way I operate – it is *de rigueur* for you to immediately go buy June's husband a drink. Look the fellow right in the eye when he drinks it. Makes the crime all that much more gratifying, savor the kill so to speak, don't you agree?"

"Sounds a bit…"

"I always say 'to hell with husbands' – actually, it was one of my ex-wives who liked to say that. Come along Major, I shall introduce you."

That did not sound like such a great idea to Maj. Stone. Everyone went armed at all times in Kenya; however.... *when in Rome.*

At first blush, Maj. Stone had the impression he had died and gone to heaven. Only later did he realize the Muthaiga Country Club was really hell.

MAJOR GENERAL JAMES "BALDIE" TAYLOR WAS LAUGHING SO hard that he thought he might actually injure himself. He was sitting in the safe house that Force N Rear used as their headquarters, receiving an intelligence briefing from the brand new Force N IO, Captain Oliver Goodwood. The report consisted of a batch of recent Y-intercepts.

Both the Force N Rear commander, Captain Taylor Corrigan and Capt. Goodwood were more than a little taken back at the semi-hysterical laughter that greeted each new entry on the wall map covering the Force N AO in central Abyssinia. Maj. Gen. Taylor was not known for having a runaway sense of humor, at least he had not demonstrated one lately. When it came to reports about Force N he had been decidedly brittle.

On an operational map, overlay grid coordinates indicating enemy positions are marked in red grease pencil and friendly positions are marked in blue. Capt. Goodwood was wearing out a blue grease pencil marking capital Ns.

Every time he added a new blue N, Maj. Gen. Taylor shouted "Go, Johnny, go!" Tears were running down his deep, tanned cheeks. There were hundreds of the blue letters on the map. The IO was holding a ream of paper and had a long way to go before he finished logging in the rest of them.

"Get General Platt on the horn," Maj. Gen. Taylor shouted to his man who was in the outer room reading a newspaper. "Tell him I said to get over here in the next fifteen minutes. No... make that ten minutes!"

Capt. Goodwood continued marking the map and Maj. Gen. Taylor kept right on laughing and shouting "Go, Johnny, go!"

Neither Capt. Goodwood nor Capt. Corrigan had any idea of the true significance of the Ns – they were merely plotting them from a list of coordinates on a piece of paper. Since neither officer felt inclined to ask, not knowing the general all that well, they had no idea what the outburst was about. If Maj. Gen. Taylor wanted to tell them, he would.

He did not, so they remained mystified.

Major General William Platt arrived in the requisite ten minutes, swishing his flywhisk. He was not the kind of man who cared to be summoned. For three years, the Kaid had been the "Leader of the Army" in the Sudan, which to his mind made him a virtual pharaoh.

"Sit down, Bill," Maj. Gen. Taylor ordered, laughing. "Take a look at that map."

"I can read a map, General," the Kaid snapped peevishly, remaining standing. "Why not let me in on the joke. What do all those Ns stand for?"

"The Wops have probably the worst radio discipline of any army in the world at the tactical level. It is just awful. Our local Y service people can read their daily traffic faster than they can."

"I know that."

"Take a close look, General. Everywhere Captain Goodwood is placing an 'N' indicates a location that the Italians have reported finding one painted on a road marker, fence, truck, building, tree or something. One report had them painted on the sides of cows.

"Two days ago the Duke in Addis Ababa queried all subordinate commanders to report if there were any unusual incidence of letter 'N' appearing in their area of operations. The response was there are hundreds of them, maybe thousands. Mysterious 'N's are showing up everywhere, and the Italians are working themselves into a frenzy about them."

Maj. Gen. Platt asked, "What do you interpret it to mean, General?"

"It means while we have been worrying ourselves sick that Maj. Randal and his team were KIA, our lad has been out there playing bloody havoc all over his area of operations like his orders called for him to do. Those Ns stand for Force N!

"You see all those blue stars Captain Goodwood has drawn on the map? Well, those indicate road ambushes," Maj. Gen. Taylor pointed, making a grand gesture. "All in his general AO. Seeing there are no significant numbers of road ambushes being reported anywhere else in Abyssinia, the only thing that makes sense is for Randal to have somehow actually organized guerrilla units and started taking it to the Wops.

"The Major has deployed his guerrillas to points on the handful of Italian roads, and the reason the blue stars are spread out all over the place is that he is constantly on the move hitting and running."

"What do the red arrows indicate?" Maj. Gen. Platt asked.

"The arrows are the reason I called you here, General. I wanted you to see them for yourself," Maj. Gen. Taylor explained, suddenly turning serious. "The red arrows are Italian units converging on the Force N area of operations in pursuit of whoever is conducting those ambushes and painting those Ns. Each arrow represents a colonial battalion of approximately five hundred men."

"How many arrows are there?"

"Sixty-three, sir," Capt. Goodwood answered.

"You are sure about your numbers, Captain?" the Kaid said.

"They came directly out of the Y intercept of Italian daily reports, sir. There may be more. These are only the latest batch to be delivered."

"And it gets better," Maj. Gen. Taylor said. "We have a report that one Italian general has cabled Addis Ababa that he never leaves his base unless he has a one thousand-man escort. Looks like Maj. Randal is really getting under those Eyeties' skin. Go, Johnny, go!"

"Sixty-three battalions committed to hunting a three-man party," Maj. Gen. Platt said in a tone that conveyed the double impression of his being both skeptical and mightily impressed at the same time. "I have to admit, that is significant Economy of Force. Randal – the young American who told me he never read Lawrence's book – said he wanted to be a Confederate raider – the Gray Ghost, John S. Mosby."

"Randal has no interest in politics," Maj. Gen. Taylor said. "Claimed he did not believe certain parts of Lawrence's *Seven Pillars of Wisdom* so he quit reading it."

"Sir," Capt. Goodwood offered, "there is additional information I did not have time to brief you on before General Platt arrived. In the last two months there have been over twelve hundred reported incidents of vehicle sabotage in the south central region of Abyssinia in the same general area the Ns are showing up."

"What kind of sabotage?"

"Mostly road spikes, sir. The Italians are reporting an enormous number of flat tires. They are quite upset about it due to a shortage of spares. Reports indicate the road sabotage by insurgent forces has reached a crisis stage."

"That's Randal," Maj. Gen. Taylor whooped, pumping his fist. "Confirmed! Right before the advance party took off, I ordered him to go for the tires. The Italians failed to stockpile spare tires before the war started, and now they have no way to bring in replacements.

"Hot damn, John is really taking it to them!"

"Your Force N, if it is them, General, has provided me with the first piece of genuine good news I have heard in the last eighteen months," the Kaid said with a swish of his flywhisk. "What do you make of it, Jim?"

"What this means, Bill, is that when you kick off your offensive, there are going to be a lot of Italians tied up in the Abyssinian interior on counterinsurgency operations chasing Johnny Randal instead of dug in on the border where, by all rights, they ought to be lying in wait for you.

"Merry Christmas, General!"

"Merry Christmas to you too, General."

14
WORLD'S GREATEST POUNCER

SQUADRON LEADER. PADDY WILCOX, CAPTAIN HARRY SHELBY and Commodore Richard "Dickey the Pirate" Seaborn were standing around a table at remote Camp Croc looking at a map of Abyssinia. They were in the process of selecting the second staging base for Force N, to be called "N-2." Now it was time to move up the chain of lakes closer to the heart of IEA – closer to where Force N should be. Their first effort at N-1 had been successful even though they had been forced to fly in the base security company and all the supplies with just the three Commodores. The RN was being difficult about parting with a Catalina to augment their aging fleet of amphibians.

Tasked with flying training missions for Major Sir Terry "Zorro" Stone's parachute battalion as well as ferrying supplies into N-1, the old Commodores were being stretched to the limit of their endurance. Maintenance was a looming issue that was certain to grow even worse as time went by.

The Canadian bush pilots were performing their mission brilliantly. The pilots were flying around the clock, dropping trainee parachutists by day and doing intruder resupply missions to the secret base on Lake Margherita by night.

The bush pilots represented the textbook, picture-perfect example of 'Right Man, Right Job,' even if their demeanor was a tad unconventional militarily. Their uniform of choice was Hawaiian shirts with khaki pants tucked into beat-up, pointy-toed cowboy boots, topped off with teardrop-shaped Ray-Ban aviator glasses, which the pilots virtually never, ever, removed – even at night. Headgear consisted of a wide assortment of baseball caps – no two alike.

They were a rowdy, hard-drinking crew when off duty – getting drunk and sniping at the yellow eyes of crocodiles they spotlighted in the lake at night with their personally-owned revolvers, for which the choice of grips tended to run to mother-of-pearl. They never killed any of the giant reptiles but always trooped back from their safaris along the bank of Lake Rudolf claiming to have given a few "migraines." When not flying, drinking or shooting their pearl-handled revolvers at crocodiles, the pilots spent the rest of their time racked out.

Capt. Shelby eventually became so concerned with the pilot's safety that he assigned a squad of askaris to accompany them on their nocturnal anti-crocodile expeditions to make sure they did not accidentally stumble over one laying on the bank in the dark and get more than they bargained for. True to form, the pilots accepted the escorts with good cheer, nicknaming the askaris "The Benevolent Lake Rudolf Bush Pilot Protection Detail."

The askaris reported back that the Canadians tried to get them drunk – every night. The bodyguards claimed they never accepted anything to drink.

There were several candidate islands that appeared on paper to be suitable for the second clandestine re-supply base, N-2. After deliberation, which was not a particularly well-informed decision-making process due to the almost total lack of hard intelligence about the lakes in the chain, Lake Ziway became the leading contender. Selecting it as the best location for N-2 was a guess, actually. The lake was situated approximately sixty miles due south of Addis Ababa, as the crow flies.

The primary reason for the lack of intelligence had to do with the fact that only Lake Tana, far to the north on the very edge of the Force N assigned AO, had ever been of much interest to anyone. And Lake Tana was only important because it was the source of the Blue Nile, which had aroused a great deal of curiosity among European explorers in the last century.

When the Italians conquered Abyssinia in 1935, they saw no reason to go to the trouble to patrol large, isolated, virtually unpopulated bodies of water.

Because lakes in Abyssinia had never been explored and the local natives never boated out of sight of land, islands in the middle of the lakes were the ideal places to set up secret military bases supplied by amphibious aircraft flying by night. However, it also made selecting the right lake and the right island a hit-or-miss proposition. Few military decisions are pure science, but this one was like throwing darts at a mapboard.

Lake Ziway had five known islands, which include Debre Sina, Galila, Bird Island and Tullu Gudo. The most prominent of the islands, Tullu Gudo, was reported to be the home of a monastery said to house the Ark of the Covenant. The other islands were believed to be uninhabited.

While none of the Force N officers actually believed the Ark of the Covenant was on Tullu Gudo, the island was struck from the list of potential N-2 sites straightaway. No Force N officer wanted to take responsibility for selecting a base that, if discovered by the Italians, would in all likelihood be bombed by the Regia Aeronautica, which might result in the destruction of the ancient religious relic. No one in their right mind would want a thing like that on their conscience, and besides, who is to say what would happen if the Arc were to be bombed? Might not some supernatural destructive force be unleashed? They had enough problems.

Why take a chance?

After some debate, it was also decided to eliminate any island with a name as a potential site for N-2 because it was either too large to easily defend, might have a small native population living on it or be known to the Italians. That meant another high-risk aerial reconnaissance was required to locate an unnamed island.

Sqn. Ldr. Wilcox immediately began to plan the mission while Capt. Shelby went off to alert a RF Commando to stand by for the operation. Cdre.

Seaborn boarded a Walrus for a return flight to brief Maj. Stone on progress with N1 and N2 at his training base outside Nairobi.

WHEN COMMODORE RICHARD "DICKEY THE PIRATE" SEABORN walked into Major Sir Terry "Zorro" Stone's headquarters, he met Major Lawrence Grand who was exiting. The major was in battledress uniform – complete with Royal Engineer insignia. The two men knew each other from having been observers on an operation to France in the HMY *Arrow*, which had been commanded by the Commodore's son, Lieutenant Randy "Hornblower" Seaborn, DSC. That operation, colorfully named BUZZARD PLUCKER, had inserted a party of Lovat Scout snipers on a clandestine mission. They had also both been on OPERATION RUTHLESS when RF had boarded a German E-boat in the Channel to capture a German Enigma machine. Neither man had any idea what the device was – that fact was classified "Most Secret Need to Know" – and neither officer had a need to know.

Maj. Grand said, "Commodore, would you care to hitch a ride back to Nairobi with me?"

The SOE chief of Section D (Destruction) did not elaborate on what it was he was doing at Maj. Stone's battalion headquarters. Cdre. Seaborn vaguely knew Maj. Grand had something to do with SOE, but at this time he had no need to know what that was, so he did not.

"Quite nice of you to make the offer. I shall be glad to accept, provided you do not mind waiting for me to conclude my business with Maj. Stone. I should not need more than a half hour at most."

"Excellent, that shall give me time to take a quick look around the area," Maj. Grand replied, putting on his smoked glasses.

Cdre. Seaborn gave Maj. Stone a concise rundown on the state of affairs at Camp Croc. When Maj. Stone heard the explanation of why Tullu Gudo Island had been eliminated as a potential base he laughed, "Blow up the Ark of the Covenant? That would be a blot on your service record!"

When the two concluded their business, Maj. Stone immediately called for the ammo carrier that he used as his personal command vehicle to be brought around, and he beat Cdre. Seaborn and Maj. Grand to Nairobi. His driver deposited him at the Kenya Colony Police Headquarters building. Inside, he was shown to the office of the Commissioner of the Kenya Police, Richard Cavendish.

Commissioner Richard Cavendish listened stoically as his visitor identified himself as an MI-6 officer by the employment of the code word "MAYFAIR." The Commissioner was himself an asset of the SIS. He knew Maj. Stone by reputation because his son had attended Eton with him.

"What service may I perform for you, Sir Terry? Your wish is my command," he inquired, feeling a certain clutch of apprehension. There was no telling what task he might be asked to perform for King and Country. Being acquainted with the record of the officer sitting in front of him, it could be anything!

"I need the name of the best man in your police intelligence department," Maj. Stone explained. "And I would appreciate an introduction. I shall require the use of his services for the next month to six weeks, possibly more."

"Intelligence – or do you possibly mean Internal Security?"

"Specifically what I need is a counterintelligence specialist if you have an officer assigned that function."

"That would be Chief Inspector Ronald McFarland, ex-Special Branch Metropolitan Police. He is the top man in his field. We were deuced lucky the day he retired and chose to seek employment out here in the colony," Commissioner Cavendish said. "Nothing goes on in Kenya that escapes the Chief Inspector's attention for long. McFarland is your man."

"How do we arrange the introduction?" Maj. Stone asked. "Keep in mind, the Chief Inspector does not have a need to know of my connection to SIS."

"Leave that to me," Commissioner Cavendish said as he scribbled on a scrap of paper. "Drop around to this address in an hour. The Chief Inspector will be there, and you can spend as much time together as you care to in complete privacy."

The address on the paper turned out to be that of a private residence located on the edge of town, in a compound behind a high, whitewashed wall – what is commonly called a safe house. The compound was a prudent choice for a clandestine meeting.

When Maj. Stone arrived at the appointed time, he found Chief Inspector Ronald McFarland to be a big, red-faced man with a huge, bushy, cinnamon-colored mustache that curled up at the ends. He had dead-black eyes that bored straight through you. The policeman chewed constantly on the tip of a giant curved pipe. He had not gone to Eton, nor had any members of his family, but he knew quite a bit about Sir Terry.

"Chief Inspector," Maj. Stone said, gazing straight back at black eyes that contained about the same malevolence one would expect to find when looking down the twin barrels of a sawed-off shotgun. "Captain the Lord Joss Hay, Military Secretary of Manpower, is a Nazi spy reporting to the Italians. This is from an unimpeachable source. The fact that you received it from me is classified "Most Secret." Since you have signed the Official Secrets Act, you are aware of the consequences if you should ever reveal what I have just informed you of or where it came from."

"Are you threatening me, Major?" the Chief Inspector asked, unruffled, not seeming in the least surprised by what Maj. Stone would have expected to have been a bombshell of an accusation about a prominent member of the British aristocracy, a high Kenyan government official and a well-known member of the colony's social set.

"Yes, I am," Maj. Stone replied. "You reveal to anyone we had this conversation, and you will be lucky if you get the post of traffic control officer at the North Pole for the duration."

A small smile played around the corners of the Chief Inspector's lips behind the tightly-clinched pipe. Apparently he had a sense of humor, though he certainly did not look like the type. The Chief Inspector was the quintessential professional policeman down to the ground.

"My assignment," Maj. Stone said, "is to organize a parachute battalion that will jump into Abyssinia in the near future. My mission is to rescue a team gone missing – lost somewhere in the central part of the country – lead by Major John Randal. You may have heard of him… the Commando raider."

The Chief Inspector nodded without comment or any flicker of expression.

"Until such time as my battalion goes into Abyssinia, I shall be assisting a Special Operations Executive team tasked with conducting a counterintelligence operation here in the colony. The SOE team's mission is to identify the Nazi's agent in Kenya Colony. The team is not currently in possession of the name of the enemy operative. For reasons I am not at liberty to go into, we need for them to discover the identity of the spy on their own. Failing that, *you* will reveal Captain Lord Hay to the SOE people as their man, never mentioning that you obtained the information from me. Is that clear?"

"Yes."

"Commissioner Cavendish has seconded you to my command for the duration of this counterintelligence operation."

"I'm all ears, Sir Terry."

"Here are your initial instructions. Affect contact with Captain the Lady Jane Seaborn as soon as possible and volunteer to assist her in her quest. Do not mention my name. Do not reveal that you are working with me."

Chief Inspector McFarland nodded his understanding without comment.

"Be very careful, Inspector. Lady Jane is nobody's fool. She will, in turn, put you in contact with Major Lawrence Grand of Special Operations Executive who is in charge of the SOE team. You will work directly with both of them. At some point they may or may not introduce you to me. If that should happen, you are to act as if it is the first time we have ever met."

"Is that all?"

"Actually, no," Maj. Stone answered, studying the ex-Special Branch Policeman carefully. "I want you to spin an airtight web around the Earl. Report to me where he is, where he has been, and where he is going at all times. From this moment forward you are to never let him out of your sight for a minute. Any objections to or comments about, your assignment thus far, Chief Inspector?"

"Only this, Major. You do not quite have your facts straight," Chief Inspector McFarland explained as he tapped his pipe on his palm. "Captain the Lord Joss Hay, 22nd Earl of Errol, is a fascist, not a Nazi. In fact, he is the Supreme Leader of the British Union of Fascist's movement here in Kenya Colony.

"The Earl is in contact with the Italian High Command in Addis Ababa through the Blackshirt cell in Tanganyika. He does not have any direct means of communications with Addis Ababa from here in Kenya.

"Also, as a side enterprise, the Earl is the head of a criminal ring trafficking in stolen military equipment. The crooks are diverting it to Italian East Africa and selling it to the enemy for profit.

"In his role as Military Secretary of Manpower, Captain Lord Hay is personally responsible for all officer assignments in the colony. The Earl is playing a shell game, assigning officers to jobs they are not qualified for, then moving them around the country re-assigning them to other jobs they are equally unqualified for. In that way, nothing ever gets done, and Kenya is effectively contributing no more than lip service to the war effort.

"Initially, Captain Lord Hay became a BUF party member when he dabbled in anti-communist politics like a lot of other people in England of his social class, including, no less, our unfortunate recently-abdicated King, the Duke of Windsor. Nowadays the man is only in it for the money. The Duke of Aosta dangled the promise of being appointed military governor of the colony when the Italians conquer Kenya, and the Earl went for it hoping to line his pockets.

"Finally, Major, I have already spun a web around the traitor so tight that it is a bloody miracle the man can even breathe."

"Very impressive," Maj. Stone said, bowled over by the extent of detailed information. "Are you quite sure about the Duke of Windsor being a fascist?"

"There is one other thing," Chief Inspector McFarland added, ignoring the question and pointing his pipe for emphasis. "My favorite nephew was a private in a territorial searchlight company assigned to Calais. In the fighting, his unit disintegrated, and he found himself hiding under a dock, separated from his mates and surrounded by Germans. An officer from The Rangers came along out of nowhere, leading his men out to the end of the dock. With no questions asked, he took the lad under his wing. That officer was an American named John Randal, and he brought my nephew home safe and sound when everyone else in his unit was lost to the bloody Nazis.

"If in truth you are planning to attempt to rescue Maj. Randal the way you say, teach me how to parachute and I shall gladly go with you. There is nothing I would not do for the man."

"Well said, Chief Inspector," Maj. Stone responded. "Good of you to volunteer. Very sporting, old stick. That said, it is quite clear we are going to have a greater need for your talents here. When were you planning to share your information on the Earl?"

"I have been waiting for someone like you to show up, Sir Terry. It could only be a matter of time."

"Well, I am here now," Maj. Stone said. "What are your questions?"

"Find what you were looking for in that cloak closet at the Muthaiga Country Club?"

Uh-oh!

"I need about a dozen good hostilities-only colonial officers for my battalion," Maj. Stone said, hoping to change the conversation. "Would it be possible for you to provide me with a list of suitable candidates?"

"You will be wanting the usual suspects… white hunters, explorers, adventurers, ex-mercenaries and the like, I presume?"

"Precisely."

"A criminal history is not an automatic disqualifier, I presume?"

"Actually, no."

"I have just the men," the Chief Inspector said, taking out a pen. "Captain the Lord Hay has them all assigned to pushing paper or guarding some remote military site of little military value in the middle of nowhere. These lads will make fine paratroops."

"Outstanding."

HIDDEN IN THE JUNGLE OUTSIDE OF THE CAPITAL CITY OF Addis Ababa, Major John Randal and a small band consisting of Rita Hayworth, Lana Turner, Waldo Treywick, GG, Kaldi, and Bimbashi Butch

"Headhunter" Hoolihan plus a dozen of his Bad Boys, lay in wait for the sun to go down. Two Caproni bombers painted in mottled green camouflage flew over at treetop level heading south. The bombers were outbound on anti-shifta patrol, which meant they were searching for Force N instead of doing something militarily productive like bombing Khartoum or Nairobi.

Tonight at 0230 hours, Maj. Randal and the others were planning to enter the city, steal into the nerve center of the Italian High Command and stealthily commandeer a radio. They would then transmit a brief message to Force N Rear in Khartoum providing the grid coordinates to a location where they would be waiting forty-eight hours hence from the time the message went out.

The idea was for Force N Rear to fly in a replacement means of com-munication. Once they had a working radio on the ground, then arrangements could be made to begin parachuting in men, arms, ammuni-tion, equipment and the all-important Maria Theresa thalers needed to finance the insurgency.

When word got round that Force N was handing out big, round, silver Fat Ladies – actually delivering on the promise of hard cash – recruiting was going to explode. Recently the Italians had not been paying their askaris regularly. That was a policy which could only be described as suicidal lunacy for an unpopular, occupying colonial army. With any luck, some of the disgruntled veteran Blackshirt askaris might be encouraged to change sides. Deserters make good guerrilla soldiers.

Maj. Randal had spread out a small tarp and was sitting under a tree cleaning his weapons in anticipation of the night's work ahead. The stubby little Italian submachine gun he had captured lay field-stripped in front of him. The finely-built weapon was a 9mm Beretta MAB-38A called a MAB-38A. In his professional opinion, the handy little carbine was the best full automatic small arm he had ever handled, and at this point in his career he was acquainted with most of the world's submachine guns.

The MAB-38A had several features that particularly appealed to him. The rifle-styled stock allowed the weapon to be fired from the shoulder and it pointed like one of the best grade sporting shotguns Beretta was internationally famous for producing. There were two selective fire triggers. The first trigger was for firing semiautomatic shots while the second was for full automatic work. The action was blowback-operated and fired from the open bolt. And most importantly, for balance, the thirty-round box magazine loaded from the bottom of the receiver.

The carbine sported a barrel encased in a perforated steel tube, giving it a deadly "rough and ready" combat look. There was a muzzle brake with four compensator slots milled on the top. The sighting arrangement consisted of a simple post front and tangent-type rear sight. The MAB-38A was a shooter's weapon. It was very controllable on full automatic.

Maj. Randal loved it – the Beretta MAB-38A was the perfect raiding tool and a very handy saddle gun.

He especially appreciated the way the slings were arranged on the stock. Unlike American weapons systems, they were not located on the bottom – the Beretta's were bolted on the left flat side of the butt and forearm. This allowed the submachine gun to be slung across the front of his chest, muzzle down, to ride there flat but readily available to be swung up and fired at an instant's notice. This gave him the ability to have both hands free and still have the weapon ready at a second's notice.

Maj. Randal wished he'd had the MAB-38A under his overcoat when he'd walked into the Blue Duck bar that cold winter night – in now what seemed like another life.

The plan tonight was as simple as it could be crafted. GG, dressed in the uniform of a lieutenant they had killed in a road ambush, along with Lana and Rita – dressed as Italian askaris – accompanied by Maj. Randal and Waldo, would simply ride up to the front gate of the capital and seek admittance. Once inside the walls they would proceed to GG's old Brigade Headquarters, sneak in and use the radio to contact Force N Rear in Khartoum. Once contact was made, they would sneak back out unobserved, with no one the wiser.

If asked, their story was that the two Americans were freelance reporters who wished to spend the night in town. Since America was a nonbelligerent, this story should be believed. GG planned to say the two had been captured by shifta while traveling in the interior and only recently released after paying a ransom.

While this tale might seem a little thin, at 0230 hours on a chilly night it would most likely be believed. Unlike in the movies, soldiers pulling guard duty late at night are generally not crack troops or trained military policemen overly suspicious of every little detail. More often than not, gate guards are simply regular soldiers from a headquarters company who draw the duty on a rotating basis.

Maj. Randal knew that in most cases the men pulling sentry duty have already put in a full day's work. Most sentries really are interested only in being relieved by the next shift. Italians on guard duty expect to encounter problems with wild animals, shifta and the odd, troublesome local natives, but not from American reporters covering the war who did, in fact, turn up from time to time.

Foreigners were not supposed to travel around the country unescorted without the proper credentials, but the American press had a reputation for ignoring the finer bureaucratic details. Most Italian soldiers wanted to visit the U.S., if not relocate permanently someday. They generally liked Americans and tended to overlook their transgressions as harmless. Besides, what were the gate guards going to do, shoot them? Or a fate worse than death in Abyssinia – turn them away?

Addis Ababa was a great-walled, medieval city. The wall kept out most intruders, like lions and hyenas, but it was not airtight and not all that effective at keeping out anyone who really wished to pay a nocturnal call. The main gate had two giant iron doors and a complicated mechanized system of closing the heavy panels.

Luckily for Maj. Randal's plan, the mechanism had broken down years ago during Emperor Haile Selassie's inauguration ceremony – about six days after it was installed. The gate had never been repaired. Now it was rusted open.

The Italians had given thought to the idea of pulling it shut with an armored car in an emergency. However, no preparations had actually been put in place to station an armored car at the gate with a tow chain or even have one nearby on call. Why bother – the town had never been attacked.

Tonight, Maj. Randal was willing to take the risk of entering through the front gate because he wanted to have the mules with them. The distance from the gate to the Brigade Headquarters they intended to infiltrate was over a mile. He wanted to get in and out fast.

Bimbashi Hoolihan, Kaldi and the Bad Boys were going over the wall at several pre-selected points beginning at 0245 hours. The Bad Boys were all equipped with cigarettes and packets of paper matches collected from captured Italian rations. While Addis Ababa was a show city with many European-style buildings, most of the roofs in the residential section were made of thatch.

The Bad Boys were planning to scale the wall, spread out through the city and bury the packs of matches in the straw on the upwind side of likely thatch-roofed buildings. The match covers would be folded shut and a lit cigarette tucked in behind the paper matches. The result was a primitive, field-expedient, incendiary device. When the cigarette burned down, the matches would ignite. It was very effective, only the timing was ragged, as not all cigarettes burn at the same speed.

That was fine – this part of the operation was not designed to go down with military precision. None of the Bad Boys possessed watches to synchronize – they would not have been able to tell time even if they did. Besides, surgical precision is something generally confined to the drill field or the imagination of armchair tacticians. It virtually never ever happens in real combat situations.

Roofs would be going *whoosh* all over the city beginning approximately 0255 – and that was all that mattered.

Unfortunately, Force N did not have any explosives or Bimbashi Hoolihan could have set them off to simulate an air raid. However, fifteen or twenty buildings catching fire at different times at different locations over a half-hour period should create a significant diversion. The Bad Boys were looking forward to putting the Addis Ababa fire department to the test.

One of RF Rules was 'Plan raids backwards. Know how to get home.' Hopefully, the outbreak of fires would create enough confusion to cover the withdrawal of Maj. Randal and company. He knew a lot of elements have to be taken into consideration when planning a small-scale operation, but hope should not be one of them.

On the other hand, sometimes a commander has to go with what he has

15
CALLING HOME

THE MUTHAIGA COUNTRY CLUB WAS A NAUGHTY GARDEN OF Eden in a wild African frontier colony. Membership was exclusive – gentlemen farmers, white hunters, socialite settlers and expatriate impoverished members of the English aristocracy living in semi-exile for one reason or another. Nevertheless, it was ultra-restricted. Untitled colonial government officials, tradesmen and churchgoers need not apply.

What went on at Muthaiga was the subject of a great deal of conjecture with the truth clouded by distortion, incestuous innuendo, exaggeration, quite a bit of puffing and more than a little downright lying. The truth was, it was a swinging place. Morals were checked at the door. Men and women knew it going in.

There was speculation that the altitude and the exposure to the equatorial sun had something to do with the licentiousness at Muthaiga. Most likely, it was the heavy drinking and hard drug use. Hedonism was the name of the game. The members reveled in the club's wickedness. That is why they joined and what debauched visitors traveled out to Kenya from all over the world to experience.

The two major Muthaiga social events took place at Christmas and in midsummer for Race Week. Christmas was now just a couple of weeks away. Around Africa, the U.S. and the fleshpots of Europe, dissipated millionaires, jaded movie stars, and degenerate aristocrats were making arrangements to rendezvous at Muthaiga Country Club to party with the Happy Valley set. One and all were coming to town with the idea to burn the place down.

Christmas in Nairobi was a scene of debauchery right out of Hollywood where the Wild West meets a Roman orgy.

Extravagant exhibitionism – the more outrageous the better – was the purpose of the exercise. There was not a lot of peace on earth, nor good will to men. The singing of Christmas carols was held to a minimum.

The club was booked to capacity during Christmas. Even members had to do battle for a room. The overflow was forced to stay in either Torr's Hotel, aka "Tarts Hotel," or the Norfolk.

Bachelors slept – though not always alone – in the "military wing." It was said the Spartan rooms were of the type you might expect to find in an affluent monastery. The quarters were tiny, but taking a page out of the Roman orgy theme, the bathrooms were super luxurious. One veteran member had been heard to comment that he preferred the military wing because "at least you do not have to suffer the bloody theatre of husbands hammering their wives into submission at night."

Melodrama was thick on the ground at Muthaiga Club.

Even though women could hold membership, the bar was "stag only" evenings between six and eight.

THERE WAS A STRICT DRINK PROTOCOL AT THE CLUB, WHICH was followed to the letter. During the Christmas season the drinking started immediately after the noon hour, not counting of course, the Pink Gins before lunch. Twelve o'clock was like the Oklahoma Land Rush – you could get killed in the stampede to the bar. Gin fizzes followed the Pinks at teatime. Then at sundown came the cocktail hour, the choices being a Trinity, Bronx or a White Lady. During the hours of darkness, it was whiskey and champagne until lights out. Only there was no lights out.

The club did not admit to a formal protocol for drugs. However, it had one. A drug dealer was on premises at all times.

The dances were black tie. Initially, the members sipped their cocktails in formal evening attire at sunset, with a lot of eye contact between tables. After dark, things spiraled out of control, pulled down by a whirlpool of alcohol, drugs and reckless sex that eventually sucked everyone under.

The dances ended at 0600 hours. No one ever made it out of bed at the Muthaiga Country Club before 1030 hours. New cures for hangovers were much in demand, with vodka shots or more likely a line or two of medicinal cocaine, the remedy of choice.

No one even considered an aspirin.

The hard drugs, drinking and non-stop adultery was not without casualties. Jealousies seethed with marriages ruined and reputations besmirched. Every member of the club hated at least one other member, and blood feuds were as common as in the wilds of Abyssinia.

Officially, there had never been a murder on premises – homicide being against the rules. No member would dare risk being blackballed for killing someone in the clubhouse, guest quarters or on the grounds, though the subject came up often. Rumors were rife of the odd body being rolled up in one of Muthaiga's oriental carpets and spirited out in the wee hours. Being banned from the club was viewed as a fate worse than death, certainly more awful than discovering your husband or wife *in flagrante delicto* with another member.

You could replace a husband or wife. There was only one Muthaiga Country Club.

The undisputed King of the club was Captain the Lord Joss Victor Hay, 22nd Earl of Errol, the one and only "World's Greatest Pouncer." Capt. Lord Hay spent so much time there that he eventually took a house across the road from the property. The two-story bungalow was convenient for the impromptu assassinations for which he was a living legend.

For the past two weeks, Capt. Lord Hay had been meeting daily with Captain the Lady Jane Seaborn, Lieutenant Pamala Plum-Martin and Brandy Seaborn at the club for lunch, followed by a foursome of croquet.

The three women were all in agreement that Capt. Lord Hay was devastatingly handsome, exceedingly well groomed and had beautiful manners. He wore a special brand of imported cologne called "CAR", created by Truefitt & Hill of Bond Street. CAR has a very distinctive aroma and was rumored to have an aphrodisiac effect on females. It was said that any man in the colony who detected a whiff of it on his wife's clothes had strong grounds for divorce.

All three of the girls were enchanted by the Earl's old-world charm, rakish style and roguish reputation. The women looked forward to their daily lunches and croquet. Capt. Lord Hay could be delightfully attentive. The "World's Greatest Pouncer" was a man who loved women and who knew how to make them feel good about themselves when he was with them.

Very few men ever master that talent.

The fact was, all three women were emotionally vulnerable at this stage in their lives and needed to feel good. They were in varying degrees of depression with Lady Jane openly in grief. Why?

Major Sir Terry "Zorro" Stone had taken it upon himself to confide to her the report that had come out of Abyssinia by runner, which indicated that Major John Randal may have been killed. His information checkmated the report about the sighting of a man in an Australian hat. Lady Jane was feeling emotionally whiplashed by good news / bad news. Naturally, since there were no state secrets involved, she had shared the story with the other two girls.

Chances were that Maj. Randal was dead, eaten by a lion.

Following their marching orders to ferret out the Italian master spy in the Kenyan Colonial Government, the women arranged for memberships at Muthaiga Country Club. They were all clubbable. Not having any formal training in counterintelligence that any of them would admit to, they had no idea how to find a spy. The trio merely followed instructions from Major Lawrence Grand to frequent the club and keep their eyes and ears open.

Capt. Lord Hay made his move the first day they arrived. He had a reputation to maintain as the "World's Greatest Pouncer."

The fact that the Earl was widely known as a rake in no way handicapped his ability to charm other women straight into bed. In point of fact, it seemed to enhance his ability to get the girls. With his golden hair, blue eyes and happy-go-lucky self-confidence, the Earl was a deadly lady-killer.

The World's Greatest Pouncer knew he was irresistible to women, and he knew the women knew that he knew it. All of which made the game so interesting, though predictable. Once he got a woman in his sights, it was a foregone conclusion how it was going to turn out.

The man did have standards restricting his conquests to *married* women. This peccadillo carried its risks. One enraged husband had publicly whipped him with a rhinoceros whip at the Nairobi train station. Instead of being a disgrace, everyone seemed to think the incident hilarious. The episode had the exact reverse effect as intended. Capt. Lord Hay's fame as a serial seducer soared to new heights.

The World's Greatest Pouncer was famous for his contempt of husbands. Capt. Lord Hay never believed for one second that legal or moral laws applied to him. And when it came to pursuing married women, he was incorrigible.

Lady Jane, Lt. Plum-Martin and Brandy Seaborn all thought him to be great fun. The fact that he was a widower made him a sympathetic figure. His reputation as a womanizer, they concluded, had to be overblown – at least two of them did. Lt. Plum-Martin recognized him for what he was down to the ground – but being single, he did not have eyes for her.

All three secretly liked edgy men, though again, only Lt. Plum-Martin had much experience with them, specializing as she did in RAF fighter pilots. Lady Jane did have some, considering her on again/off again relationship with Maj. Randal – though he had a different kind of hard edge.

For his part, Capt. Lord Hay thought they were the best-looking three women he had ever seen in a group, even though they were not his type. In truth, he preferred plain, wealthy women of a certain age. There was room for only one peacock in the boudoir, though at 39 he was beginning to rethink the age policy.

Currently, Capt. Lord Hay was engaged to his first *younger* woman, Mrs. Diana Broughton. She had been married to Sir Jock Delves Broughton less than a month when the Earl met her at the club a few weeks ago. Now, he was beginning to think the engagement might be a mistake.

Being virtually destitute, Capt. Lord Hay needed rich women to support his lifestyle. The Earl valued the vulnerability of a wealthy aging woman. His method of operation was to captivate women past their prime, exploit their vulnerability and have his way with them – which meant get at their bank account.

Diana, his fiancée, was not older, she was fairly good looking and she was not rich. Capt. Lord Hay was already beginning to tire of their relationship. Marriage to her did not make financial sense.

Lady Jane fit the bill much better than Diana, almost. For his purposes she had two drawbacks. Besides being more beautiful than he was, she did not impress him as a woman he could ever wrap around his finger. Capt. Lord Hay knew Lady Jane would never turn over her money to him, but that was not her main shortcoming – her biggest negative was that she was reported to have a lover who had a well-established reputation for arriving unexpectedly in the dark of night and killing people.

The World's Greatest Pouncer was not afraid of dealing with jealous husbands – he had practice. He derived special pleasure from letting the other fellow know he had taken his wife and there was nothing the man could do about it. Sometimes that was actually better than the sex. However, there was a point beyond which even he feared to tread.

Maj. Randal was a stone killer.

To his way of thinking, Brandy Seaborn had an edge over Lady Jane in the eligibility department – being a few years nearer to his own age, mind-numbingly wealthy, plus she was married to a man who traveled frequently. The glittering honey-blond happy girl was his idea of the total package – with the only downside being that she was spectacularly beautiful – plain women really were best.

The prospect of adding her to his long list of conquests made him giddy. Once that happened, she would divorce her sailor husband and marry him. Capt. Lord Hay was confident – for good reason – of the results of what he called his "performance" once he got any woman in bed.

Capt. Lord Hay's day-to-day existence was entirely devoted to setting up his next conquest. The Earl did not smoke, but he always carried elegant, gold-tipped, black Balkan cigarettes in an elegant gold cigarette case along with his elegant gold lighter so he could provide cigarettes to his women and light them for them. He could turn the simple act of lighting up into an intimate erotic art form, particularly if there were witnesses.

A virtual teetotaler, he would nurse a drink at the orgies his first wife, Idina, used to ringmaster at their farm in Happy Valley. When pressed on why he did not drink more, he would explain with a devilish smile, "Why, I would never want to impair my 'performance.'"

Cap. Lord Hay had a custom-built portable bar concealed in a leather suitcase stocked with miniature bottles of spirits that he always had at hand to ply his ladies with liquor. The case also contained a small stash of cocaine and morphine along with a sterling silver syringe. Liquor may be quicker; but in his professional opinion hard drugs were virtually guaranteed.

Neither alcohol nor drugs held much appeal to Brandy. So they were probably not going to work.

Fast cars were Capt. Lord Hay's second passion, though he did not know the first thing about auto mechanics and he was hard on his vehicles. On one occasion he rolled Idina's Rolls Royce (RR) at high speed and simply went off and left it lying in the ditch where it landed. His current preference in automobiles ran to Buick Super 8s because of their powerful engines. The Earl tore around the country in a fire-engine-red sedan that had become his trademark.

Brandy was, according to all reports, a woman who liked to go fast, and he was thinking that she might like to go for a high speed-run to view the spectacular African scenery. Or possibly, he might offer to let her drive. Life was sweet – so many choices, so little time.

The Earl almost always planned his conquests in detail and in advance – like a military operation. He never left anything to chance.

BIMBASHI BUTCH "HEADHUNTER" HOOLIHAN DEPARTED THE jungle hideout first with his Bad Boys and Kaldi. Major John Randal handed his 9mm Beretta MAB-38A submachine gun to Lana Turner. She swung it across her back, muzzle down. Tonight he was wearing a big, wide, pearl gray, Tom Mix-style-style cowboy hat, as was Waldo Treywick. Both men were swathed in the traditional off-white Abyssinian togas that covered their BDUs all the way to their knees. Under the wrap he was carrying both of his Colt .38 Supers, his Browning 9mm P-35 and the silenced .22 High Standard.

Lana Turner and Rita Hayworth were dressed in the uniform of Italian cavalry askaris of the "Hawk Feathers" battalion, which was identified by a hawk feather sticking up from the side of their perky red and white-striped fez hats. Their thick, jet-black hair was tucked up under the headgear. Neither girl was wearing her trademark brass hoop ear rings tonight. Each girl had a leather bandolier strapped across her chest and a Carcano carbine slung over her shoulder. GG was dressed in the uniform of a "Hawk Feathers" lieutenant.

The weak point of the plan to enter Addis Ababa and hijack a radio was that they were totally dependent on GG since none of them spoke Italian. This was a serious flaw, and Maj. Randal and Waldo both knew it.

GG had made it perfectly clear that he had no interest in serving another day in the Italian Army. He claimed he wanted to go back to America, finish college and open a restaurant. He could be lying.

"You ever seen the Major put on one of his demonstrations where his shoots somebody's initials in a target, GG?" Waldo asked. "Gubbo Rekash had his welded right there on his shield after the Major done it. I know you seen it."

"Yes sir, Mr. Treywick."

"Well, tonight the Major is going to have that silenced High Standard .22 of his pointed right at your gizzard from under his robe, and if anything suspicious lookin' happens or somethin' goes wrong, then he's goin' to shoot your initials square in the middle a' your spine. Got that, Wop boy?"

"No problem, Mr. Treywick. This is going to be easy."

"For your sake, I hope so kid, 'cause if it ain't, my guess is the Major's not only goin' to shoot your initials, he's gonna' put a period after each G."

"Let's do it," Maj. Randal ordered, glancing at the green, coke bottle-shaped hands on the heavy Rolex watch that Lady Jane had given him. He wondered what she was doing right about now.

The little party moved out onto the road and started the mules toward Addis Ababa. The night was as dark as the inside of a well. The moon had already set. As they approached the gate a couple of spotted hyenas drifted away in the gloom.

A command rang out in Italian that sounded like it meant HALT!"

GG identified himself in a loud, authoritative voice and then they were inside the wall with no fanfare – not even having to use their story about being war correspondents. The guards at the gate waved as they rode past. They all waved back except for Lana Turner and Rita Hayworth who haughtily ignored the Blackshirt soldiers.

The gate guards had no reason to be suspicious. Normally, no one traveled at night in Abyssinia, but on the rare occasions when someone was unfortunate enough to be caught out after last light, they wanted to be allowed in the gate quickly. The guards knew the shifta owned the night and lurked out there in the shadows. Man-eating wild animals roamed the countryside. Best get inside.

Tonight confirmed to Maj. Randal that the Italian occupation troops were existing in a state of perpetual fear. Being surrounded by an evil populace that hated their guts, wanted to cut off their precious body parts, and dangerous animals that would eat them – all contributed to creating an unhealthy bunker mentality.

No one was going to deny sanctuary to an Italian national because of a lack of paperwork or not knowing the latest password. "Welcome to Addis Ababa, stranger. Glad you made it alive. Come inside where it's safe." So much for security.

GG led them through the winding streets to the 5th Colonial Infantry Brigade Headquarters a mile and a half from the main gate. The HQ was located in an elegant, three-story building that had been the private residence of the British Counsel prior to the Italian Invasion in 1935. There was no security posted outside. What would be the point? The Italian Army lived behind a guarded wall. Besides, the nearest enemy formations other than shifta – who were not capable of launching a coordinated ground attack – were in the Sudan or Kenya.

Lana and Rita waited outside in the street with the mules while GG, Waldo and Maj. Randal stepped down and went inside. The girls were fingering their Carcano carbines, not overly fond of the idea of being deep in the enemy camp.

Just inside the door, an orderly was asleep at the desk in the foyer. Next to him on the wall was a "WANTED" poster featuring a blow-up photo of a bearded Maj. Randal in his cut-down Australian slouch hat with a cigarillo clenched in his teeth, ivory-handled pistols strapped to his chest, staring straight at the camera. Some informant had surreptitiously snapped the photo and sold it to the Italians for a king's ransom in Fat Ladies.

Nothing stayed secret in Abyssinia for long.

GG ignored the sleeping soldier and proceeded straight up the stairs to the radio room located on the second floor as if he owned the place. At 0325 hours nothing was stirring, the 5th Bde. HQ appeared deserted. The communications center was situated in a corner room that looked out over the street. The walls were lined with a bank of radios that generated a moderate degree of heat inside the cramped space.

A quick head check revealed an officer and two enlisted men on duty. They were sitting in chairs in front of the bank of radios and smoking cigarettes out of a crumpled gold package of Auroras which sported a picture of a faded, chocolate-colored rooster crowing on the front.

Maj. Randal motioned silently for Waldo to take up a position from where he would have an unobstructed field of fire down the length of the hall and the stairs. The old ivory poacher pulled Maj. Randal's A-5 Browning 12-gauge shotgun with the cut-down barrel out from under his off-white shawl with a flourish.

Maj. Randal flipped the tail of his toga over his shoulder, removed the silenced High Standard .22 from its holster, then with GG trailing in his shadow he stepped into the commo room and shot all three of the Blackshirts two times each in the head. The silenced pistol made a sound no louder than a wooden match being struck.

The fascist soldiers slumped in their chairs, dead.

GG had never seen anything like it. The gunplay was all over, fast! Incredibly fast! Even in the movies he had never seen anything that fast!

"Dial in to this frequency," Maj. Randal ordered, handing him a slip of paper. "Get a move on, GG."

The radios were all turned on, making it a simple matter to tune in the designated channel scribbled on the paper. Within seconds, GG turned around and inquired, "What message do you want me to send, Major?"

"I'll do it," Maj. Randal said, shoving a dead Blackshirt out of the chair and sitting down at the key. Trust can only be carried so far. He quickly tapped out a brief series of dots and dashes. An acknowledgement came right back.

"Let's go, GG!"

They stepped out into the hall just in time to see Waldo light up an Italian soldier strolling down the stairs from the third floor. The 12-gauge Browning A-5 went *BAAARRROOOOOMMM* in the enclosed hallway! The Blackshirt cartwheeled down the stairs – that put paid to stealth.

"Time to get the hell out of Dodge, Mr. Treywick!" Maj. Randal barked.

"You first, Major," Waldo responded. "I'll cover the rear!"

They dashed down the stairs. The sleeping orderly sat up in surprise, fumbling for a weapon. Maj. Randal shot him twice with his Colt .38 Super as they ran past.

Outside, the sky was glowing. In the distance it looked like half the city was burning. Sirens were beginning to wail. Rita tossed Maj. Randal the reins to his mule. As he clambered aboard, Parachute decided to go into his rodeo routine. Lights were beginning to come on inside the 5th Brigade HQ. Shouts were ringing out, and windows were opening so the Blackshirts could look out to see what was happening.

Waldo loosed off a couple of 12-gauge rounds at the windows, causing the tinkling of broken glass and more surprised shouts in Italian. Parachute was crow-hopping. The sound of troops could be heard running toward the building. The two girls began to lay down covering fire with their Carcano carbines.

One of the fascists threw an M-35 Red Devil hand grenade out into the street from a third-story window. A squad of Italian 5th Brigade troops was coming down a side street when suddenly GG started shouting out commands in Italian and gesturing back toward the 5th Brigade HQ building.

Then the grenade exploded *KAAAAAAABOOOOOOM!* The flash lit up the night!

The Italian troops on the side street responded to GG's shouts and the grenade by unleashing a fusillade on the 5th Brigade Headquarters. The Blackshirts inside the building immediately shifted their attention to the side street and returned fire. Before long a major firefight developed. The engagement was what staff types who spend their time sticking pins in a map call a "blue-on-blue." The confused Italians were shooting it out with each other in the dark, neither side inflicting much damage on the other but making a terrible racket.

The Red Devil put a stop to Parachute's antics in mid-crow hop and he lit out like his tail was on fire. "What in the hell did you say to those troops, GG?" Maj. Randal shouted, leaning forward over the white mule's neck as they raced through the narrow streets at a dead run.

"I lied that the 5th Brigade had mutinied, Major," the young Italian shouted back with a big display of handsome white teeth.

"Nice going, stud."

Lana caught his eye and tossed the 9mm Beretta MAB-38A. Maj. Randal caught it on the run. As they clattered around a corner, a formation of Blackshirt troops appeared out of the dark. Maj. Randal shouldered the weapon one-handed and loosed off a long burst of 9mm rounds, knocking over several of the surprised enemy soldiers and causing the rest to scramble for cover.

He had brought two magazines loaded with all tracers for the night's work. The little carbine put out an impressive volume of fire magnified all out of portion by all the preponderance of tracers – normally tracer is loaded only one in six. The Italian troops scattered immediately, going to ground as the mules pounded past. The mules and their riders were around another corner before the terrified Eyeties managed to get off a single round.

As the party made their mad dash for the gate, they fired at every Italian soldier they rode past. Behind them, the battle had intensified at the 5th Colonial Brigade Headquarters. In the distance, the sky had turned a golden red from the conflagration of fires set by the Bad Boys.

Bimbashi Hoolihan's troops had certainly overachieved tonight. Maj. Randal had hoped for no more than fifteen or twenty fires max. From the looks of things, hundreds of buildings were blazing. The Bad Boys could not have possibly lit that many fires by themselves. The wind must have carried sparks – or a lot of local firebugs had turned out to take part adding to the inferno.

The blaze in Addis Ababa was raging out of control.

The mules came clattering around the final corner – the gate was one hundred yards straight ahead. GG started yelling at the guards. Maj. Randal had left his quirt in his saddlebag so he reached back and slapped Parachute on the flank with the barrel of the Beretta MAB-38A submachine gun. The mean-looking perforated steel tube that covered the barrel kept it from coming in direct contact with the mule's flesh, but it was hot.

Parachute kicked it into a gear Maj. Randal had never realized the animal had. They were literally flying at the gate. He brought up the submachine gun and let rip. The white tracers ricocheted all around the base of the gate in a dance of blazing white bright lights, looking not unlike the one hundred miles-per-hour fairies Major Sir Terry "Zorro" Stone had once described to a reporter after OPERATION TOMCAT.

The tracer rounds did not seem like fairies to the Blackshirts manning the gate. The stream of glowing bullets looked like certain death. The guards broke and ran for their lives.

Pounding through the gate, Maj. Randal could not restrain himself, "YEEEEEHAAAAAA!"

AT 0630 HOURS CAPTAIN THE LADY JANE SEABORN, Lieutenant Pamala Plum-Martin and Brandy Seaborn dragged themselves out of the elevator at the hotel they were using as their Nairobi Headquarters after a long night of partying at the Muthaiga Country Club. When they came to the door of the three-bedroom suite they were sharing, they noticed that the door was ajar. There was a light on inside the sitting room.

Lady Jane and Lt. Plum-Martin produced profusely engraved Walther PPK pistols from their handbags, startling Brandy, who had not known either was armed. She bought out her Beretta. Before they could enter, Major Lawrence Grand came to the door.

"Don't shoot. When you did not answer I let myself in," he explained. "Diligently pursuing your man, I see. Any chance you ladies are sober?"

"I am," Brandy laughed. "There are a lot of intoxicated plants at Muthaiga."

"The fern next to my table is probably going to be dead from Champagne poisoning by tomorrow," Lady Jane giggled.

"Were you pouring out your drinks?" Lt. Plum-Martin asked, surprised. She had been known to drink an entire squadron of hard-partying Battle of Britain fighter pilots under the table.

"Ladies," Maj. Grand announced without fanfare, "a message from Force N Rear in Khartoum has arrived within the hour. I wanted to deliver it personally. Tonight at approximately 0330 hours, a radio message claiming to be from Force N Advance Party was logged, giving coordinates to a DZ where a resupply drop can take place in two days' time."

The three women froze, dead still.

"The sender did not identify. However, as it happens Captain Mickey Duggan was pulling duty when the transmission came in. He recognized the hand of the radio/telegraph operator because a keystroke is like a fingerprint. Mickey says he taught the sender himself. He claims nobody could fake this message… says there is only one operator who can botch a key as bad.

"That, ladies, is John Randal."

16

THEY'RE MY SLAVES

MAJOR JOHN RANDAL, WALDO TREYWICK, BIMBASHI BUTCH "Headhunter" Hoolihan, Kaldi, and Cheap Bribe lay resting on their saddles out in the open savanna. They could see for miles in any direction. Rita Hayworth, Lana Turner and GG were holding the mules on tethers allowing them to graze. They were waiting for the RAF to arrive.

"Major, we got movement on that ridge line over yonder 'bout nine o'clock," Waldo called out as he continued to watch, never taking the Zeiss glasses he had borrowed from the Force N commander down from his eyes.

"I see it."

In the far distance a tiny black speck appeared out in the open. Several other dots appeared on the ridgeline behind it. Suddenly a green flare shot up, and the moment it began to arch down, a red flare followed. It was "Red over Green," the traditional Commando signal of "success."

"Saddle up," Maj. Randal ordered. "Let me have those glasses, Waldo."

As soon as he brought up the binoculars, a hand-held light in the distance began flashing the letter "N."

"Who are those people?" Bimbashi Hoolihan said in a concerned tone.

"Whoever it is they know who we are," Maj. Randal said. "Signal back with an "N, Butch."

The Royal Marine jumped up and started wigwagging the international Morse Code hand and arm signal for the letter designator of Force N. The immediate response was for the first tiny speck to start moving rapidly in their direction. Soon the black dot was recognizable as a man on a mule.

Sergeant Mike "March or Die" Mikkalis rode up to within hailing distance of the little group and called out "Remember Calais."

"I do, Sergeant," Maj. Randal said. "What the hell are you doing here?"

"Looking for you, sir," Sgt. Mikkalis said with a big grin. "We brought in your first supply of Springfield rifles and Maria Theresa silver thalers from the Sudan. Major, you are never in your life going to believe who is about to come riding over that ridge line leading the mule train."

When Captain "Geronimo" Joe McKoy rode up on his big blue mule "Georgie," it was difficult to determine who was the most surprised.

"Howdy, John," the handsome, silver-haired cowboy called out. He was looking tan and fit from weeks on the trail. "Holy smoke, is that you Waldo?"

The ex-slave had turned as pale as a sheet. "Yeah, it's me, 'W. O.' I was hopin' I'd never have to run into you again."

"Don't worry, Waldo I don't have any papers on you," Capt. McKoy said – only he did not sound quite convincing. "Should I?"

"You two know each other?" Maj. Randal asked.

"Back in the day when I was scoutin' for army headquarters with P.J. Pretorius, Joe was a' servin' in the same capacity with the 25th Royal Fusiliers. 'The Old and the Bold' – the craziest regiment that there ever was. Millionaires, lords, cowboys, movie stars, White Russian generals serving as privates, big game hunters – you name it, they had it," Waldo said. "Seems Joe had tracked a criminal all the way down the length of South America to Chile and over to Africa. He signed on when he heard his man had joined the 25th to try to get away from him.

"There weren't no way to get the outlaw out of the army and back to the U.S. of A. to stand trial, so old W.O. here just took him out in the brush on a two-man scout. Only Joe come back."

"W.O.?"

"Yeah – 'Widows and Orphans' McKoy. That's all that's left if W.O. ever gets on your trail – ain't never heard no 'Geronimo Joe' before."

"It's my stage name," Capt. McKoy said placidly. "The word is you was a mercenary working out here in Abyssinia. That true, Waldo?"

"Was, is right – for the last five years I been a slave. The Major emancipated me. Anything I ever done illegal, well, the statute of limitations has got to have done run out. Surely you can't be after me for poaching ivory off those damn Portuguese?"

"I'm not after you, Waldo."

"What are you doing here, Captain?" Maj. Randal said.

"I'm on vacation, John."

"Some holiday," Sgt. Mikkalis said. "We had to shoot our way through a solid wall of shifta. Not to mention a bloody Noah's Ark's worth of hungry animals that wanted to dine on us or the mules every step of the way."

"I brought you five hundred '03 Springfields with fifty thousand rounds of ammunition, twenty Hotchkiss light machine guns with another fifty thousand rounds, enough Maria Theresa thalers to open a well-heeled bank, and some other toys for big boys I just know you're going to get a real kick out of, John," Capt. McKoy said.

"Why are you here, Captain?" Maj. Randal said again.

"I'm your brand new Animal Transport Officer reporting in for duty. I know more about mules than any man in Africa. Baldie – General Taylor that is – signed me on."

Lieutenant Jack Merritt rode up and snapped a crisp parade-ground salute. "Good morning, sir."

"I thought you had more sense than to ever get mixed up with a crew like this, Jack," Maj. Randal said.

"Sir, Sergeant Mikkalis and I are absent without leave. Both of us more or less deserted our post. We are here to turn ourselves in."

"Consider yourselves under arrest," Maj. Randal said. "The punishment appropriate to the circumstances in this case will be an immediate award of the Military Cross for you, Sergeant Mikkalis and a bar added to yours, Lieutenant Merritt. That sound about right?"

"You cannot award me the MC, sir," Sgt. Mikkalis responded. "That's an officer's gong."

"That's right, Lieutenant, it is."

"Lieutenant?" the tough ex-Legionnaire said in alarm.

"You'll be the oldest one I ever saw."

"Sir, you would not do that to me! I hate officers!"

"Consider it already done. Don't blame me, Mike, you did it to yourself."

The first order of business was for Lt. Mikkalis to unpack his radio transmitter and send a message to Force N Rear announcing the link-up with the Force N Advance Party. The response came right back.

Maj. Randal was ordered to proceed at once to a location on the shore of Lake Ziway, to arrive no later than 1800 hours that evening. Since the lake was thirty miles distance, it was decided that a flying party consisting of Rita and Lana would ride to the lake with him while Waldo led the mule train to the high mountain rendezvous where the main body of Force N was waiting in hiding.

AFTER A HARD MARCH, MAJOR JOHN RANDAL AND THE TWO girls arrived on the shore of Lake Ziway. Dark had already fallen. When it gets dark in Abyssinia, it gets dark fast. Maj. Randal did as instructed and flashed his torch out into the lake, making the signal for the letter "N." Almost immediately a rubber raft appeared out of the night and grounded virtually at their feet. Two of his National Lifeboat Servicemen stepped out accompanied by two heavily-armed men he had never seen before.

"Climb in, Major. These men will take care of your mules. You have a plane to catch, sir," Lifeboat Serviceman Tom Tyler informed him. "A pleasure to see you again. We were afraid you might not be found, sir."

Maj. Randal and the two girls crawled in the raft. As soon as they were away from the shore a small outboard motor was cranked up and in no time they were in the middle of the lake pulling into a dark island. Italian opera music was playing over a loudspeaker. If they had arrived earlier they would have seen a flagpole flying the Italian flag. The idea was for anyone who flew over or paddled by to think it was an Italian outpost. Any intruder that came close enough to investigate would be summarily shot. The island was ringed with machine gun positions.

"What is this place?"

"This is N-2, your forward amphibious supply base, sir."

"I see."

They were motored straight to a waiting Walrus amphibious aircraft. Maj. Randal climbed aboard, followed by a couple of highly-dubious ex-body slaves. Neither Rita nor Lana had ever been on an airplane.

Squadron Leader Paddy Wilcox was sitting in the left seat, and he cranked up the engine the moment the three passengers were aboard. Maj. Randal sat in the right seat next to him. It took quite a bit of effort to get the two girls buckled into their safety belts in the back.

After a short takeoff run, the Walrus lifted off, skimmed across the surface of the lake and they were away in the inky black Abyssinian sky. Maj. Randal turned around and winked at Rita and Lana. The girl's eyes were as big as Maria Theresa thalers.

During the flight down the chain of lakes, Sqn. Ldr. Wilcox briefed him on the status of Camp Croc, the Commodore flying boats, the recruitment of Canadian bush pilots to fly them, and the two island bases N-1 and N-2 that had been established to leap-frog men and military stores forward into Abyssinia.

"This is a real barnstorming, flying-by-the-seat-of-your pants-type operation," Sqn. Ldr. Wilcox said enthusiastically. "It's the most fun I have ever had in an airplane. Major, I would not have missed this show for the world. When General Taylor requested I be sent out as your Air Officer, I took one look at the map, and I knew you already had it all figured out."

"Learned it from you, Paddy," Maj. Randal said.

"Major, I have to ask – why didn't you leave me detailed written instructions?"

"Why would I?" Maj. Randal said. "If flying up the chain of lakes turned out not to be the way to go, I knew you'd think of something else."

The Walrus flew direct to Camp Croc, refueled, then immediately took off again for the secret base outside of Nairobi where Major Sir Terry "Zorro" Stone was training his battalion of Abyssinian paratroopers.

They arrived in time to whisk Maj. Randal into a most secret briefing being held for the commanders of the forces that would be attacking into Abyssinia. Because of the great distance involved between their commands, this was the last chance the senior officers would have to coordinate directly with each other face-to-face before the operation kicked off

Present were Lieutenant General Sir Archibald Wavell, General Officer Commanding Middle East; Major General William Platt, "the Kaid," the Commander of the Northern pincher; Major General Alan Cunningham, Commanding, EAF, the Southern pincher, Commodore Richard "Dickey the Pirate" Seaborn; plus a number of senior aides, staff officers, and the RAF deputies for each commanding general.

Three brand new major generals, the commanders of the three divisions being formed in Kenya from the nine brigades that were now in-country, were sitting on the second row. Also present in the room were Lieutenant Colonel Dudley Clarke, Maj. Stone, Captain Taylor Corrigan, Captain Jeb Pelham-Davies, MC and Lieutenant "Pyro" Percy Stirling, MC. The two captains and Lt. Stirling were recently out from RF HQ at Seaborn House. Major General James "Baldie" Taylor conducted the briefing.

There was a stir in the room as everyone turned to stare when Maj. Randal quietly stepped inside from the rear and stood leaning against the back wall. He was wearing four ivory-handled pistols and carrying an ivory-handled whisk with a black lion's tail teaser. There was a fresh scar on his left cheek plainly visible beneath his short beard.

Other than the scar, Maj. Randal did not present the appearance of someone who had spent the last three months behind the lines on the run from the Italians, surrounded by hordes of homicidal Abyssinian shifta and a host of savage, man-eating animals. He looked tanned and fit. For a man given up for lost, now-returned-from-the-dead, he seemed relaxed, though as hard-edged as a Fairbairn fighting knife.

Maj. Gen. Taylor nodded to him and began the briefing. "The situation is roughly this – the Italians occupy Libya with approximately two hundred fifty thousand first-class, fully mechanized forces. In Italian East Africa are approximately three hundred fifty thousand troops consisting of National army units, Blackshirt units and Colonial native units – most of whom are veteran forces with long years of African service – led by Italian officers.

"Wedged between these two enemy strongholds, like a walnut in a nutcracker, is the Anglo Egyptian Sudan. There we currently have approximately thirty-two thousand men, all arms. Our immediate fear is that the Italians will attack simultaneously from both directions and crush us in a pincer movement. The possibility of this taking place sometime in the immediate future is very real. It should have happened months ago, and if does we lose the Suez Canal. Subsequently, Great Britain will be forced to abandon most of her African territories. For all practical purposes, we have already lost the Suez Canal because Italian naval and air forces operating out of bases along its coastline in Italian East Africa can interdict the Red Sea.

"The United States is preparing to initiate a program called Lend Lease. Under Lend Lease, the U.S. will provide Great Britain the war materials she needs to stay in the fight. However, unless the Red Sea can be declared a 'safe zone,' the U.S. will not allow its merchant marine ships to traverse it to the Suez Canal.

"That requirement dictates a land battle must be fought to clear the Italians from the banks of the Red Sea.

"Visualize Italian East Africa as an apple. We intend to slice it into three pieces.

"The first slice will be the much-heralded entry of the Emperor, the 2nd Ethiopian Battalion and the Frontier Battalion from the north supported by a camel caravan into Gojjam Providence with the stated goal to liberate the country and restore the King of Kings to his throne. The Emperor's return to Abyssinia is timed to draw the Italian's attention away from the Sudan.

"The second slice will be General Platt's attack on a line due east from Kassala through Kern to the all-important port of Massawa.

"The third slice will be from the south out of Kenya. General Cunningham will initially conduct a feint at Moyle, north of Lake Tana, to freeze the Italians in place – then turn and attack east along the coast, clearing in succession Brava, Merka and Mogadishu – then pivot, continuing the attack toward Harar up the rail line to Addis Ababa.

"At some point as yet to be determined, a naval force under the command of Commodore Seaborn will launch an amphibious task force out of Aden across the Red Sea to recapture Italian-occupied British Somaliland. Once that takes place, the primary military objective of the campaign will be accomplished.

"The Italians will have us badly outnumbered in operational aircraft and heavy artillery. They will be well dug in with heavily-fortified, mountainous positions in the north and protected by vast stretches of impenetrable waterless desert in the south. The Italian Army will also have the tremendous advantage of operating on short interior lines, able to shift reinforcements rapidly from one front to the other when and as desired.

"On paper there is no military reason to believe that we can defeat the Duke of Aosta. However, this fight will be fought in the field – not on paper – and we do have a few things working in our favor.

"The Italians have a vast area to defend. They are equipped with a largely road-bound army and there are only a few roads able to support military traffic. There is only one rail line in the entire country. The native population is generally not friendly to the Italian occupiers, and a large number of the fascist field troops are tied up on internal security operations at the present time. Finally, the Italians rely almost entirely on landline communications because they have very few radios.

"We are in the process of raising a guerrilla force – Force N – in the very center of the country under the command of Major John Randal. Force N will interdict the Italian road and railway system in order to prevent the enemy from being able to freely shift their forces from one battle front to the other along their interior lines, limiting that advantage. Force N is already doing a most excellent job of drawing Italian line units off defense of the border in order to chase them. There are currently at least one hundred twenty-five thousand Italian troops now operating in the interior guarding fixed locations and on anti-guerrilla patrol. Once Force N is up and running, it will be fair to expect that there will be a lot more – at least until the invasion begins. Every enemy soldier persuing Force N is one less you will have to fight.

"Maj. Randal, would you come forward at this time and brief us on the conditions inside the country and on the state of your current preparations to employ your guerrilla army to best advantage?"

Surprised to be singled out, Maj. Randal walked to the front of the room. He had not made any plans to conduct a briefing. Best, he decided, keep it short and simple.

"Force N is in the process of raising six mule-mounted companies presently being commanded by former NCOs from the King's African Rifles. We have an additional company of handpicked native personnel commanded by Bimbashi Butch 'Headhunter' Hoolihan. We also have a group, approximately battalion-strength, called the 'Bad Boys' made up of teenagers tasked to perform acts of sabotage. Recently they have been concentrating on setting road spikes to exploit the Italians' critical shortage of spare truck tires.

"The Italians instituted what they call 'Democratic Colonization.' They bring over civilians from Italy and set 'em up to farm large grants of land. Since the Blackshirts took the farmland away from the locals and gave it to white colonists, there's bitter resentment. The Italians have been forced to commit some of their combat troops to protect the settlers.

"Four weeks before you begin your attack, Force N will launch a widespread series of strikes targeted against these isolated farms. These raids will be designed to force the Blackshirts to siphon off even more combat troops to reinforce the units already tied down guarding the Democratic Colonization projects.

"Two weeks prior to the invasion, Force N will begin an intensive program of demolition raids against the railroad. Simultaneously we will carry out coordinated ambushes saturating the central road network. Once this phase begins, travel by rail or road will become problematic for military traffic.

"Forty-eight hours prior to the invasion, the Bad Boys will take down every phone line in the central part of the country... and ambush the wire cuts to inhibit repairs. This will be a wide-scale sabotage operation."

"Bloody preposterous!" Maj. Gen. Platt exploded, unable to constrain himself any longer. "Sounds like you are planning to win the campaign single-handed, Randal. Why not simply have your bloody bandits march on the capital and save us the trouble? Are you quite sure you have not left anything out? "

"Just this, sir," Maj. Randal said. "Before you kick off your operation, sir, Force N will conduct a raid on every airfield in South Central Abyssinia except for those located inside the major metropolitan areas. We intend to take out a good portion of the Italian air force on the ground."

The room grew uncomfortably silent at this pronouncement. Clearly, most of the senior officers wanted to believe him. With the exception of Lt. Gen. Wavell, however, the generals present had no experience employing guerrilla troops to augment conventional operations. They had nothing to judge by.

The Kaid sneered, "I took the trouble to read your book about the Confederate raider. Are you planning to operate like Mosby's Rangers and live off the land – or will you constantly be hounding my staff with demands for more and more of everything under the sun like that great bloody beggar, Wingate?"

Lt. Gen. Wavell glanced over his shoulder at his aide and raised an eyebrow. That officer leaned over to Maj. Gen. Platt's aide and whispered, "General Wavell desires a copy of that book."

"Absolutely, it's yours!"

"I don't need anything other than what has already been agreed on, sir – officers to command the indigenous troops, light weapons, ammunition and Maria Theresa thalers," Maj. Randal said.

"Any other questions, gentlemen?" Maj. Gen. Taylor asked, wanting to move things along in order to not have this get out of hand. "If not, I have one. Have you seen any indication of a Patriot revolt, the kind Major Wingate has been promising?"

"No, sir," Maj. Randal said. "You have Amhara, Tigreans, Shoans and the Galla – the major tribes, and they all hate each other. Within each tribe you have those who support the Italian occupation and those who oppose it. Anyone tells you the Abyssinians will rise up in a cohesive rebellion doesn't know what they're talking about."

Since that was exactly the opposite of what they were being told on a daily basis by Major Orde Wingate – to expect a major, unified uprising the moment the Emperor crossed the border into Abyssinia – this pronouncement was met by stony silence. Many of the generals may have despised Maj. Wingate for his outrageous personal habits and abrasive personality, but every senior officer in the room was hoping for the massive Patriot revolt he was predicting to help ease the way for the invasion.

The briefing continued for another hour with Maj. Randal being followed by Sqn. Ldr. Wilcox, who was followed by Major R.E. Cheesman, an intelligence expert on Abyssinia who had written a book on Lake Tana and the Blue Nile, who was followed by a logistics expert... and on and on.

Finally, Maj. Gen. Taylor concluded with the announcement that there would be a private conference of the three main commanders immediately after. Following that, Lt. Gen. Wavell, Maj. Gen. Cunningham and Cdre. Seaborn were scheduled to fly up to Lake Rudolf and inspect the operations at Camp Croc. Maj. Gen. Platt, the Kaid, had declined the opportunity and would be immediately returning to Khartoum. The rest of the officers were dismissed with the exception of Maj. Randal who was asked to remain outside in the event there were any more questions for him.

The happy reunion of Maj. Stone, the three RF officers and Maj. Randal was short-lived. When they moved out of the room onto the long breezeway outside, they found Captain the Lady Jane Seaborn in conversation with Rita and Lana.

The officers surrounding Maj. Randal suddenly felt a pressing need to be somewhere else and scattered with the alacrity if someone had shouted "Incoming."

Lady Jane stood up, "Hello, John."

She was without any question the most beautiful woman Maj. Randal had ever seen. The months in Abyssinia had in no way diminished her physical impact on him. The first time he met her he had known no other woman would ever do. As usual, when he was around her he could not think of one single thing to say.

"Are you going to say hello to me?"

"How are you, Jane?"

"I am well," she replied, reaching out and gently tracing the scar on his cheek with her finger. "Oh, John, I heard you were killed by a lion."

"Not yet," Maj. Randal said, fairly confident his I.Q. went down anytime they were within ten yards of each other.

"I have been talking to Rita and Lana," Lady Jane said. "What enchanting names."

"Watch yourself – they're priestesses in the Zār Cult, which makes them semi-extortionists."

"Really?"

"The way it works, the girls use magic to cure sick people, and then demand a monthly retainer or they'll uncure 'em."

"Rita and Lana tell me they are your concubines," Lady Jane informed him with a twinkle in her sea-green eyes.

"They're not concubines – they're my slaves," Maj. Randal said, realizing that did not sound right.

"The girls say you do not beat them very often or sleep with them enough," Lady Jane said. "How do you tell them apart?"

"Rita wears my Ranger's insignia," Maj. Randal said, wondering how his conversations with her always seemed to spiral out of control like this, and making plans to kill both girls first chance he got. "Lana wears Butch's Royal Marine globe and anchor."

"So I see," Lady Jane said. "Ever think they might switch pins?"

Rita and Lana, who had been following the exchange with the inquisitiveness of divorce attorneys, now suddenly found items of immediate interest elsewhere around the breezeway. Neither girl would look anywhere near his direction.

Before he could come up with a response, Lt. Gen. Wavell's aide stepped out in the hall and said, "Maj. Randal, the general requests your presence, sir."

"What language were you speaking to the girls in?" Maj. Randal asked as he turned to go.

"They speak fluent English, John."

Taking his arm, Lady Jane said in her soft, husky voice, "Be advised, Major, when I get you home you're going to pay a price for running off to Africa and making me worry so."

Maj. Randal found himself back in the briefing room where a purple-faced Maj. Gen. Platt was in the act of throwing the mother of all temper tantrums. The outburst was so fantastic it seemed as if the Kaid was a man possessed. Lt. Gen. Platt was literally foaming at the mouth, screaming incoherently, "I shall not have any want-to-be Lawrences anywhere near my area of operations! I will not tolerate it, I say!"

The officers in the briefing room were all embarrassed by the outburst. Being forced to witness the meltdown was an ugly experience. Anyone who has served in the military for any length time has seen their share of ranting and raving, but the Kaid's performance was truly impressive.

Maj. Gen. Taylor translated deadpan, "General Platt has elected to... ah... decline the services of Force N, Maj. Randal. Confine your guerrilla operations to the central region of the country and to the south in support of General Cunningham's attack out of Kenya. You are not to allow any of your indigenous troops within twenty kilometers of General Platt's front lines. Is that clear, Major?"

"Yes, sir."

When he went back out to the breezeway, Lady Jane had vanished. Rita and Lana were sitting in wicker chairs looking as innocent as cherubs. Well, he had a surprise in store for those two troublemakers.

The girls were going to Jump School.

17
ALL IS FAIR

MAJOR JOHN RANDAL PUT ON A PAIR OF BORROWED swimming trunks, strolled down the stairs of the Earl's house, then outside and across the road to the Muthaiga Country Club. Major Sir Terry "Zorro" Stone had arranged with Captain the Lord Joss Victor Hay, 22nd Earl of Errol, for Maj. Randal to use his spare bedroom while he was in Nairobi. The "World's Greatest Pouncer" had cheerfully evicted the current occupant, one of his old pals from Happy Valley, to make space for the visiting Commando officer.

"I stay there every weekend I am not on field maneuvers, old stick," Maj. Stone said. "The place comes equipped with revolving women. Joss is a splendid host with more girlfriends than he can possibly handle at any given time, and he is willing to share. Simply be careful not say anything to him you would not want to read in the newspapers. The man likes to kiss and tell."

Capt. Lord Hay's women were no exaggeration. Maj. Randal had been in the field for a long time. He was no longer engaged – if he ever had been.

Nothing had actually ever been formalized confirming the engagement before his intended fiancée's dead husband had turned up alive – which had a chilling effect on any plans along those lines. Now he was making up for lost time in a hurry, though he was trying to be semi-discreet. Captain the Lady Jane Seaborn was absent, but one of her relatives or girlfriends was in the area at all times.

A string of jaded ladies in slinky evening dress, invited and uninvited, dragged their furs up the steps to his quarters at Capt, Lord Hay's house. Sometimes they passed each other in the night. The Earl's house was that kind of place.

Women would show up in the late hours and announce themselves by scratching on the door to his bedroom with their lacquered nails. The place was like a nonstop adult frat party, only no one ever had to get up in the morning to go to class. The thing that impressed Maj. Randal was there were no regrets and a complete absence of drama. When a woman came to "The World's Greatest Pouncer's", she was not there to play canasta.

In the Sudan when Major General James "Baldie" Taylor was informed about the lodging arrangements, he immediately went into closed conference with Lieutenant Colonel Dudley Clarke, who was in from Cairo. The commander of A-Force saw an opportunity.

Together, the two officers cooked up a story that they wanted to introduce to the Earl in hopes the spy would pass it along to the Italian High Command in Addis Ababa.

Lt. Col. Clarke, the officer who had originally selected Maj. Randal to organize RF for pin-prick raids on the French Coast, flew on to Nairobi. On arrival, he took the Force N commander aside and briefed him in private on the importance of freely discussing certain of his experiences in Abyssinia with Capt. Lord Hay, putting heavy emphasis on his plan to go back shortly to continue raising a guerrilla army – with one noteworthy exception.

Under no circumstances was he to reveal to anyone the detail that IEA was to be invaded by Imperial Forces out of Kenya – that was Most Secret. Maj. Randal was instructed to mention that the Emperor was planning to make his return in the near future – coming in from the north out of the Sudan with the stated purpose of taking back his throne.

Maj. Randal was not informed that Capt. Lord Hay was a spy, or even that there was a spy. He did not have a need to know. The commander of Force N would be parachuting behind enemy lines soon where he might be captured and subjected to interrogation. If he did not possess information, he could not reveal it. That's how "Need to Know" works.

"Force N is no longer a completely covert operation, though certain aspects of it are still highly classified and quite probably always will be," Lt. Col. Clarke explained. "Never mention Camp Croc, N-1, N-2, or any of the details of how we are planning to supply you. We want the Wops' attention focused on Force N actions, not operational details."

"The idea is to keep the Italian High Command concerned about internal security. We want them to believe the Emperor's return to his country will signal a large-scale insurrection. Your story is that Force N is the advance party to pave the way for the Emperor's return – tell that to Lord Hay."

"I understand, sir," Maj. Randal said. "I work for the Emperor."

"Correct, we have good reason to believe the Italian's greatest fear is a general uprising of the natives led by a charismatic British officer – meaning you. We want the Blackshirt's attention focused on the return of the Emperor and you leading an uprising."

"Won't that tip our hand, sir?" Maj. Randal asked.

"No. The Italian High Command is anticipating a British-led insurgency," Lt. Col. Clarke explained. "We also know they *suspect* the Emperor might come in from the Sudan someday at the head of a Patriot column. Wingate keeps holding press conferences to that effect.

"The Eyeties also suspect we might invade out of the Sudan someday, but they have no idea we are even vaguely considering a southern pincer. We want to keep it that way. Our story is that the only reason we are building up troop strength in the colony is because we need to be able to defend the Kenyan border from *Italian* invasion."

"Got it, sir," Maj. Randal said.

"Never miss an opportunity to point out that the Abyssinian National Patriot Movement is primed like gun power," Lt. Col. Clarke ordered with a straight face, "waiting for the spark that will cause the entire country to explode into open rebellion."

"Roger that, sir," Maj. Randal said, knowing full well there was no Abyssinian National Patriotic Movement and there was not going to be any rebellion.

"If you tell enough people here in Nairobi what your intent is, they will gossip. Their servants will pick up on the story, and you can bet it will make its way back to Addis Ababa – mark my word," the A-Force commander lied. His misinformation target was Capt. Lord Hay. Only he could not tell that to Maj. Randal.

Lt. Col. Clarke also carefully coached Maj. Stone on his role in the deception. He was instructed to confide to Capt. Lord Hay the classified details of his upcoming combat mission in the strictest confidence after giving him the appropriate secret Etonian old boy handshake and wink, pledging the Earl to "never reveal what I am about to tell you to a soul."

The next evening, following Col. Clarke's orders to the letter, Maj. Stone confided to Capt. Lord Hay privately, "My paratroopers are standing by to launch. We go the very moment a wing of Royal Air Force Whitley troop transports arrive in Nairobi to fly us to our drop zone deep in Abyssinia.

"When you see those Whitleys come in, old stick, that's the signal all the hard work you have been doing at the Manpower Office is getting ready to pay off."

"I am still rather browned off at you for going around me to have so many of my best Kenyans assigned to your parachute battalion," Capt. Lord Hay sniffed, not evidencing the slightest interest in his new friend's future military adventures. "Quite unsporting to pinch them like that."

"All is fair in love and war," Maj. Stone replied cheerfully, hijacking Capt. Lord Hay's favorite idiom.

"That it is."

The details of the parachute operation were pure fiction. The purpose of the story was to trick the Earl into drawing the conclusion that there would, in fact, be an invasion of IEA out of Kenya despite all the evidence to the contrary. And that the arrival of a squadron of Whitleys would be the trip-wire for it to start. The idea was to lull him into waiting until the Whitleys actually landed in Kenya before triggering his "invasion imminent" alert to the Italians.

Military deception is a fine-run thing. Sometimes it is necessary to reveal the actual truth – cloaked in a believable lie – to the enemy in order to protect your main secret. In this case, the truth was that there was going to be an invasion out of Kenya. Maj. Stone was telling the Italian's man in Kenya that the British were coming from the south while every other fascist intelligence source in the Middle East was being fed the big lie that there was not going to be an attack from Kenya Colony. The primary secret was the actual date when the invasion was going to take place – it had to be protected at all costs.

The Whitley airplanes were a false indicator.

In fact, Maj. Randal and Maj. Stone were privately telling Capt. Lord Hay two completely different stories. What was the spy going to believe, that which he heard or that which he could see? The best guess was he would believe that which he could see – and what the Earl saw was Maj. Stone training paratroops. And he could also see that there were not enough troop transports to drop them except in penny packets, so the Whitley story made perfect sense.

Was he going to believe an American stranger or an Eton man? Well, that was a given – the old school tie trumped everything.

There was no wing of RAF Whitley troop transports en route to Nairobi and there never would be. The Earl would be waiting for a long time to send out his "invasion eminent" warning. By the time he realized there were no Whitleys, it would be too late. The southern pincer of the invasion would have already launched.

Lt. Col. Clarke was the world's reigning master of military deception, and he played for high stakes.

BRANDY SEABORN WAS LYING BESIDE THE POOL IN A TINY black swimsuit sipping a tall glass of iced mint tea brought to her by one of the pool boys as she waited for Major John Randal to join her poolside. There was a sizeable circle of men around the pool and a few in the clubhouse peeking out windows watching her watch for him.

The spectacular golden girl gasped when Maj. Randal removed the towel he had casually draped around his neck and tossed it on the back of the lounge chair next to her. The lion claw marks raked across the left side of his chest. Additionally, there was the pocked bullet hole from the Blue Duck. She had been there the night he was shot.

"You should see the lion, Brandy."

"Doubt he could look hurt much worse than you do, handsome."

"That's his tail on my riding crop."

Shortly, Lieutenant Pamala Plum-Martin, Lieutenant Penelope Honeycutt-Parker, RM and the sensational Clipper Girl, Red, arrived poolside. When they saw the scars they went "Oooooooh!"

Sexy Lt. Plum-Martin teased, "Pick those up in Istanbul?"

Maj. Randal shot her a look.

"Istanbul?" Brandy inquired with a raised eyebrow.

"Inside joke," Maj. Randal said.

"Your two slave girls are missing you, John," Lt. Plum-Martin laughed. "Karen and I have been swapping off escorting them through their parachute training. Mad Dog has them scheduled to make their first jump later today."

"I miss them too, Pam," Maj. Randal said, which was not entirely untrue. The two girls had been his constant companions for months. He felt strange not having them around.

Red, the Flying Clipper Girl, was responsible for Major Sir Terry "Zorro" Stone's banishment to the Middle East by personal diktat of His Majesty the King because of her behavior in the Life Guards Officer's Mess one memorial evening. Red had been discovered in the act of drinking a Black Strap – the official drink of the Life Guards – which regimental tradition stipulates must be drunk standing on your head.

That particular practice is not intended to extend to female guests. By some oversight, neither Maj. Stone nor any of his brother officers present at the time had remembered to mention to her that exception to the rule.

Red was now on the payroll of MI-6. When she was no longer needed in Kenya, the plan was for the Clipper Girl to return to flying status, where she would be free to travel the world under no cloud of suspicion that she was a British intelligence agent.

Statuesque Lt. Honeycutt-Parker was out from Seaborn House where she had been in charge of the women's Royal Marine detachment in Captain the Lady Jane Seaborn's absence. During the Dunkirk evacuation, she and Brandy had made five trips together in the Seaborn family houseboat to rescue troops. Her husband, a Royal Dragoon officer, was currently serving in the Cavalry Division in Palestine. Unknown to Maj. Randal or Lt. Honeycutt-Parker, he had recently volunteered for hazardous duty with Force N.

Lady Jane had recently departed for the United States, and the two women had been brought in to take her place shadowing Captain the Lord Joss Victor Hay.

The hunt for the Italian master spy had also been augmented by the addition of Lieutenant Commander Ian Fleming, RN, of the Naval Intelligence Division (NID). He had recently flown to Kenya Colony with Major Lawrence Grand and been press-ganged to serve on the pick-up surveillance team. Being a romantic and a ladies' man of some note in his own right, Fleming jumped at the chance for counterintelligence duty. The suave naval officer melded into the Muthaiga Country Club scene like a chameleon.

For his part, Maj. Randal was unaware that there *was* a counterintelligence operation.

Capt. Lord Hay was standing in the club lounge doing what every man in the establishment or around the grounds was doing right this minute – staring out at the pool gaping at the five stunningly beautiful women in skin-tight bathing suits and wondering what they could possibly see in Maj. Randal. The male membership of Muthaiga Country Club was literally counting the days until he parachuted back into Abyssinia. "Good luck, Godspeed, old boy, and do try not to return any time soon," was the prevailing attitude.

Unlike the other men, the Earl was relatively unfazed by the stunning sunbathers surrounding his houseguest. For one thing, with the exception of Brandy and Penelope, the girls were all too young for his taste. And in truth, those two also were. While he was conflicted about any woman who might possibly be better-looking than he was, Capt. Lord Hay planned to bag them all, if for no other reason than he could. Rules were made to be broken – even his own.

There was one person conspicuously absent at the pool – Lady Jane. The Italian's man in Kenya wondered where she might be. The fact that she had a relationship with Maj. Randal was widely known at Muthaiga, where there were few secrets. He would have expected her to be with him poolside.

Capt. Lord Hay knew Lady Jane's husband, Commander Mallory Seaborn, RN. When the HMS *Wind* had put in at Mombasa two years ago, her skipper had come up-country to Happy Valley to visit, spending a week at his house during the peak of the orgy season. He had been a star.

The Earl had pointedly not mentioned their acquaintance to her. He planned to reveal that detail when the time was ripe for the picking, to throw her off balance emotionally before he pounced. That's how the World's Greatest Pouncer operated – every move planned in advance with military precision.

At 1230 hours Maj. Randal was joined poolside by Lieutenant "Pyro" Percy Stirling, Captain Taylor Corrigan and Captain Jeb Pelham-Davies. The officers agreed to meet in the lounge. Since swimsuits were not allowed in the club, Maj. Randal walked back over to the Earl's house and changed into uniform before heading back to meet his officers for a light lunch.

Muthaiga Country Club was particular about its dress code.

The Commandos selected a private but highly visible corner of the lounge where they could be seen but not overheard... well, maybe a little. Maps were produced, and Maj. Randal made a great show of briefing his three officers on their upcoming mission. In fact, this had already been done in private and the performance today was a charade orchestrated by Lieutenant Colonel Dudley Clarke.

That being said, Maj. Randal was not going to waste the opportunity to go over the plans with his key officers one more time.

"Any of you men interested in the position of being my executive officer?" Maj. Randal casually inquired. "Thought not. In that case – Taylor, you and Jeb are slated to command irregular guerrilla mule battalions.

"You two men will operate south and east of the capital. Right now we have six companies formed under long-service King's African Rifles NCOs and a small company commanded by Butch Hoolihan.

"Jack Merritt has two platoons of Sudanese that will be expanded into a company, and Mike Mikkalis has a company of mercenaries that will be expanded into a battalion – the '1st Mercs.' Harry Shelby has a company of ex-Blackshirt Abyssinians called 'Shelby's Scouts.' He has been using them for security duties at Camp Croc, N-1 and N-2. They should be available to deploy up-country as soon as replacements for them can be brought forward.

"Percy, you will have a roving demolitions job operating primarily against the rail system. A promotion to go with it. Congratulations, Captain.

"That means the six companies we've raised will all be assigned to your guerrilla battalions, three each. You will be expected to raise three more companies from volunteers in your area of operations. When you do, reorganize your command to your own liking.

"Getting the two battalions formed in the field will be our first order of business when you arrive in-country. Terry has recruited some hostilities-only officers locally, and others will be coming in from the Sudan. Volunteers have been going through a school run by RF personnel outside of Khartoum. The ones selected should begin arriving in the next few days.

"You're going to have to make do with what we have, which is Cavalry Division volunteers, locally recruited explorers, big-game hunters, mercenaries, farmers and the like, all given the rank of Bimbashi in the event they do not already hold a commission. They're men who have experience in Africa but not necessarily formal military training. There's a real leadership challenge ahead of you.

"Commission your strong NCOs – I have the authority to make Bimbashis out of anyone worthy. Use your best judgment. Don't hesitate to take a chance and do not get hung up on who has date of rank. Promote your best combat leaders.

"Soldiers apply for special service for a variety of reasons – not always because they want to see action. My guess is we're going to discover a fair share of bad apples in this volunteer O group. When you do, get rid of 'em. I don't care who they are or what their pedigree is. I'll back you up.

"The natives you're going to command are good in the attack but excitable. You can't order them out on operations. You have to lead them from the front. They like to follow what they call a '*tillik sau,*' meaning big shot. Act like one – it goes with the job.

"The kind of missions you can expect will be small-scale raids and road ambushes – most of them of your own choosing, unless from time to time I send you a codeword target; then you'll drop whatever you're doing and execute it. You'll be operating independently for the most part, and you'll be breaking your battalions down into company-sized elements responsible for operating over a wide-ranging area. Within your AO you have absolute authority.

"When you take the field, you men are going to become warrior kings."

The Commandos listened as if hypnotized, though they had heard all this before. Maj. Randal was giving them the assignment every officer dreams about – an independent combat command with little to no interference from higher authority and virtually unlimited powers.

They would have jumped into hell with him.

Turning to Capt. Stirling, Maj. Randal said, "You remember what they said after the Blackshirts took control in Italy?"

"That Mussolini made the trains run on time, sir?"

"They make that brag in Abyssinia, too, but you're the little boy who's going put a stop to it, Percy."

"Roger that, sir!"

"There's a single rail line that services the entire country all the way from Addis Ababa to the Red Sea," Maj. Randal said. "It's all yours to take down – about a thousand miles worth. Have you given any thought on what you're going to need to accomplish your mission?"

"After a perfunctory map study, sir, I believe the best way to neutralize the railroad is to divide it into three sections approximately three hundred-plus miles in length. My plan is to organize three demolition parties – each augmented by a platoon of hard-hitting mule cavalry – and assign each one their own individual section of track to work over.

"We can blow every bridge, railway trestle and culvert in Abyssinia and we can cut the rail line at will, but the Italians are good railway men. To prevent them from making rapid repairs, we need to ambush our cuts. My plan is to blow the rail line, hit the repair parties when they show up, and run."

"You'll get your three guerrilla platoons," Maj. Randal said.

"Major, in that case, the Italians' trains will not only be late – there won't be any trains running at all."

"That's why I sent for you by name, stud," Maj. Randal said. "That goes for all of you. Never forget, 'Right Man Right Job.' And gentlemen, that means Raiding Forces personnel in all the key positions. Is that clear?"

"Clear, sir," the three officers chorused.

"We jump into Abyssinia before sunrise tomorrow."

18
PREGNANT GUPPY

WHILE THE COUNTERINTELLIGENCE OPERATION IN NAIROBI continued without her, Captain the Lady Jane Seaborn was making her way across the Atlantic by air to recruit aircraft mechanics willing to travel to Kenya to service the three Commodore flying boats. The long, hard service seaplanes were literally flying themselves to pieces, and there were no specialist amphibious aircraft mechanics available to perform maintenance on them.

Preliminary arrangements had been made for her to attempt to hire private contract mechanics from the Consolidated Aircraft Corporation located in San Diego, California. Lady Jane also intended to negotiate a private purchase of spare airplane parts to be shipped via Mombasa.

After a flight halfway around the world, Lady Jane was met at the San Diego Airport by a representative from the British Consular Office, Mr. Derek Chatham-Weatherford. She was whisked directly to the Consolidated Aircraft Corporation headquarters in an official car. Consolidated had been founded by an abrasive, hard-nosed businessman, Ruben Hollis Fleet. On the side of the Consolidated plant, printed nine feet tall and four hundred eighty feet long, was his company motto – "NOTHING SHORT OF RIGHT IS RIGHT." She thought it hard to find fault with the man's work ethic. Clearly, every employee in the company knew exactly where the founder stood on the subject of quality control.

Consolidated built the PBY Catalina Flying Boat. The company had sold and delivered two hundred of them to the U.S. Navy, but in 1940, with isolationist policies being the driving force behind all American politics, there were no new orders on the horizon.

Ruben Fleet had no idea who Lady Jane was. When the British Ambassador in Washington had called him personally out of the clear blue sky to set up the appointment, it had come as a complete surprise. The purpose of the meeting was not entirely clear to him. He hoped she might have some connection to the RAF. He would dearly love to sell airplanes to the RAF.

When the mahogany-haired beauty swept into his office he was surprised to find she was so young. She was wearing a uniform that bore the insignia of the Royal Marines. Ruben Fleet had enough experience with the British military from contract negotiations to recognize the insignia, but he had not been aware until now that the Royal Marines had a women's auxiliary. Maybe the Marines could use PBYs.

Lady Jane did not waste time. "Mr. Fleet, I am here to seek your assistance in hiring contract mechanics willing to travel to Kenya for a minimum of six months to perform maintenance on a small flight of Commodore flying boats."

"Lady Seaborn, I doubt you couldn't have asked me for anything I am less inclined to do. My mechanics are all committed to servicing existing contracts. It's our bread and butter."

Undeterred, Lady Jane said, "I am also here to purchase spare parts for the Commodores."

"We'll be delighted to sell you all the spares you need. Consolidated is in the business of selling airplanes and parts," the businessman said, having no wish to be rude to the woman. "However, trained mechanics with the ability to work on both boat hulls and airplanes, the requisite two skills necessary to repair Commodores, are as rare as golden eggs.

"Ours are all tied up on contract helping train the U.S. Navy to transition into maintaining its fleet of PBYs on its own. I'm afraid finding mechanics to travel out to Africa at this time would be out of the question."

"Mr. Chatham-Weatherford is here with me to negotiate the purchase of a squadron of Catalinas equipped for anti-submarine convoy patrol for the Royal Navy," Lady Jane said. "Provided you supply the mechanics and parts I need for the Commodores.

"Failing that, Mr. Fleet, I wish to arrange a time for my U.S. business manager to fly out from New York to work out the details necessary to purchase Consolidated Aircraft Corporation. You are a publicly-traded company, and should you decline to sell, we are quite prepared to initiate a hostile takeover."

"*You* want to buy my company?"

"No, but I will if you refuse to supply me with the mechanics I require," Lady Jane said in a take-no-prisoners tone.

"Forgive me for my straightforwardness, Mr. Fleet. I have traveled a long distance, time is short, and 'no' is not an acceptable answer. My presence is required back in Kenya immediately – so we need to resolve the issue of mechanics quickly."

Owning an airplane manufacturing company was Ruben Fleet's life. His company was not for sale, but if they did not sell some airplanes soon it would be – or bankrupt. Offering him the chance to sell a squadron's worth of Catalinas (he believed there were fifteen aircraft in a RN squadron... he would have to check that detail) was like throwing a drowning man a life raft.

The aircraft manufacturing industry was feast or famine. With the entire world at war, the U.S. had decided to sit this one out. The British were broke, and he could not – and would not – sell to the Axis Powers. He wondered if his visitor was aware that Consolidated was in financial straits. Odds were she did – he would bet on it.

"What sort of mission are the Commodores flying, Lady Seaborn?"

"They work out of a primitive base supplying a guerrilla army operating behind enemy lines," Lady Jane said. "The Commodores fly around the clock and are starting to develop serious maintenance problems."

"How many of our Commodores do you have operational?"

"Three. We purchased them from the Rio Tinto Mining Company in Brazil."

"Ouch!" Ruben said. "Those are hard-service aircraft, prototypes – probably had the worst maintenance program imaginable down there in Latin America."

"We are at the point of having to cannibalize one of them to keep the other two flying," Lady Jane said. "We need your help, Mr. Fleet."

"How about this, Lady Seaborn. You arrange to let me sell Mr. Chatham-Weatherford a squadron of Catalinas for the Royal Navy. Then I will draft a separate contract, contingent on that sale, for spare parts and have Consolidated Aircraft Corporation mechanics come out to set up a maintenance program for you in Kenya. We will supply the personnel to run it for six months – after that we renegotiate."

"Splendid!"

A lightbulb flashed in the airplane company founder's brain. He was a chief executive officer highly respected for being fast on his feet. Consolidated had already designed and manufactured several prototypes to be the PBY Catalina's successor – designated the Model 31 – it was the best amphibious airplane in the world.

The problem was, the U.S. Navy refused to buy Model 31s even though they were vastly superior to the PBY. The Navy did not want to pollute its supply line for the two hundred PBYs already in inventory by adding additional parts for another type aircraft to it. The U.S. Navy understood logistics and the importance of keeping it short and simple.

Maybe if the British saw the Model 31 in action they might be interested.

The new plane was state-of-the-art design. Its advanced body style was able to carry a maximum amount of cargo, was easy to load and offload quickly, was revolutionary, and would influence transport aircraft design far into the future. The Model 31's engines were so powerful that they were being considered to run the Top Secret U.S. Air Corps B-29 Superfortress currently under development.

Because of its powerful engines and a short wingspan of a revolutionary new design, the Model 31 was extremely versatile – able to take off in as short a distance on the water as it could on land, even with a heavy payload. In addition, it was a true amphibian – meaning capable of landing on either land or water. For the kind of operations Lady Jane had described, it was perfect.

"How are you planning on returning to Kenya?"

"By commercial air."

"What if I were to offer you our newest, most modern amphibian to fly you and the team of Consolidated mechanics out to Kenya?" Ruben said grandly, "Then I could allow you to keep the plane and crew on loan as a demonstrator. Between the two of us, I know the President is getting ready to announce a program called 'Lend Lease' any day now. We'll jump the gun here and have our own little version of lend but no lease."

"I think that would be marvelous, Mr. Fleet. Tell me about the new airplane."

"The aircraft is officially designated the Model 31 – however, around here we all fondly refer to it as the 'Pregnant Guppy.' It's light-years ahead of any other amphibious aircraft."

"What a quaint name."

"Well, that's exactly what the plane looks like. You'll understand the moment you lay eyes it."

"How long will it take for you to fit it with static lines?" Lady Jane asked.

"Static lines?"

"The cable parachutists hook their snap links to that automatically activates the rip cord to deploy the parachute."

"Not long," Ruben responded. He was not completely sure he knew what a static line actually consisted of – a steel cable most likely. The United States Army did not have parachute units, though they were reported to have organized a Test Platoon at Fort Benning experimenting with parachute jumping. They might know the answer. "I'll have my chief engineer get right to work installing them."

No one had ever suggested parachuting troops out of a flying boat, at least not to him. Maybe there was a future in it. The idea might make money or help market his airplanes by giving them another capability. He wondered if he could get a patent on it.

"There is one small request."

"Request?" Ruben froze, feeling sick to his stomach. This was generally how deal-killers sounded when they were tossed out at the last minute, coy and innocent. He really needed to make this contract happen. If not, he probably was going to be working for her.

"Would you paint the Pregnant Guppy black for me?" Lady Jane said, lighting off one of her heart attack smiles. "Her destiny is to be a creature of the night."

"Consider it done!"

Ruben Fleet was a battle-scarred executive, particularly good around acquisitions and mergers and a hard man to put one over on. He had phenomenal instincts. The businessman sensed Lady Jane was emotionally invested in the outcome of the negotiations, too much for it to be a straight-up government contract. She had to have an angle.

He wondered what it was.

The answer was simple, though Ruben Fleet would never ever hear it. If the Commodores did not keep flying, Major John Randal's Force N would be cut off with no way to be resupplied. Once the invasion of Abyssinia began, as the Italian Army folded back in on Addis Ababa, attacked by armies from two directions, his small guerrilla army would gradually be surrounded by hundreds of thousands of enemy troops in an ever-tightening noose. If some way could not be found to adequately resupply it by air, Force N would eventually be overwhelmed.

Lady Jane was prepared to do whatever was necessary to prevent that from happening. Randal's Rule for Raiding laid down 'The first rule is there ain't no rules.' And that meant, under present circumstances, she was prepared to crush anyone who stood in the way of her getting the aircraft mechanics and spare parts needed to keep the Commodores in the air.

Fortunately, she did not have to. This was the first business negotiation she had ever conducted. It had not seemed all that difficult. Did Lady Jane have what it took to be a cutthroat businesswoman? She thought not. Then again… she *had* Tommy-gunned a BMW full of Nazi pilots outside the Blue Duck. That had been out of character.

And they were stone dead.

19

TYRANNOSAURUS CROC

MAJOR JOHN RANDAL TROTTED TO THE WAITING WALRUS followed by Rita Hayworth and Lana Turner. Captain Roy "Mad Dog" Reupart, late of the Army Physical Training Corps and No.1 British Parachute School before joining RF, was waiting by the steps to the airplane. The Walrus's motor was kicking up red dust off the dirt road that it was using as an airstrip. The little bi-plane with the unwieldy motor bolted on top of the fuselage was a true amphibian – it could set down on land or water.

This was the girls' first parachute jump. The plan was to make five training jumps this afternoon, one right after the other, then take off for the return flight to Camp Croc and then on to Abyssinia. Maj. Randal hoped the girls were as anxious about it as he was. He had never liked heights, and no matter how many times he jumped, that pre-jump knot in his stomach showed up every single time. He had thought it would eventually have gone away over time – but it never did.

"Ready, ladies?" Capt. Reupart bellowed over the roar of the pusher engine overhead. "When I give the command 'GO,' Maj. Randal will exit the aircraft. Rita, you will immediately move up into the door and take his place. I will give you an individual command to 'GO.' Is that clear?"

To Maj. Randal's astonishment the ex-slave girl quickly responded, "Clear, Captain Mad Dog!"

"Lana, when Rita exits the aircraft you will immediately move up to the door and take her place. I will then give you the individual command to 'GO.' Is that clear?"

"Clear, Captain Mad Dog!"

"Make me proud."

The little airplane roared to life, raced down the dirt road and leapt into the air. The pilot did a quick racetrack, gaining altitude, then leveling out and flying parallel to the straight stretch of the road where they had taken off. The landing zone (LZ) they were jumping into was a cleared field next to the road. The pilot would land, they would immediately strap on new parachutes and re-board for their next jump. Lieutenant Karen Montgomery was on hand with a truckload of parachutes for the five scheduled jumps.

Capt. Reupart hung out the door of the Walrus, then swung back inside and immediately motioned for Maj. Randal to take up his position. The girls had tight, serious looks on their chiseled faces. Maj. Randal gave them a wink then moved to the door.

"GO!"

As usual, the adrenalin kicked in when he made his exit. After the X-type parachute deployed, Maj. Randal performed the automatic motion of checking his canopy. He could see both of the girls had come out hard on his heels. No hesitation on their part. The two Zār priestesses must have ice water running through their veins.

But then, he already knew that.

Three hours and four more jumps later, they boarded the Hudson bomber that Lieutenant General Sir Archibald Wavell had loaned Captain the Lady Jane Seaborn and took off for Camp Croc. The GOC's personal pilot was in the left seat. Flying co-pilot was Squadron Leader Paddy Wilcox, who had bumped the regular occupant of the right seat for this mission.

On board were Maj. Randal, his two ex-slave girls, Captain Taylor Corrigan, Captain Jeb Pelham-Davies, Captain "Pyro" Percy Stirling – the legendary destroyer of lighthouses – and five handpicked subalterns from the Cavalry Division who had volunteered for duty with Force N. The Hudson rolled out, headed north. Rita Hayworth and Lana Turner, exhausted from their five jumps, curled up clutching their Carcano carbines and went straight to sleep. Maj. Randal went up to the cockpit and spent the entire trip going over the current state of Force N air operations with Sqn. Ldr. Wilcox.

When they arrived at Camp Croc, the Hudson landed on the black, crushed-lava airstrip. Using Turkana labor, it had originally been constructed by Lady Jane's father for his Nile perch-fishing camp. Captain Harry Shelby was at the strip to greet the plane. He immediately buttonholed Maj. Randal as he stepped off the aircraft.

"I want a fighting command, sir," the Sherwood Forrester's officer informed him. "Maj. Stone can detail one of the colonial officers to take over my security duties. There is no way I am going to sit out this entire campaign guarding supply bases, even if they *are* behind enemy lines, sir."

"I don't have a command to give you until we can replace your men at N-1 and N-2," Maj. Randal said as they walked off the airstrip. "But we'll form one. Get your gear – you can jump in with us tonight. We'll call your outfit 'Harry's Hell Raisers!'"

"Major, has anyone ever called you a poet?"

"No, Harry, they never have."

Sqn. Ldr. Wilcox turned out the pilots to meet the Force N commanding officer. The Canadians were not the kind of men who appreciated being "turned out." The bush pilots, dressed in their Hawaiian shirts, baseball caps and tear-drop Ray-Ban aviator glasses, reminded Maj. Randal of the Gold Coast tugboat skippers who had transported RF during the raid on Rio Bonita, only cooler. The bush pilots saw themselves as dashing flyboys even though they were now middle-aged, well past their prime.

Maj. Randal performed the obligatory pistol demonstration, shooting a capital "C" for Camp Croc in a large, rusted tin square that was immediately nailed up on the wall of the main building. The pilots seemed suitably impressed with the pistol work until one challenged, "Shootin' targets is one thing, Major, how you reckon you'd do on big lizards?"

These were pilots who flew rich trophy hunters into remote mountain lakes armed with an exotic variety of the latest elk and big-horned sheep rifles. They had seen men who could shoot quarter-sized patterns on paper targets fail to fill their licenses time and time again. There is quite a bit of difference between shooting targets and bagging a trophy. Besides, it was a trick question. Everyone at Camp Croc knew it was impossible to kill a crocodile with a pistol. The bush pilots had been trying every single night for months.

The group strolled down to the edge of Lake Rudolf, which was uncommonly green in the twilight. There were always crocs lying offshore, semi-submerged with only the humps of their eyes showing above the water, studying the activity at the camp. They were just waiting for someone to do something stupid.

Since the pilots had started their shooting safaris, the giant reptiles stayed considerably more distant from the land than they had in the past. Previously, they had lurked inches off the bank waiting to leap out, snatch a victim and haul it down to their underwater lair.

One set of giant yellow eyes periscoped from what was obviously a monster reptile lying about fifty yards offshore. The crocodile was a veteran of the shooting safaris, a giant affectionately known to the pilots as "Tyrannosaurus Croc", or "T-Croc" for short. Depending on how much the men doing the guessing had been drinking, T-Croc had variously been estimated anywhere from twenty-five to thirty feet, though that was clearly impossible.

Crocodiles never grow that large.

Maj. Randal produced one of his ivory-handled Colt .38 Supers and took up a relaxed two-handed stance. To kill a crocodile you had to shoot it dead-on in the brain, in a tiny spot the size of a tea cup located slightly above and behind the eyes.

"Nobody can hit a croc with a handgun from that far!" one of the pilots said as the Force N commander settled into a shooting position.

BOOOMMMMM!

The Colt .38 Super is a wonderfully flat-shooting pistol cartridge designed to penetrate the engine block of speeding automobiles. The round smacked into the huge crocodile right above and behind the ears, turning its brain into jelly, killing the monster instantly. The only response to the shot was a sharp meaty *Whaaap!* when the high-velocity bullet struck. T-Croc never moved an inch. The giant reptile simply floated, dead in the water.

The crocodile did not even flap its giant tail.

The bush pilots stood in silence. Not one of them had ever killed a single crocodile in all their many nights and hundreds of rounds expended trying. Two of the Life Boat Service Ratings piled into a rubber raft and paddled out to secure the dead reptile. The skin was worthless because of the concentration of salt in the water; however, they planned to nail T-Croc's hide up on the wall of one of the buildings as a trophy.

The pilots showed a particular interest in Maj. Randal's 9mm Beretta MAB-38A submachine gun. The aviators all agreed they would love to have one stashed in their cockpits when they flew into IEA. In the event they developed engine trouble and had to make a forced landing, it might come in handy. They had all heard the stories about what the shifta liked to do to downed pilots. Abyssinians were known to waste no time trying to distinguish between friend and foe – they just went to work with their spears and knives.

"I'll send some down for you, men," Maj. Randal said.

When it was time, the party going up-country boarded the Hudson and roared off into the moonlit night. Instead of the plush accommodations the plane had boasted when it was flying a theatre commander, now there were only canvas fold-down benches running down both sides of the fuselage. Maj. Randal gathered his new subalterns around him and spent most of the trip getting to know them, briefing the men on conditions inside the country and detailing the types of operations that they could expect to be conducting.

Once they arrived, there was not going to be a lot of time to get oriented. He wanted them to hit the ground running. The Force N officers could expect to be assigned to their troops one day and dispatched on operations the next.

Capt. Reupart came back from the cockpit, went to the tail of the airplane and opened the door on the left side of the fuselage and tied it down. The wind howled in.

"Ten minutes!" he bellowed over the howling and the roar of the engines. The plane banked and rolled in on its final approach. The release point was in sight ahead. Far in the distance a glimmering light could be seen on the DZ. As the plane droned, the light became recognizable as a series of small fires built so that they formed a giant "N."

Maj. Randal stood up in his parachute and waddled back to where Capt. Reupart was standing. He was moving in what was known as the "Airborne Shuffle," never raising his boots off the floor so he would not trip. Movement was not easy in the heavy parachute plus the equipment he would be jumping.

"Do not forget, sir, you bloody-well promised me a position in the field."

"Don't worry, Mad Dog," Maj. Randal said. "Maj. Stone and I are arguing over who's going to get you. It's your call."

"Sir, in that event, it shall be my pleasure to inform Sir Terry I have been assigned to Force N HQ."

"I'll expect you in-country within the next two weeks."

"Thanks, Major," Capt. Reupart, said. "Six minutes, sir."

"Stand up and hook up," Maj. Randal ordered, turning to the parachutists. This was the first time he had jumped from the door of an airplane standing up and he liked the way it felt a lot better than exiting through a hole in the floor. The jump commands were slightly different. Capt. Reupart had rehearsed them with him at Camp Croc before takeoff.

Lana Turner and Rita Hayworth were going to be following him out the door with the rest of the officers in the stick behind them. Maj. Randal gave the ex-slave girls a thumb's up. The two had not shown any reluctance to jump, but he knew they had to have butterflies in their stomachs. He sure did.

"Check static line!" he shouted, as he rattled his static line and jerked on it to make sure it was locked tight on the steel cable running down the roof of the fuselage and that the safety pin was through the hole and bent down on the far side. The sound of metal rasping on metal filled the aircraft.

"Check your equipment!"

Maj. Randal turned back to the door, braced both feet on either side and grabbed the inside rim of the door above his head on either side. Standing in the door spread eagle, like a gingerbread man, he arched his back until he was outside the airplane. Up ahead he could see the letter "N" burning clearly on the DZ. The wind was howling, making his eyes water and distorting his facial features. He swung back inside.

"Sound off for equipment check!"

"OK, OK, OK,...."

"Close on the door!"

The jumpers all shuffled forward until they were pressing against each other, packed together like sardines. Maj. Randal looked them all over, then turned back to the door. He braced himself again, only this time his hands were outside the door on the skin of the airframe, palms down flat.

When the brightly burning "N" was one inch in front of his right boot he leaned back inside and shouted, "Let's Go!"

Then he vigorously thrust himself out the door, feet and knees together with his head down. The prop blast from the powerful propellers tumbled him in a raging river of turbulent air – then he heard the whishing sound as the static line deployed the canopy, and he felt a gentle tug as the silk parachute popped open. He was suddenly riding easy in the saddle of the harness of his X-chute.

The stars were shining bright – the night was clear and cool. Maj. Randal had always been afraid of heights, but loved the exhilaration of jumping at night. He could see people on the ground standing around the fire as he drifted in, slipping forward for a rare change. On most of his jumps, for some reason he usually came in backwards.

He remembered to relax his legs and wobbled his boots to make sure his feet and knees were together, knees *not* locked. Landing with locked knees was a sure way to break something he did not want to break. The ground blazed below him, then he was down and rolling, keeping his elbows tucked in tight, making a picture-perfect five point of contact landing fall exactly like they had taught him at No.1 British Parachute School.

Bouncing up immediately, he quickly recovered his parachute. Suddenly, Bimbashi Butch Hoolihan was at his side. Maj. Randal hammered the quick release on his chest, dropping his harness on the ground. "Assume the position of attention, Butch."

"Sir!"

Maj. Randal reached inside the pocket of his sand green parachute smock and produced a set of single diamond rank insignia. He walked over to the young Royal Marine who was virtually quivering while standing at a rigid position of attention. "There are five lieutenants landing on this drop zone tonight, Butch, so we have to get this over with in a hurry." He pinned a diamond insignia on the epaulet on each shoulder. In the dark the former Royal Marine private could not see what was happening.

"Congratulations, Lieutenant."

"Lieutenant?"

"Yeah, it's permanent, Butch," Maj. Randal informed him. "Just don't tell anyone when it happened. I don't want any of these new arrivals to try to pull grade on you because they have date of rank."

Lieutenant Butch "Headhunter" Hoolihan felt weak in the knees. Bimbashi was a temporary rank. He had been expecting to revert back to private once this operation was over, though he had hoped the major might promote him to corporal. To become a permanent grade officer was something he had never considered, even in his wildest imagination. Jack Merritt had done it, but he was probably the best soldier in the entire army. This was unbelievable.

And the way it happened was fantastic. The melodrama was typical of Maj. Randal. During the jump on *TOMCAT*, right the middle of the raid with a firefight raging, the major had pinned his parachute wings on him. No other officer he had heard of had ever done anything like that.

"Battlefield commission," Maj. Randal said. "It doesn't get any better than that, stud."

"You must be desperate, sir."

"Is March or Die on the ground tonight?"

"Right here, Major," the gravelly voice of his former Swamp Fox Force senior NCO responded as he stepped out of the dark. "Have a nice relaxing vacation, Major?"

"Stand at attention there, Mike!"

"Sir!"

Maj. Randal produced a set of three-diamond insignia from his sand green parachute smock. "On behalf of His Majesty's Government, the King, the House of Lords or whatever else they credit at a time like this, I'm promoting you to the acting grade of Captain. I intend for you to be one of my battalion commanders and you can't do it as an acting Lieutenant."

"Sir, did the Major land on his head?"

"Probably," Maj. Randal said. "With this temporary rank goes a permanent promotion to the grade of Lieutenant. I will promote all three of your Foreign Legion corporals to Bimbashi. We're going to expand Mikkalis' Mercs to battalion strength – the 1st Mercs – and they'll be commanding companies if you so choose."

"Major, have you gone completely off your rocker? Me – officer material?" the tough-as-nails King's Royal Rifle Corps (KRRC) sergeant said. "I knew you were going to be trouble from the day you showed up in Calais."

"You can thank me later, Captain."

When Maj. Randal moved off to check on Rita and Lana, Lt. Hoolihan confided to Captain Mike "March or Die" Mikkalis, "The major looked like trouble to me, too, the day on the train when he pulled me out of a lounge car to guard his private compartment. Nothing in my life has ever been quite the same since."

"Butch," Capt. Mikkaliis said, "my guess is we will probably make the two worst officers in the history of British Forces."

Waldo was holding the reins to Parachute and the girls' mules. He had brought additional saddle animals for the arriving officers. After securing all the equipment containers, everyone mounted up and rode high into the rugged mountains for four hard hours. Maj. Randal was surprised at how good it felt to be back.

When they rode into the Force N mountain base camp, it was bustling with activity. Sqn. Ldr. Wilcox had been pushing men and equipment up the line hard and fast in the five days he had been gone. A dozen new officers and an equal number of other ranks had arrived since he left. M-1903 A-1 Springfield rifles were being issued as fast as they could be uncrated. Hotchkiss LMGs had also begun to arrive. Two were authorized per mule company, each operated by a British corporal or sergeant machine gunner extensively trained in the care and maintenance of the notoriously unreliable weapon.

While Maj. Randal had been away, Captain Mickey Duggan had flown in to take up the post of Force N communications officer. He was quickly becoming the busiest man in the command. Without question, the Royal Marine signaler was the single most valuable person in the unit. Coded messages were pouring in at all hours, night and day. The former Royal Marine sergeant and hero of Swamp Fox Force at Calais brought with him additional radios and a team of radio operators supplied by Captain David Niven of the super-secret signals unit known as "Phantom." There were enough radios for each of the battalion's HQs to have a radio and a two-man phantom team to operate them, one per company and one for each platoon of the railroad-busting team that Capt. Stirling was slated to command.

Force N was going to conduct operations over a wide-ranging area, and the need for good communications was vital.

Cheap Bribe loped up on his mule and shouted excitedly at Kaldi, gesturing up the mountain behind him.

"The Italians are coming!" Kaldi translated. "He and Captain McKoy spotted them from their observation post on the peak."

Maj. Randal leapt on Parachute and with Waldo and the girls tailing right behind him on their mules, rode out of camp at a gallop. The shifta chieftain was whipping his steed as he led the way. They rode high up the mountain until finally they had to dismount and climb up the steep side of a sheer, razor-sharp ridge that ran below the peak. There they found Captain "Geronimo" Joe McKoy manning an observation position that gave a panoramic view into the valley far down below.

"We got us a squadron of Wop cavalry headed this way, John," Capt. McKoy said conversationally. "That's their *Tenente Colonnello* on the white stallion. Italian officers won't stoop to riding mules."

"They're sportin' black crow's feathers in their headgear," Waldo said looking through a pair of captured Italian binoculars.

"There are over fifty Italian banda battalions in the field looking for us nowadays," Maj. Randal said as he unlimbered his Zeiss glasses.

"How far do you make that, Waldo?" Capt. McKoy asked.

"I'd say about a mile and a half, Joe."

"Well, in that case, it's just about time for me to go to work."

"What are you talking about?" Maj. Randal said, not taking the binoculars down from his eyes.

"I'm gonna' shoot that fancy colonel off his white horse just as soon as he moves up about another five hundred yards closer."

"With what?"

Capt. McKoy pulled the tarp off an ungainly-looking tripod rig, "This here .55 caliber Boys Anti-Tank Rifle."

Still looking through the fine German glass, Maj. Randal said, "The Boys is the most worthless anti-tank weapon ever made, but it's good on thin-skinned vehicles out to four hundred yards."

"Take a look," Capt. McKoy said. "I made a couple of modifications to this one that might be of interest to you, John."

When Maj. Randal lowered the glasses he saw a .55 caliber Boys AT Rifle mounted on a heavy general-purpose tripod sandbagged to the ground. There was a telescopic sight on the weapon. He had never seen the combination before.

"The problem with the Boys is that it ain't an anti-tank weapon at all, but British military ordnance morons keep insisting on calling it one. What it really is, John, is the world's best long-range sniper rifle.

"I've mounted a No. 32 Mk1 scope on this one that was originally designed to go on Bren guns –it's all steel constructed so the Boys recoil, which will definitely make your teeth rattle, won't shake the reticule loose. Then, as you can see, I placed the Boys on a Hotchkiss 'Omnibus Tripod,' which is a general purpose universal machine gun tripod, because the Boys will really stomp you with its recoil. Then, just to be on the safe side, we sandbagged her in. I purely tamed this puppy."

Capt. McKoy slid in behind the Boys, sitting cross-legged, and adjusted the traversing mechanism on the machine gun tripod. "Best plug your ears, boys. Not only does she kick but she's real loud."

Down below, the column of enemy cavalry had snaked out into the valley. The officer on the white horse stopped to scan the distance with his own binoculars, though he was not looking up into the mountains. His more immediate concern was what might lay in wait for him on the far side of the valley. Shifta were notoriously rotten shots, and he was not worried about anything farther out than two hundred yards.

That was a tactical mistake.

KAAAAABOOOOOOOOOM! The big .55 caliber rifle spoke with authority. The sound echoed and re-echoed through the mountains, which made it virtually impossible to distinguish with any certainty where the shot came from.

For what seemed like a long time, nothing happened. Then the rider of the white horse seemed to explode and the horse broke in half. Apparently, the huge .55 caliber armor-piercing round had torn right through the Italian squadron commander at waist level and traveled at a downward angle, killing his horse too.

Panic gripped the startled native cavalrymen. In the blink of an eye, they scattered, turned tail and were galloping away in the far distance. The enemy troops were racing for their lives, not entirely sure what it was they were running from. None of the men took the time to go back and check on their commander or his white horse. Soon the entire squadron was completely out of sight.

There was dead silence on the mountaintop.

Cheap Bribe looked like he had witnessed a miracle.

"The Boys is going to be your mobile, line-of-sight, direct-fire artillery, John," Capt. McKoy said matter-of-factly. "Combined with the Omnibus Tripod, it weighs in at around one hundred ten pounds, which is about the same weight as the tube, bipod and base plate for a four-inch mortar. But the shells, well, you can carry fifty rounds or so for the Boys to one mortar shell. In addition to being your Animal Transport Officer I'm now you're Chief-of-Artillery.

"Oh yeah, I got a dozen more of these Boys rigged up with scopes and tripods ready to go. Some of your old Green Jacket Swamp Fox Force riflemen are going to be the gunners. Paddy'll start flying 'em in just as soon as you give the word."

Down below in the valley, vultures began to circle overhead, and several hyenas had slunk out of the brush to investigate. The black crow's feather on the hat of the dead Italian *Tenente Colonnello* sprawled out next to his beautiful white stallion and rippled gently in the breeze.

"Impressive," Maj. Randal said. "We're going to be able to sit up high in the mountains and plink trucks until the Italians run out of 'em."

"That's kind of what I had in mind when I rode in, John," Capt. McKoy said. "You didn't really think I came all this way out here to be a mule skinner, did you?"

"When this here circus is over, Joe, what say you and me head down and poach us some of them long-toothed Portuguese elephants with one of your big bangers?" Waldo said wishfully. "With a weapon like that we could become ivory millionaires in no time!"

"You like it in that prison the last time you was incarcerated there, Waldo?"

"I did get tired a' cockroach sandwiches now that you mention it."

"Let's ride down and see if the colonel was carrying anything of intelligence value," Maj. Randal suggested.

"Good idea, Major," Waldo agreed. "I need me a new time piece."

INTELLIGENCE REPORT NUMBER 2

FOR THREE MONTHS, MARSHAL RODOLFO "BUTCHER" Graziani had been encamped inside Egypt with his Tenth Army, forming the giant northern pincer of the claw that held Egypt and the Sudan in its powerful grip, not doing very much. That was a mistake. On 9 December 40, Lieutenant General Sir Archibald Wavell launched OPERATION COMPASS, a "reconnaissance in force" against the northern tip of the Italian pincer located at Cyrenaica on the Mediterranean coast. After initial unforeseen success Lt. Col. Wavell quickly reinforced to exploit the situation. Then he delivered a lightning follow-through attack that smashed the Blackshirts at Sidi Barrani.

In a stunning turn of events no one had anticipated, Empire Forces routed the vastly superior Italian Army, capturing thirty-eight thousand prisoners, two hundred thirty-seven pieces of artillery and seventy-three tanks. British casualties were six hundred thirty-four killed and wounded. The battle of Sidi Barrani turned into one of the most lopsided victories in modern history, and while it was a local disaster for the Fascist Army in Libya, the battle had a catastrophic effect on the military situation in far-away IEA.

The hope of Mussolini squeezing the two pincers together to crush Egypt and the Sudan went up in a puff of smoke. In a single stroke the Italian High Command in Abyssinia suddenly found itself left twisting in the breeze in a remote corner of darkest Africa. Addis Ababa was thrown into a state of pandemonium, according to radio intercepts read with mounting glee by Major General James "Baldie" Taylor in Khartoum. The Viceroy Duke of Aosta panicked. In classic comic opera style he insisted on reading every communiqué and debating every decision. Orders were given, then countermanded – nothing was accomplished.

The only reason Italy had declared war on Great Britain in the first place was because it seemed clear that the Germans were going to win it in a few short weeks. Benito Mussolini pictured himself as a modern Caesar and did not want to be left out of a share in the spoils. It was becoming painfully obvious Il Duce had miscalculated. Italian moral at home and at the front plummeted. Now it was going to be a long war.

Standing on his balcony in Rome, posturing with his thumbs in his belt, The Leader made a public statement after the defeat of his Tenth Army, "Marshal Graziani is another man I cannot get angry with, because I despise him," he declared, shaking his tanned bullet-shaped head as if that explained it all away.

An "I hate my generals" speech was not what the despondent crowd below wanted to hear.

Broadcasting from London on public radio, Prime Minister Winston Churchill was euphoric as he spoke directly to his enemy, "Our army is tearing and will tear your African Empire into shreds and tatters…"

In Cairo, Lt. Gen. Wavell, engaged in fighting a constantly evolving, multi-front, extraordinarily complex war, did not have time for theatrics. At this decisive point in the campaign, he made a move that marked him as a strategic genius. With little fanfare, he shifted the victorious 4 Indian Division from the northern front where it was in the vein of the attack, to the Sudan, and placed them under the command of Major General William Platt.

The transfer was a bold, unselfish military decision. By making it, the General Officer Commanding sacrificed the glory of scoring an even bigger victory in the desert. Few commanders would have been so noble as to shift the right troops to the right place at the right time where they could be put to the best use for the overall good – at the cost of personal glory.

Originally it had been planned to send the 6th Australian Division to the Sudan. However, the idea was shelved because Maj. Gen. Platt did not have any experience commanding Australians, who can be a touchy body of men to control, particularly in their off-duty leisure hours. The Kaid, however, had plenty of service on the Indian Northwest Frontier. With that in mind, 5 Indian Division had been assigned instead.

The veteran 4 Indian Division, flushed with success from licking Italians at Sidi Barrani, was paired with it. They were reinforced with a company of I-Tanks and a battery of six-inch howitzers. Now the Kaid had a corps of the best type of soldiers the British Empire could produce.

20

1 GUERRILLA CORPS (PARACHUTE), FORCE N

HIGH IN THE ABYSSINIAN CENTRAL HIGHLANDS IN A SECRET base camp, Major John Randal was standing in a parachute tent next to an improvised briefing board. He was working through the Table of Organization and Equipment (TO&E) for the four Mule Raider Battalions (MRB) that Force N was forming in the field. The size of the units had been modified to meet the need to increase the number of battalions from two to four, making the MRBs smaller and more flexible. Now each one would only have approximately two hundred fifty men to start, though each battalion commander was expected to recruit more men once they took the field. The Force N TO&E was constantly evolving.

The primary reason for increasing the number of the MRBs was to accommodate the desires of highly talented officers who wanted a command. The battalion commanders were going to be Captain Taylor Corrigan, Captain Jeb Pelham-Davies, Captain Harry Shelby and Captain Mike

"March or Die" Mikkalis, all RF officers. Each MRB would have five raiding companies of forty-five men plus a small headquarters company. The MRB companies would consist of two platoons each with a small headquarters element. This was almost the exact TO&E that Commando Battalions used – except they did not ride mules.

Emphasis was on extreme mobility. The plan was for all of the battalions except for one to be supported by an Operational Center (OC) consisting of volunteer officers and other ranks from the Cavalry Division. The OC's mission would be the raising of local shifta units – like Cheap Bribe's – to operate in conjunction with its MRB. Again, with the exception of one, each MRB would also have a detachment of Bad Boys for sabotage missions.

The sole exception to the rule, the 1st MRB "Mercs" commanded by Capt. Mikkalis, did not need the assistance of an OC or the Bad Boys. The former Legionnaire was headed far south to the area northeast of Lake Rudolf on the Kenyan border, where he could count on the indefatigable Captain Jack Desmond Taylor's legion of tough desert fighters for support.

The other three battalions – designated the 3rd, 4th and 5th MRBs – were to be assigned AOs completing the corners of a rough diamond-shaped formation stretching from Addis Ababa to the Danakil Depression. Each battalion was assigned to operate independently, and they would be free to roam over a vast area. The MRBs would be entirely supported by air – the first time in history that feat had ever been attempted.

There was some question whether or not Squadron Leader Paddy Wilcox would be able to accomplish the air supply mission with the limited number of obsolete aircraft available; however, the patchwork fleet was all Force N had.

Within a battalion's AO, companies would operate detached with their own individual operating areas. A MRB company-sized AO would encompass hundreds of square miles of wild Abyssinian countryside, which was the company's private hunting preserve.

Maj. Randal's idea was for Force N to be constantly on the move, avoiding a concentration of troops for any length of time in any one place – thus preventing the Italians from being able to locate, attack and destroy them in a single battle. And he intended for Force N to be spread out over as wide a range of territory as possible which would, in turn, compel the enemy to stretch out its forces searching for them. He knew from personal experience, having operated against Huk bandits for two years in the Philippines, the beauty of being a guerrilla is in never having to be strong anywhere except at the point of attack. And then not for very long.

The Force N strategy would give the Duke of Aosta no choice but to attempt to project a powerful military presence everywhere. Either that or risk the appearance of being weak everywhere. Maj. Randal knew it would be very unwise for the Blackshirts to ever appear impotent, even for a minute. Any sign of vulnerability in Abyssinia invited instant attack from the shifta who were always out there hiding and watching in the shadows like hyenas.

Maj. Randal's plan was simple. He intended to induce the Italians to *self degrade* their numerical advantage.

To accomplish his objective, he needed to force the Italians to guard every outpost, every installation, every fascist agricultural project, and patrol every road in central Abyssinia. To that purpose, Force N would carry out an intensive series of small hit-and-run raids and ambushes. The Italians would be forced to respond by deploying ever-growing numbers of their soldiers in the defense of unimportant places of little military value that would never be attacked, or never attacked again unless they were. Many other Blackshirt troops would be committed to conducting patrolling operations and searching for the elusive raiders in the interior.

Before he realized it, the Duke of Aosta would find his manpower advantage soaked up like a sponge.

All the while, Force N would be going from strength to strength. Highly mobile, free to rove and attack at will, picking their targets, hitting them and then dispersing into the countryside. After each action, the RF-led MRBs would scatter, planning to reassemble and do it all again somewhere else at a prearranged time and place of their own choosing. And that meant Maj. Randal would be dictating the time, place, type and pace of operations to his enemy.

Now, *he* would have the initiative when that happened.

With the single exception of Capt. Mikkalis, the MRB commanders were all young men in their twenties. The battalion commanders and the company and platoon commanders were going to have enormous responsibility and wide latitude in the conduct of their guerrilla operations. They would be free-roving warriors/ kings over a vast territory – the master of everyone and everything in their domain. Few men ever experience the degree of absolute power the Force N officers were going to exercise.

Today was the big day. Force N was being formed. There were twenty-six officers assembled in camp. They would be the key commanders with other junior officers and NCOs being dropped in to the individual battalions by parachute as they arrived in theatre and became available for deployment. Assigning the company-level officers to the battalions was an issue of intense interest and spirited debate.

Once again, Capt. Mikkalis would not take part. Acting on Maj. Randal's recommendation, he had promoted his three Foreign Legion corporals to Bimbashi and made them company commanders. While his three newly-designated company commanders had been learning English from the time they marched out from the Sudan to locate the missing Force N Advance Party, it was a requirement for any officer assigned to the 1st Mercs to be fluent in French, which limited choices and ensured he got the best French-speaking Cavalry Division subalterns.

The 1st Mercs were going to have the most eclectic combination of officers in Force N. The rank structure made things complicated. Bimbashi is a field grade rank in the Sudanese Army but is junior to a British lieutenant. That meant the three Bimbashi company commanders could only have Bimbashi platoon leaders. Capt. Mikkalis would have three companies commanded by ex-Foreign Legion mercenaries led by temporary officers and three commanded by the bluest of the blue bloods from the most exclusive Cavalry regiments in the British Army.

Maj. Randal, with Captain "Geronimo" Joe McKoy assisting, allowed the MRB commanders to conduct the selection process by putting all of the officer's names up on the board, then letting them make their picks in rotation. He was careful to ensure the procedure worked as fairly as possible. The chemistry between the troop commanders was of exceptional importance. A guerrilla force operating behind enemy lines is not the place for personality conflicts.

Capt. Corrigan had the advantage of knowing most of the Cavalry Division officers – or at least knowing someone each one of them knew – because the cavalry is a small family in the British Army. When it came to the locally commissioned hostilities-only officers, Capt. Shelby had the edge, having grown up visiting Kenya since he was a boy. He had met quite a few of the volunteers over the years when he came to hunt on his family's farm, and most of them knew each other – at least by reputation.

The only battalion commander who did not have personal knowledge of any of the new Force N officers was Capt. Pelham-Davies. Because of the handicap, he was awarded the first pick. He selected Lieutenant Jack Merritt, the sole RF officer up for grabs. Maj. Randal thought it an inspired choice. As a member of the Guards polo team Lt. Merritt had met quite a few of the volunteer Cavalry Division officers, which helped level the playing field when it came to making the remaining selections.

Lt. Merritt would be taking over command of Lieutenant Butch "Headhunter" Hoolihan's old outfit. His original command was going to the 1st Mercs, to be expanded into a company. Neither officer was pleased to be giving up troops they had raised, trained and led in battle; however, the exigencies of war do not allow for the luxury of becoming emotionally attached to people, places or units – soldiers serve where they are assigned.

When Lt. Hoolihan realized his name was not up on the board for selection, he immediately came to Maj. Randal to register a protest.

"I've got something else in mind for you."

"Exactly what I was afraid of," the Royal Marine said despondently, still not fully recovered from the shock of losing his "Headhunters." "Palace guard for Headquarters is not my cup of tea, sir."

"I'm organizing a Force Raiding Company, Butch – penciled your name in for it," Maj. Randal said as he lit an Italian cigarillo with his old, worn Zippo lighter with the U.S. 26th Cavalry Regiment crossed sabers on the front. "The only thing you'll ever secure is Captain McKoy when he sets up his .55 Boys sniper rifle to plink something interesting."

"Bloody fantastic, sir!" Lt. Hoolihan whooped. "Does that mean I continue working directly under you?"

"Except when you're operating independently – can you handle that, Marine?"

"Maj. Randal, I will not let your down, sir."

"I was counting on that, stud."

At his base outside Nairobi, Major Sir Terry "Zorro" Stone had been ordered to stand by to dispatch a picked company to be dropped in to act as the Force Raiding Company. The current commander of the company selected for the assignment was the Royal Dragoon husband of Lieutenant Penelope Honeycutt-Parker. Captain Lionel Honeycutt-Parker would surrender his command to Lt. Hoolihan and in turn become the Force N Adjutant, a post for which he was highly qualified.

Captain Mickey Duggan handed Maj. Randal a decoded message. The communiqué, signed by Major General James "Baldie" Taylor was succinct, "COMMENCE OPERATIONS EFFECTIVE IMMEDIATELY." He stuck the flimsy in his pocket.

There was a drumbeat of excitement in the air as each of the MRB commanders huddled privately with their new company commanders and went over the list of remaining lieutenants and Bimbashis. This was serious business, the first strategy session the MRBs would conduct as official organizations, and Maj. Randal did not hurry them. The list of names being evaluated included officers already in camp as well as those in Kenya and the Sudan waiting to be flown in.

Maj. Randal strolled around and listened in on the debate, studying his officers at work. He could feel an electric thread of anticipation crackling through the group. Right here in this tent, Force N as a fighting command was being born.

Capt. McKoy pinned up a list of the remaining candidates.

"This is real interesting, John. The only other time I ever actually saw a regiment getting formed was at Camp Mabry down in Austin, Texas when we raised the Rough Riders before shipping out to Cuba. I like the way you're doing it a whole lot better. Back then Colonel Roosevelt drew names out of a hat."

When the next round of selection started for the platoon leader positions, the first officers to be chosen were those already in-country with Force N. As soon as they were selected, the men were brought into the tent and formally assigned. At this point the battalion O groups went back into private session again to evaluate the list of prospects still in Kenya awaiting air transport.

In this manner, no Force N officer was picked blind. Someone in each MRB either vouched for or blackballed every candidate. If none of his people knew an individual, the battalion commander passed. While a man had to be invited in, the process was categorically not a popularity contest. The only standard was military aptitude. There was some horse trading between battalions and companies within battalions to get the exact right mix. The tension could be cut with a knife. The officers coming together as a team were keenly determined to make their MRB or company the best in Force N.

Selection was serious business.

At the end of the process, five officers awaiting assignment in Kenya or the Sudan, along with one subaltern from the 10th Lancers in camp, did not make the cut. The young 10th Lancer looked to be about fifteen years old and seemed incapable of saying the letter "R," it being pronounced the same as a "W." He sounded exactly like Bugs Bunny.

Maj. Randal glanced at the names, not recognizing any of them. He handed the list to Capt. Duggan. "Advise Maj. Stone to have these men returned to their units."

When Capt. Mikkalis noticed that no one had taken the young 10th Lancer he said, "Give him to me, Major."

The 10th Lancers were rumored to be the most expensive regiment in the British Army. They were variously known as the "Dandy Tenth" or the "Shiny Tenth." By all accounts, its officers were snobs. Nobody liked them very much, but that did not seem to bother the officers of the Tenth. It was said that they would rather talk to each other at parties than dance. "The Tenth don't dance," was the unofficial regimental motto ever since one officer famously said it to the hostess of a party thrown in their honor when she inquired why none of them were participating in the festivities.

Why the tough ex-Legionnaire would take the lieutenant when no one else seemed to have any use for him was a mystery.

"He's yours, Mike," Maj. Randal said, "Why do you want him?"

"Well, he can't speak English, Major, but he's fluent in French and passable in Italian," Capt. Mikkalis said. "Besides, he looks like a fire-eater to me, sir."

"Really?"

"Reminds me of you, sir" Capt. Mikkalis said with a gleam in his pale blue eyes. "Besides, we have a lot in common. I don't dance either."

The next item on the agenda was to assign individual battalion AOs. Capt. Mikkalis would be heading far south almost to the Kenyan border. His indigenous troops were all from the desert region and not happy in the high mountain altitude of central Abyssinia. Merritt's Marauders, all lowland men, were assigned to the 1st MRB for the same reason.

The most Western AO abutted the capital, Addis Ababa. It was assigned to Capt. Corrigan's 3rd MRB.

The Northern AO was allocated to Capt. Pelham-Davies' 4th MRB.

The Eastern AO went to Capt. Shelby's 5th MRB, which would also be responsible for the area between the Southern AO and the secret supply base, N-2.

Captain "Pyro" Percy Stirling was responsible for attacking the single rail line that ran the length of the country. The Death or Glory Boy's original responsibility had also included the short line that ran west from the port of Mombasa toward the Sudan. However, due to the fact that Major General William Platt, the Kaid, had banned Force N from operating on his front, that section of enemy rail transport was stricken off the target list.

The three reinforced platoon-sized demolition groups that Capt. Stirling was slated to command had initially experienced an organizational hiccup. Commodore Richard "Dickey the Pirate" Seaborn vetoed the idea of bringing out the two Kent Fortress Royal Engineer officers from Seaborn House. The two engineer officers were currently committed to other Most Secret operations RF was conducting against targets in enemy-occupied France, rating equal priority to Force N operations in IEA. Strategic RF was living up to its name, carrying out vital missions on two continents.

To replace the no-show Kent Fortress Royal Engineer demolition platoon commanders, three mining engineers in Kenya had been located. The men had plenty of experience with explosives and long service overseeing indigenous personnel – exactly what was needed for Capt.

Stirling's railroad-busting mission. The three engineers were immediately commissioned as Bimbashi, rushed through training and were now ready to be dropped in to Force N.

The next step in the organizational process was to introduce the Force N officers to their new commands. Maj. Randal made this an informal affair. He simply led each MRB commander and his subordinates down to the mule lines and presented them to the Abyssinian officers who had raised and trained the companies.

There was a tremendous ripple of excitement among the native troops. The former KAR NCOs, who had been given Abyssinian Army commissions, had been preparing them for the big day for a long time. At this point, the proceedings became decidedly formal and followed a solemn protocol.

Each of the MRB commanders brought with him several heavily packed duffel bags. In the bags, compliments of Captain the Lady Jane Seaborn, were brightly-colored cummerbunds she had tailor made in Nairobi. Each MRB had its own distinct color and pattern.

Wearing of the colored silk garments was something unique to this part of Africa. The cummerbund was worn around the waist under a trooper's web gear. Every Force N officer arrived at their new commands already wearing his unit's cummerbund.

When a commander was assigned to his company, his first order of business was to hold a formation, and in conjunction with his two platoon leaders, personally issue a cummerbund to each soldier with instructions that the distinctive item of clothing was to be worn at all times thereafter. The ceremony was not unlike the ritual pinning of jump wings or placing on of the forest green Commando beret after graduation from the Special Warfare Training Center at Achnacarry.

The native troops took the matter with a great deal of gravity. The new company commander, accompanied by the new leader of the platoon, personally issued a cummerbund to each man. The act symbolized his command authority. The colored cloth signified membership and commitment – not to a country or king, but to the unit – what soldiers really fight for. The unique symbol created an instant bond between officers and men.

Waldo rode into camp with a mule train bearing supplies and more officer reinforcements from N-2. Maj. Randal consulted his roster, and the new arrivals were quickly sent down to their battalions. One of them was Lieutenant Dick Courtney, the former Gold Coast Border Policeman just out from having completed all his training at No.1 Parachute School and the Special Warfare Training Center at Achnacarry. He brought with him his two trackers, X-Ray and Vanish, from the Gold Coast Border Police (GCBP).

Lt. Courtney was assigned to Lt. Hoolihan's Force Raiding Company as an extra officer until suitable employment would be found for a man of his skills.

A big, totally bald officer, Captain Hawthorne Merryweather, who resembled a happy porpoise, pulled the Force N commander aside and discretely introduced himself as the super-secret PWE operative Maj. Randal had requested. He was loaded down with enough gear to outfit a small army. It took six mules to pack all his equipment in from N-2.

"What am I supposed to call you, Captain?"

"Why not your Propaganda Officer, sir?"

"What's in all those boxes?"

"My mobile printing press," Capt. Merryweather beamed proudly, "To whip up leaflets and the like. And there are some loudspeakers and record players along with a selection of opera records to serenade the lonely Italian troops in their isolated camps at night."

"A printing press?" Maj. Randal said in disbelief.

"Lady Seaborn acquired it for me, sir," the PWE officer explained with a big, happy grin. "She had to buy out a Chinese calling card printing company in Nairobi."

"I see."

"Look, Major, I ran these off for your Force N officers after General Taylor informed me you highly recommended the book." Capt. Merryweather enthused as he pulled out what looked like a small catalogue from the large bellows pocket of his brand new BDU jacket. "It's a condensed version of *Colonel John Mosby: The Gray Ghost*... the way they do in *Reader's Digest*. I edited out everything except the parts about

Mosby's Rangers organization, tactics and operations. We have enough to provide a copy to each of your officers to read around the campfire at night."

"Outstanding," Maj. Randal thumbed through the thick little pamphlet. He was impressed.

"I printed up your 'Rules for Raiding' in small card form. Each Force N man passing through Camp Croc is issued one."

"Keep up this level of work, Captain, and I just may not mind hauling your gear all over kingdom come on a mule," Maj. Randal said. "I've always admired PWE ever since one of you studs dreamed up the idea to tell the Germans the Royal Navy was stocking the English Channel with Great White sharks."

"Ah, actually that would have been me, sir."

"Dropping dead pigeons on Occupied France?"

"Me again, Major."

"Parachutes weighted down with blocks of ice?"

"Guilty."

"Welcome aboard, Hawthorne."

Maj. Randal gave his people four hours with their new commands before holding an Officers Call. At this time, all Force N officers were issued their Operations Order. This was when the reality set in for some of the cavalry subalterns and hostilities-only Bimbashi – they were going to war!

As the sun was setting through the mountains to the west in a blaze of brilliant golden orange, Maj. Randal called the Force N officers together for what he was reasonably sure would be the only time the guerrilla leaders would all be in a group. He wanted to set the tone for the fighting ahead. Since this was his one and only chance, he needed to get it right. For this briefing he abandoned the traditional format and cut straight to the "Concept of the Operation."

"There will be three phases to Force N's war," he announced crisply, standing in front of the assembled officers, idly swishing his lion-tailed whisk against one leg. "Phase I where the guerrilla, meaning Force N, earns the respect of the population has concluded. 'Headhunter' Hoolihan, Mr. Treywick, Kaldi and I did that. Phase II, active operations by organized guerrilla units, is set to commence immediately upon conclusion of this briefing.

"In this second phase of operations, you men will launch an increasing crescendo of small-scale raids and ambushes targeting the Italian infrastructure. There will, in fact, be five distinct segments of Phase II: 1) attacking isolated Italian civilian projects; 2) ambushing the roads; 3) cutting the rail lines; 4) taking out the enemy's means of wire communications; and 5) raiding airfields. While you are authorized to attack any of these targets at will, from time to time you will be notified to shift your priority from one type of target to another.

"Phase III will consist of active operations in support of conventional friendly forces attacking through your AO. You will receive additional instructions regarding these missions at a later date.

"When you move out to your assigned AOs tonight, you are cleared to attack targets of opportunity en route.

A shiver of excitement ran through the audience. The officers looked around at each other. The war was coming at them fast now.

"In short," Maj. Randal said, "your mission is to create havoc throughout your individual AOs, with the overall objective of causing the Italian Army to divert more and more of their combat troops to guard convoys, protect fixed installations and to hunt you down.

"Remember, Force N's primary goal is to live to fight another day. We are in the raiding business. Do not allow yourself to be drawn into fighting set piece battles. Do not try to assault fixed military objectives such as the small Italian forts that dot the countryside. And never, ever, under any circumstances, defend anything. Stay alive, stay in the fight, cut, slash and run, and then move on to continue the mission somewhere else.

"Now our, ah, Special Warfare Officer, Captain Merryweather, is going to brief you on certain aspects of the psychological and propaganda campaign Force N intends to conduct. Psychological Operations are a central part of our plans and will be run in conjunction with your direct action missions. It's crucial to our success to have the people support you and the enemy fear you – Captain Merryweather..."

Making his way to the front of the tent, the PWE officer stopped briefly to show Maj. Randal something he had scribbled on the small notepad he carried in the breast pocket of his jacket. The Force N commander studied the pad, then nodded. "I like it, let's do it – go ahead, tell 'em."

"Within your individual AOs, deploy your Bad Boys to conduct combined sabotage and propaganda missions," Capt. Merryweather began, beaming at his new title. Special Warfare Officer sounded substantially more bloodcurdling than Propaganda Officer. "Think of them as juvenile delinquents. Have them cut telephone wires and spread nails on every road around every enemy base camp. Keep the Bad Boys well supplied with paint so they can slap the letter "N" on every solid object in Abyssinia. Use the Bad Boys to pass out the propaganda leaflets we will be printing up and dropping in with your regular aerial resupply of Maria Theresa thalers, ammunition and foodstuffs.

"Propaganda is an important aspect of guerrilla warfare. It will raise our profile and deliver our message to encourage the Patriots to rise against the Italians. I'd better not hear my leaflets make good toilet paper – spread 'em all over your AOs. Is that clear?"

"Clear!" the assembled men roared with a laugh.

"We are not trying to win hearts and minds," the PWE officer continued, knowing full well most fighting men tended to view propaganda as a complete waste of time. "Force N is in the business of scaring the bloody hell out of all the Italians we don't kill. If the Blackshirts live in terror the locals will sense it and start to pick off Italians on their own from time to time when they see an opportunity.

"Our propaganda campaign will be scientifically crafted to promote the belief that a general Patriot uprising is ready to explode at any minute. It's not, so do not count on it, but the more we have the bloody Eyeties looking over their shoulder expecting a spear up their backside at any second, the easier your job will be.

"Bearing that in mind, there are two things the Italian High Command worry most about – British-led guerrilla forces operating in the interior of the country, and parachute raiders that might drop in unannounced while they are asleep in their beds. To stir the pot on these fears, Maj. Randal has authorized me to inform you that from this moment forward we will be known as '1 Guerrilla Corps (Parachute), Force N.' Starting immediately the battalions will style their communications as 1st, 3rd, 4th and 5th MRB, 1 Guerrilla Corps (Parachute), Force N – that should give the brass hats in Addis Ababa something to ponder.

"I will order unit flashes made up and dropped in with your resupply. Extras will be included. Have your troops sew them on and have the Bad Boys nail up the extras outside every Wop base in your operating area. I have stickers printed with a pair of wings over a moon with an 'N' over the top that you can have the Bad Boys slap on everything solid. It pays to advertise.

"In conclusion, as Virgil wrote in his narrative of the *Battle of Troy*, *'Dolus an virtus, quis in boste requirat'* – which for you non-Latin speakers means, 'It won't matter to the enemy whether you beat him by guile or valor.' "

"Thank you, Captain," Maj. Randal stepped back to the front. "I'd say that pretty well covers everything you men need to know on the subject of psychological operations.

"Guerrilla direct action tactics are based on actionable intelligence, detailed planning, rapid movement, concentration of forces at the point of attack, violent execution, quickly breaking contact, disappearing into the countryside and regrouping. Force N will not seize and hold anything. We do not capture territory or defend a fixed position.

"Stay mobile, be nimble, pick your targets, maintain the initiative and strike only when you're ready. Plan carefully, rehearse your operations beforehand and carry them out utilizing the elements of surprise and speed coupled with violence of action – break contact, withdraw, reorganize, then go out and do it all over again. Give the Blackshirts guerrilla war and plenty of it.

"The success or failure of Force N will depend entirely on the leadership demonstrated in the field by you men sitting in this tent."

A hush had fallen over the assembled troops. The officers listened, mesmerized by Maj. Randal's nonchalant, almost casual, explanation of how to execute what most military professionals would view as a suicide mission cooked up by a delusional maniac. Every man in the tent, RF officer, cavalry subaltern or hostilities-only Bimbashi was struck by the fact their commander clearly did not think it delusional or suicidal.

Maj. Randal *intended* for them to go out and do exactly what he said.

The only sound was a guinea fowl screeching in the distance.

"Lieutenant Hoolihan is now going to come forward and give you the benefit of his views on commanding indigenous troops," Maj. Randal said.

"Listen up – the Headhunter is the best small unit guerrilla leader in the business, Butch ..."

The young Royal Marine marched out front and center to conduct his first-ever briefing as a commissioned officer to a group of other officers. Dazzled by the major's glowing introduction, he was amazed to discover his audience was staring at him in wide-eyed anticipation from beneath their slouch hats, astounded that the officers would want to hear what a former Royal Marine private had to say about anything.

Lt. Hoolihan was not aware he had become a virtual living legend.

"T.E. Lawrence liked to compare an irregular army to gas – guerrillas can disperse and vanish into thin air," "Headhunter" informed his rapt group of listeners. "The major and I would rather you to think of Force N like an artillery shell that screams in from out of nowhere, explodes without warning and sends red hot shrapnel ripping out in all directions."

In the back of the parachute tent Capt. McKoy elbowed Maj. Randal and whispered, "Listen at him, a' quotin' *Seven Pillars of Wisdom* –I never knowed 'ole Butch was a Lawrence man."

Maj. Randal fought back a smile as he looked down at his unpolished canvas-topped raiding boots, so scuffed they were worn white.

"Never abuse the askaris you command, the shifta hangers-on or the local tribesmen you encounter. We need their good will," Lt. Hoolihan continued, warming to his subject. "Abyssinians respect power figures – *tillik sau*, or 'big shots' as the term translates. Conduct yourself as one at all times. But keep in mind – a heavy hand does not work with these people. You lead and your troops will follow you.

"Never trust the locals. Never take the friendly demeanor of the population for granted. The tribes are shot through with collaborators, sympathizers, spies and paid informants. They will sell you out to the Italians in a heartbeat. Most of the natives have at least one family member currently serving in the enemy army, so while they may hate the fascist invaders they still have mixed emotions about helping us.

"Truth is, the people are more interested in warring with their neighbors over local water rights or some ancient blood feud than fighting the Italians anyway. Never get involved with regional politics. Never take sides in a tribe-on-tribe fight. No matter what the locals tell you, there are no good guys. So the rule is – never pick sides.

"Utilize the shifta to gather intelligence, as guides, to screen your operations and to act as force multipliers. The bandits, I mean… Patriots will sweep in and help out in a fight once it's clear you're going to win. Only don't bloody expect them to hang around if things do not go well.

"Reward the Patriot leaders generously. Following a successful action, allow the shifta to keep the spoils after your troops take what they need. Remember, the Patriots are pirates, robbers and outlaws – but they're *your* pirates, robbers and outlaws.

"Properly led Abyssinians make good fighting men, though excitable – particularly, for example, during a wild rush into the kill zone of an ambush to get at the loot. The men are excellent spearmen but rotten shots. Work your troops in close and count on volley fire if you expect them to hit anything. Generally speaking, the Patriots are braver in groups.

"The lads tend to focus on being the first to the booty and once the shifta believes a prize is within their grasp, they are indifferent to casualties and very difficult to control. Then again, the Abyssinians do not much like taking fire in a static position and tend to retire early if taken by surprise or if the mission does not go according to plan.

"The lads can be moody.

"Finally, do not be put off when your men never say 'thank you' for anything," Lt. Hoolihan said. "Those two words do not exist in their vocabulary. Keep in mind it's not necessary to love the troops you command. You simply have to make them fight.

"Gentlemen, this concludes my portion of the briefing."

To a man, 1 Guerrilla Corps (Parachute), Force N personnel stood up and loudly applauded Lt. Hoolihan's performance as Maj. Randal worked his way forward with Cheap Bribe and Waldo Treywick trailing behind. Clearly the young lieutenant knew his stuff.

"Now my… ah… Patriot Commander has a few words. He's going to perform the official Force N shifta war chant – Mr. Treywick will interpret."

The snaggle-toothed, one-eyed bandit was looking particularly sharp today. He was sporting one of Maj. Randal's brand new jungle-green BDU jackets (a gift from Lady Jane), bandoleers crisscrossed over his chest, a

Beretta automatic in a flap holster, sword, shield with his initials shot in it and a wicked-looking dagger on his belt. Crushed down on top of his big bee-hived hairdo was an Italian officer's hat he had recently taken to wearing, sporting a heavy, gold, scrambled eggs braid on the bill. He was wearing a pair of Ray-Bans over one of Sqn. Ldr. Wilcox's black eye patches.

Several of the cavalry subalterns in the audience, the sons of various dukes and viscounts, noting the superb double-stitching on the button holes wondered how the blazes the evil-looking buccaneer could have possibly come into possession of a Pembrooks tailored jungle jacket.

Gubbo Rekash chanted:

"The wild fig tree, the fool, bears fruit without flowering.
How can one of them fear unless the other one is killed?
Let's hit! Let's hit him! Let's hit him, this is good!
Saying later or tomorrow rejuvenates the enemy.
Hit him! Hit him, and let him flee into the brush,
It's when saying 'I've got it that a dog bites."

After it became clear that there was no more to the chant, the officers of Force N clapped politely wondering what it meant exactly. Suddenly the wily old bandit shouted out a last fierce admonishment.

"Kill 'em all and let Allah sort 'em out!" Mr. Treywick translated, managing a perfectly straight face.

There was a moment of stunned silence, then the tent broke into loud cheers. The audience knew exactly where that phrase originated – *Jump on Bela* had been mandatory reading for all Force N personnel waiting to go into the field.

"Phase III will be the invasion of Abyssinia by conventional forces launching out of the Sudan and Kenya," Maj. Randal repeated. "When it kicks off, our mission will be to work close in the rear of the Italian forces immediately in front of the attacking East African Forces out of Kenya.

"Our goal will be to make the Italians believe their position is untenable. Force N will accomplish that by means of a deception program designed by Captain Merryweather, combined with a relentless campaign of aggressive raids and attacks carried out by your MRBs. We want the

Blackshirts to feel isolated, alone, and very, very afraid. I will notify you when to begin planning, coordinating and executing Phase III operations.

"Now, Captain 'Geronimo' Joe McKoy has a few final words."

The sun-bronzed old soldier marched to the front of the audience. He looked lean and dangerous with his flat-brimmed campaign hat slanted down over his eyes. He was squinting out at the crowd like a gunfighter sizing up an opponent.

"Captain Merryweather will be passing out a pamphlet upon the conclusion of this here briefing," the sliver-haired cowboy announced, "a condensed version of a book on Col. John S. Mosby's guerrilla operations during the American Civil War. READ IT! The major wants you to operate exactly the way Mosby did.

"Now, it'd be a real good idea for anyone ah' thinkin' about conductin' his own personal guerrilla campaign to pay particular attention to the parts in it on how the Gray Ghost keeps his plans to hisself, never assembles his Rangers until it's time to conduct a raid, strikes like blue lightnin' from out of nowhere, then steals away in the night and melts into the countryside with his plunder before the dust settles.

"There just so happened to be this one other Confederate, a general named Nathan Bedford Forrest – 'The Wizard of the Saddle.' Most experts agree he was the best cavalry commander on either side and may have been the best America has ever produced. General Forrest's favorite tactic, which I'd like to pass along to you, was to 'throw a scare into 'em and keep a scare in 'em.'

"Words can't describe better than that what it is you hardcases want to do to the garlic-eaters. This is war to the knife! When you ride outta' here today, hell's gonna' be a' poppin' – take it to 'em, boys!

"One day when your grandkids ask what you did in the war you're gonna' be proud to say, 'I rode for John Randal.' "

The Force-N officers leapt to their feet, thundering their enthusiasm and cheering as Capt. McKoy did a snappy right-face and marched to the back of the tent. "Geronimo Joe" virtually always had that effect on fighting men.

"You've got your orders," Maj. Randal said in conclusion. "Good hunting, gentlemen. Let's go do it!"

21
IF I'M NOT HERE…
WHERE AM I?

MAJOR GENERAL JAMES "BALDIE" TAYLOR BOARDED A Commodore for the flight to Camp Croc on Lake Rudolf. All the interior compartments of the airplane had been stripped out by Squadron Leader Paddy Wilcox to reconfigure it into a freight hauler. The plane was loaded to maximum lift capacity with crates of rifles, ammunition, saddles and bridles. For this flight, they had to improvise passenger seats.

Upon landing on the green lake, he was met by Sergeant Major Maxwell Hicks, DCM, recently arrived from Seaborn House to be the Camp Croc Commandant. Camp Croc was now a bustling military base in a barren no-man's land. There were four amphibious bi-winged Supermarine Walrus RN spotter aircraft bobbing in the lake shrouded in camouflage nets. Commodore Richard "Dickie the Pirate" Seaborn had been true to his word and supplied them for the operation. He was having a more difficult time providing the RN Catalina he had promised.

Sqn. Ldr. Wilcox had recently returned from a second whirlwind trip to Canada to recruit more multi-engine-qualified bush pilots. The men he brought back were aviators who could fly anything with wings in all weather conditions, land on a mud puddle and make any repair that might be necessary with a pair of pliers and a ball of bailing wire.

The bush pilots were all middle-age men with thousands of flying hours in their logs. Signed on as civilian contractors, they were never told exactly who it was they were officially employed by. The Canadians were perfect for the type missions Sqn. Ldr. Wilcox had in mind. Fly deep into enemy territory at night in an obsolete, overloaded airplane and land on an uncharted lake by moonlight – no problem.

Sgt. Maj. Hicks briefed Maj. Gen. Taylor on the ongoing military operations in the area. Since the northern tip of the lake straddled the border and encroached into Abyssinia, he was running cross-border reconnaissance operations out of outboard motor-mounted rubber rafts using a combination of RF Commandos, Lifeboat Servicemen and Turkana tribesmen.

Just across the wire, the Italians had the Merrille tribe working for them. At least they thought they did. Jack Desmond Bonham had been recently traveling among the Merrille, recruiting them to turn against their Italian masters.

Dressed in shorts, wearing desert shoes with no socks, a battered bush shirt, carrying his favorite .275 Rigby rifle and always accompanied by "Kim," his mixed breed Airedale dog, the colorful frontier character was waging a private desert border war without benefit of military rank or authorization from any authority.

For sport, Jack liked to disappear across the border with his small army of Somali cutthroats and ambush the askaris working for the Italians and the fascist colonial troops operating in the area. He was also running guns to the Merrille, who had agreed to stage an uprising against the Blackshirts at the appropriate time – for a price.

Whoever controlled the water holes controlled the desert, and Jack knew them all.

"The only two wells of any note along the entire vast twelve hundred-mile border region are two thirty-foot-deep pools at a place called Wajir. Somehow they have been hacked out of solid, lava-covered limestone straight down through the black desert rock." The guerrilla fighter said to Maj. Gen. Taylor, "There are two schools of thought on how the wells came to be.

"Some say they were dug by a tribe of one-armed giants who were only vulnerable to bee stings.

"Others claim the wells were dug by little slave boys dangled down by ropes tied to their ankles who chopped through the lava rock and then the limestone with hand chisels until they passed out. Take your choice, General."

"I think we can safely dismiss the one-armed giant story," Maj. Gen. Taylor said. "As of right now you are working for me, Jack. I am promoting you to the temporary rank of Captain. When the time comes you will fall under the tactical control of the officer commanding Force N, Maj. Randal – any problems with that?"

"Not a ruddy one, General. Reckon you could issue me a chit for my back pay?"

"Consider it done – at the grade of captain from the beginning. Speak to Lady Seaborn later and provide her the particulars. Anything else I can do for you?"

"Could use a case of Two-Seven-Five solids – I'm running low."

"My people will corner the market and send you all they have in Nairobi," Maj. Gen. Taylor promised. "How many Merrille do you estimate will respond to your call when the balloon goes up, Jack?"

"Oh, I recon about sixty thousand lads, give or take a few."

Staggered by the number, Maj. Gen. Taylor said, "You raise that many, I shall personally see you decorated."

Sgt. Maj. Hicks added, "Jack and I have been coordinating our local operations. The Turkana and the Merrille have been feuding for ages. Somehow Jack brokered a ceasefire between the two tribes until the Blackshirts are driven out. After that, all bets are off."

"Excellent," Maj. Gen. Taylor said, "Any security problems to report?"

"Only getting the natives to trust us," Sgt. Maj. Hicks responded. "About forty years ago some rogue trader lured one of the local tribes into a tent and blew it up with a keg of gunpowder laced with two-penny nails so he could steal their ivory. After that, the locals – no matter what their tribe – have not been trusting of white men in these parts. The sight of a nail keg tends to make them scatter like quail."

"I can see why it might."

"Does this promotion mean I'm going to be required to fill out paperwork, General," Capt. Bonham asked skeptically, "duty rosters, daily reports and the like? I ain't real good with forms, General."

Maj. Gen. Taylor looked the sun burnt desert warrior in the eye, "Captain Bonham, we never keep records in this outfit, there are no forms or reports. This operation does not officially exist. In fact, Jack, you are not even here. Get the picture?"

"If you say so, General. Only, if I'm not here, where am I?"

LIEUTENANT BUTCH "HEADHUNTER" HOOLIHAN WAS STRIDING DOWN A road Somewhere IN THE mountainous plateau of Abyssinia past one of the stone kilometer markers with a fasces carved on it. This was the sign of ancient Rome that the Italians placed on all the strategic roads. Someone had already painted a crude "N" on the rock symbol. Lt. Hoolihan had his Australian slouch pulled down low to shade his eyes from the bright, midday sunshine. His beloved Thompson submachine gun was cradled in his arms; and trotting along behind him lugging his M-1903 A-1 Springfield rifle was his pageboy. He was getting in one last operation before flying down to take command of his new Force Raiding Company.

Minutes before, Cheap Bribe's men had executed a road ambush on a small convoy of four Italian supply trucks. Strangely, these trucks were not Fiats. They were a mixed bag of Ford, Chevrolet and Chrysler models, painted a splotchy, amateur, homemade camouflage. The trucks looked like farm vehicles that had been pressed into military service. The question in Lt. Hoolihan's mind: where would the Wops get old American-manufactured farm trucks? Certainly not from Abyssinian farmers – they did they have roads to drive them on.

His Force Raiding Company troops were busily looting the shot-up trucks. They were working fast, it not being a good idea to hang around a road you have just ambushed deep in enemy territory. Lt. Hoolihan was planning to give the command to withdraw in a few more minutes.

He came to one battered Ford that none of his men were bothering with. That was peculiar – usually the lads would be swarming all over any vehicle looking for booty. Without hesitation he swung up into the bed of the truck and found it was piled high with crates of ammunition. Normally his boys would have already carted off every single round of ammunition. Bullets were money. There was something wrong with this picture.

Bending down to inspect a partially opened ammo can, he found to his surprise it contained brand new green boxes of Remington .22 caliber bullets. Counting the boxes, then the ammo crates, it looked like there was close to a million rounds in the back of the truck. No wonder his men were ignoring this truck – they had no use for .22 caliber ammunition, the tiny little bullets had no trade value.

Lt. Hoolihan ordered two of his men to secure enough of the Remington ammunition to keep Major John Randal supplied with bullets for his silenced High Standard H-D Military Model for the rest of his life. Then he doused the truck in gasoline from the cans strapped to the running board. After giving the command to "Rally," he waited until his men had cleared the killing zone of the ambush before tossing a match into the back of the Ford. The camouflaged truck went up with a *WHOOOOSH*!

Loping away from the ambush site with his men on mule back, Lt. Hoolihan began to ponder the implication of where the Italians might have obtained American trucks and American .22 caliber ammunition. The closest place he could think of was Kenya. Was it possible someone in Kenya could be smuggling farm vehicles across the border to the Italians? If so, that was treason!

In the distance he could hear the sharp, furious staccato crackling of the .22 rounds cooking off on the burning Ford truck.

22
BROWN SHIRTS AND PINK SWASTIKAS

MAJOR GENERAL JAMES "BALDIE" TAYLOR FLEW BACK TO Nairobi where he immediately went into a closed-door session with Commodore Richard "Dickey the Pirate" Seaborn, Major Sir Terry "Zorro" Stone, Major Lawrence Grand, Lieutenant Commander Ian Fleming, Captain the Lady Jane Seaborn and Lieutenant Pamala Plum-Martin at the private, high-walled compound belonging to Chief Inspector Ronald McFarland. Absent were Lieutenant Penelope Honeycutt-Parker, Mrs. Brandy Seaborn and Red, the Clipper Girl, because they did not have a need to know the information to be discussed at the meeting.

The counterintelligence team had not made any progress in uncovering the Italian's master spy. Time was growing short, and so the decision had been made to give them help. Maj. Grand, the dapper Chief of SOE Section D (Destruction), who was, in actuality, a longtime member of the British SIS, chaired the meeting. He went straight to the main point.

"I have some late-breaking information that has come to my attention, uncovered by Chief Inspector McFarland. The inspector has broken the case. The Italian's man in Nairobi is an individual known to you: Captain Lord Joss Hay, 22nd Earl of Errol aka the World's Greatest Pouncer."

"Joss is far and away too narcissistic to risk his neck spying," Lady Jane said. "The man does not even own a gun or participate in blood sports. Are you absolutely sure, Lawrence?"

"Quite!"

"Personally, in my opinion, I think the Earl is a psychopath," Lt. Plum-Martin said. "He believes the universe revolves around him, has no conscience and does not care who he hurts as long as he has his way. That said, I simply cannot picture him being an enemy agent."

"Known the Earl for ages," Lt. Cdr. Fleming chimed in. "Never had an original thought in his entire life. The proof had better be awfully strong to convince me he is anything but an unsuspecting dupe of the Italians. Now *that* is entirely possible!"

"After Chief Inspector McFarland's report I doubt you shall remain unconvinced," Maj. Grand said. "The Chief Inspector is uncommonly talented at the art of counterintelligence. The evidence is irrefutable – judge for yourself."

The big burly Chief Inspector walked to the front of the room. He was wearing a rumpled corduroy suit. With his bushy, cinnamon, walrus mustache that curled up at the ends and his curved-stem pipe, he looked like he had stepped straight out of a Sherlock Holmes novel. The image was one he cultivated.

"My area of expertise at Special Branch was 'External Threats.' I spent over twenty-five of my thirty years' service as a counterintelligence officer. When I retired to Kenya, I quickly grew bored, so more as a hobby than anything else, I volunteered to work for the Commissioner of Police performing the same counterintelligence duties as I had for Special Branch."

He pulled out a notebook and flipped through the pages, "Joss Victor Hay, born 1901 to a family, The Earls of Errol, the Hereditary Lord High Constables of Scotland since 1315, a position that entitles them to walk directly behind the Royal Family at coronations. Attended Eton, was asked to leave prematurely. His story – he bought a stolen motorcycle not knowing it was hot. Eton's official line – he was caught sleeping with one of the chambermaids and expelled.

"Sir Terry, you are an Eton man. What would you estimate the odds of one being sacked from that learned institution for boffing a chambermaid?"

"Precisely zero, old stick."

"Commander Fleming?"

"Ditto."

"In fact, he was caught with one of the boys who delivered coal to the rooms."

This bombshell caused the men to clear their throats uncomfortably and the two ladies to look at each other crestfallen. In their minds, the virtue the Earl had going for him was his idolization of females.

He was the man who loved women... or maybe not.

"1920 to 1922 served with the Foreign Office, Military attaché, High Commission Berlin. During this time, Hay met and socialized with many of the men who are currently running Nazi Germany. In particular, Hay was known to have had contact with a shadowy group called the 'Pink Swastika,' a hush-hush cabal of homosexuals who claim to have masterminded the rise of the Nazi Party and by some accounts were the actual brains behind Hitler's early political career.

"During the Night of the Long Knives and immediately following, Pink Swastika went underground after Hitler ordered their liquidation along with the Brownshirts and their openly homosexual leader, Ernst Röhm, also a founding member of Pink Swastika. Röhm was shot, along with hundreds of Brownshirt and Pink Swastika members.

"1924, Hay came out to Kenya in the company of Lady Idina Gordon, a woman eight years his senior. The two established the Happy Valley Social Set – a hedonistic group of white farmers who in time grew to be known for excess drink, drugs, wife swapping, orgies and overt displays of flagrant overindulgence – married Lady Gordon the same year.

"1928, inherited title upon father's death – divorced Lady Gordon though they remained on good terms.

"1930, married Mary 'Molly' Ramsay-Hill, a moneyed woman several years his senior.

"1934, joined the British Union of Fascists, also known to frequent the Cliveden Set – a group variously described as a ginger group, a junta, a camarilla, a cabal, an inner circle and/or a secret committee. The Set was a group of super wealthy, powerful people who established Gods Truth Ltd., whose pronouncements on British Government policy have been described as Olympian in tone – openly pro-fascist, pro-Nazi before the outbreak of hostilities.

"1936, served as Secretary to the Production and Settlement Board, Kenya, and was a member of the Legislative Council.

"1939, became Assistant Military Secretary for Kenya Colony, Chairman Manpower Committee.

"1940, widowed; wife died following a protracted decline brought on by drug addiction to morphine and cocaine."

Inspector Ronald McFarland snapped his notebook shut. He looked at the small audience. "My interest in the Earl was first pricked when he returned from a trip to England in 1934, started making political speeches on behalf of the British Union of Fascists and began wearing a custom-made silver fascist's badge with his kilt at Happy Valley parties.

"The question I asked myself was, why would a notorious playboy, resolutely committed to a life of carefree sensuous pleasure and hardcore debauchery, suddenly take an active interest in radical rightwing politics? The mystery was solved when I discovered the precariousness of his personal finances. In short, the Earl is penniless. Alas, the family squandered its fortune. Hay was basically reduced to marrying women of a certain age for their money. He saw radical politics as a means for personal pecuniary profit.

"The Earl neither smokes nor consumes drugs, though he is a provider of both to his paramours, and only drinks moderately. He views the sex act as 'his performance,' openly boasting he would never want to 'impair it.' The man has had countless affairs but there are two ironclad rules he has never broken, until recently – he never touches any woman who is not married, and all his paramours are older women. The single glaring exception is his fiancée, Diana Broughton, who at age 27 is younger than he is. The upcoming nuptials are slightly complicated by the inconvenient fact that she is currently married to Sir Jock Broughton – has been for a period of two months.

"Six men and one woman have made verbal threats to shoot the Earl for his philandering, including Diana's cuckold husband, Broughton. Hay recently installed bulletproof glass in his Buick Super 8 after his window was smashed. He claimed his pet cigarette-smoking chimpanzee threw a rock and shattered the original windscreen. The auto mechanics who installed the security window report the damage was a bullet hole.

"Lady Seaborn was incorrect when she pointed out the Earl does not indulge in blood sports. While he loathes hunting and is one of the few men in the colony who does not own a single firearm, Hay breeds fighting roosters and enjoys cockfighting, which, as I am sure you are aware, is a bloody battle between birds wearing steel spurs – fought to the death.

"The Earl was furious recently when one of his servants cooked one of his prized fighting roosters by mistake.

"Recently he has taken up wildlife photography. Quite a lot of his photographs happen to be of animals grazing in places of certain military interest to our enemies. Most of the photographs disappear shortly after he has them developed.

"As the Chairman of the Manpower Committee, the Earl personally oversees all officer assignments. One night the building housing the Manpower Committee's offices burned down. Every single military officer's personnel file in the colony was destroyed by the fire. Hay has been reconstructing the records from 'memory.' According to the Nairobi Fire Inspector, the fire started in the Earl's office. It was not an electrical fire and, as stated, the man does not smoke. He worked late that evening – alone.

"Using his position on the Manpower Committee, Hay has been able to place confederates in strategic assignments around the colony. These men siphon off military stores, spirit them across the border and sell them to the Italians. Hay takes a commission off the top.

"Before the war, the Duke of Aosta was a known frequenter of the Happy Valley party scene when he visited Kenya. It was at that time the Duke recruited Hay, putting him on the Italian payroll. Unfortunately for the Earl, the money he earns spying is paid in Lira and is sitting in a numbered account in Addis Ababa.

"Behind his back men openly label Hay a gigolo – in Kenyan frontier society, a man is expected to stand on his own two feet, not be supported by wealthy older women.

"I could go on and on, but these are the salient points – questions?"

"Joss was reported to be a caring and devoted husband while his wife was dying," Lady Jane said. "You make him sound like an evil ogre."

"Hay instructed the house servants to provide his wife, Molly, all the morphine she desired anytime, in any amount she asked for. He did not seek out a doctor's care or attempt to have her institutionalized to treat her drug addiction. In point of fact, the Earl put his wife down for what little money she had left after he had run through her fortune."

"You have very specific private information, Inspector," Lt. Plum-Martin said, looking up from filing her scarlet red nails. "Are you quite sure it is reliable?"

"In Kenya, nothing never ever happens without the servants knowing," Inspector Ronald McFarland said. "Household staff make the world's best informers. Particularly when they come from different tribes, then they spy on each other. I can provide you the down and dirty on every large domicile in the colony.

"Drop by my office, Lieutenant. I shall walk you through the entire Hay file."

"Thank you, Chief Inspector," Maj. Gen. Taylor said, bringing the session to a close. "At this point, our efforts will shift from investigative to surveillance. Lady Seaborn, you and Lieutenant Plum-Martin can resume your normal duties, though you may be recalled for brief periods.

"Now that we have identified the Earl as our man, what we require is to have his movements monitored. I want Red, Mrs. Seaborn and Lieutenant Honeycutt-Parker glued to him like a shadow. Fleming, you will assist their efforts.

"Bear in mind Joss Hay is a purveyor of hard drugs, a black-market war profiteer, a premeditated murderer and a traitor to his country in time of war. Do not let his good looks, pedigree, suave personality or peerless manners mislead anyone."

ALL MEMBERS OF THE MUTHAIGA COUNTRY CLUB AND – FOR a rare change, nonmembers also – were invited to assemble on the golf course to witness a demonstration jump by the 2nd MRB "Lounge Lizards," 1 Guerrilla Corps (Parachute) Force N. Nearly the entire population of Nairobi turned out for the event. At 1200 hours sharp, three black painted Commodores arrived over the country club, flying in trail formation. Standing in the door of the lead aircraft was Major Sir Terry "Zorro" Stone.

Down below, he could see hundreds of people lining the fairway. Along the road leading to the country club for a mile or more, cars were parked end to end with people standing out beside them to see the show. None of the civilians in attendance – or military personnel for that matter – had ever witnessed a mass parachute drop. The "Lounge Lizards" did not disappoint.

"Go!" Maj. Stone shouted to the men in his stick, then leapt out into the clear Kenyan sky with his troopers piling out right behind him. By the time his X-chute popped open he could already hear the screams of the excited throng below. He came down near the first hole making a picture-perfect parachute landing fall (PLF).

As soon as they assembled, the demonstration jump unit consisting of the battalion's officers and NCOs formed up and marched past the reviewing stand on the polo grounds. The Governor, Nairobi's Mayor, Major General Alan Cunningham and the President of the Muthaiga Country Club were there to take the salute. Captain the Lady Jane Seaborn presented Maj. Stone with his battalion colors, a pennant that she'd had specially made with what appeared to be a spread-eagle, fire-breathing, turquoise gecko stitched on it with the letter "Z" in the upper right-hand corner.

While faking a huge smile for the crowd, Maj. Stone threatened through gritted teeth – not for the first time – "I shall pay you back for this, Lady Jane, if it is the last thing I ever do!" The "Lounge Lizard" moniker had dogged him ever since Major John Randal learned that Lady Jane had once described him as one; and the major had never let him live it down.

"I shall not blame you one bit if you do, Sir Terry."

As soon as the NCOs were bused back to their base, the 2nd Lounge Lizard officers proceeded with military precision into the country club main building, and the party was on. Maj. Stone was the hero of the hour.

ACROSS THE STREET FROM THE COUNTRY CLUB IN THE GUEST bedroom of Captain the Lord Joss Victor Hay's house, Major Sir Terry "Zorro" Stone was upstairs, entwined with the fabulous Clipper Girl, Red. At 0230 hours he heard the front door loudly close on the first floor. That was the signal the Earl was home from an evening of carousing and wanted to share the salacious details of his escapades. The World's Greatest Pouncer liked to deliver a blow-by-blow account of his dalliances – and he required an audience.

Quietly, so as not to wake Red, Maj. Stone slipped out of bed, put on a pair of tennis shorts and padded down to the kitchen. As expected, Capt. Lord Hay was waiting impatiently. He proceeded to describe in exquisite detail every intimate minute he had spent with his fiancée, Lady Diana Broughton. Then, after dropping her off at her husband's house out in the country, he had swung by the club and managed a quick assignation in the back of a parked RR with some up-country farmer's wife and her teenage daughter, which he also detailed in a graphic, blow-by-blow account.

You have to hand it to him, Maj. Stone thought, *the man never lets up.*

After the Earl wound down his telling of his night's extracurricular activities, he mentioned in passing, "Quite an afternoon's entertainment, Sir Terry. Inspiring sight, to see you and your lads come spilling out of those giant black airplanes."

This was exactly the moment Maj. Stone was waiting for and the real reason behind the demonstration jump, which had been the brainchild of Lieutenant Colonel Dudley Clarke. Now the Lounge Lizard's commanding officer made his move, playing the opportunity to perfection.

"Exactly what it was, old stick, pure theater. A mere diversion to make the Wops waste their time worrying about something that shall never ever happen."

"Are you implying it's all a sham?" Capt. Lord Hay asked. "Your battalion is not actually preparing for an invasion?"

"Surely you never actually believed I would risk my neck parachuting into darkest Abyssinia? The syphilis rate is abysmal," Maj. Stone laughed. "Invasion – if you bought that story, old stick, I have been doing a better job duping people than I thought. There is not going to be any invasion. It is all a hoax. General Cunningham's troop build-up is purely defensive to protect the Kenyan border."

"You sly cad," Capt. Lord Hay said, shaking his golden head. "Really put one over on me, Sir Terry, and everyone else in Nairobi I dare say."

"And you can never tell," Maj. Stone said, man-to-man. "This conversation never happened – classified information, Most Secret. It's the Tower of London if you do."

"Tell? Why, who would I tell?" the Earl smiled from under hooded eyes. "My lips are sealed, sport."

The Duke of Aosta was reading a transcript of the conversation within 24 hours.

23

ALLAH DO IT

CAPTAIN "PYRO" PERCY STIRLING WAS HAMMERING AWAY AT the railroad. The single-track, three-foot, one and three-eights-inch-gauge Imperial Abyssinian Railroad, nowadays modestly called the Roman Railway by the proud Italian High Command, ran from Addis Ababa to the coast, approximately one thousand miles in length as the crow flies. Along the track were thirty-nine tunnels, sixty-five bridges and viaducts, some of which spanned major rivers – and fifteen hundred culverts – more or less. The aggressive young RF officer was determined to blow them all.

To carry out his attack, he broke the rail line down into three target areas. The far northern section closest to the capital was assigned to one of his Bimbashi; the far southern section closest to the Red Sea to his other Bimbashi; Capt. Stirling took the central sector. His demolitions group was divided into three equal reinforced platoon-sized elements, each with a scope-mounted .55 Boys AT Rifle with a two-man team of Green Jackets from RF attached to each to operate them – all original Swamp Fox Force men. The .55 caliber armor piercing (AP) rounds were proving deadly against steam locomotives.

The idea was to chip away at the line around the clock. Nights, Capt. Stirling's troops mined the track, blew the culverts and lit huge bonfires of brush to burn the wooden trestles of the bridges. During the day "The Railroad Wrecking Crew" sniped rolling stock with the long-range .55 Boys and ambushed their cuts in the rail line to prevent work crews from being able to make repairs.

The attacks drove the Italians crazy. Romans take great pride in their ability to build roads and make the trains run on time. It was the one thing they did well. Unfortunately for them, Capt. Stirling was a self-starting go-getter. A cavalry officer commissioned in the famed 17/21 Lancers, he was hell-bent on living up to the regimental motto "Death or Glory." The hard-charging young Lancer was determined to see to it the trains never ran at all – much less on time.

The rail interdiction program came right out of the condensed copy of Mosby's Rangers. After reading it, Capt. Stirling immediately put up an ostrich feather in his Australian slouch hat like the one Colonel John S. Mosby, the *Gray Ghost of the Confederacy*, had worn. Placing him in charge of attacking the rail line was a classic example of "right man, right job."

The challenge the Italians faced was that it was virtually impossible to defend a rail line twenty-four hours a day without tying up their troops, all three hundred fifty thousand of them – especially a line that ran through some of the most rugged terrain in the world. At least that many troops, if not more, would be necessary to prevent Capt. Stirling from sneaking in to blow up a culvert, demolish a section of track or burn down a trestle whenever he chose. The around-the-clock attack on the rail system was hit-and-run guerrilla war against a strategic target at its finest.

The immediate effect of the rail interdiction operation was that the Italians were forced to rely more and more heavily on motor transport. The convoys running the few roads that existed in the mountainous terrain began to increase in frequency and in size, which provided even more juicy ambush targets for the MRBs of 1 Guerrilla Corps (Parachute), Force N.

Militarily, Force N was now dictating to the occupying Blackshirt Army how they could go about conducting their logistical operations. And the precise moment that happened was the tipping point in time where Major John Randal went over from being the hunted to the hunter.

CAPTAIN "GERONIMO" JOE MCKOY HAD HIS BIG .55 CALIBER Boys AT Rifle muscled up the tall mountain by a sweating squad of men. He had handpicked his gun team from Hoolihan's Heros before the rest of the Heros had been re-assigned to Lieutenant Jack Merritt. He set up on a ledge beneath the peak where there was an excellent enfilading view of a road that snaked through the mountains. One side of the road was a sheer drop-off of one thousand feet or more, and the other side was a fairly steep slope up for nearly five hundred feet.

Spread out along the top of the ridge above the winding road, waiting in concealment, was Cheap Bribe and his merry band of brigands. Since he had allied himself with Force N, the outlaw's force had increased ten-fold in size, with new shifta volunteers coming in daily. Gubbo Rekash was coming up in the world of banditry. Mercenaries love a winner.

The brigand marched up to where Major John Randal was studying the killing zone through his Zeiss binoculars, stomped his sandals in the approved fashion and saluted, saying "Allah do it!"

Maj. Randal solemnly returned the snaggle-toothed Patriot commander's salute with his riding crop. He repeated Major Robert Rogers' First Standing Order to his Rangers from the French and Indian War, "Don't forget nothing."

Not understanding more than a handful of English words, Gubbo Rekash responded happily, "Allah do it," one more time for effect. He was hooked on his new foreign-language capabilities.

The plan was to ambush a column of trucks known to be making a daily run down this stretch of highway. Capt. McKoy would open the ball by shooting the lead truck through the engine block, forcing the convoy to a halt.

The winding road was too narrow to allow the Italian drivers to turn their trucks around. Boulders would be rolled down on the roadway to block any possibility of retreat by backing up. After firing on the convoy from the ridgeline to soften up resistance, the plan called for Cheap Bribe and his men to carry out the shifta version of an online infantry assault into the killing zone of the ambush. It remained to be seen if the Patriots would actually carry it out.

Studying the carefully selected ambush site, Maj. Randal was glad he was not going to be riding in the Italian convoy. With a crew of bloodthirsty Patriots lying in wait, drooling in anticipation of the plunder, under orders from their shifta chief to "Kill 'em all and let Allah sort 'em out" and Capt. McKoy caressing the finely-tuned trigger of a .55 Boys AT Rifle with a No. 32 Mk1 scope mounted, the Blackshirts were in for a nasty surprise.

The whine of trucks shifting gears as they labored up the distant incline wafted up the ridge. Maj. Randal felt the old familiar tingle of adrenalin. Ambushes were his specialty, and this one was organized and set to perfection.

Then the line of trucks rolled into view. There was the usual oddball collection of Italian Army ground transport intermingled with civilian vehicles manufactured in four different countries – all camouflaged in tawny yellows, milk chocolates and different shades of mottled olive – and one five-ton fuel tanker. The caravan looked more like a drive-by of itinerant migrant workers than a military convoy.

Concealed in his position with him was Lieutenant Pamala Plum-Martin, along to observe her first Force N combat operation. Maj. Randal had not known the snow-blond Royal Marine was going to be parachuting in to join the guerrilla unit until the night she arrived. SOE was the only organization that allowed women to participate in actual combat operations in the field – with the exception of RF on rare occasions – and that was only because the women insisted on doing it. Maj. Randal was more than a little worried she might get hurt today.

Also along today in the ambush was Captain Hawthorne Merryweather.

The enemy convoy snaked below. *BAAAAAAA-RRRRRRRROOOOOOOOMMMM!* The big .55 Boys boomed in the thin mountain air. *CAAAAAWHAAAAANNNNNKKKK!* The AP round slammed into the engine of the mottled-green Fiat in the lead, sending up a plume of steam from the punctured radiator and blowing up the motor. The Italian truck slammed to a halt.

BAAAAAAAARRRRRRROOOOOOOMMMMM! The Boys spoke again. This time the round shrieked down the length of the convoy and sliced into the engine of the last truck in the convoy, eliminating the need to block the retreat with boulders. Now the Italians were in real trouble. The trucks were trapped with three hundred-odd shifta on the mountain above fingering their curved swords, crazed by the thought of getting at all the loot in the vehicles.

BAAAAAAAARRRRRROOOOOOOMMMMM! The five-ton tanker erupted in a giant, orange, mushroom-shaped fireball fifty feet high.

Maj. Randal stood up. Shouldering the M-1903 Springfield with the aperture sight, he fired offhand as rapidly as he was able to work the butter-smooth bolt, putting an armor-piercing round through the driver's compartment of the first five trucks. Then without turning his head, he handed the weapon back to Lana Turner to reload, took his second M-1903 Springfield with the ivory post front from Rita Hayworth and rapidly emptied it at the next five trucks in the line. Handing the empty rifle back, he repeated the process until he had put a .30 caliber armor-piercing round through the driver's side cab of every truck in the convoy – all twenty-three of them.

That many vehicles under prudent convoy security discipline should have been traveling dispersed for at least a mile – making a shoot like his impossible. But today the truckers were running closed up practically nose-to-tail, feeling a false sense of security by being all bunched up. It was a fatal mistake. There was no way to tell how many drivers he had hit, but those not killed or wounded were now cowering on the floorboard.

Cheap Bribe's men laid down a withering fire, though being miserable shots it was doubtful they hit very much. Nevertheless, three hundred-plus high-caliber military rifles of assorted models banging away would tend to induce high-intensity anxiety in anyone downrange – whether anything was being hit or not.

So far, the Italians had not loosed off a single round in return. Since every truck in the convoy had a pedestal-mounted Breda Model 37 heavy machine gun in the bed, they had plenty of firepower if they opted to use it.

The problem was that standing up in the back of a truck to fire a machine gun was as close to committing suicide as you could possibly get, short of hara-kiri, so the truckers in this convoy chose not to man theirs.

The question now was whether or not the Patriots would actually carry through and launch the final assault. There was no guarantee that they would, and in that case, the Plan B called for Capt. McKoy to fire a .55 Boys AT round through the engine block of each of the trucks before Force N withdrew.

In spite of careful planning, things did not come about exactly the way intended. Without warning Capt. Merryweather rose up with his trusty loud hailer and in fluent Italian commanded, "Exit your vehicles, move to the rear immediately and you will not be castrated!"

The result of this impromptu proclamation was impressive. As Maj. Randal was in the act of exchanging rifles with Rita Hayworth, a mass exodus of Blackshirts literally exploded from the trucks. The scene below was like something out of a Hollywood prison movie when one of the convicts yells "jailbreak!" Panicked men scrambled out of the stalled trucks, many not even bothering to take their personal weapons. Screaming in terror, they made a mad dash back in the opposite direction of travel, as instructed.

The Patriots had been showing signs of restlessness, impatient to get at the booty from the moment they realized the Italians were not shooting back. When they saw the drivers fleeing, the troops acted on their own initiative and launched a mass assault down the mountainside, shrieking unintelligible blood-tingling war cries at the top of their lungs. The shifta were carrying their rifles and shields in one hand while waving their wicked curved swords in the other. Most still retained eight-foot spears. Running full bore down a mountain with both hands full of highly-lethal weaponry is a military skill not to be underestimated.

Caught off guard by the timing of the attack, the Force N commander, a lead-from-the-front type, found himself left behind with no choice but to turn and sprint after his hard-charging troops. To his advantage, Maj. Randal was unencumbered by a robe, toga, spear, shield or a sword; in fact, he was empty-handed.

From high above on the peak, Capt. McKoy and Waldo Treywick observed the fast-breaking melodrama unfolding. "What do you reckon 'ole Merryweather bull-horned them Wops, Joe?"

"I don't know, Waldo, but would you look at those Mussolinites haul ass!"

"Personally, Joe, I never put much truck in all that psychological warfare mumbo jumbo myself. I've always reckoned it was somethin' cooked up by college boys and staff weenies."

"Me neither," Capt. McKoy said, "but I'm beginning to get more open-minded on the subject."

Maj. Randal caught up with the mob of Patriots shortly after they swept over the convoy. Not understanding Italian, he had no idea what Capt. Merryweather had shouted at the Blackshirts either. But he realized that whatever the PWE officer had said had prevented a bloodbath.

The surviving Italians were long gone before Cheap Bribe's men could leg it to the killing zone.

The panic-stricken truck drivers and their equally frightened security element had nothing to fear in the way of pursuit from Cheap Bribe's boys. The shifta's sole concern was racing each other to the treasure. The rule in banditry being "first come, first served," they had no interest in chasing after the Blackshirts. There was no profit in it.

The Italians were far from safe, however. They had to worry about making it back to friendly lines on foot through thirty miles of territory studded with nomadic gangs of unaligned shifta, always on the prowl to pick off easy prey. Since many of the convoy personnel had abandoned their personal weapons as they ran away, they had no way to defend themselves against the wild, bloodthirsty outlaws. And the Blackshirts could count on the sound of the gunfire and the tall columns of greasy smoke from the burning trucks to draw the local land pirates like a hungry pack of hyenas.

As Cheap Bribe's men were swarming the trucks to get at the booty, Maj. Randal was working his way down the line of vehicles. He stopped at each truck, reached up and swung open the driver's side door with one hand while aiming his Colt .38 Super inside the compartment with the other. All he found were dead or dying drivers or empty cabs. Down the convoy, a short burst of gunshots flared, accompanied by a shrill crescendo of high-pitched Patriot voices shouting excitedly. Maj. Randal reached back, expecting Rita Hayworth to place the Beretta .9 mm submachine gun in his hand, only to discover it was Lt. Plum-Martin edging up against him – not his trusty gun girl.

"You were under orders to stay put in the ambush site," he said, less than pleased. "Escort her back to the mule line, Lana – do it now!"

The shooting turned out to be a petty disagreement between two of Cheap Bribe's men over a division of plunder, not an Italian counterattack. Maj. Randal continued working his way down the line of motor vehicles until he came to the shifta chief. "Tell Gubbo to set fire to the trucks and be prepared to move out in five minutes, Rita," he ordered briskly, thinking they had been out in the roadway long enough.

There was a flurry of activity as the Patriots scrambled frantically to unload all the remaining cargo preparatory to lighting off the trucks not already on fire. In a matter of minutes, flames were crackling as one after another of the line of vehicles were torched.

There were no Force N casualties except for a couple of shifta wounded in the exchange of friendly fire as a result of the squabble over property rights to a spool of concertina wire that was too heavy to carry back to the mule lines anyway. Eighteen Blackshirts were KIA, their heads now grinning from poles lining the road.

Within twenty minutes the Force N ambush party was a good mile away, putting the quirt to their mules. Behind them in the widening distance the raiders could hear a string of thunderous booms as the gas tanks of the burning trucks began to explode. The concussion echoed loudly through the thin air of the high mountains.

A happy band of Patriotic Abyssinian bandit warriors rode into the Force overnight position. The party started immediately upon arrival. Waldo came into the HQ tent to find Capt. McKoy peeking out the far flap. "Each and every one a' those crazy bandits is claimin' a kill. The booze is flowin' down at Cheap Bribe's and they're a' smokin' some dope. Funny ain't it, how only drivers got themselves shot."

"Real amazing," the old Arizona Ranger responded over his shoulder without turning his head.

"What you studying on, Joe?"

"John is 'ah tearing a strip of the three girls. I'm not exactly sure what it's about."

Outside the tent a little way from the camp, Maj. Randal had Lt. Plum-Martin, Lana Turner and Rita Hayworth lined up with their heels locked, standing at the ridged position of attention. He was walking up and down the line, reading them the riot act. Neither man had ever seen the young officer so steamed up.

"I think he just told Rita and Lana he was thinkin' about rentin' 'em out to Gubbo," Waldo offered as he looked out the tent.

"Before you got here I thought I heard him threaten to bust Pam down to buck private and make her peel potatoes."

"What's going on, Joe?"

"Best I can figger, he ordered Pam to remain in the ambush site and for one of the girls to stay with her until he gave the all-clear. Apparently Pam ignored the order and charged down the hill with the rest of Bribe's boys. Now John is giving her the what-for and blaming Rita and Lana for dereliction of duty. It's real entertaining."

"The Major's got hisself a complicated life when it comes to women, don't he Joe?"

"You might say that is your basic vast understatement, Waldo. Not too long ago in Istanbul he gunned down the best-looking woman you ever saw, just as cool as ice."

"Yeah, I heard somethin' about that. By the way, before I forget – Merry Christmas."

"Is today Christmas? I didn't know – Merry Christmas to you too, Waldo."

"Maybe we can all get together and sing some Christmas carols a little later on. Now, tell me about that trouble in Istanbul. Kaldi has a cousin livin' in Turkey and he'd heard somethin' about it. Said the rumor was that the lady John shot was some kind of a Nazi spy."

"Classified, Waldo. You don't have a need to know, but what I *can* tell you is, the woman was a barn-burner in the looks department and John shot her deader than world peace."

"I understand his ex-fiancée jilted him bad," Waldo said. "A Dear John can take a toll on a man. I've noticed the major ain't packin' real heavy in the sentimental department. Parachute generally shows warmer feelin's than he does, and that's one stonehearted mule."

"No fiancée done him wrong on purpose, but that don't change the fact John's a' carrying a torch for a certain special lady," Capt. McKoy said. "A real poignant story. You ain't cleared for that one neither, Waldo, so don't ask."

"Well, Joe, you're the man brought it up," Waldo said. "Sounds to me like you might be a little worried about the major. That what it is, you concerned about the state of our chief's emotional well bein'?"

"I could be, Waldo. Then, on the other hand, maybe not," Capt. McKoy said. "For the record, this conversation is concluded. In fact, we never had it."

"What conversation?"

24
THE PROBLEM IS
THE SOLUTION

MAJOR JOHN RANDAL SAT IN HIS CANVAS CAMP CHAIR IN HIS
Force N HQ tent with his Special Warfare Officer, Captain Hawthorne
Merryweather, reading through a stack of intelligence reports. The reports
were courtesy of Lieutenant Pamala Plum-Martin. The Vargas Girl-looking
Royal Marine had a thick stack of intelligence material she had been
gathering while biding her time in Nairobi waiting her chance to go into the
field. The sound of Beretta 9 mm Kurz pistol rounds were popping outside.

The firing finally ceased. Captain "Geronimo" Joe McKoy was
introducing Rita Hayworth and Lana Turner to the gentle art of combat pistol
shooting using captured Italian Beretta handguns. The girls were eager
pupils, picking up the skill as quickly as any students he had ever trained.
The cowboy showman was giving some serious thought to incorporating
them into his Wild West show after the war. The girls were a cinch to be a
big draw.

Capt. McKoy and Waldo Treywick strolled into the tent. They pulled up canvas chairs and lit a couple of long, thin Italian cigars – booty from one of the ambushes.

"Captain McKoy," Maj. Randal said, "I need direction from my Animal Transport Officer."

"Fire away, John," the silver-haired cowboy responded, waving the cigar expansively. "That's what I'm here for, giving sage advice and plenty of it."

"Maj. Stone will be jumping his battalion in-country sometime in the next few weeks. Where am I going to find four hundred mules to mount his men?"

"That's a lot of mules," Waldo said. "There ain't that many spare long-ears available to be bought."

"You know, I took a junior college correspondence course one time back when I was a' workin' the Mexican border conducting stakeouts for smugglers and bootleggers. Had a lot of spare time on my hands sittin' in those hide positions," Capt. McKoy said as he studied the growing ash on the tip of his cigar. "It was in Business Administration."

"You was thinkin' on givin' up law enforcement to become a businessman?" Waldo inquired.

"Naw, I was just bored and needed something to do to keep me occupied. The name of the course was Problem Solving 101."

"What's that have to do with Terry's mules, Captain?" Maj. Randal asked carefully. He had enough experience dealing with the old Arizona Ranger, Rough Rider, etc. to know he should at least make a show of avoiding one of his traps.

"Well, John, the title of one lesson was styled 'The Problem is the Solution.' "

"What the fool does that mean, Joe?" Waldo asked. "That's crazy!"

"Exactly what it says," the Capt. McKoy said. "According to the curriculum, you say the problem out loud and she pops right out – the solution."

"You been smokin' your rope?"

"Well, let's give 'er a try, boys – take a shot, Waldo."

"Ain't no four hundred mules to be bought. Now what?"

"There you go, you done answered the question."

"I did?"

"Well, yeah – halfway. Why ain't there four hundred mules to be bought?"

"Because the Italian Wops have done confiscated all they is in this entire part of the country, that's why."

"See, John, clear as a bell."

"Why don't you expand on the solution part, captain?" Maj. Randal said, glancing over at Capt. Merryweather. The PWE officer was intently following the conversation but artfully keeping his mouth planted firmly shut.

"We'll have us a regular stampede," Capt. McKoy said, slapping his thigh. "It'll be just swell, like back in the olden days, downright Western."

"A stampede?" Waldo asked. "What's that?"

"It's the problem providing the solution, just exactly like my correspondence course said it would. The professors who write those things are the smartest men in the world."

"Maybe you better spell it out for us, Captain." Maj. Randal said. "We don't all have the benefit of your education."

"Well, John, the reason we can't buy mules," Capt. McKoy replied, "is because the Italian Army has got 'em all. So all we have to do is go get 'em from the Blackshirts, and then we'll have mules. We sneak in stealthy-like and stampede the entire Italian mule herd, run 'em over to Terry's drop zone in time to mount his boys up – the problem is the solution. Waldo and a handful of Bad Boys is all I'll need to get 'er done."

"Anything else, Captain?"

"Be a good idea to have Zorro's men parachute in a' carryin' saddles and tack, unless you want his troopers to be ridin' bareback."

"The problem is the solution," Waldo said. "That's a good 'un, Joe. I'm gonna try to remember that next time I get myself in a scrape. I remember one time when P.J. Pretorius and I was a' sittin' in a stinkin' Portuguese prison…"

Capt. Merryweather had developed a grimace like you might expect to see on a man who has discovered an abscessed tooth.

Maj. Randal went back to his reading.

The next document in the folder was a list of the annual salaries (which meant bribes) paid by the Italians to certain Abyssinian chiefs. The two leading lights of the Abyssinian Orthodox Church were on the bribe list – in fact they topped it, each being paid 525,700 lira each annually. Ras Haylu Takla Haymanot was the highest paid nobleman in the country at 490,492 lira with the next highest being Ras Kabade Mangasha at 172,000 lira. After that the amount paid per bribe dropped off precipitously. Down almost at the bottom one familiar name appeared – Gubbo Rekash 23,750 lira per annum. Cheap Bribe was on the Italian payroll!

The bandit chief had a boot – in his case a dirty sandal, in both camps. In U.S. dollars the amount came to approximately $350 a month. On the local economy that was a fortune. Who was to blame Gubbo? In 1940 Abyssinia it was every robber for himself. Still, the information was worth knowing. Probably a good idea, Maj. Randal decided, to match the Italian bribe in Maria Theresa thalers.

CAPTAIN "GERONIMO" JOE MCKOY, WALDO TREYWICK AND A squad of Bad Boys rode out to go on a "mule safari" – a test run to steal sixty mules prior to the four hundred-mule raid. Waldo had performed a detailed reconnaissance of an Italian FOB's mule herd conveniently located within ten miles of the DZ Lieutenant Butch "Headhunter" Hoolihan and his Force Raiding Company would be parachuting into at 2330 hours later that night. Major John Randal felt a tinge of uneasiness about letting the two set off unsupervised. They were acting like a couple teenagers heading out to go hell-raising on a Saturday night.

Actually, the Force N commander wished he was going with them. However, a commander needs to have the discipline to know where to position himself to be most effective. Tonight's first priority was the DZ.

Shortly after nightfall, Force N broke camp and moved out on a cross-country march to the DZ. The night was cool, and before the moon came out, the brightest thing in the deep purple sky was the glittering Southern Cross. Four hours of riding brought them to a long, flat valley that was the designated location of the evening's entertainment. When the column snaked down out of the mountains, a small herd of mules was already there ahead of them, grazing peaceably on the grassy floor of the valley.

"How did it go, Captain?"

"Just swell, John. We slipped in easy like, snatched up these animals and rode out yipping and firing our pistols in the air. You should a' been there."

"The Italians didn't try to come after you?"

"On what? We rustled all the riding stock – got a few head extra."

Five minutes early the distant sound of aircraft could be heard approaching from the south. Maj. Randal gave the command to light the signal fires. The beacons had been arranged in the shape of an arrowhead pointed in the direction of flight toward a giant letter N. Extreme care was taken to insure that all the grass around each one of them had been cleared in a large circle so there was no possibility of the fire spreading. To be on the safe side, a guard was on duty watching each beacon.

One thousand feet up, three dark shapes – the Pregnant Guppy with two Commodores flying in trail formation – lined up on the beacons for their run in and reduced their airspeed. Inside the Pregnant Guppy, Lt. Hoolihan shouted out the series of jump commands. Then he took up his position standing in the door. Looking down he could see the burning arrowhead below on the DZ – then the burning N. The cold wind was whipping at his sand-green parachute smock. When the tip of the "N" was just off the toe of his left boot, the young Royal Marine leaned back inside the cabin and shouted to his Force Raiding Company paratroopers, "Follow me. Go!"

From down below, the specks of the jumpers came spilling out the lead aircraft and were soon followed by more specks dropping from the other two planes. The black dots came out fast and seemed to fall rapidly, unchecked at first, then a thin ribbon of a shadow appeared above them that blossomed into a wider, mushroom-shaped shadow. Except for the powerful drone of the airplane engines, the night was perfectly silent.

There was a rustle of silk, then Lt. Hoolihan was touching down, executing his PLF. When he bounded to his feet, Maj. Randal was standing there. Rita Hayworth and Lana Turner ran to chase down his canopy. Across the DZ, Cheap Bribe's men were assisting the rest of the Raiding Company troopers as they drifted down.

"Welcome back, Lieutenant Hoolihan."

"Good to be here, sir."

"Get your men mounted. I want to move out as quickly as possible."

"Can I introduce you to my new platoon commanders, sir?"

"We'll get around to courtesies later, Butch. We need to move out as soon as possible," Maj. Randal said. "A lot of really mad Blackshirts are likely to be out tonight looking for these mules."

In less than an hour, the Force Raiding Company was saddled up and moving. Even if the Italians knew where the DZ was, there was little to no possibility they would be able to react rapidly enough to mobilize an attack on it.

Even so, Maj. Randal was not taking any chances.

25
THE BEAUTIFUL ONE
HAS ARRIVED

A SIGNAL ARRIVED AT FORCE N HQ ORDERING MAJOR JOHN Randal to unleash the Bad Boys on the Italian's communications systems. The order also contained the directive that within ten days Force N was to be ready, on command, to raid as many airfields in central and southern IEA as possible, to try to prevent the Regia Aeronautica from interfering with Major General Alan Cunningham's upcoming offensive out of Kenya. The message plunged Force N HQ into a frenzy of activity. Orders were drafted and sent to each of the battalions.

Bad Boys were dispatched all over the central highlands on a mission of mayhem. The young Abyssinians fanned out across the countryside on an orgy of government-sanctioned juvenile delinquency. Since the Italians had virtually no radio communications, they relied almost entirely on landlines, which were ridiculously easy to sabotage. The youngsters pulled down or cut every phone cable they came across. At night Captain Hawthorne

Merryweather arranged for burning telephone poles to be seen flaming for miles in all directions from known Italian installations, a sight that did not do much for the morale of Blackshirt soldiers sitting in isolated FOBs on lonely hilltops late at night pondering their prospects.

The Italian communications system was in shambles within seventy-two hours.

Twelve landing grounds were targeted for Force N units to attack. The majority of the air bases were small, single-squadron aerodromes hosting less than a dozen aircraft each. Some landing grounds had CR-42 fighters, while others were home to Savoia bombers. Airfields are notoriously soft targets because most are not defended in depth. The trick to attacking a landing ground is to penetrate the outer first line of defense. Once the perimeter is breached, airfields are relatively easy to take down.

Regia Aeronautica doctrine called for each individual base commander to draft his own installation's defense scheme, which meant the senior air force officer at each airfield had to make a hard choice between two radically different options. Base commanders had to decide whether to disperse their airplanes so that the aircraft were not vulnerable to mass destruction from air attack by the RAF or South African Air Force (SAAF), or park them close together wingtip to wingtip in order to make it easier to protect the planes from saboteurs. There is no school solution – either choice has its advantages counterbalanced by its risks.

And there is no third option.

Minefields and layers of concertina wire surrounded most of the Italian airfields. Guard towers were strategically placed around the outer perimeters. Roving security patrols circled inside the wire day and night. Heavily-armed ready reaction platoons were on standby at a central location ready to spring into action at all times. At least that was Regia Aeronautica SOP for Airfield Security – on paper.

In reality, air base defenses on landing grounds all across Abyssinia had fallen into a state of disrepair over the years. Most of the land mines had been put down in 1936. More than a few mines were no longer serviceable, while those exploded by the odd zebra or gazelle had never been replaced. Worse, the local natives had a habit of driving their goat herds through the minefields, leaving plainly marked trails for anyone to see.

Generally there were not enough security troops stationed at the airfields to make the roving patrols meaningful, much less to staff a ready reaction platoon. In practice, it was virtually impossible for the Italians to motivate their men to stay out at night alone or in pairs in the watch towers – they knew a bloodthirsty shifta was likely to be lurking behind every bush waiting to pick them off. Officers could not see anything to be gained by walking the perimeter in the dark to check on the sentries – a bandit or a trigger-happy guard might get you.

Due to the shortage of airfield security forces and the reluctance of the troops to stand isolated guard or conduct roving patrols around the perimeter in the dark, most base commanders elected to concentrate their aircraft in one location. It made the planes easier to guard. Besides, the Regia Aeronautica owned the sky. RAF or South Africa Air Force (SAAF) bombing attacks in the interior of Abyssinia were virtually unknown.

Maj. Randal had spent a lot of time studying the vulnerabilities of enemy landing grounds during OPERATION BUZZARD PLUCKER, the Most Secret RF clandestine operation that employed Lovat Scouts to snipe Luftwaffe fighter pilots at their airfields in France. The lessons learned then came in handy now.

Commanding his 1 Guerrilla Corps (Parachute), Force N MRBs in the field he had four of the finest officers to ever wear a uniform. There was no doubt in Maj. Randal's mind that at the prescribed time, all twelve Regia Aeronautica bases would be hammered. The only question was how to go about it with the men and equipment available and the tactical constraints dictated by the individual landing ground's location and terrain.

Since Lieutenant Butch "Headhunter" Hoolihan did not have the benefit of formal training, Maj. Randal helped him craft his plan for the raids on the two airfields assigned the Force Raiding Company. The Force N commander entered the project in the spirit that the exercise was a teaching process as well as deadly serious military business. It was the way he had been mentored in the Philippines by his team sergeants "Hammerhead" and "Tiger Stripe."

The wise commander finds a way to give ownership in the final product to his junior officers, NCOs and the troops who will be executing the plan. The way to accomplish that is for the commander to issue a mission-type order, and then stand back and allow his subordinates the freedom to develop the actual plan. Mission planning is not the place for prima donnas, egotists or a tactical planner with a Messiah complex. What is needed is input and ideas from everyone participating in the mission.

The best military plans are always simple.

"Time spent on reconnaissance is rarely wasted" is a military truism a combat commander ignores at his peril. Maj. Randal had no intention of disregarding it. Several days were spent conducting a leader's recon of the Force Raiding Company's two objectives.

One of the airfields presented a straightforward setup. The target consisted of a picturesque pink adobe village adjoining a small landing strip located at the edge of a patch of jungle. Between the airstrip and the town was a tank farm of aviation fuel storage tanks. The facility presented an irresistible target for a demolition team, operating stealthily under cover of darkness to sneak through the village and blow up. The resulting explosion should, Maj. Randal reasoned, create enough of a diversion to cover an attacking force that wanted to approach unobserved through the jungle, breach the minefield, penetrate the perimeter and attack the fifteen closely parked CR-42 fighters clustered below the control tower.

Not easy, but doable.

The second air base assigned the Force Raiding Company posed a significantly greater challenge. Located in the middle of a wide valley, it was completely surrounded by miles of flat savanna grassland. There was no covered approach. Even at night, the base was going to be difficult to attack with any reasonable hope of achieving the element of surprise.

However, like most military airbases, its location had been selected by airmen for ease in constructing a landing strip, not with an eye to siege by an attacking army, and its defense contained a flaw. A small, treeless, cone-shaped hill of the type described as a kopje was located three-quarters of a mile south of the installation. If an attacker placed artillery or mortars on the reverse slope of the anthill-shaped mound, then they could command the landing ground. That vulnerability would have been obvious to a line infantry or artillery officer but may not have been apparent to the IAF engineer who chose the location.

Lying on a mountaintop two miles away, studying the target through his Zeiss binoculars, Maj. Randal spotted the chink in the defense the moment he clapped eyes on it. The trouble was, he did not have artillery or mortars to give to Lt. Hoolihan to place on the reverse slope of the hill. Captain "Geronimo" Joe McKoy borrowed the glasses, took one look, grinned and shook his long, gunfighter-style, silver mane. "Me and Waldo'll take out this objective for you, Butch – all by ourselves."

"We will?" Waldo queried, with a certain amount of trepidation. More than a little apprehensive, he was wondering if the problem was going to turn out to be the solution again. Privately the ex-ivory poacher preferred to have more direct input into his personal life path than trusting to some random, correspondence-school, problem-solving process designed by educated idiots.

"How do you intend to go about it, Captain?" Lt. Hoolihan asked as he scanned the target area through his own binoculars.

"Easy, we'll haul my scoped Boys .55 up on that hill yonder. I'll mark up a range card zeroing in on each one of those Savoia bombers parked along the airstrip, and then when the time's right I'll drill an armor-piercing slug through the engine housing of every airplane sitting out there on the flight line – that'll put 'em outta' business for the duration. Once I dial in the click adjustments and log 'em on my range card, using the vertical and horizontal traversing mechanism on the tripod, I can even do the shoot in the pitch dark if you want me to."

"Can you do that?" Lt. Hoolihan asked. He knew that's a skill level generally reserved to highly trained machine gunners.

"Like shooting fish in a barrel, young lieutenant. Don't you worry none, Butch – it's a done deal."

Upon their return to Force N HQ a Warning Order was issued to Force Raiding Company. Then a giant terrain map of the target airfield was constructed on the ground. The topography and built-up area were modeled roughly to scale using rocks, twigs, pieces of paper and anything else they could think of to represent the airfield. The result was a crude but effective field-expedient sand table. Maj. Randal, Lt. Hoolihan, his two Bimbashi platoon leaders and Lieutenant Dick Courtney spent hours carefully working out the exact details of every move. Then Force Raiding Company troops were brought in to receive their Operations Order prior to conducting rehearsals.

A supercharged sense of impending action was in the air. In hidden encampments all over the central highlands of Abyssinia, 1 Guerrilla Corps (Parachute), Force N officers were going about the same reconnaissance, planning, briefing and preparation cycle with the Force N native troops in the MRBs under their command. On the big night, simultaneous attacks would be launched countrywide in a highly-orchestrated show of force.

Force N's guerrilla war was moving inexorably toward the classic phase, where the guerrillas come out of hiding and attack fixed military installations using conventional ground attack tactics. The anticipation to get started was building.

Just as blowing the railroads had increased the volume of truck traffic, the Bad Boys taking out the phone lines resulted in fleets of motorcycle dispatch riders taking to the roads in previously undreamed-of numbers. Motorcycles are easy targets. Every day Cheap Bribe and his men were out in force on every road, tract, or trail – lying in wait. The Patriots let the large, heavily-armed parties pass unmolested, but the smaller convoys and the motorcycle dispatch riders were being slaughtered.

The bandit chief had reached the zenith of his criminal career. He was getting rich, paid a retainer by the Italians and now by Maj. Randal, and raking in the loot from the relentless pace of the road ambushes. The Force N commander had magnanimously provided him 50 M-1903 A-1 Springfield rifles to arm his personal bodyguard, greatly increasing his prestige in the eyes of his followers.

Gubbo Rekash was in shifta heaven – living the life.

The Patriots were pointedly not included in the planned attack on the airfields. In fact, they had no idea such an operation was even in the works. For reasons of security, this was strictly a Force N affair. To keep them in the dark, the shifta were deliberately directed to ambush locations miles from any Italian airfields. For the first time, they were allowed to operate entirely without supervision. Cheap Bribe and his lieutenants took that as a sign of trust.

Nothing could have been farther from the truth.

The order arrived giving a specific date to launch the raids on the Italian airfields. Tension at Force N HQ reached pressure-cooker level. On the morning Force Raiding Company was preparing to move out for the big show, the overworked Signals Officer, Captain Mickey Duggan, came running up waiving a flimsy toward Maj. Randal, who was sitting on Parachute. Semi-hysterical, he shouted, "Urgent message for you, Major!"

"What's in it, Mickey?"

"The signal is marked 'Eyes Only,' sir, Most Secret."

"You decoded it – what's it say?"

"Orders for you to select a stretch of road somewhere the Hudson can land for pick-up tonight, Major. You are wanted in Khartoum, sir, most immediate."

"Khartoum?" Maj. Randal snatched the flimsy and studied it in disbelief. The orders were clear. He was to fly out tonight. His first reaction was outrage. He started to wad it up and ignore the order; then it dawned on him the message designator read "FROGSPAWN."

"Hoolihan!" he barked. The young Royal Marine was at his side in an instant. "Take charge of your company; move out. Execute your mission as ordered!"

"Sir?" the young Royal Marine responded with a catch in his voice.

"You heard me, Lieutenant."

"Without you, Major?" There was a spark of what might have passed for momentary panic in his eyes.

"Change of plans; my presence is required elsewhere. You're in command, stud."

"Yes, sir!"

"Light 'em up good, Butch."

The two men locked eyes. Then Force Raiding Company's CO snapped a crisp salute. Maj. Randal returned the gesture lazily, making a studied effort at nonchalance – an emotion he most definitely did not feel.

He was flashing back to the first time he had led a group of men on a desperate venture. Being a commander is different from being a leader. Maj. Randal did not like the way it felt right this minute.

Capt. McKoy trotted past on his fast-stepping mule "Georgie," followed by Waldo Treywick leading the pack train carrying the scoped

Boys .55 caliber AT Rifle. Waldo was followed by their squad of hard-eyed Patriot security guards. "Don't fret, John, have a good time on your R and R," the handsome old Rough Rider called as he rode by. "Them Wop flyboys ain't even gonna' know what hit 'em when me and Butch get done with 'em."

"Good luck, Captain."

With the troops gone, Force N HQ felt empty, even though the staff was busy at appointed tasks. Maj. Randal hated being there. Sensing his mood, Lieutenant Pamala Plum-Martin tried to sooth his feelings by reminiscing, "I recall the day Jane and I were waiting at the station when you walked off the train. Butch was trailing along carrying your bag, wanting to volunteer for Raiding Forces. Now he's a company commander. Cheer up, John. 'Headhunter' can carry this off without you along to hold his hand."

"At least," Maj. Randal said, "I won't have to be worried about you crawling through the wire with a knife in your teeth."

Time seemed to stand still until his party moved out to the extraction location. The moment the lime green hands on Maj. Randal's Rolex watch lined up at 2000 hours, the small signal fires lining a long, straight stretch of road were lit. Before the last one was ignited, the drone of an incoming aircraft could be heard. Appearing out of the majestic purple sky, the Hudson glided down and greased a perfect landing.

Maj. Randal jogged up to the aircraft followed by Rita Hayworth and Lana Turner. The trio tossed their gear inside, jumped up, grabbed the sides of the fuselage and swung aboard. Major Sir Terry "Zorro" Stone slammed the door shut and signaled the pilot to take off. The Hudson revved its engines and roared down the road before lifting into the air.

"This had better be good," Maj. Randal said as he slumped onto one of the canvas bench seats. "What's the flap in Khartoum?"

"I rather think you shall find it is pretty good, old stick – and we are not flying to Khartoum." Maj. Stone offered him a Player's cigarette out of his elegant silver case. "That part of the signal was a rather clumsy cover story. Actually we are inbound Nairobi."

"What ...?"

"Straightaway before we talk about anything else, and you are going to owe me for this, the 'N' in Force N stands for Nefertiti, got that?"

"What the hell is a Nefertiti?"

"An Egyptian queen – the name means 'the beautiful one has arrived.' Don't forget it. I did you a favor, old stick."

"If you say so..."

Captain the Lady Jane Seaborn stepped out of the pilot's compartment and made her way back to where the two officers were sitting. As usual, whenever she was in the immediate vicinity, Maj. Randal felt it difficult to breath. Possibly tonight it could be blamed on the altitude.

"Remember... Nefertiti," Maj. Stone repeated under his breath, "and you picked the name."

"Roger that," Maj. Randal said, making eye contact with Lady Jane. "Nefertiti – got it."

The two ex-slave girls perked up when they saw the Royal Marine officer, like she was a long-lost girlfriend.

Lady Jane walked down the aisle, leaned down, threw her arms around Maj. Randal and gave him a long, lingering kiss – ignoring the other three completely. Except for the throb of the airplanes engines, you could have heard a pin drop in the back of the converted Hudson bomber as it hurtled through the Abyssinian night.

Later – actually much later – Maj. Stone came up from the tail of the airplane where he and the two girls had retreated. "Time to break it up you two."

"Go away," Maj. Randal ordered.

"Sorry, we have to talk and there simply is no time."

"Unfortunately, he is right, John," Lady Jane said regretfully. "We need to discuss a rather delicate situation."

"Like I said before," Maj. Randal said, "this had better be good."

"Good!" Maj. Stone laughed out loud. "What I am going to tell you, John, is so preposterous it's difficult for me to believe any part of it. And I have been living with it for the better part of the last two months."

"Agreed," said Lady Jane.

The Life Guards officer began a brisk, no-nonsense briefing, and he was right –Maj. Randal could hardly believe what he heard. Had he not been sitting in the back of the General Officer-in-Command of the Middle East Command's personal airplane, having just been snatched from behind enemy lines in the middle of a major guerrilla combat offensive to hear the story, he probably would not have believed a word of it.

A flip chart was needed to diagram all the assorted players…misdeeds, high crimes, and who was sleeping with whom. The saga had all the elements of an Academy Award winning movie script.

When Maj. Stone finished, Maj. Randal said, "Let's see if I've got this straight. Joss Hay is the Italian's man in Kenya, SOE has dispatched a hit team from Cairo to terminate him, a group of gay Nazis called the 'Pink Swastika' have sent out their own team to kill him, one of the enemy alien Italian settlers he interned has put out a contract on him, at least five men and one woman have verbally threatened to shoot him for reasons of their own, and you believe the World's Greatest Pouncer will alert Addis Ababa of General Cunningham's intentions to invade Abyssinia the second he can confirm them.

"I miss anything?"

"Bang on the high points, old stick. There are a few minor odds and ends I purposely left out for brevity."

"I see."

"Probably not – the story has a lot of twists and turns," Maj. Stone said. "As we both know, General Cunningham is almost ready to go. In your professional opinion – what will the result be if the Italians get wind of his plan of attack before the balloon goes up?"

"The Blackshirts will launch a preemptive strike. They'll blow right through Force N if they do. They have the manpower to do it."

"Our own assessment, almost verbatim. The lads who are getting ready to go over the top deserve better than for us to stand idly by and let that happen to them, do they not?"

Maj. Randal said, "If the Earl's a spy, why not just shoot him?"

"I was rather hoping you would see it that way," Maj. Stone replied. "You would not have any qualms helping me kill him then?"

"Why should I? Those are my boys the Italians will be cutting through."

"Excellent, we are in agreement," Maj. Stone said. "The time for sitting around hoping for any of the other people to eliminate him for us has now passed. The SOE bunglers out of Cairo are so amateurish it's farcical.

Those fools have been traveling incognito to Kenya for over three weeks now by boat and train, changing identities, wearing disguises and doing silly Keystone Cops, movie spy thriller stuff. They have not been checking in as instructed, so who knows where they are?

"Our people lost track of the Pink Swastika hit team last week. As for the others, someone *did* take a pot shot at Joss recently, but they missed. What it boils down to is if we want the job done, we are going to have to do it ourselves."

"Not *us*, Terry. You've got a battalion to command. Your primary responsibility is to be with your troops. I'll handle this, but let's make it quick so I can get back to mine," Maj. Randal said.

"All right, if that's the way you prefer to handle it."

"What's the plan?"

"Pretty bare bones. You and I were simply going to drive out to Lady Diana's house in the country late tomorrow night, waylay the Earl on the road after he drops her off at home following the usual evening of carousing at the Muthaiga Country Club, and shoot him."

"I can do that," Maj. Randal said.

"After neutralizing Joss, you will be flown out same night to Camp Croc, then parachute back in to Force N the next, and no one will ever be the wiser," Maj. Stone said. "As far as anyone will ever know, you were never in Nairobi."

"Hard for me to picture Hay as a spy."

"Quite right, that's pretty much the same response of everyone in on this who knows him. Not a story one would likely invent – it's all true."

"Why would a British aristocrat from an ancient family commit treason?"

"For the money, old stick."

"One last question, Terry."

"Ask away."

"What's that stuck on your hat?"

"Why, an ostrich plume, of course," Maj. Stone drawled, "Mosby's Rangers!"

"Oh no…"

"If I am ever allowed back in my regiment, which appears unlikely, I fully intend to make *Gray Ghost of the Confederacy* required reading for all ranks. The plume does lend a certain tone to the uniform, does it not?"

Lady Jane failed in her attempt to suppress a giggle. Maj. Randal shook his head. Passing out the condensed book had been a stroke of pure military genius on the part of Capt. Merryweather.

AS THE HUDSON BOMBER THUNDERED THROUGH THE DARK African sky, Force N units were moving into position all over the central highlands region of Abyssinia. The plan laid down that no attack could go in before 2400 hours. The raids were not synchronized to go off simultaneously – that would have been coordination on a grander scale than 1 Guerrilla Corps (Parachute), Force N was capable of achieving. Since it was impossible to synchronize the attacks precisely, they were set to commence any time in a four-hour window.

As the Hudson crossed over into Kenyan air space, Captain "Geronimo" Joe McKoy and Waldo Treywick were settling into position. The two had left their mules in defilade on the reverse slope at the base of the hill, under guard. With the help of their security detail, they had hauled the .55 caliber Boys AT Rifle up to the top one hour before sunset. A range card was carefully prepared in the remaining minutes of daylight, checked for details and rechecked. The gun was sandbagged to prevent its massive recoil from jarring the tripod loose, and a folded tarp was laid over the barrel with a camouflage net over the top of the tarp to prevent any possibility of muzzle flash giving away their firing position.

At the designated time, which by their own choice was one minute after midnight, Capt. McKoy placed the big steel-butt plate of the Boys against his shoulder and dialed in the first target. Waldo was lying under a blanket holding a flashlight on his watch, and when the hand swept past the appointed time he gave the command "Fire when ready, Joe."

KAAAAABOOOOOOM!

As the big .55 caliber shell screamed toward its target, Capt. McKoy cranked the bolt back and manually loaded a second round into the chamber. The Boys AT Rifle came equipped with a five-round magazine, but the No. 32 Mk1 scope blocked the magazine well, thus reducing the weapon to single shot. From under the blanket where he was studying the range card in the glowing yellow light of the hand-held torch, Waldo called out the click correction for the second target. The adjustment was quickly dialed in.

KAAAAABOOOOOOOM!

The process was repeated again and again until fifteen rounds had been pumped down range. On the Italian airfield, three-quarters of a mile away, there was no sign of life. Nothing stirred. Surreal as it seemed, the Blackshirts did not appear to be aware they had been attacked. However, fifteen Savoia bombers sitting on the flight line were now nothing more than scrap metal, their engines shot out. After the last round boomed out and the concussion wafted off into the night, silence set in on the hill as the two men waited and watched. The results seemed more than mildly anti-climactic.

"You think you hit anything, Joe?"

"I nailed 'em, all right! We'll give it a few minutes – then I'll give 'em another dose a' .55 medicine."

In the distance, a tiny red glow appeared as a fire inside the fuselage of one of the Savoia bombers began to burn. The glow grew gradually brighter and brighter until the airplane unexpectedly exploded in a massive fireball. The Savoias were sitting on the flight line topped off with high-grade aviation fuel and a full bay of bombs – ready for an early-morning mission. The sound of the detonation rumbled across the savanna to the hill. The explosion caused a chain reaction, and while the two men watched in delight, all fifteen bombers cooked off, one after another, in a spectacular show of high explosive pyrotechnics. The ground rumbled with each detonation.

Down on the airfield a spirited firefight broke out. The Italian gunners were shooting straight up, blazing away into the sky firing at phantom aircraft under the mistaken impression they had been bombed! The battle against imaginary aerial invaders raged for over two hours and did not slow until the gunners finally ran out of ammunition.

As the battle raged, Capt. McKoy and Waldo made their getaway. Miles away, looking down from the top ridge of a mountain they were crossing as the firing fizzled out, Capt. McKoy said, "Too bad Cheap Bribe didn't come along, ain't it, Waldo."

"Yeah, Bribe's boys could a' waltzed right in and slit everybody's throat after them Wops ran out of bullets. P.J. Pretorius would a' loved to seen what you just done, Joe. He'd a' got a real kick outta' it."

"Wonder how ole' Butch is doin' right about now?"

Fifty miles away Lieutenant Butch "Headhunter" Hoolihan was on his belly working his way through the enemy minefield to his target. Kaldi and the rest of his men followed, wiggling behind him in single file like Indian Scouts. Tonight's work did not exactly require skilled sneakers and peekers. Force Raiding Company was crawling along a goat path packed as hard as asphalt from all the goat traffic. A blind man could have followed it. The only threat the raiders had encountered to this point was a trail of fresh goat droppings.

On the far side of the airfield, Captain "Pyro" Percy Stirling was hard at work with a team of his Railroad Wrecking Crew in the middle of the aviation fuel tank farm, setting the last of their demolitions in place. The Death or Glory Boy had not been able to resist the lure of a full-scale raid. Instead of detailing one of his Bimbashi to handle the assignment, he had come himself. Even though he outranked Lt. Hoolihan, he was not in command – tonight was the "Headhunter's" show.

Once the explosives were in place, Capt. Stirling and his team silently exfiltrated the area and made their way back to where their mules were being held. The Railroad Wrecking Crew party was miles away when the first fuel storage tank blew sky-high. The result was a mind-numbing explosion, not particularly loud, but the flash was absolutely brilliant and the luminous fireball could be seen for miles and miles and miles. The first detonation was followed by eight more, virtually turning night into day.

The instant the first fuel tank blew, Lt. Hoolihan leapt to his feet and ordered in a loud whisper, "Move out!"

Kaldi quickly translated the command.

Carrying his cherished Thompson .45 caliber submachine gun at the high port, the Royal Marine charged across the runway straight toward the clustered CR-42 fighters parked on the far side of the tarmac. A sentry standing near the planes called out when he saw the ghostlike figures in the shimmering white light created by the flaming fuel tanks.

Lt. Hoolihan chopped him down with a short burst of fire without breaking stride. Behind him his men began screaming unintelligible tribal war cries while firing their M-1903 A-1 Springfield rifles from the hip as fast as they could cycle the bolt.

When he reached the first CR-42, the Royal Marine pulled a Mills bomb out of the canvas satchel he had slung over his shoulder, armed it and tossed it into the open cockpit of the fighter. Not waiting around to see the results, he dashed down the flight line tossing one in each of the twelve fighters that were parked wingtip to wingtip. The grenades cooked off in a steady, muffled cadence, *WHUUUMPH! WHUUUMPH! WHUUUMPH!* turning the interiors of the enemy aircraft into smoldering wrecks.

At that point, his mission accomplished, Lt. Hoolihan shouted, "Break contact, Rally" to each of his two platoon leaders, who were busy supervising the shooting-up of the control tower and the adjoining buildings. Then he led the way off the north end of the airfield to where Lieutenant Dick Courtney was positioned at the edge of the wire with his two trackers, X-Ray and Vanish, holding a hooded flashlight to guide them through the minefield to their waiting mules.

Force Raiding Company trotted out through the perimeter wire, once again following a clearly defined goat trail. Shortly they were away, gone in the night. From beginning to end the raid did not last a full eight minutes. Colonel John S. Mosby, the Gray Ghost, would have been proud.

Behind them, the battle was joined. Initially the Italian airfield defenders had gone to ground but now they returned to their defensive positions, stood to their guns and did their duty with a will. The Blackshirts put out an impressive volume of automatic weapons fire in every direction. Apparently the Regia Aeronautica's preferred method of firing a machine gun in the static defense was to hold the trigger down and run the entire belt of ammunition in one long burst. This technique instills a great deal of confidence in the machine gunner, though it rarely causes harm to anyone downrange and is highly wasteful of ammunition. Some of the Italian machine gunners even managed to perform the feat while keeping their head completely down below the firing slit.

In the excitement of battle, the airfield mortar crews stood to, manned their tubes, panicked, and fired the base Final Protective Fire, which was a last-ditch fire mission intended to be reserved until the absolute last second when the airfield was in danger of being overrun by a wave of ground attackers. When the mortars started registering the FPF, desperation set in among the defenders and every airman, mechanic, cook – anyone who could pull a trigger, stood to and joined the fight. All personnel understood full well the implications of firing the FPF. They were all going to die! The Regia Aeronautica men fought their hearts out.

All across Abyssinia, at ten other carefully selected locations, 1 Guerrilla Corps (Parachute), Force N was carrying out similar operations.

The next morning at dawn, the RAF, flying out of airfields in the Sudan, and the SAAF, flying from bases in Kenya, struck from out of the sun, carrying out a series of carefully-planned air strikes on the same airfields, coordinated by Pilot Officer Gasper "Bunny" Featherstone.

The RAF and SAAF claimed every one of the airplanes destroyed by Force N – all one hundred fifty-seven of them.

The jubilant pilots, who were not even aware of the existence of 1 Guerrilla Corps (Parachute), Force N due to it being classified, were elated to find that they encountered little or no enemy resistance. For all practical purposes, the Regia Aeronautica in the central southern half of Abyssinia had ceased to exist as a fighting force. The Italians had lost their air superiority in a single night.

When the invasion kicked off, the Imperial Forces would find the odds against them dramatically whittled down.

26

QUIET LITTLE MURDER
IN THE COUNTRY

MAJOR JOHN RANDAL WAS STANDING ON A STREET CORNER IN downtown Nairobi. He was dressed in mufti, wearing smoked Ray-Ban aviator glasses, and had the brim of his cut-down Australian bush hat pulled low over his eyes. Since the only people he knew in the colony were jaded Muthaiga Country Club women of the night-crawler set who never got out of bed before full-on noon, there was no way he was going to run into anyone who would recognize him. He was scanning a copy of the *East African Standard* newspaper as he waited at the curb.

The news was bad. The Battle of Britain was over, but the Blitz was going full bore. The Luftwaffe was bombing English cities every night. Invasion was still expected at any minute. Rationing was being strictly enforced, and women were being drafted in unimagined numbers. In the Atlantic, U-boats were on a rampage. The Japanese were rattling their sabers in the Far East. On a happier note, he read the King was away on an extended shooting vacation in the country.

Standing in the middle of a friendly city in broad daylight seemed oddly peculiar. Maj. Randal felt distinctly underdressed, as the only weapon he was carrying was his ivory-stocked 9mm Browning Hi-Power tucked in the skeleton holster in the back under the khaki safari jacket. For the first time in quite a while he was not primed for fight or flight.

A pretty woman about his own age walked up and handed him a small white feather.

"Thank you," Maj. Randal said.

The girl gave him an annoyed look, then turned away as a nondescript black Ford pulled up at the curb with Captain the Lady Jane Seaborn at the wheel. In the back were Rita Hayworth and Lana Turner outfitted in new Royal Marine BDUs. They were wearing cream-colored turbans with Royal Marine insignia and their parachute wings pinned on the front. Rita had Maj. Randal's old regimental badge from the Rangers Territorial Regiment of the KRRC on the right breast of her blouse so that he would be able to tell the girls apart, though by now he no longer needed it. The two new recruits were wearing their 9mm Kurtz Beretta automatics on highly polished Sam Brown belts.

"Joined the Marines, ladies?" Maj. Randal said with an arched eyebrow as he climbed into the passenger seat. It was perfectly clear that they were no longer working exclusively for him. Lady Jane had shanghaied his slave girls. As Rita and Lana twittered, Lady Jane put the Ford in gear and they pulled out into traffic.

"Strange town," Maj. Randal said, "some woman back there gave me a white feather."

Lady Jane laughed. "That was her way of saying you should be in uniform. She called you a coward, John, to your face."

"Really? Good for her."

Today they were off to make a reconnaissance of Broughton House, sometimes called Karen House because it was located seventeen miles outside of Nairobi near Karen. The object of the exercise was to select a site for the ambush of Captain Lord Joss Victor Hay, 22nd Earl of Errol later that night. Maj. Randal wanted to inspect the lay of the ground himself.

Ambushes were his specialty. Typically for him, he was not going to leave anything to chance – time spent on reconnaissance, he knew, was rarely wasted.

Outside of town the pavement stopped abruptly. The highway dropped off, and from that point on it was gravel. The road was badly potholed. In Abyssinia, Maj. Randal noted, the Italians maintained better highways than the British Colonial Authorities in Kenya.

"Joss drives a scarlet red Buick Super 8 outfitted with bulletproof glass," Lady Jane said. On weekends, the Happy Valley colonists race each other along this stretch to see who can reach the Muthaiga Country Club first. They say he goes like a bat out of hell."

"Hang out with the Pregnant Guppy aircrew much, Jane?"

"Why do you ask?"

"Bat out of hell... girls talk like that at your Swiss finishing school?"

Flashing one of her patented heart attack smiles, Lady Jane pressed on with her briefing, "The Earl shall not be driving his Super 8 tonight. The Buick is conveniently in the shop for service. Discrete arrangements have been made for the mechanics to keep the car there until our work is done. Joss will be driving a loaner, another Buick – black."

"Why do so many people want the man dead?"

"Pink Swastika is acting under the impression the Earl is providing information about their membership to British counterintelligence, who in turn have been feeding it back to the Gestapo to round up and execute them. British counterintelligence, MI-5, simply loves to help Nazis liquidate other Nazis."

"What's the Gestapo have against gay Nazis?"

"There is a possibility that Hitler was a charter member of Pink Swastika. Rumor is he used to be a male prostitute in Vienna. Ever since becoming Chancellor, the Führer has attempted to wipe out any trace they ever existed. Even the name is banned in the Third Reich."

"How would an underground organization of Pink Nazis ever find out Hay was informing on them?" Maj. Randal asked, thinking the Hitler story sounded like something right out of Captain Hawthorne Merryweather's PWE dirty tricks playbook.

"Why, we told them of course," Lady Jane said. "If you think Pink Swastika sounds like bad fiction, wait until you hear the reason why one of the Italian internees is plotting to murder Joss."

"Why might that be?"

"The Earl arranged to have himself placed in charge of interning the colony's enemy aliens, a job no one else had any desire for. Most of the people classified as aliens in Kenya – Germans and Italians alike – have been here for years and are fine upstanding citizens, or at least they were before the war. Everyone knows everyone in Kenya, and the idea of putting friends in prison was not something most people wanted any part of.

"Joss coveted the job so that he could be in a position to have the wealthy aliens pay him a bribe to order house arrest instead of putting them in one of the internment camps. After accepting the payoff, Joss has them interned anyway. Then he sends a team of crooks out to pilfer their empty estates of all their valuables, knowing no one will be home."

"Really?"

"Count Mario Rocco, the owner of a marvelous mansion on Lake Naivasha, paid a fortune in bribe money, but Joss double-crossed him, claiming he was plotting to escape to Abyssinia in a hot-air balloon."

"Anybody believe that story?"

"Actually, yes. Coming from the World's Greatest Pouncer – the more outrageous, the more believable," Lady Jane laughed. "Police informants report the Count has imported a Somali hitman to kill Joss and then disappear back across the border."

"Hot-air balloon – I'm still having a hard time buying Pink Swastika."

"They are a real organization, John. I can vouch for their existence," Lady Jane said. "Mallory belonged to a smart mob called the Cliveden Set before I married him.

"Terribly political, an applicant was required to have impeccable pedigree to be invited in. Lady Astor hosted the meetings on one or another of their fabulous country estates over long weekends of croquet, tennis and politics.

"Sounds like fun," said Maj. Randal, who hated politics.

"Fascism was all the rage. Mallory believed he could advance his Navy career by being active. Joss attended from time to time, as did Winston

Churchill and King Edward before he abdicated. Mallory saw it as a super sort of patriotism where England's interest came first above everything else."

"Your husband is a fascist?"

"He flirted with the idea, along with a lot of other highly influential people at the time. We were terribly naïve and, of course, possessed of a certain conceit. Occasionally the Cliveden Set invited select foreigners for the weekend to speak. Pink Swastika sent representatives more than once."

"Mallory's a fascist?"

"He was, or *thought* he was and Mallory is well acquainted with Joss. When his ship was out here, he took full advantage of the Happy Valley party scene. I found his entry in the Muthaiga Country Club guest book, "When Vikings die they go to Valhalla. Personally, I hope to go to a place like the Muthaiga Club – beats the hell out of heaven.""

"Man must have enjoyed his shore leave."

"I am sure he did," Lady Jane said, her knuckles turning white on the steering wheel. "Smacked across the top of Mallory's entry was the full imprint of some woman's lips in fire engine red lipstick – sealed with a kiss."

"I…" Maj. Randal said. "Jane, I didn't…"

"My marriage was a charade," Lady Jane cut him off, "only I never knew it. Seems everyone else did, naturally. Now I realize I only married Mallory because it was expected of me. He was so handsome and dashing in his uniform. Everyone thought we were the perfect couple – the ideal match. In the Six Hundred that means everything.

"Then the war came, the *Wind* was sunk, I met you, John and I realized love had never entered into my relationship with Mallory. I did not even know what love was, actually, not really."

"Jane…"

"You should know I thought I was simply going to die when you ran away to Africa without telling me goodbye." There were tears rolling down her cheeks. "The girl who gave you the white feather was right – you are a coward."

Maj. Randal had a different recollection of events, but he still felt guilty. Lady Jane had a way of making him do that from time to time. No other woman ever had.

"Another thing. You better hope no more wanton Happy Valley women slink up to me at the Muthaiga Country Club to make inquires. I have had it with debauched party girls confiding to me they understood we 'used to be close.'"

"Not my fault."

"Like hell!"

In the rearview mirror, Maj. Randal could see two sets of smoldering amber eyes as big around as silver Maria Theresa thalers. Terrific, all he needed was a couple of Zār Cult priestesses down on his case. Luckily, the black Ford reached a fork in the road approximately sixteen miles north of Nairobi – one and a half miles, as the crow flies, from Sir Jock Delves Boughton's house, which cut short the conversation.

The road formed a V with Karen Road running to the left and Ngong Road to the right. Approximately a mile and a quarter north of the V, Karen Road joined Marula Lane to the right. One half mile farther up on Marula Lane, at the junction with Tree Lane, sat Sir Jock's house, also on the right-hand side of the road. Tree Lane was a seldom-used cut-through that ran between Ngong Road and Marula Lane.

Viewed on the map, the road network was an uneven rectangle resembling a pyramid with the top lopped off. Boughton House was in the northeast upper right-hand corner. Langata Road ran diagonally across the rectangle, slicing it into two fairly equal triangles of property. A footpath from the junction of Karen Road and Ngong Road ran straight as an arrow through the bush to Broughton House. All the roads were gravel. The footpath was not much more than an animal trail about a mile and a half long.

They cruised slowly up Karen Road, took a right turn on to Marula Lane, cruised past Broughton House, turned right and drove down Tree Lane, then turned right again onto Ngong Road, which was the road to back Nairobi.

A person leaving Broughton House en route to Nairobi was able to choose from two gravel roads. Whichever was taken, Marula Lane or Tree Lane, the driver ended up at the junction of Karen and Ngong Roads. Past that junction on the north side of the highway was a murram pit. Maj. Randal decided to intercept the Earl's car before he reached the pit.

"Joss has never taken Tree Lane in all the nights we trailed him," Lady Jane said as they rolled by the country house. "He uses Marula Lane religiously."

The Karen/Ngong Road junction was the ideal ambush site. It created an isolated choke point the target had to pass through. Maj. Randal could wait at the junction and intercept Capt. Lord Hay no matter which road he traveled. A hide position was selected where the Ford could be parked off the road in concealment east of the junction facing back toward Nairobi ready for a quick getaway.

Not wanting to remain in the neighborhood any longer than necessary, Lady Jane pointed the car back toward town. "Joss will be unarmed. The man loathes firearms, does not own one – never even signed out his issue service revolver from the armory."

"I like it when the opposition can't shoot back," Maj. Randal said.

"Sir Jock will instruct the Earl to have Diana home by 0300 hours tonight."

"How did you manage to arrange for the jilted husband to tell his wife's boyfriend what time to bring his fiancée home?"

"Believes he is working for MI-6, the fool."

"Pretty tricky," Maj. Randal said.

"Broughton has no idea what is going to happen tonight."

"Well, it's a cinch he's going to be blamed for it."

"Sir Jock is expendable, repayment for letting the side down ages ago," Lady Janes said. "He owns a revolver similar to the one you are going to use to shoot Joss – same caliber but of a different manufacturer. His is a Colt, you are going to use a Smith & Wesson. We hope to get him off at trial because the ballistics will show the bullet that killed the Earl does not match the rifling found in his pistol."

"You think this up?"

"The gun is in the glove compartment," Lady Jane said, ignoring him.

Maj. Randal opened the box to find a .32 caliber Smith & Wesson Hand Ejector and a box of ammunition. He cracked the action and saw the weapon was loaded. After checking in both directions to make sure there were no other cars in sight, he stuck the Smith & Wesson out the window and pulled the trigger six times, rapid fire. To his surprise the revolver was stoked with black powder ammunition of a type not manufactured in years, maybe not even in his lifetime. A volcano of gunpowder erupted from the barrel every time the weapon fired. Was there a reason for the ammunition?

He carefully reloaded the little pistol, dropped it in the bellows pocket on the right-hand side of his khaki safari jacket and placed the green cardboard box of Remington ammunition into his left pocket.

"John, your mission, code named OPERATION HIGHLAND CLEARANCE, is to shoot Captain Lord Josh Hay with the Smith & Wesson provided. Later, when you pass through Camp Croc, you will toss the handgun into Lake Rudolf to rest forever with the crocodiles," Lady Jane ordered in her official tone – which Maj. Randal always thought very sexy. "Questions?"

"Negative."

Maj. Randal was dropped off at a safe house on the edge of Nairobi. Lady Jane had a busy afternoon ahead to prepare for the night's action. The ex-slave girls were scheduled to make their first-ever visit to a beauty salon with her. That promised to be a circus.

Maj. Randal walked inside the white stucco, thatch-roofed bungalow. This was the first time Rita and Lana had not been at his side in months except for the few days they went to Terry's jump school, and he felt strangely alone. With several hours on his hands, he did what fighting men always do when they have spare time before a mission: cleaned his weapons; and then hit the rack, dead to the world.

However, it would have been a bad idea to try to sneak up on him.

BY SUNDOWN THE MUTHAIGA COUNTRY CLUB WAS ROCKING. Captain the Lord Joss Victor Hay, 22nd Earl of Errol, arrived between 1830 and 1900 hours with Lady Diana Broughton and June Carberry, a woman described by one knowledgeable source as "an unnatural blonde who, if you cut her in half you would find mostly gin." June was known to be sleeping with both Joss and Diana, though it was thought not at the same time.

Sir Jock Delves Broughton joined them about 2000 hours, and the drinking of champagne commenced with the occasional Bronx for variety. As usual, the World's Greatest Pouncer abstained, pacing himself. Broughton, the jilted husband of a failed two-month-old marriage – a man who knew when to cut his losses – proposed an awkward toast to "Diana and Joss."

At approximately 2015 hours, on the way to purchase cigarettes for Lady Diana, the Earl encountered a tousled, clearly intoxicated Captain the Lady Jane Seaborn in the hall. She was carrying an open magnum of champagne by its gold, foil-wrapped neck. He noted that the Royal Marine officer looked extraordinarily physically fit in her skintight black evening sheath, which reminded him of a story a recent houseguest, Major John Randal, had once told him about a woman who's abdominal muscles rippled through her evening gown.

He had never actually seen that before – until now.

Lady Jane informed him she would arrive at his house at 0330 hours sharp and leave promptly at 0345 hours if he had not arrived home alone by that time.

Realizing that his ship had come in, he was practically euphoric – though not particularly surprised – this was the sort of thing that happened from time to time to the World's Greatest Pouncer. Capt. Lord Hay departed the Muthaiga Country Club at 2030 hours with Lady Diana to go dancing at the Claremont Road House, abandoning Sir Jock and June who switched from champagne to gin fizzes. At the Claremont, the lovers danced until the stroke of midnight, 2400 hours, and then the pair drove to the Earl's house where they went inside and up the stairs to his bedroom for a "short performance."

At 0030 hours Maj. Randal stepped out of Lady Jane's black Ford, walked up the driveway to the Hay residence, and with the steel skull crusher on the hilt of his Fairbairn knife, broke out the left rear brake light on the Buick loaner the Earl was driving. He then returned to the Ford, where he waited with the three women sitting inside. Lady Jane was at the wheel no longer dressed in her evening attire. She was not the slightest bit intoxicated. Rita Hayworth and Lana Turner were in the back seat.

Everyone was armed.

June Carberry and a staggering drunk Sir Jock departed the Muthaiga Country Club at 0140 hours and were driven to the house on Karen Road by his chauffeur.

After a brief one-hour "performance," Joss and Diana came downstairs, put her three suitcases into the Buick and roared off in the direction of Karen Road, not detecting the damaged brake light or noticing the Ford parked across the street. Unknown to the occupants, the Ford tailed the Buick for sixteen miles, dropping off at the V of the Karen/Ngong Road junction. The broken taillight made the job of following easy.

At the Karen House, Sir Jock's chauffeur helped him stagger inside at 0210 hours. Mrs. Wilks, Lady Diana's maid, met them at the door. June went up the stairs to the guest bedroom, stripped nude and went straight to bed. She did not go to sleep because, for her, the night was still young.

Capt. Lord Hay and Lady Diana arrived at Karen House at 0215 hours. They went inside with her luggage. Mrs. Wilks offered The World's Greatest Pouncer a cocktail, which he declined.

"Do drive carefully, darling," Diana said.

"Carefully yes, but not slowly," Italy's man- in Kenya replied suavely as he rushed back out to his automobile.

Capt. Lord Hay did not bother to mention to his fiancée that he was running late to meet a late date for what he intended to be the most sensational performance of his entire career.

As the Earl peeled out of the drive spewing gravel, Lady Diana tripped lightly up the stairs, stripped, and slipped into bed with June. Sir Jock was in his bedroom across the hall in a drunken stupor, rattling the walls with his snoring.

Maj. Randal was standing at the apex of the V of Karen/Ngong Roads wearing his sand green parachute smock and cut-down Australian slouch hat. He was armed to the teeth with five pistols, although he was only planning to use the S&W .32 in his pocket for tonight's work. The moon was out, bathing the African scenery in pale, mellow light. He was pacing back and forth, swishing his ivory-handled riding whip against his leg.

The lime green hands on his Rolex read 0223 hours.

Lana Turner was standing in the shadow of a blue gum tree on the north side of the road. She had been given firm instructions to move up and cover the Earl with her Beretta 9 when his loaner Buick came to a stop, but NOT to shoot him under any circumstances. Rita Hayworth and Lady Jane waited in the black Ford parked in concealment. They had a clear view of Maj. Randal standing at the junction.

Both women had pistols at hand.

In the distance, the headlights of a car with the headlamps taped into slits like a pair of cats eyes – in compliance with Kenyan blackout regulations – could be seen approaching from the direction of Sir Jock's house. In Abyssinia, Maj. Randal stayed clicked on all the time. Someone was always trying to kill him or something always trying to eat him. When he flew into Kenyan airspace, he must have de-compressed.

Never able to think clearly around Lady Jane, he had not been dialed in when he planned tonight's ambush. Everything had seemed so easy – waylay an unarmed, unsuspecting man who knew him on a desolate stretch of road late at night and shoot him. No problem.

A pair of lions hunting in the bush between the V and Boughton's house coughed. Maj. Randal realized he had made a serious mistake – the same one Lieutenant Butch "Headhunter" Hoolihan had made on his first-ever ambush.

Too late, the phrase "a bat out of hell" popped back into his head. There was no way he was going to flag down the oncoming car. Kenyan roads are notoriously dangerous at night. Someone had already taken a potshot at the Earl along this same stretch of highway. The World's Greatest Pouncer was not going to stop for anyone, not tonight. He had a date with Lady Jane – or thought he did. Who could blame him?

A native on a bicycle swished past silently out of the dark from behind. Maj. Randal turned, taken off guard. The rider looped around lazily, pedaled back and stopped with one sandaled foot on the ground right next to him.

"Why you here, mon?"

"Go away," Maj. Randal ordered, "NOW."

Unruffled, the native bike rider opened his ragged jacket to reveal the oil-stained walnut grip of a Belgian Army Nagant 7.62mm revolver tucked in the waist of his pants. "Go away yourself, mon, if you know what's good for you."

The bicyclist was extremely sure of himself, very in-charge. They were standing inches apart and Maj. Randal could smell the native's minty breath. Bhat? Africans in Kenya did not, as a matter of practice, speak to a white man in the manner the bicycle rider had – much less threaten one.

Maj. Randal glanced up the road at the approaching headlights and noted, as predicted, the Earl was driving like a bat out of hell. He turned to look the bicyclist full in the face and saw his ugly brown eyes gleaming wickedly in the moonlight. Pressing the checkered metal stud below the engraved Lion of Judah on the butt of his horse whisk, he plunged the razor-sharp stiletto concealed inside straight into the native's sternum, running it all the way in up to his knuckle – hard.

The black man looked puzzled – not quite so confident. As he coughed blood, he keeled over in the middle of the right-of-way, falling in a tangle on top of his bicycle. The Buick roared up and swerved to avoid the fallen rider but did not pull over when Maj. Randal waved and shouted "STOP JOSS!"

The Earl was not stopping. Not tonight. Not for anyone or anything. He was a man on a mission, with visions of rippling ab muscles dancing in his head. If he could win Lady Jane with her fantastic fortune, he would be set for life. Once in bed she was his – all women were. He was not called the "World's Greatest Pouncer" for nothing. She would divorce that fool Mallory in a fortnight.

When Capt. Lord Hay swerved the Buick to dodge the bicycle but failed to heed the call to stop, Maj. Randal fired a round at him from the .32 Smith & Wesson as he brought it up out of his pocket. *CRAAAACK!*

A snapshot fired in desperation with an unfamiliar pistol in uncertain light, the bullet cracked past – inches from the Earl's left ear – and slammed into the headboard. The car ran off the roadway at a high speed nearly chopping down Lana under the blue gum tree, and then crashed into the murram pit.

Quickly the ex-slave girl darted to the driver's side and pointed her Beretta 9mm Kurtz in the window. Capt. Lord Hay was semi-comatose, having struck his head on the steering wheel. Groggily regaining consciousness enough to recognize the pistol in his face, he crawled down on the floorboard under the steering wheel facing the passenger door and put his hands up as if praying, begging, "Please do not harm me."

Traveling in the wake of the Buick was a motorcycle with sidecar, running with its lights off. It roared up, skidded sideways and came to a halt in a cloud of dust. The machine's operator was a man sporting round driving goggles. A woman wearing a blue and black paisley scarf wrapped over her blond hair was riding in the sidecar.

Pointing a Smith & Wesson at him exactly like the one Maj. Randal was holding, the lithe blond screamed. "Stand back or I will bloody well shoot you!"

CRAAAACK! A tiny hole appeared off-center in the woman's forehead. *CRAAAACK, CRAAAACK, CRAAAACK!* Maj. Randal pumped three .32 caliber rounds into the driver's chest as the man fumbled inside his leather coat. The motorcycle sputtered and quit.

While the gun smoke from the black powder cartridges was still clouding the scene, a dark touring sedan traveling fast thundered up from the direction of Nairobi. Six blond, crew-cut men wearing tuxedos were crammed in the car. Silhouettes of the skinny barrels of 9mm Lugers and P-38s were showing in the windows. The automobile skidded to a stop, sliding hard on the gravel road surface. The car might as well have had a glowing neon pink swastika hood ornament instead of the Mercedes emblem.

Maj. Randal dropped the Smith & Wesson .32 back into his pocket, drew his right hand Colt .38 Super, bringing it up into a two-handed grip, and commenced firing the instant the gold bead on the front sight came level: *BLAAAAM, BLAAAAM, BLAAAAM...* shooting fast until the magazine ran dry.

Inside the Mercedes, 9mm pistols were popping like flash bulbs, and the men in evening dress were jinking around stiffly like marionettes in a light show. Maj. Randal was not actually aware of individual shots directed at him. Events seemed to be taking place in slow motion. He was experiencing tunnel vision, focused on the car's compartment.

Maj. Randal was firing, concentrating on the front sight, though not actually seeing it, shooting at movement. The .38 Super rounds from his blazing Colt 1911 stitched the windows with white stars. As soon as the Colt ran empty he holstered it, drew his Browning Hi-Power 9mm and fired thirteen more rounds fast, even though all return fire had ceased. From start to finish the gunfight was over in a handful of seconds, though it seemed to have gone on for a long time.

The sensation of slow motion dissipated. The tunnel vision cleared. Moving fluidly like a big cat, never taking his eyes off the car, Maj. Randal holstered the Browning and produced his second fully charged Colt .38 Super as he stepped over to the Mercedes to inspect the damage. Lady Jane and Rita came running up with their weapons drawn. Lady Jane had managed to get off five rounds with her 7.65 Walther PPK. They took up positions on both sides of the bullet-riddled auto, pistols at the ready.

The six well-dressed occupants were dead.

"Bring the car, Jane," Maj. Randal ordered, "before someone else shows up who wants to kill the Earl."

Out of the darkness from the direction of Karen Road, a tall, slim figure strode into sight tapping a Player's cigarette against his elegant silver case. The gravel on the road was crunching loudly under his canvas-topped raiding boots. Maj. Randal covered him with his Colt .38 Super.

"Remember Calais, old stick. Any bullet holes? It's not nice to point."

"Not in me," Maj. Randal said, lowering the pistol.

"Somali hit man, I presume. Those two must be the SOE team who failed to check in upon arrival in Nairobi, as per instructions – fatally bad tradecraft, what! Pink Swastika put in their appearance, too," Major Sir Terry "Zorro" Stone said as he studied the carnage. "These lads have been seen hanging around Nairobi masquerading as dairy production experts from South Africa partied at Muthaiga tonight, no doubt.

"Let's see, two of ours, one independent and six of theirs, quite a body count even for you, John."

"Jane was firing too," Maj. Randal said. "You're supposed to be with your battalion, Terry."

"Change of plans," Maj. Stone replied. "My apologies for how this turned out. You were Plan B tonight. Fleming and I intended to take Joss outside Boughton's house. The one night out of the last twenty the Earl would choose to drive down Tree Lane, extraordinarily bad luck. So much for a quiet little murder in the country."

"Fleming, Ian Fleming," Maj. Randal said, "missed his chance again."

"I was the designated shooter, actually. HIGHLAND CLEARANCE is sanctioned by the highest authority," Maj. Stone said. "Up the road apiece are two observers who by all rights should not be in Africa, and, in fact as far as anyone will ever know, never were. Traveled out at great personal risk to see this thing carried out properly, this job is so vital."

"Who might they be?"

"I am not at liberty to divulge identities but one did authorize me to inform you, provided you were still standing, that once again you have upheld the finest traditions of your regiment, speaking as your Colonel-in-Chief."

"The King's on the ground tonight?" Maj. Randal said. "Newspaper claimed he was on a shooting vacation in the country."

"And so he is – only the article did not specify what country, and you did all the shooting. One should never attempt to blackmail a member of the Royal Family with racy photos, especially not the King's older brother. Royals consider that sort of thing exceedingly bad form. We are not having this conversation, by the way."

"What conversation?"

"I am obligated to corroborate the Earl's passing – a mere formality, no doubt?"

"He's not dead," Maj. Randal said. "At least I haven't killed him."

"You don't say?"

The two officers strolled over to where the Buick was crashed. Lana was standing by the driver's window, aiming her pistol inside at a cowering figure still crouched on the floor under the steering column. Capt. Lord Hay was blubbering like a baby, terrified to even raise his eyes.

"Who... help!"

"We're from the government," Maj. Randal said. "We're not here to help you."

"You have been a bad boy, Joss," Maj. Stone chided. "Really let the side down. His Majesty ordered me to admonish you if you were still in this world by the time I arrived. He rather enjoyed the photos, by the way.

"Sir Terry, is that..."

"The Chief of Secret Intelligence, your former brother-in-law, requested I mention that he never much cared for you, if I had the opportunity to do so before we shot you. And Lady Jane, well, there was never any chance she would actually be waiting at your house. In fact, Jane is here with us tonight. As for myself, well, old stick, I would simply like to add… it's always darkest before pitch black."

"Please, please, this is all some kind of a ghastly mistake I can explain…."

CRAAAACK! Maj. Randal shot him point-blank behind the ear with the little .32 Smith & Wesson.

"I'd be careful walking back up the road if I were you, Terry," Maj. Randal said as they hiked to where Lady Jane waited in the Ford with the motor running. "There's a couple of lion working the brush off to the left."

"Oh, you don't say?"

"Those cats probably aren't man-eaters but then there's no way to tell for sure until they eat you."

"How about giving me a lift," Maj. Stone asked, peering into the darkness. "Partway?"

"Love to," Maj. Randal said. "Let's get the hell out of Dodge."

"By the way, I have been intending to ask," Maj. Stone inquired as they walked toward the car, "what exactly *does* the 'N' in Force N stand for?"

"'Nothing.' Robert Rogers' first Standing Order to his Rangers – 'Don't Forget Nothing.' Seemed appropriate."

"We never forgot you."

"No, you didn't."

The long-planned invasion of Abyssinia, OPERATION CANVASS, was getting underway as the two climbed into the Ford.

The Raiding Forces series continues…all the way to VE Day.
To be on our notification list for the next book, contact
phil@philward.com

~~~

THE MISSION CONTINUES IN GUERRILLA COMMAND
COMING SOON

THE BATTLE OF
THE PLAIN OF REEDS

~ ~ ~

After an intensive six-week campaign of airmobile operations in the Mekong Delta, Alpha Company played a key role in the climactic Battle of the Plain of Reeds, which resulted in the 1st Recondo Brigade, commanded by the legendary Colonel Henry "Gunfighter" Emerson, being awarded the Presidential Unit Citation.

On 3 June 1968, the third morning of a four-day running battle in the Plain of Reeds, Alpha Company air-assaulted into a hot LZ, charged across one hundred meters of open rice paddy straight into the teeth of a dug-in main force Viet Cong regiment that was throwing everything at them but the kitchen sink; carried the enemy left flank, penetrating their first line of bunkers; and pinned the VC in their emplacements and fixed them in place until the rest of the 1st Brigade could arrive, encircle and destroy them. This was accomplished despite A Company having landed outside the range of artillery support, with the company commander killed in the first minutes, and fighting in 110-plus-degree heat – with no shade, no water – armed with M-16 rifles that would not function in those conditions. They were outnumbered more than ten to one. The initial air strike had to be called in on their own position to prevent A Company from being overrun, which was complicated by the lack of even a single smoke grenade or any other signaling device to mark their location.

One senior officer described Alpha Company's charge and refusal to allow the VC to break contact as the "finest small unit action ever fought" – and maybe it was.

Six Huey helicopters flew out all the troops in the company that were left standing – 37 men.

ABBREVIATIONS
ORDERS & AWARDS

Bt	Baronet
CB	Companion of the Bath
CMG	Companion of the Order of St. Michael & St. George
DFC	Distinguished Flying Cross (Royal Air Force)
DSC	Distinguished Service Cross (Royal Navy)
DSO	Distinguished Service Order
GCB	Grand Cross in the Order of the Bath
KBE	Knight Commandeer of the British Empire
KCVO	Knight Commander of the Royal Victorian Order
MC	Military Cross
MVO	Member of the Royal Victorian Order
OBE	Order of the Empire
VC	Victoria Cross

ACRONYMS

AO	Area of Operation
AP	Armor Piercing
AT	Anti-Tank
BCDSAP	Big Cat Down Shoot Again Procedure
BDU	Battle Dress Uniform
CP	Command Post
DZ	Drop Zone
EAF	East Africa Force
EAFHQ	East Africa Force Headquarters
FOB	Forward Operating Base
GOC	General Officer Commanding
GCBP	Gold Coast Border Police
HQ	Headquarters
IEA	Italian East Africa
IO	intelligence officer
KAR	King's African Rifles
KISS	Keep It Simple, Stupid /Keep It Short and Simple
LMG	Light Machine Gun
LZ	Landing Zone
MRB	Mule Raider Battalion
NCO	Non-Commissioned Officer
NID	Naval Intelligence Division
NYRBA	New York, Rio and Buenos Aires Airline
OC	Operational Center
PLF	Parachute Landing Fall
PWE	Political Warfare Executive
RF	Raiding Forces
RR	Rolls Royce
SAAF	South African Air Force
SIM	Servizio Informazioni Militare, (Italian Military Intelligence Service
SIS	Secret Intelligence Service
SOE	Special Operations Executive
SOP	Standard Operating Procedure
TO&E	table of organization and equipment

LIST OF CHARACTERS

Brandy Seaborn
Brig. Collin Gubbins
Capt. Jack Desmond Bonham
Capt. Taylor Corrigan, MC, Horse Guards
Capt. Douglas Dodds-Parker
Capt. Mickey Duggan, DCM, MM, RM
Capt. Oliver Goodwood
Capt. Lionel Honeycutt-Parker
Capt. "Geronimo" Joe McKoy
Capt. Hawthorne Merryweather
Capt. Jeb Pelham-Davies, MC
Capt. Harry Shelby, MC, Sherwood Foresters
Capt. George Steer
Capt. "Pyro" Percy Stirling, MC
Capt. the Lord Joss Victor Hay, 22nd Earl of Errol
Capt. the Lady Jane Seaborn, OBE, RM
Cdr. Mallory Seaborn, RN
Cdre. Richard "Dickie the Pirate" Seaborn, VC, OBE, RN
Chief Inspector Ronald McFarland
Col. Stewart Menzies, DSO *aka* "C"
Col. Dan Sanford
Commissioner Richard Cavendish
FM Rodolfo "Butcher" Graziani
Gubbo Rekash *aka* Cheap Bribe
Guido "GG" Grazinni
Haile Selassie, His Imperial Majesty, Emperor, Lion of Judah, King of
Kings, Elect of God
June Carberry
Lana Turner
Lifeboat Serviceman Tom Tyler
Lt. Dick Courtney
Lt. Hugh Thompson "Hughsie Daisy" Dickinson
Lt. Penelope Honeycutt-Parker, RM
Lt. Butch "Headhunter" Hoolihan, MM, RM
Lt. Jack Merritt, MC, MM
Lt. Karen Montgomery
Lt. Pamala Plum-Martin, OBE, RM
Lt. Randy "Hornblower" Seaborn, DSC, RN

Lt. Cdr. Ian Fleming, RN
Lt. Col. Dudley Clarke
Lt. Gen. Sir Archibald Wavell
Lt. Mike "March or Die" Mikkalis, DCM, MC.
Maj. Courtney Brocklehurst
Maj. Edwin Chapman-Andrews
Maj. R.E. Cheesman
Maj. Lawrence Grand
Maj. James Hamilton
Maj. John Randal, DSO, MC
Maj. Sir Terry "Zorro" Stone, KBE, MC
Maj. Orde Wingate
Maj. Gen. Alan Cunningham
Maj. Gen. William "the Kaid" Platt
Maj. Gen. James "Baldie" Taylor, OBE
Mr. Derek Chatham-Weatherford
Mr. Ruben Hollis Fleet
Plt. Off. Gasper "Bunny" Featherstone, DFC
PM Winston Churchill
Red
Rita Hayworth
Sgt. Roy "Mad Dog" Reupart
Sgt. Maj Maxwell Hicks, DCM
Sir Jock Delves, Broughton, 11th Baronet
Sqn. Ldr. Paddy Wilcox, DSO, OBE, MC, FC
Waldo Treywick

ABOUT THE AUTHOR

Phil Ward is a decorated combat veteran commissioned at age nineteen. A former instructor at the Army Ranger School, he has had a lifelong interest in small unit tactics and special operations. He lives in Texas on a mountain overlooking Lake Austin.

~ ~ ~

OTHER BOOKS IN THE RAIDING FORCES SERIES:

Those Who Dare

Dead Eagles

Blood Wings

Guerrilla Command

Necessary Force

Desert Patrol

Private Army

Africa 1941

The Sharp End

Raiding Rommel

Strategic Services

Tip of the Sword

Always So Few

The War That Never Was

Printed in the USA
CPSIA information can be obtained
at www.ICGtesting.com
LVHW052018150823
755366LV00006BA/133

9 780989 592246